P9-EMC-060

APR 27 2011

Demon Hunting in Dixie

No Longer the Property of
Hayner Public Library District

HAYNER PUBLIC LIBRARY DISTRICT
ALTON, ILLINOIS

OVERDUES .10 PER DAY, MAXIMUM FINE
COST OF ITEM
ADDITIONAL $5.00 SERVICE CHARGE APPLIED TO
LOST OR DAMAGED ITEMS

HAYNER PLD/ALTON SQUARE

Demon Hunting in Dixie

LEXI GEORGE

BRAVA

KENSINGTON PUBLISHING CORP.

www.kensingtonbooks.com

BRAVA BOOKS are published by

Kensington Publishing Corp.
119 West 40th Street
New York, NY 10018

Copyright © 2011 Lexi George

All rights reserved. No part of this book may be reproduced in any form or by any means without the prior written consent of the Publisher, excepting brief quotes used in reviews.

All Kensington titles, imprints and distributed lines are available at special quantity discounts for bulk purchases for sales promotion, premiums, fund-raising, educational or institutional use.

Special book excerpts or customized printings can also be created to fit specific needs. For details, write or phone the office of the Kensington Special Sales Manager: Kensington Publishing Corp., 119 West 40th Street, New York, NY 10018. Attn. Special Sales Department. Phone: 1-800-221-2647.

Brava and the B logo are Reg. U.S. Pat. & TM Off.

ISBN-13: 978-0-7582-6309-4
ISBN-10: 0-7582-6309-0

First Kensington Trade Paperback Printing: May 2011

10 9 8 7 6 5 4 3 2 1

Printed in the United States of America

b19549891

To Megan Records—
Thanks for "getting" me and for giving me this chance.

To Jill Marr—
Thanks for having my back.

To Carla Swafford—
You are my guardian angel.

Chapter One

Addy glanced up at the rumble of thunder, her pace slowing to a jog. Alabama summers were a pressure cooker of high temperatures and humidity, and thunderstorms came up in a hurry.

"Whatcha think, Dooley, is it gonna rain?"

Dooley whined and tugged at her leash, eager to continue their late-night run in the quiet, gated community they called home.

"Okay, but you're sleeping in the kitchen if we get wet." Addy allowed the dog to urge her toward the trees at the end of the park. "Eau de Wet Dawg is not my favorite cologne, especially on my new sheets."

She set off down the smooth path at a comfortable pace with Dooley panting at her side. Running was her stress reliever. And between owning and operating her own floral business and lending a hand at the family funeral parlor, Addy had a lot of stress.

As they rounded the curve, she eyed the clump of trees ahead with unease. A sense of quiet expectancy had settled over the little park. She and Dooley had made this run a hundred times before, but tonight the cluster of oaks seemed brooding and sinister, the shadows beneath their branches a living, breathing thing. She ran a little faster, anxious to get past the trees and reach the safety of the lights beyond. The steady slap of her running shoes against the pavement and the sound of Dooley's snuffling seemed loud in the stillness.

She heard a second clap of thunder and skidded to a halt, tightening her grip on the leash. Dooley feared no mailman, but she was a major weenie when it came to thunder. She glanced down, expecting to find the dog trembling with fear. To her surprise, Dooley stood stiff-legged beside her, hackles on end, her unblinking gaze fixed upon the murky thicket. The dog rumbled low in her chest and took off without warning, jerking the leash from Addy's hand.

"No, Dooley, no!" Addy rubbed her stinging palm against her thigh, watching in growing dismay and dread as the Lab headed straight for the trees and disappeared into the darkness. "Come back here, you stupid mutt!"

"Damn!" She took off at a run after Dooley. "Why couldn't I have been a cat person?"

She plunged into the woods and faltered. The trees had *changed,* the dozen or so familiar oaks mushrooming into a forest of birch, elm, maple, beech, and ash. She squinted into the gloom. The trees seemed to be waiting; the forest hushed, but for the steady, faraway sound of Dooley's barking.

Addy's heart pounded as she picked her way through the woods. The thick carpet of leaves dulled the sound of her footsteps. Here and there a birch tree shone ghostly white in the darkness. She stumbled over fallen branches and scratched her arms and legs on briars and vines. Muttering under her breath, she pushed her way deeper into the forest. Stubbornness and concern for Dooley were all that kept her moving forward. If she stopped to examine things too closely—like how and why an entire forest of hardwoods had sprung up overnight in the middle of her boring little park—she knew she'd be too scared to go any farther. Better to keep her mind focused on the task ahead. Find Dooley and strangle her. She climbed over a fallen tree trunk and stepped into a clearing. The damn fool dog stood in the middle of the open glade barking like mad at . . . at *nothing.*

"Shh!" Addy marched up to the dog and tugged on her collar, her unease increasing by the minute. "Stop it, you big doofus. I'm totally creeped out. I want to go home."

To her chagrin, her voice shook. Her big brother Shep would have a field day if he could see her now. Addy Corwin scared of the dark. She was no stranger to the woods, had tagged along with Shep many a time when he and his buddies went camping, hunting, and fishing. She'd learned to be tough—one of the boys—so he wouldn't send her home. No whiney pants girly-girl stuff allowed. But this was different. This was *wrong*.

Something lurked in the surrounding darkness.

It was out there, watching her.

The dog pulled away and growled low in her throat, her gaze on the shadows in front of them.

Addy knelt beside Dooley and laid her hand on the quivering dog. "What is it, girl?"

Unbidden, an old superstition came to mind. Look between a dog's ears and you can see the devil. Without thinking, she glanced over the top of Dooley's head into the woods beyond. To her horror, something moved in the trees, a misshapen, undulating form darker than the blackness around it. The smudge of darkness flowed into the clearing, bringing with it a sickening sense of wrongness. Terror slammed through her, white-hot and paralyzing and all too brief, and then the thing was upon her, touching her with clammy, skeletal fingers. Bone-chilling cold seeped into her limbs, robbing her body of strength and sapping her will to fight. In the distance, she heard Dooley barking.

A third rumble shook the glade, and the evil being drew back with an angry hiss. The icy grip on Addy's heart eased, and she slumped to the ground, struggling to draw breath into her shriveled lungs. Dooley whined and stuck her cold nose against Addy's cheek. She rubbed the dog's ears with trembling fingers. That horrible thing was gone, thank God, and Dooley was here. Everything was going to be all right.

Some small creature stirred in the underbrush, and Dooley took off like a shot.

Addy sat up with an effort and pushed the hair out of her eyes. Dooley was nowhere to be seen. So much for doggie loyalty. Heart thumping, she looked around. The little clearing was empty, but the evil thing waited in the trees beyond. She could feel it. Addy swallowed the lump of terror clogging her throat. She had to go into those trees to get her dog. Oh, God, she did *not* want to go in there. But what choice did she have? None.

Great. Just freaking great.

A tiny pinpoint of light caught her attention. A rectangular opening appeared in mid-air and widened. Blinding light poured into the dark clearing. She blinked at the brightness. A man stood in the doorway, his tall, broad-shouldered form silhouetted by the patch of white light behind him, his face in shadow.

The portal snapped shut behind him. Without warning, the thing from the gloom struck.

"Hey, buddy, watch out behind you!" Addy cried.

To her astonishment, the man drew a flaming sword and spun to meet the attack. The thing screeched and drew back in alarm, circling the warrior warily. Light from the man's shimmering sword illuminated his face. Above the shining blade his eyes burned like bits of flame in the darkness. Addy gaped at him, too stunned by the sheer beauty of the man to be afraid. Wow, this guy was something else, a study in perfection, his features cold and unyielding, expressionless as carven stone.

I'm dreaming, Addy thought, staring at him in shock. Yeah, that was it. She was dreaming. This could not be real. No one could be that gorgeous.

A flicker of movement drew her attention from Mr. Perfect. A second wraith-like smudge of darkness slid into the clearing, bringing with it the same rotten, soul-sucking sense of evil as the other. Rising on ragged wings, the new attacker swooped down upon the unsuspecting warrior like an evil bird.

Dream or no dream, the hunky guy with the glow-in-the-dark sword was about to get his butt kicked by Mr. Nasty and his creepy sidekick.

Addy leaped to her feet. "Look out, mister! There's another one."

He whirled and lifted his sword, impaling the smoky figure

upon the blade. The wraith wailed in agony and vanished into the flames. With a furious shriek, the first wraith pushed past Addy and fled into the night. She swayed, staring in shock at the jagged knife of black ice that protruded from her chest. The knife sizzled and dissolved in a puff of oily smoke. Burning cold seeped from the wound and curled around her heart. With a sigh, she slipped into darkness.

Addy awoke on the couch with a groan. Her chest ached and her head throbbed. She took a deep breath and tried to ignore the stabbing pain in her ribs. Stabbing pain? What had happened to the thing in the woods, and how did she get home? And she *was* home, thank God. The scent of the new pineapple-sage candle she'd burned earlier in the evening still hung in the air, and the clock on the mantel ticked its steady rhythm. Dooley whined and licked her hand.

She patted the dog on the head. "Some dream, huh, girl?"

Addy opened her eyes and looked down. A large, charred hole marred the front of her favorite T-shirt and the sports bra she wore underneath. Surely, the freaky little thing in the woods hadn't been real? Supernatural woo-woo was way out of her league. Who was she kidding? The stuff she'd seen tonight didn't happen to anybody. It was too Syfy Channel for words.

She nudged the ruined material aside with the tip of one finger. An irregular black mark marred her right breast in the exact spot where Mr. Nasty stabbed her. She was still trying to absorb the ramifications of this discovery when a very deep, very *male* voice startled her.

"You should rest. I have repaired the damage to your organs from the djegrali blade. You will live, but I fear some of the poison is still in your system."

Addy shot off the couch like she'd been bitten. The sword-carrying, creature-of-darkness-fighting dude from the park gazed down at her without expression. In the semidarkness he'd been handsome. In the bright light of her living room he was devastating, a god, a wet dream on steroids. Tall and powerfully built, with wide shoulders and a broad chest that tapered down to a lean waist and hips, he was the most handsome man Addy had ever seen. His long, muscular legs were encased in tight-fitting black breeches, and he carried a sword in a sheath across his back. He was also a stranger, a very big stranger, and he stood in her living room.

"Who the hell are you?"

"I am Brand." He spoke without inflection. "I am a Dalvahni warrior. I hunt the djegrali."

"Of course you do." Hoo boy, the guy was obviously a nut case. Real movie star material, with his shoulder-length black hair and disturbing green eyes, but a whack job nonetheless. Addy grabbed the back of the couch for support as a wave of dizziness assailed her. "That would explain the flaming sword and the medieval getup you're wearing. Nice meeting you, Mr. . . . uh . . . Brand." She flapped her hand in the general direction of the door. "If you don't mind, I'm a little freaked out. I'd like you to leave."

"I cannot leave. The djegrali that attacked you will return."

Addy clung to the couch for dear life as the room began to spin. "Look, I appreciate the thought, but I'll be fine. Really." She closed her eyes briefly and opened them again. "Dooley will protect me."

He crossed his arms on his chest, his expression impassive. "Dooley? You refer, I presume, to the animal that led me to this dwelling?"

This guy was unbelievable. His superior attitude was starting to tick her off.

"The 'animal' is a dog and, yeah, I mean her."

"This I cannot allow." He spoke with the same irritating calm. Dooley, the traitor, ambled across the room and sat at the man's feet, gazing up at him in adoration. "She would not be able to defend you against the djegrali."

"Cannot allow—" Addy stopped and took a deep breath. She was dealing with a lunatic. He wouldn't leave, and she couldn't run. She was too woozy to make it to the door. Best to remain calm and not set the guy off. Besides, the spike in her blood pressure made the dizziness worse. "Okay, I'll bite. What exactly is this juh-whats-a-doodle thing you keep talking about?"

"The djegrali are demons." He raised his brows when she gave him a blank stare. "Evil spirits. Creatures of dark—"

"I know what a demon is." The guy thought he was a demon chaser, for Pete's sake. "Okay, just for grins, let's say this demon business is for real. What's it got to do with me?"

"The demon has marked you. He will return. He will be unable to resist."

"Oh, great, so now I'm irresistible. Just my luck he's the wrong kind of guy. Don't worry, I've got a thirty-eight, and like any good Southern girl I know how to use it, so you can leave." She waved her hand toward the door again. "I'll be fine. If this demon fellow shows up, I'll blow his raggedy butt to kingdom come."

The corner of his lips twitched, and for a moment she thought he might smile.

"You cannot kill a djegrali with a mortal weapon."

"I'll rush out first thing tomorrow morning and get me one of those flamey sword things, I promise."

Again with the lip twitch. "That will not be necessary. I will protect you."

"Oh, no, you won't!" Addy straightened with an effort. Her chest still hurt like a son-of-a-bitch. "I'd never be able to explain you to my mama."

"This mama you speak of, she is the female vessel who bore you?"

"Yeah, but I wouldn't call her a vessel to her face, if I were you."

"You fear her?"

Addy rolled her eyes. "Are you kidding? The woman scares the crap out of me. *Thirty-two hours of labor, and don't you ever forget it,*" she mimicked. *"You owe me. Big time."*

The eye-rolling thing was a mistake, because the room started to spin again.

"The mama will not be a problem," he said.

"You're darn tootin' the mama won't be a problem, 'cause you're not going to be here!"

She stepped away from the couch, and her knees buckled.

One moment he was across the room, his shoulder against the wall, the picture of aloof boredom, and the next she was in his arms. She closed her eyes and swallowed a sigh as she was lifted against his hard chest. The man sure had muscles, she'd give him that.

"You will recline, at once." His tone was stern.

Okay, muscles and a few control issues.

She opened her eyes as he lowered her to the couch and saw a grimace of pain flash across his features. It was the first expression of any kind she'd seen on his face, unless you counted the lip twitch thing. The man could give a marble statue lessons in being stoic.

She caught his arm as he started to rise. "That thing hurt you!"

He stilled, his gaze on her fingers wrapped around his wrist. "You are mistaken. The djegrali did not injure me. It is your touch that disturbs me."

Addy stiffened and drew back. "Well, excuse the hell out of me."

He caught her by the hand. "You misunderstand. You do not repulse me."

He knelt beside her, put his fingers under her chin, and tilted her face with gentle fingers. Addy stifled a gasp. Who was this guy? The merest touch from him and her breasts tingled and she felt hot and wobbly inside. What was the matter with her?

"Look at me," he commanded.

Sweet Sister Ruth, he had a voice like whiskey and smoke. She shivered and raised her eyes to his. He stroked her cheek with his thumb, a rapt expression on his face. His thumb drifted lower to brush her bottom lip. "You must be patient with me, Adara Jean Corwin. The Dalvahni do not experience emotion. It would be superfluous. We exist for one purpose and one purpose alone, to hunt the djegrali. For ten thousand years, that has been my objective, until now."

"Ten thousand years, huh?" With an effort, she squelched the sudden urge to scrape the pad of his thumb with her teeth. No doubt about it, she was in hormonal meltdown. "Sounds boring. You need to get a new hobby, expand your horizons."

"Earth is but one of the realms where the Dalvahni hunt the djegrali."

Oh, brother, too bad. He was paying a visit to schizoid-land again. Then the impact of his words percolated through the fog of lust that set her brain and her body on fire.

"Hey, wait a minute, I didn't tell you my name!"

"The animal you call Dooley informed me of many things, including how to find this dwelling."

"You don't say? Funny, she's never said a thing to me in four years."

He put his hand on her shoulder as she tried to sit up. "You will not rise," he said with annoying calm.

"Oh, yeah? That's what you think, bub."

She pushed at his arm, an exercise in futility. The man was built like the proverbial brick outhouse.

His hand slid over her abdomen and down her running shorts to her legs. She froze. His hand felt hot against her bare skin.

"Dooley, come here," he said.

The dog rose and trotted over to the couch.

Brand traced an intricate pattern with his fingers along the skin of her inner thigh. Addy began to shake. What was happening to her? This was so unlike her. All her life she'd struggled to rein in her reckless nature, the wild streak that made her mama wring her hands in despair. Self-control was her hard-earned mantra. Think first and feel later. But this guy . . . this guy really got her going, made her want to throw caution to the wind. She wanted to arch her hips against his hand, a *stranger's* hand.

"Speak, Dooley," Brand said with his gaze on Addy's face.

"Dooley love Addy. Love, love, love," the Lab said in the growly voice of a three-pack-a-day smoker. Flinging up a back paw, she scratched her ear. *"Can Dooley have chicken leg in cold box? Can Dooley?"* Her head snapped around. *"Oh, look, a bug!"*

There was a long moment of silence as Addy gaped at her dog in shock. Slowly, she raised her eyes to Brand's.

"Who *are* you?"

A slight crease appeared between Brand's brows. The expression in his eyes grew puzzled. "Until tonight, I thought I knew."

Lowering his dark head, he kissed her.

Chapter Two

Never been kissed . . .

N The thought spun through Addy's mind as Brand's lips met hers. Lightning streaked along her nerve endings, and her toes curled. Good grief, her toes *curled*.

This was beyond absurd. A thousand giddy butterflies did the happy dance inside her stomach, and the man had barely touched her. She was a grown woman. She'd been kissed lots of times. Why . . . ?

The tip of Brand's tongue touched the corner of her mouth, and she forgot everything else. He traced a lazy path across her bottom lip, tasting her, his touch leisurely, lingering, as if he wanted to memorize the shape and texture of her mouth.

Oh, Lord. Addy's thoughts grew hazy. Maybe she only thought she'd been kissed. Heavens, but the man had a wicked mouth! The glide of his lips across hers was sinful, exquisite. Giving in to the heady temptation, she sighed and kissed him back. Their tongues danced together, warm velvet on warm velvet. She licked his firm bottom lip.

He groaned and cupped the back of her head in his hands, deepening the kiss. Tearing his mouth from hers, he rained a trail of hot kisses down her throat and across her chest. He paused when he reached the spot where she had been stabbed. He murmured something indistinct and pushed aside the edge of her ruined shirt to lick the dark mark on her breast. Addy gasped and arched her back, wanting more, wanting everything.

"If you would disengage your mouth from the female, we could converse," a bored voice came from behind them.

Addy shrieked and tumbled off the couch, landing in a heap at Brand's feet. A flaxen-haired man with silver eyes stood in the middle of her living room. Instead of a sword he carried a long bow and a quiver of arrows. Like Brand, he was tall and muscular and drop-dead gorgeous. Also like Brand's, his handsome features formed an expressionless mask.

Brand lifted Addy to her feet and stepped in front of her. "What brings you here, Ansgar?"

His calm, detached tone hit Addy like a bucket of ice water, cooling her ardor in an instant. He spoke without inflection, no trace of his earlier passion discernible in his deep voice. She'd been on the verge of doing the horizontal mambo with a stranger, and the guy in question was, from all appearances, unaffected. Cool as a cucumber, a regular the-ice-man-cometh *not!*

How. Humiliating.

Seething with mortification, she stepped around Brand. "Look here, Mr. Ansgar, I don't know who you are or how you got in here, but I want you to get out of this ho—"

She froze, her eyes widening. Dooley hung suspended a few inches off the floor, caught in mid-pounce. The dog's ears were perked, and her tongue lolled out of her mouth like a big pink snail.

"Dooley, baby," Addy cried.

She stumbled over to the dog on wobbly legs and ran her fingers through Dooley's thick yellow fur. The Lab felt warm but stiff as a board to the touch. Addy found a heartbeat and breathed a sigh of relief. She stroked Dooley's head. No response. The dog wore the same frozen look of surprise as the deer her brother Shep shot and had mounted on his den wall.

Addy glared at the two Adonises who'd invaded her living room. Anger sizzled through her veins. She rose to her feet, her earlier dizziness forgotten. "What the hell did you do to my dog?"

The man called Ansgar flicked a look of cool disinterest in

her direction. "I silenced it. Such creatures are annoying and invariably noisy."

Addy pointed a shaking finger at the front door. "Out. Both of you."

"The djegrali—" Brand said.

"I don't give a rat's behind about your demonic little buddy." Outrage seethed in Addy's veins, making her feel stronger. "I want you two bozos out of this house. Now."

"Bozo?" The blond hunk looked thoughtful. "This appellation is unfamiliar to me. Is this a term used to signify hunters in this realm?"

"It's a term signifying I'm going to get my gun if you don't leave, and pronto."

Ansgar raised a brow. "You refer, I assume, to the metal tube you grasp?"

Addy looked down. She balanced a shotgun in her hands. The wooden stock felt cool against her palm. She broke open the gun. It was loaded with bird shot.

"Yeah, that would be the one." She closed the shotgun with a snap and pointed it at the two men. "Get out."

Brand and Ansgar exchanged glances and strode toward the door.

"Hold your horses, Blondy!" The big blond turned, and Addy jerked a thumb in Dooley's direction. "What about my dog?"

"I would advise against releasing the creature," he said. "It is bound to create a disturbance."

"And I would advise *you* to un-whammy my dog." Addy swung the barrel of the shotgun toward him. "Or else. It's been a long night, and I'm starting to get a little cranky."

He looked at her without blinking for a long moment and waved his hand at Dooley. Dooley landed on the carpet and erupted in a frenzy of barking.

"Obnoxious, is it not?" Ansgar's expression was pained. "You cannot say I did not warn you."

"Yeah, yeah, you told me." Addy waved the shotgun in the general direction of the door. "Beat it, both of you."

The two men walked out of the house without a word. With a final triumphant *woof*, Dooley ran to the door and sniffed. Satisfied she had done her duty, the dog trotted up and nudged Addy's leg with her nose.

Addy dropped the gun. It hit the floor with a dull thud.

"That's telling 'em, Dooley," she said, staring at the door with a pang of regret.

Brand left, without saying good-bye. Waggle a shotgun in a guy's face, threaten him with a little mayhem, and he ran fast enough to make a girl's head spin. Well, who needed him?

Staggering to the door, Addy flipped the dead bolt and made her way through the living room. What a night. She felt drained and exhausted. She needed a hot shower followed by the bed. She got all the way to the bedroom before it hit her.

She didn't own a shotgun.

Brand stood in the shadows watching the house. Long minutes passed, the night quiet but for the rustle of the wind in the leaves and the soft chirruping of insects.

"The human interests you?" Ansgar asked, breaking the silence.

"Yes."

"You have lived a hundred of her lifetimes. She is but a child."

Brand thought of Addy's soft lips moving beneath his, the feel of her smooth skin against his palms. He itched to touch her again. Adara Jean Corwin might be many things, but she was no child.

"If it is emptiness you seek, why not avail yourself of a thrall?" Ansgar persisted. "Is that not their purpose?"

Brand's gaze moved to the back of the house. A shapely form passed briefly in front of the curtained window and disappeared. "Perhaps it is not emptiness I seek."

"The emptiness serves its purpose, *our* purpose. We can ill afford distractions . . . no matter how tempting the distraction might be."

Ah, so Ansgar found the human enticing also.

Something hot and unfamiliar unfurled inside Brand.

He gave the other warrior a cold look. "You have not answered my question, Ansgar. Why are you here?"

Ansgar ran a loving hand along the curve of his bow. "I tracked my quarry to this place and lost it. I sensed the presence of another hunter and sought you out. What brings you to this place?"

"I followed two of the djegrali to this realm. One I slew, the other escaped, wounding the female human in the doing of it."

Ansgar grunted. "Three djegrali in one locus—odd, is it not? What do you think it means?"

"I do not know."

"You mean to linger here?"

"I do."

"Is that wise?"

Brand shifted his gaze to the other man. "The djegrali marked the female. It will return. When it does, I will be waiting."

"So, you mean to use the human as bait." Ansgar nodded in understanding.

Brand turned back to the house. "What else?"

"For a moment, I thought . . ." Ansgar shrugged. "No matter. It is a good plan. I will leave you to it then. To the hunt."

He raised a hand in farewell and vanished.

Brand studied the house for a long moment. "To the hunt," he said softly.

Addy made her way to the bathroom. Her chest still ached, but some of the dizziness was gone and she felt stronger. She took out her contacts and got into the shower, letting the warm water ease the tension from her muscles. It had been a hell of a night, and her nerves were worked. There was a rational explanation for what happened tonight—what she thought had happened tonight—wasn't there?

Uninvited, an image rose in her mind of the thing in the woods, its black scabrous hands reaching for her. The bathroom door banged open, and Addy jumped. She whirled around in the shower, lost her balance, and scrambled to keep a foothold on the slippery tile. She squinted and tried to focus her nearsighted eyes on the new threat. Instead of a soul-sucking fiend, she spied a familiar buttery blob through the glass shower door.

"Dooley Anne!" Addy clutched her chest. "You almost gave me a heart attack!" She opened the shower door a crack. "Nothing to say for yourself, huh? Good, 'cause you sure had plenty to say a little while ago. I gotta tell you, it seriously freaked me out. I guess that Brand fellow hypnotized me. I mean, it's not like dogs can talk, right?"

Dooley wagged her tail in answer and trotted out of the bathroom and into the adjoining bedroom. She sat down near Addy's queen-size bed, her ears perked at attention and her gaze on something only she could see.

Addy shut the shower door with a shake of her head. The Lab had an unnerving habit of staring at nothing. "Dooley-vision," she muttered.

Her Aunt Muddy said dogs could see things that humans could not, like spirits . . . or demons.

She shivered, then reached for the bar of soap. As the sponge glided over her wet body, she closed her eyes and allowed the soothing scent of lavender and chamomile to dispel her dark thoughts.

Brand waved his hand and the dead bolt turned with a satisfying snick. The door to Addy's house swung open. He frowned. The djegrali could have done the same thing with ease. The woman needed a keeper. He set a number of protective spells around the property's perimeter to alert him to the demon's presence and stepped inside the house. He stood in the darkness for a moment, listening. Faint sounds and a sliver of light drew him to the back of the dwelling. Silent as a shadow, he entered the bedroom and looked around. A large bed stood against one wall, the coverlet turned back to reveal green and white linens. Overhead a ceiling fan lazily stirred the air.

From the adjoining room he heard the unmistakable sound of flowing water. The dog trotted into the bedroom, and Brand mentally kicked himself. He had made himself invisible to humans, but he'd forgotten about the animal. Dooley's eyes lit up when she saw him. She sprang forward, her ears cocked in recognition. He raised an admonishing finger, and she swallowed her yip of welcome and sat down on the carpet. Wagging her tail, she gave him a doggie grin. Satisfied he had the animal under control, Brand glanced through the open door into the connecting room and received a shock. Addy stared back at him from the other room . . . some kind of bathing chamber, he realized dimly, unable to take his eyes off her. She could not see him—her gaze was on the dog—but he could see *her,* every delectable inch of her. She was naked, utterly, gloriously naked. The water coursed down her satin skin, and her wet hair hung in damp curls against the nape of her neck. She gave Dooley a nervous look and resumed her bath. Brand eyed her hungrily, drinking in the tantalizing view of her backside. A wave of lust hit him that nearly brought him to his knees. Perhaps Ansgar was right, he thought through a haze of desire. He should have availed himself of a thrall. Such strong emotion could not be productive.

Addy turned off the water and stepped out of the shower. He caught a brief glimpse of damp, gleaming skin.

"Thanks, hound doggie, for letting in all the cold air," she scolded, shutting the door.

Brand closed his eyes, thankful his view of Addy's lovely body had been blocked. He heard a mechanical whir from behind the closed door. Some kind of grooming apparatus, his muddled brain surmised. Taking a deep breath, he tried to curb his racing pulse. His heartbeat had scarcely slowed when the door to the bathing chamber opened and she stepped into the bedroom. She wore nothing but a towel. Her cap of light brown hair was still slightly damp. He stared at her, transfixed. His traitorous heart thundered as she walked toward him. Somehow, he retained the presence of mind to step out of her way before she bumped into him. He caught a tantalizing whiff of lavender as she sauntered past. The scent shot up his nostrils and straight to his groin. With an effort, he shook himself from his stupor and followed her on silent feet across the room. She stopped before another door, opened it, and disappeared inside.

Brand stole forward. Addy stood in the center of some kind of storage room. Garments hung on racks in neat rows, and a large number of drawers marched along the walls on either side. He edged closer. Some of the shelves held an alarming number of shoes.

Her back to the door, she opened a drawer and retrieved a patch of sheer white cloth. Dangling the scrap of cloth from one finger, she yanked a shapeless piece of gray material out of another drawer. She dropped the towel without warning. Brand's vision blurred and blood pounded through his veins as Addy wiggled the snippet of cloth up her firm thighs and over her curvaceous rump. He watched, fascinated by the way the filmy material hugged the lush curves of her backside. It was a ridiculous garment, designed to serve little practical purpose other than to inflame the male senses. Brand wanted to run his tongue along the edge of that lacy scrap of nothing and tear it off with his teeth. He swallowed a groan and closed his eyes.

When he opened them again, she had slipped the gray garment over her head. Oversized and shapeless, the shirt hung to her thighs and covered her backside. His tortured gaze followed her as she strolled back into the bedroom. The thin fabric teased her swaying breasts as she walked. Mercifully, she got into bed and pulled the blankets up to her chin. He took a deep breath, struggling to regain his customary calm. His reaction to this woman was an aberration. He willed his galloping heart to return to its normal rhythm. Now that she was in bed, her delicious form hidden beneath the covers, his raging libido would subside and he could do what he came here to do: kill the djegrali. He exhaled in relief, comforted by the thought.

His heavy sigh was audible in the quiet room.

"Who's there?" Wide eyed, Addy sat up and looked around. She spotted the dog and relaxed against the headboard. "Oh, Dooley, it's you. Come here, girl."

Dooley gave Brand a look that said, *Sorry, duty calls,* and ambled across the room. The dog shoved her long nose into Addy's hand.

" 'Course it was you, wasn't it, Doodle Bug?" Addy rubbed

the dog's ears. "I'm being silly, I guess. Truth is I'm still a little freaked out. Things were nuts tonight, you know?" A wave of lust hit Brand at her throaty little chuckle. "Come to think of it, you were a bit on the bizarre-o side yourself this evening, old doggie, old pal. For a while there, you looked like a window display in Skeeter's Taxidermy Shop. It was creepy, I gotta tell you." She scowled. "That was Blondy's fault though. Should have shot him when I had the chance. *Such creatures are invariably noisy.*" She mimicked Ansgar's haughty tone. "Jeez, what a pain in the rump. Right, Dooles?"

The dog gave a sharp bark in answer.

"Right." She rubbed the dog's ears again. "Glad we agree. What say we crash? Old Man Farris's funeral is tomorrow afternoon, and he's got a butt-load of relatives. Going to be a big day at the flower shop."

With a soft snuffle, Dooley curled up on her dog bed and laid her head on her paws.

"Good girl," Addy said.

With a yawn, she turned off the lamp and settled in the bed. A moment later, the light clicked back on.

Dooley raised her head and gave her mistress a questioning look.

"I think I'll leave the light on," Addy told the dog. "You know, just for a little while."

Brand's gut clenched when he heard the slight tremor in her voice. She was frightened. The knowledge hit him like a steel-clad fist. More shocking still was the overwhelming urge to take her in his arms and comfort her. He ground his teeth, stifling the impulse with an effort. He was a warrior, not a nurse maid. Swallowing a growl of frustration, he retreated to the far side of the room. He needed distance from the female if he was to control these ludicrous whims. He sank to the floor and folded his arms across his chest, his gaze on Addy's supine form. He was here to protect her. That was all. He could not allow himself to have feelings for her.

Feelings. He suppressed a snort of derision at the thought. Such a *human* concept.

The very idea was laughable or would be if he possessed a sense of humor. But the Dalvahni did not indulge in levity. Theirs was an immortal race created for one purpose and one purpose alone. To hunt the djegrali and return them to their proper plane of existence or slay them as need be. The Dalvahni did not *feel*. There was no place for emotion.

Brand shifted in sudden unease. A Dalvahni warrior did not lie, even to himself. Something had happened to him when he encountered this female.

He *felt*.

Some of the emotions he recognized. Lust, for example; the Dalvahni knew well the sharp claws of desire, especially in the wake of battle. Thus the need for the thralls, although never to this degree, and never in combination with other more dangerous emotions . . . such as the odd sensation he experienced earlier this evening when he realized Ansgar also found the human female desirable. It was as if a demon had taken residence in his chest and tried to claw its way out. He wanted to howl with rage and tear the other man limb from limb. Ansgar, a brother *warrior*!

Most unsettling.

He scowled. And then there was the pleasurable sensation he felt when the woman said and did certain things, a lightness that rose up inside him and made him want to smile. What was that? And what name did one attach to the desire he'd experienced a moment before when he sensed her fear and wanted to hold her?

He was a warrior, a man renowned among a stoic race for self-restraint. Yet in the space of an evening, thousands of years of self-control had been decimated by one maddeningly unpredictable female. The woman had to be a sorceress, her enchantment magic of the most powerful kind. She was dangerous, more dangerous than a hundred demons. If he knew what was good for him, he would hunt down the demon and leave this place.

If he knew what was good for him.

Chapter Three

Brand closed his eyes and recited the creed engraved on the walls of the Hall of Warriors. *We are the Dalvahni. We seek the djegrali through space and time. We do not tire. We do not fail. We hunt.*

He faltered, the familiar words wiped from his mind by a soft rustling movement across the room. No matter how hard he concentrated, he could not ignore the woman in the bed. Once she'd fallen asleep, he turned out the light, thinking the darkness would be his ally. Wrong. Her scent filled the air. He heard each breath she took. The whisper of her smooth skin against the sheets, her gentle sighs in her sleep played like a siren's song upon his tortured nerves, luring him to his doom. Again and again his unwilling feet carried him to the bed. He stood over her and watched her sleep, trembling with need. Each time, sanity returned, and he retreated to the far side of the room. No battle he ever fought had left him so exhausted. He had been in a fever of lust for hours, imagining his limbs tangled with hers, his tongue laving her pebbled nipples, his hardness thrusting into her silken heat. The heated images left him sweaty and shaken, filled with longing for a dawn that would not come. Never had he imagined such agony.

Never had he felt so alive.

He rose and strode to the window to look out. Not long until dawn. The knot in his belly eased. The longest night of his very long existence was almost over. At daybreak he would resume the hunt. He would find the djegrali, slay it, and depart this place. He would repair to the Hall of Warriors and slake his desire upon a thrall. He glanced down at the bulge in his leather breeches. Two thralls, maybe three. He would not think of the human female again. He would forget the uncomfortable emotions she evoked, return to the familiar emptiness. He would avoid Earth for a few hundred cycles. He would forget.

He was Dalvahni . . . He would forget.

With a muffled grunt of impatience, Addy rolled over. Brand froze at the window, his back to the bed. The soft swoosh of the blankets told him she'd thrown off the covers. He closed his eyes and gritted his teeth. He would not look. Sweat beaded on his forehead with the effort not to turn his head. His neck muscles moved of their own accord. He opened his eyes and saw her. She lay on her side, her long legs bared to his perusal, the gray garment bunched around her waist. His gaze roamed up the firm curves of her calves and thighs and stopped. The ridiculous snippet of cloth she wore over her heart-shaped ass had ridden up on one side, exposing the bottom half of a lusciously rounded buttock. All the blood drained from his head and went straight to his groin. With a groan of defeat, he moved toward the bed.

Warm hands caressed Addy's skin, slid up her calves past her thighs and inside her panties, stroked and kneaded her bottom. A deep voice murmured wicked words in her ear. *I need you,* the seductive voice whispered. *I want you. Pleasure me, little one. Let me pleasure you.* Her shirt eased up. Rough palms cupped her breasts. Hot breath brushed her bared nipples. She arched her back in silent entreaty, begging for more. A velvet tongue licked the tip of one breast, and then the other. *That is it, little one. Give yourself to me.* Addy shivered as cool air drifted across the wet buds. It felt wonderful, sinful, beyond anything she'd ever imagined, the most erotic dream of her life. She didn't want it to end.

A callused thumb grazed her aching nipples. She stretched, seeking the caress with hungry eagerness, and rubbed up against a warm, hard chest.

Her eyes flew open. She sat up in bed, wide awake, but the dream did not end. Invisible hands tugged her T-shirt over her head, leaving her naked except for her panties. Numb with shock, she watched her shirt sail across the room and land in a rumpled heap on the floor. She squeaked in surprise as unseen fingers traced a delicate path along her collarbone and over the slopes of her breasts. Her eyes widened as her breasts were fondled and lifted. A hot, wet mouth fastened upon one nipple and then the other, suckling. She gasped and dropped her head back with a moan of protest. The smooth slide of a phantom tongue soothed the tortured peaks. Heat flared in her belly and between her legs.

This could not be happening. Either she was crazy as her great-aunt Etheline, who talked to lampposts and saw flying cats, or she was being made love to by a ghost.

"Son-of-a-bitch," she said, coming to her senses. She swung her arm at her amorphous seducer. To her surprise, she contacted solid flesh. Solid *unyielding* flesh.

"Ouch." She rubbed her bruised arm.

Brand materialized on the bed beside her, a frown creasing his perfect brow. He scooped her up in his strong arms and deposited her in his lap. "You have harmed yourself," he said, examining her arm. "This I cannot allow."

"*You.*" She scrambled to the floor and crossed her arms over her naked breasts. "I told you to leave. How did you get back in my house?"

"I entered through the door of this domicile, in the usual manner of your species." He rose and stalked her around the room, backing her against the bed. "I found it pitifully easy to breach your defenses."

In more ways than one, Addy thought, her cheeks growing hot at the memory of her wanton response to him. She raised her chin. "Oh, yeah? Well, I don't remember asking you to protect me."

"It is my duty, in case the djegrali returns."

"Are you telling me you've been here *all night*?"

"Yes. All night."

He pounced without warning and pushed her onto the bed. Pinning her arms above her head with one hand, he trailed his other hand over her breasts and stomach and farther down, past the top of her panties. "I watched you sleep, you know." His tone sounded conversational as he traced a lazy pattern between her legs with his fingers. "Counted every sigh, every breath you took."

She twisted beneath him as he stroked her through the outside of her panties. "Oh, my God, that feels so . . . Oh, *please.*"

He lowered his head. His long hair tickled the skin of her breasts and stomach. "I sat in the lonely darkness, listening to the whispered sigh of your hair across the pillow as you stirred."

His tone no longer sounded neutral. Alarm and something else skittered along Addy's nerves at that low, rumbling growl.

"I ached for you throughout the endless hours of the night, imagined the silken kiss of your hair and lips upon my flesh." His mouth grazed hers. "I burned. All night I burned for you." He slid his hand inside her panties, his fingers tangling in her damp curls. His fingers found and teased the sensitive nubbin between her legs. "I am the sun, Adara Jean, and you are the flower. Such sweet petals. That's it. Open for me, little flower."

"You should have heeded my advice and availed yourself of a thrall, my brother," a low, disapproving voice said. "Such strong emotion is not advisable in a warrior."

Brand jerked Addy beneath him, covering her nakedness with his body. "Ansgar." His voice was without inflection. "What is your purpose here?"

The blond warrior shrugged. "What else, but the hunt? I tracked the djegrali into the village near here and lost him. I thought, perchance, we might join forces. But you pursue game of a different sort, I see."

"How came you past the safeguards I set in place?"

"You timed your spells to end at sunrise." There was a hint of mockery in Ansgar's cool tone. "The sun is up, my brother, and you have yet to continue the chase. Or is that the djegrali you grapple with, cleverly disguised as a . . . flower, was it?"

"Let me up." Addy was mortified beyond belief. God, she was such a skank, a hoochie mama, a slut of biblical proportions.

What was the matter with her? She'd come within an inch of . . . well, within an inch of *coming* and letting this guy do her.

Brand's cold gaze flicked over her and back to the other warrior. "No. You are unclothed. He will see you. This I cannot allow."

"Cannot allow? Cannot *allow*? That's it. I've had enough of this macho crap." Addy shoved against Brand's broad shoulders, but he did not budge. "Get off of me, you big ape."

"Not while you are unclad."

"Then tell that blond horse's ass to get out of my room." Addy decided to take refuge in fury. "Better yet, tell him to get out of my house And you, too, while you're at it." Her head whipped around at a sudden thought. "Wait a minute, where's Dooley?"

"Do not distress yourself. The animal is unharmed." Ansgar sounded bored. "She chases a stag through the smallish wood situated at the edge of this demesne."

"Stag? You mean a deer? This is a gated community. There aren't any deer here." Addy's blood pressure rose. "You've done something to my dog. Again. That tears it. Out. Both of you. Out of my house. NOW!"

One moment, the heavy weight of Brand's muscular body pressed down upon her, warm and hard and unbelievably sexy, and the next instant he was gone. Addy sat up and looked around. Ansgar had disappeared, too.

"Good riddance," she mumbled. She wiped her stinging eyes with the back of her hand. Tears of humiliation and outrage, that's what they were. No way was she crying because that big jerk got her all hot and bothered and turned into Icicle Man once his buddy showed up. She stomped over to the closet and pulled on a pair of shorts and a clean T-shirt. Shoving her feet into a pair of flip flops, she stormed out the back door in search of Dooley.

Brand landed on a wide stretch of mown grass beside a paved road, his senses still spinning with Addy's intoxicating warmth and scent. He looked around. To his left, the wind sang through a forest of pines. On his right, an immense field of freshly tilled earth stretched like a fallen red clay giant in the early morning sun. It was a peaceful scene, at odds with the firestorm of lust and frustration raging within him. He was rock hard and aching with lust. He wanted Addy. Wanted to lose himself in her sweetness and warmth until the devil's brew of desire and emotion she aroused in him was spent.

Barring that, he wanted to slam his fist in Ansgar's smug face for interfering.

As if summoned by his thoughts, the air shimmered and Ansgar appeared.

Brand schooled his face into an expressionless mask. "You have a purpose for bringing us to this place, I assume?"

Ansgar raised his brows. "I? I thought this was your doing."

"No."

"How . . . unsettling. I hoped you had perchance come to your senses and abandoned the wench."

"In good time," Brand said through his teeth. "But first I will use her to trap the djegrali."

"Very clever of you. I suppose it was necessary to disrobe the human in order to—er—bait the trap?"

Something dark and unfamiliar clawed its way from the deepest recesses of Brand's soul. The sensation was strange and disquieting, and it was a moment before he recognized it. Jealous; by the sword, he was *jealous*. Ansgar had seen Addy in all her unclad glory, her exquisite body bare but for an inconsequential wisp of fabric that hugged her delectable backside. The other warrior's eyes had roamed the graceful curves of her back and long, smooth legs. Perhaps he even caught a glimpse of Addy's luscious breasts before Brand pulled her beneath him. The knowledge made Brand want to kill Ansgar with his bare hands, to wipe the memory of Addy's body from the other man's mind. With an effort, he tamped down his anger. Such emotion was undesirable in a warrior. He was a demon slayer, he reminded himself. In a race of disciplined fighters, he was renowned for his self-control. He would not lose his temper.

"She is amusing, I will admit." He shrugged. "But the Dalvahni are immune to human wiles, as you well know."

"So I thought, but she is a most distracting female, is she not?" Ansgar's cool voice held a thread of amusement. "Such spirit and fire contained in a delicious package. Small wonder if you were distracted, brother. It makes me want to—er—check her snare myself."

The demon of jealousy burst forth. Brand slammed his fist into Ansgar's face and knocked him to the ground. He stood over the other warrior, fists clenched. "You will keep your distance, *brother*," he snarled. "If you value your life."

Ansgar climbed to his feet, his expression one of stunned disbelief. "You hit me. You hit me over a *woman,* Brand. Such unbridled spleen is unsuitable in a warrior. I should report you."

"But you will not. Because that would mean abandoning the hunt, and that you will not do."

"No, I will not relinquish my prey. But that is not all that keeps me here." Ansgar rubbed his bruised jaw and gazed at the smudge of trees on the far side of the plowed field. "Strange forces stir in this place. The djegrali gather here, but to what purpose? And then there is your behavior. Most uncharacteristic. In the eons I have served beside you, you have always been a model of restraint. But no more, it would seem. Why, I ask myself? My curiosity is aroused, as well as my hunter's instincts. I have questions, and I mean to find the answers." He turned to Brand, his silver-gray eyes sharp. "For instance, if you did not transport us to this place, and *I* did not, then who did? This, at least, is a mystery I think you can answer. How came we here, brother?"

Brand tightened his jaw and measured his words with care. What he was about to admit was unprecedented. "In thinking the matter over, it is perhaps possible that Adara—uh—I mean, the female may be responsible."

Ansgar gazed at him without blinking. "She is a sorceress, then?"

"No. As I told you last night, she was harmed during the fight with the djegrali."

"Harmed in what manner?"

"An ice dagger. The creature stabbed her in the chest as it fled. 'Twas a mortal injury. I repaired it."

For the first time in Brand's memory, Ansgar's perpetual air of imperious complacence wavered.

"A mortal wound and you repaired it? Such a thing is not permitted. If she is responsible for transporting us here, then that means . . ." Ansgar's eyes widened. "It means you gave a human a portion of your essence! It is forbidden."

"She came to my aid and in doing so was injured. Healing a human comrade wounded in battle is not unknown, although I will admit it is unusual and generally discouraged. As for the other, where is it written? I do not recall such a prohibition."

It was Ansgar's turn to clench his teeth, a circumstance that gave Brand some small measure of satisfaction. "You do not recall it because it has never been done," Ansgar ground out. "We are immortal. The consequences of what you have done could be disastrous."

"Don't you think I know that? That is why I mean to keep a close eye on the human."

"It wasn't your eyes I noticed on the female, Brand."

Brand ignored him and strode up the road. "I take full responsibility for my actions, including the consequences. I bid you good hunting. I must return to my charge, lest the djegrali find and harm her in my absence."

Ansgar trotted after him. "I will accompany you. The demon I seek will no doubt be drawn to its fellow creature."

"As you wish."

They rounded a curve in the road and saw a number of buildings in the distance.

Ansgar stopped in front of a faded metal sign on the side of the road. "*Brand.*"

Anxious as he was to get back to Adara, something in the other warrior's voice gave Brand pause. He retraced his steps.

"What is it?" Ansgar stood unmoving before the sign, a peculiar expression on his face. Swallowing his annoyance, Brand joined Ansgar. "What troubles you, Ansgar?"

Ansgar raised his hand and pointed. With growing impatience, Brand turned and looked at the strange squiggles painted on the worn metal marker. The Dalvahni were blessed with the gift of languages, a necessary talent in their travels between worlds. After a moment's concentration, the unfamiliar marks shifted and blurred into something recognizable.

"It is a sign proclaiming the name of this hamlet. What of it?"

"Look at it again, Brand. And this time, speak the words out loud."

"Han-nah-a-lah." Brand read the strange script aloud. Startled, he stepped back. "By the sword, it cannot be."

Ansgar nodded. "Han-nah-a-lah. How many times have you heard those words? *The Dalvahni shall be bound to the hunt until Han-nah-a-lah,* or so the old saying goes. We always assumed Han-nah-a-lah meant until the end of time. The end of time, it would seem, is upon us."

"Dooo-ley." Addy trotted down the paved path in the park, slowing when she saw the clump of trees ahead. Even in daylight the shadows in the wood seemed menacing. She did *not* wish to go back into those trees. She cupped her hands to her mouth and called the dog again. "Dooley Anne Corwin, you come here. Don't make me come after you." She heard the Lab's excited barking from the belly of the woods and decided to try bribery. "Be a good girl and come here, and Addy will give you a piece of cheese."

"Lost your dog?" a voice drawled.

She spun around. She relaxed when she recognized Darryl Wilson, the strapping security guard hired by the home owner's association to keep an eye on things. Darryl finished high school a few years ahead of her and was harmless enough. There were six Wilson brothers. All but one played football at Hannah High. Like most of his brothers, Darryl worked hard and played harder, which around here meant hunting, drinking, and running around raising hell in his pickup truck. The gig as security guard, he once confided to Addy, was, he hoped, a stepping stone to the local police force.

"Oh, hey, Darryl, you startled me." She flung him a distracted smile, her thoughts on her dog. "Yeah, Dooley got out, and I'm trying to round her back up. How you doing?"

Darryl did not answer. Addy glanced back and found him staring at her chest, mouth ajar. Her face grew hot. She'd rushed out of the house without putting on a bra, and her nipples were on high alert, pushing against the thin fabric of her T-shirt. Her first instinct was to cross her arms and slink away. Nice girls did *not* go out of the house without a bra. From the look on Darryl's face, you'd think he'd never seen a pair of undomesticated casabas, which Addy knew for a fact wasn't true. Darryl's girlfriend, Raeleene, was rough as a cob and a threat to get drunk and hang out the window of Darryl's truck, her bare boobs flapping in the breeze. Addy straightened her shoulders. Well, Darryl could get over it, 'cause these puppies weren't going back in the crate until she found Dooley. She hoped Mama didn't find out she'd been running around without proper undergarments. Sheesh, the thought of the bear jawing she'd get made her wince.

"Yoo hoo, Darryl." She waved her hand at him.

"Huh?" He dragged his eyes off her breasts. "Say, Addy, your hair looks different. Kinda crazy sexy, if you know what I mean." His gaze moved to her bare legs and stuck there. He swallowed like he had a potato stuck in his throat. "Y-you wanna go out sometime? I got my own truck."

Lord love a redneck, Addy thought with a mental eye roll. "Thanks, but I don't think Raeleene would like it."

"Oh, yeah, I forgot about her." He looked alarmed for a moment and then wistful. "Would she have to know?"

"It's a small town, Darryl."

"Yeah, but I wouldn't want to carpet it."

Oh, brother, a comedian. She really did not need this.

"Aren't you the funniest thing?" Addy gave him a bright smile and edged down the path. "Well, nice to see you, Darryl. Tell your mama I said hi. I'd best go look for Dooley."

A deep bay from the stand of trees drew her up short.

"That your dog, Addy? He sounds hepped up. Maybe he's treed him a cat or something."

"She," Addy said absently, her gaze on the woods. Dooley was chasing something, and she sounded excited about it. "You seen any deer around here, Darryl?"

"In River Bend? Not unless you count them ornamental ones Miz Hiebert has on her lawn. She dresses them thangs up for holidays. Puts bunny ears on 'em for Easter and gives 'em fangs for Halloween. It's wrong." He spat. "I can't wait until I get me a real police job. It's deadsville working in a retirement community. Bunch of blue-haired little old ladies mostly. You still house-sitting for your great aunt?"

"Yeah, I'm staying in River Bend while Aunt Muddy does the world tour thing."

"That Muddy's whatcha might call a gen-u-ine character, ain't she?" He was staring at her chest again with that deer-in-the-headlights look. *Her* headlights. The poor guy practically drooled. "Why, I 'member one time when I was a boy, she—"

A loud snort interrupted him. An enormous white deer with silver antlers trotted out of the grove. Dooley bounced behind the gigantic animal barking like mad. The buck ignored the yapping canine with magnificent disdain and danced across the park, his hooves skimming the surface of the grass.

"Holy shit." Darryl's eyes bugged out of his head. "Take a look at the rack on that buck. I ain't never seen a spread that wide. Where's my gun?"

He dashed off in the direction of the gatehouse and his truck.

"Typical guy," Addy muttered. "Always going for the bigger rack."

The stag cantered past her and cleared the eight-foot wrought-iron fence that encircled the subdivision with room to spare. Dooley tore after the gigantic ruminant and threw herself against the fence with a last emphatic woof as if to say, *There, and don't come back.* Tongue lolling, she turned and galloped up to Addy for approval.

"Bad dog," Addy scolded. "What would you do with that

thing if you caught it?" Dooley hung her head and whined. "I cannot believe you went back into those woods. Didn't you learn anything last night?" Hands on hips, Addy glared down at the dog. "Well, young lady, what have you got to say for yourself?"

The Lab rolled over and showed her belly. *"Sorry, Addy. Sorry."* Dooley looked up at Addy with soulful eyes and sprang to her feet. *"Ooh, Addy, Addy! Can Dooley have cheese?"*

Chapter Four

The shrill ring of the telephone greeted Addy as she stepped into the house. She grabbed the receiver off the cradle. Balancing it between her shoulder and ear, she rummaged through the refrigerator looking for dog cheese. Dooley watched her open the drawer and remove the block of cheddar, ears perked and eyes bright with interest.

"Hello?" Addy grabbed a knife and sliced off a piece of cheese to give to the salivating dog.

"Addy." Her mother's voice on the other end of the line sounded tense. "You need to open the shop early this morning in case there are any last-minute orders for the Farris funeral. It's a morning service, you know."

"Yes, Mom, I know." Addy resealed the cheese and shoved it back in the drawer. "I always open early when there's a funeral. I'll be there in a few minutes."

"And wear something appropriate. Don't think about wearing jeans, or, God forbid, spaghetti straps. A funeral is not the place for cleavage."

"Oh, I don't know, Mama. A little T and A might be a surefire way to make certain Old Man Farris is dead before we stick him in the ground. From what I hear, he was quite the womanizer."

"I'll have you know, Adara Jean Corwin, that your brother is a professional. His customers come in here dead, and they stay that way! And don't speak ill of the dearly departed. It's disrespectful."

"Yes, ma'am." Addy put her hand over the mouthpiece. "But the man was still a dog, if you'll pardon the expression," she told Dooley. "I've heard her say it more than once. I don't see what's wrong with saying so just 'cause he's dead."

"What's that? I can't hear you," Mama said. "Addy, are you talking to that dog again? People are going to think you're as crazy as Aunt Etheline if you're not careful. I swear you need a husband, someone you can carry on a real conversation with."

Addy glanced at the clock. Fifty-five seconds before her mother dropped the "h" bomb. Predictable, but nowhere near her world-record time. Mama was off her game today.

All her life she'd tried to please her mother, to stay inside the lines when she was a color-outside-the-lines kind of girl. But her stubborn nature balked at Mama's attempts to get her hitched. She would not marry someone to please her mother. But that didn't mean she didn't feel guilty about it.

"You'd be surprised what a good conversationalist Dooley is, Mama," she said. "Listen, I gotta go."

She hung up the phone with a sigh, snagged her favorite mug out of the cabinet, and fixed a cup of hot tea. After a moment's hesitation, she went to the liquor cabinet and added a liberal splash of Grand Marnier. She took a small swig, enjoying the spicy orange flavor the liqueur added to her Irish Breakfast tea. Normally she wasn't much of a drinker, especially in the morning, but between her Close Encounter of the Absurd Kind with Darryl and Bambi from *Land of the Giants,* and her conversation with Dooley the Loquacious Labrador, she thought she was entitled to a little tonic for her nerves. Sipping her drink, she padded into her bedroom and made the bed, then laid out a black skirt and blue silk blouse to wear. No spaghetti straps, no jeans. As if she didn't have more couth than to show up at a funeral with her girls hanging out. She finished her cup of tea and felt a little calmer. She could do this. The trick was to handle one thing at a time. Sure, a talking dog was a little unusual, but that didn't necessarily mean she was losing her mind. And if it did, she didn't have time to worry about it. She had too much to do.

She stripped off her clothes and tossed them into the hamper in the closet. As she stepped into the bathroom she spied her contact case on the counter by the sink. The case was still closed. She did a quick recap of the morning. Nope, she hadn't put in her contacts before she left the house.

Moving like a sleep walker, she went over to the sink and plucked her glasses out of the case. She'd been blind as a bat since third grade. Without contacts or glasses, things should be hopelessly blurred, but she could see great. Better than great, in fact. She had perfect vision. Stunned, she looked up and saw herself in the mirror.

"Holy cow," she squawked, stumbling back. She caught her foot on the rug and fell into the shower, banging her arm on the way down. Nursing her bruised wrist, she scrambled to her feet and rushed back to the mirror. Her hair was a pure white blond, the same color it had been when she was a child. A color only nature—and no hairdresser—could produce. In addition to the startling color change, her hair had grown four inches overnight. It floated around her shoulders in soft, wild curls that gave her a tousled just-been-bedded look. She remembered Brand with a blush. And she nearly had been, hadn't she? Who would have guessed her inner whore lurked so close to the surface.

She glanced down and gave a little shriek. The hair *there* had turned blond, too. She dragged her gaze upward to study the woman in the mirror. She looked different and yet the same. Same nose, same chin, same mouth, but better. Addy to the twelfth power. Super Addy with flawless skin, glowing cheeks, and a sultry, pouting pink mouth. She leaned closer. Her brows and lashes were golden brown, not blond like the hair on her head, thank God. Blond eyelashes and she'd look like a roach in a flour barrel.

She touched the jagged, black mark above her left breast, the single blemish on her otherwise flawless skin. Even the little white scar below her right eye, the one she got falling off her grandmother's porch when she was eight, had vanished. As she watched, the angry, purple and red lump on her arm faded and disappeared, too. What was happening to her? This was way past

Aunt Etheline crazy. This was *Twilight Zone* stuff. Hannah was a very small town. People were bound to notice and comment on her new makeover. Mama would notice that was for darn sure. Oh, God, her *mother.*

Addy jumped in the shower to get ready for work.

Thirty minutes later, she deactivated the alarm system and entered the flower shop through the back door. Stepping inside the stockroom, she took a quick mental inventory of the floral supplies that lined the shelves on the wall, a ritual that seldom failed to soothe and ground her. The shop was her home away from home, had been since the eighth grade when she fled the horrors of Dead Central to work after school in her great-aunt's flower shop. It was a betrayal her mother had yet to forgive or forget. Two years ago, Aunt Muddy had sold her the business and sailed off to see the world, leaving Addy, at twenty-five, the proud new owner of the only floral business in town. She remodeled the shop, which hadn't been changed since the late sixties, adding two open display coolers banked along one wall that invited customers to browse a wide selection of flowers. Several large worktables and sinks in the middle of the space allowed patrons to observe floral arrangements being made, and a separate workstation in one corner contained balloons, a helium tank, rolls of ribbon, and balloon weights. In addition to the cosmetic changes Addy had made, the shop's inventory now included a small number of tasteful gift items and monogrammed stationery. Last, but not least, there was a line of exquisite handmade candles, soaps, and lotions made by her best friend, Evie Douglass.

Addy entered the front room of the shop. She flipped on the lights, unlocked the front door and booted up the computer. Within fifteen minutes, she received three more orders for the Farris funeral. She was putting the final touches on a sympathy vase of Stargazer lilies, snapdragons, Fuji mums, and alstromeria when the bell on the door chimed and a woman came in wearing a shapeless ankle-length dress, a wide brimmed gardening hat, and Birkenstock knock-off sandals. She staggered inside, her face obscured by the large cardboard box she carried.

Addy smiled. "Morning, Evie."

"Green tea and banana bread for breakfast and brownies for later." Evie set the carton down on the counter and gasped in surprise. "Addy, your hair! Oh, my God, why didn't you tell me you were thinking of going blonde?"

Oh, Lord, here we go, Addy thought with an inward groan. What on Earth was she going to tell people? What on Earth was she going to tell *Evie*? They'd been friends since elementary school. She'd never be able to buffalo Evie Douglass. Evie had a sixth sense about such things. She'd know in a second if Addy lied to her.

For that matter, so would anybody else, Addy reflected glumly. She was a terrible liar.

"Uh, I didn't exactly plan it." Addy avoided Evie's gaze. "It—uh—just kind of happened."

"What do you mean, it just kind of happened? Did you trip and fall into a vat of peroxide on the way to work?"

Addy snorted. Evie could always make her laugh. It was one of the things she loved about her. Not that Evie shared her sense of humor with many people. She was way too shy.

"No, smart ass, I didn't."

Evie came around the worktable. "No way you got this done at the Kut 'N' Kurl. You went to one of those she-she salons in Mobile, didn't you?"

The hint of accusation in Evie's voice made Addy smile. A trip to the big city was a rare treat. "Calm down. I didn't go to Mobile without you."

"I should hope not." Frowning, Evie examined one of Addy's curls. "I have to admit, it's a great dye job. It looks so natural. But the upkeep is going to be a bitch, and all those chemicals are going to ruin your hair."

"Relax, Granola Girl, I didn't dye my hair."

"You didn't? So, what happened then? Somebody scare the crap out of you and make your hair turn white?" Evie gave her a squinty-eyed glare. "Your hair is straight as a stick, not curly. And it's grown to your shoulders overnight. Explain that." Her expression eased. "Oh, it's a wig, isn't it? Gosh, girl, you had me going. Can you imagine what your mother would say if you dyed your hair? She'd have a cow." She waved her hands in the air. "She'd have a whole *herd* of cows."

"I didn't dye my hair, and it's not a wig."

"But, Addy—"

Addy shoved aside the bouquet she was working on. "Look, Eves, I have to tell somebody or I'm going to explode. Something happened last night, and I—"

The front door chimed, and a petite, fashionable blonde sailed into the shop on designer sling-back heels.

"Later." Evie sounded panic stricken. "Death Starr at two o'clock."

"Great," Addy said. "Just what I needed."

Summoning a smile, she turned to greet her customer. "Good morning, Meredith. What can I do for you today?"

"Good heavens, what have you done to yourself, Addy? You look wonderful." Meredith Starr Peterson ignored Evie and set her Fendi leather baguette on the counter. She placed her left hand on top so that the huge diamond ring she wore sparkled in the light. "You went to Mobile for a makeover, didn't you, you sly thing, and didn't tell me!"

"Evie and I went together." Addy winced as she received a sharp kick in the ankle from Evie. "It was a lark, you know. One of those glam shot things at the mall."

"You and The Whale went?" Out of the corner of her eye Addy saw Evie cringe as Meredith's attention shifted to her. Meredith's upper lip curled as she looked Evie up and down. "Looks like the same old Whaley Douglass to me. I'd say you wasted your time and your money."

Meredith had been a thorn in Addy's side since seventh grade, but that was nothing to how she'd mistreated poor Evie over the years. For some unknown reason, Meredith *hated* Evie. To make matters worse, Evie was now the bookkeeper in the Peterson Land Office, the business owned and operated by

Meredith's husband, Trey. This seemed to make Meredith hate Evie worse and gave the Death Starr more torture time.

"Grow up, Meredith, and stop picking on people," Addy said. "This is not high school."

Meredith raised her arched brows. "This is a small town, Addy. It will always be high school. Only we're in the twenty-first grade instead of the twelfth." She drummed her long, red nails on the counter. "And in case you've forgotten—though how you could when it was 'the' social event of the season three years ago is beyond me—I'm Mrs. Trey Peterson now. What I say goes, same as in high school."

"You mean, because Trey has money."

"Exactly. Something you'd do well to remember as a business-woman."

Addy swallowed her retort as Brand and Ansgar strode into the shop. Brand looked bigger and more intimidating and—God help all females—more handsome in broad daylight, even in that ridiculous getup. Nobody in their right mind wore leather in Alabama in the summertime, unless they were into something kinky or on the back of a motorcycle. Or maybe both. Ansgar looked around him with interest, but Brand seemed indifferent to his surroundings, bored even. And then he looked at her. His expression might be impassive, but his green eyes blazed with fury. Whew, she had one seriously pissed-off medieval dude in her shop. She edged away from the counter. Maybe she could make a run for the back door. But, that would leave poor Evie with Macho Man and Testosterone Pal *and* the Death Starr to deal with. That would be a rotten thing to do, especially to a friend. Besides, she was pretty sure Brand would catch her before she got out the door.

"Well, well, w-e-l-l, and who is this?" Meredith propped her manicured hands on her size two hips and eyed the men with appreciation. "It's a little early for Halloween, but I like it. Shiver me timbers, me buck-os."

"They're not pirates, Meredith. They're warriors," Addy said. "The big sword and the bow and arrows ought to be your first clue."

"The only sword I see is the one Tall, Dark, and Sinful is carrying in his pants. Impressive," Meredith purred. She turned her attention to Ansgar, her gaze lingering on his crotch. "Ooh, his friend is packing heat, too." She gave a fake shiver. "Delicious."

What was up? Couldn't Meredith see the great big sword Brand carried or Ansgar's longbow and arrows? Evie didn't seem to see them, either. How strange.

"So, what brings you boys to town?" Meredith said, oozing femininity with all the poisonous charm of a cobra.

Back in high school, Meredith was Miss Everything. Prom queen, homecoming queen, head cheerleader, emphasis on the *head*. After high school, she got her hooks into Trey. Marrying into a socially prominent family landed her front and center in the Hannah social scene. Meredith thrived on attention. She demanded attention, particularly from males. But Brand and Ansgar, bless them all to pieces, ignored her. The Death Starr! Nobody ignored the Death Starr. The expression of disbelief and outrage on Meredith's face was priceless. It made Addy feel warm inside.

Until Brand glared at her, that is, and the warm fuzzies turned into the cold willies.

"Adara, I must speak with you," he said.

Well, actually, he *growled*.

Meredith grew visibly more peevish by the second. "Who *are* these men, Addy?"

Addy thought quickly. "Actors, from the medieval dinner theater in Orlando."

"What are they doing in Hannah?"

"They're—uh—here for the Farris funeral."

"Hmm." Meredith tapped one dainty little foot. "Long-lost relatives?"

"That's right." Addy smiled with relief. The Death Starr seemed to buy her story, thank God. Maybe she wasn't such a bad liar, after all.

Meredith cocked her head like an inquisitive sparrow. "Just blew into town?"

"Uh huh."

"If they just got here and they're so long lost, how come you know so much about them?" the Death Starr asked sweetly, going in for the kill.

Addy gaped at Meredith. "Uh . . . well, um, you see . . ." And that was it. Her brain shut down and went on vacation. For the life of her, she could not think of a single intelligent thing to say. Or a not so intelligent thing to say. She was screwed, glued, and tattooed. She was the planet Alderaan, and she was toast. Score one for the Death Starr.

Evie stepped forward, bravely drawing the Death Starr's fire. "Her mother told her. She called Addy this morning and told her to expect them. They have to rush back to the theater right after the funeral, which is why they're dressed so funny. They've each ordered a spray for the funeral, which I think is awfully sweet. The large sprays, too, not the dinky ones like—" Evie faltered, but Addy knew what she'd been about to say. *Like the dinky ones you ordered for your father's funeral, Meredith.* From the expression on Meredith's face, she knew it, too. Addy saw Evie dart a nervous glance at Ansgar, and away again before continuing. "N-nothing but roses and white lilies. There won't be a single white rose left in the shop today after Addy fills their order."

The Death Starr turned her super lasers on Evie and opened fire. "I don't recall speaking to you, *Whaley,* but since you're such a know-it-all let me tell you this. I'm here to place an order for the very exclusive luncheon I'm having in the Gilded Room at the club today. Six centerpieces, all white roses and baby's breath. Since you're Addy's little gofer, I suggest you shag your lumpy ass over to Paulsberg and get me some white roses pronto. But, make sure you have the florist wrap them in cellophane first. Don't you dare touch them, you hear? I don't want fat girl cooties on my flowers."

Evie wilted under Meredith's barrage of venom. Something inside of Addy snapped.

"Evie is not fat." Addy jabbed the floral scissors in her hand at Meredith for emphasis. "She never was. That's something you made up out of spite in the seventh grade, because Evie got boobs first and you were jealous. You, on the other hand, have always been a rude bitch. I put up with it in school, but I'm tired of it. Apologize to Evie at once."

"Me, apologize to that stupid cow? I don't think so. And you'd better watch your mouth, Addy Corwin, if you hope to keep my business. I'm a very important person in this town."

The blood sang through Addy's veins. She was strong. She was invincible. She was tired of Meredith's crap.

"Here's the thing, Meredith," she said. "I don't want your business. In fact, I don't want you in my shop. Ever again. You're a nasty, mean person, and I hope you get pimples all over your tiny little butt so bad you have to eat off the mantel for a month."

Addy knew she'd scored a direct hit when the Death Starr's skin went all blotchy and her eyes bugged out.

"You'll regret this, Addy," she said. "By the time I'm through with you and Tub O' Lard you'll—"

Meredith gave an unladylike grunt and whirled around. "Something stuck me. Somebody jabbed a pin in my—" She tucked in her pelvis, jerking like a marionette. "Stop it! Ouch, oh, my God, that *hurts*. Help! Somebody help! Ow, ow, *ow!*"

Clutching her bottom in both hands, she ran out the door.

Chapter Five

A nsgar shut the front door, drowning out the shrill sound of
Meredith's wails.

He turned to Addy with a frown of disapproval. "You see
what comes of imparting our gifts to humans, brother?" He
spoke with that superior drawl that set Addy's teeth on edge. "A
petty misuse of power."

His gaze shifted to Evie and softened. "Although in this case,
I will admit, the punishment may have been justified. She was
a most unpleasant creature, much like the three-tongued adder
harpies of Gorth. Still, I cannot think Conall will approve."

Addy bristled. "Who the Sam Hill is Conall? What are you
on about, Blondy? What 'petty misuse of power'?" She waved
her hands in the air. "Never mind, I don't have time for this."

Brand stepped closer, his expression intent. "Adara, we must
speak. It is of the utmost importance."

Evie cleared her throat. "Uh, Addy, you haven't introduced
me to your friends."

"They're not my friends."

"Introduce me anyway."

Addy blew out an impatient breath. "Oh, all right." She
flapped a hand in Brand's direction. "Evie, this is Brand. The
blond guy with the stick up his butt is Ansgar. I met them last
night. If you'll excuse me, I have a million things to do."

She hurried into the supply room and shut the door. Sagging
against the frame in relief, she closed her eyes. She could hear
Evie and Brand talking. Their words were indistinct, but the

muffled sound of Brand's deep, rumbling baritone made her want to cry. What was the matter with her? Her skin felt too tight. She was jumpy and on edge, like she'd overdosed on caffeine. One moment she was tearing Meredith a new one—oh, my God, she called the Death Starr a bitch to her face, the small-town equivalent of committing hara-kiri, but boy, it felt good!—and the next moment she wanted to burst into tears.

Her emotions were all over the place. What happened to her hard-won self-control? Must be hormones kicking in. Surely, she wasn't acting like a lunatic because she was happy to see Tall, Dark, and Frosty again? He walked through her door and her heart started rabbit-kicking like Thumper on speed. Nah, her palpitations had nothing to do with him.

Maybe she had a heart condition. Yeah, that was it. She was probably walking around with a bad ticker. What a relief. She took a deep breath and opened her eyes. In the meantime, she needed to get a grip. Places to go, people to plant. The Farris funeral was two hours away.

"Umph." She stumbled forward as Brand pushed his way into the supply room. He balanced a thermos and a paper plate in one hand.

"I have sustenance, thanks to the beneficence of your friend Evie." He set the plate and the thermos on a shelf. "You will eat."

Addy stiffened. You *will* eat, says the alpha male. Not you should eat or, Addy, won't you please eat something, but you *will* eat. "See here, bub, I don't—"

He jerked her into his arms and kissed her. It took Addy by surprise, that hot, devastating assault on her senses. The man sure knew how to kiss. It also shut her right the hell up; no doubt what he intended all along, the macho jerk. What surprised her was her response. She kissed him right back. No struggling, no murmured protests, no coy attempts to evade his kiss. He put his mouth on hers, and she went from zero to ninety like that. She was heart pine and he was a blow torch, and she went up in flames. She loved it. She couldn't get enough of it. She wanted to climb the man like a telephone pole.

"You sent me away." Wrapping his hands in her hair, he pulled her head back and trailed a path of kisses down her throat and along her collarbone. "This I cannot allow. Suppose the djegrali returned and I was not here to protect you?"

There he went again, telling her what she could and could not do. He touched the pulse at the base of her throat with the tip of his tongue and dragged his hot mouth up her throat to nibble at her lips, and she forgot all about being indignant. He coaxed her mouth open and dipped his tongue inside, tasting her, exploring her, his tongue tangling with hers. Her head spun, and her insides went all shivery. She clutched his arms and held on for dear life. She was on fire, she was flying apart. She was losing her mind.

"Let me go, I can't breathe," she gasped, trying to break free. It was no use. The man was six feet plus of pure, hard muscle. "I want—I want—"

"I know. I know, little one." He ran his hands down her back and hiked her skirt over her thighs. His fingertips teased the curves of her buttocks. "It is the first time you've used the power, and you burn."

Power, what power? Her thoughts were hazy with lust. Burn didn't begin to cover it. More like spontaneously combust. She gave a cry of protest when he slid his hand inside her panties.

"Shh, easy," he whispered. "Let me help. I know what to do."

His fingers parted the tender folds and found the sensitive nubbin of flesh hidden within them, and she went off like a rocket. The Big O, *la petite mort,* only there was nothing little about it. He caught her scream of release in his mouth and held her until the first violent wave of trembling passed. Boneless and weak, she collapsed against him, too spent to object when he pulled out a crate and sat down on it with her in his lap. She relaxed, enjoying the comfortable silence that stretched between them. After a moment, he retrieved the thermos and the plate of banana bread from the shelf.

Breaking off a bite-size piece of the bread, he held it to her lips. "Eat, and then we will talk."

She shook her head. "No, thanks, I'm not hungry."

"Nonetheless you will eat." She shook her head, and his voice deepened to that low, purring growl that sent shivers up and down her spine. "For me, you will do this."

"Oh, all right." Unable to resist the entreaty in his voice, she parted her lips and allowed him to slip a piece of bread in her mouth. "Though I can take care of myself."

"I like taking care of you."

"Yeah? I kinda like it, too, but I don't think I should get used to it." She glanced at him through her lashes. "It's not like you're going to hang around or anything, right?"

His arms tightened around her. "I will abide here for the time being. Han-nah-a-lah appears to be a hub of demon activity. It is most curious. Ansgar and I agree the situation warrants further investigation."

"Han-nah-a-lah?"

"Is that not what this hamlet is called?" Brand slipped another morsel of bread into her mouth. He opened the thermos and poured green tea into the top, then held the cup to her lips. "It was the name on the marker at the outskirts of this place."

Addy swallowed a sip of the sweetened tea. "Are you talking about that old sign at the south end of town? I'm surprised you could read it. Hannah, *Alabama,* is what it says, but half the letters are gone. The city council has been talking about replacing it for years."

"To the Dalvahni, Han-nah-a-lah means *the end of all things.* Perhaps that is why Ansgar and I—like the demons, it would seem—have been drawn here, to fight the final battle."

"Hannah a hotbed of supernatural woo-woo? You've got to be kidding. No self-respecting demon would be caught undead here. Heck, we're so podunk we don't even have a Burger Doodle."

"Demons find this Burger Doodle attractive?"

"Nah, if I had to guess, I'd say they're more into soul food." She clapped her hands over her mouth. "Oh, God, I made a pun. Slap me."

"You are giddy from the power. It is natural. Now that you

have taken in nourishment and found sexual release the symptoms should subside."

Sexual release? The blood rushed to Addy's face. Oh, no, he did not say that out loud. And so matter-of-factly, too. *Pardon me, milady, but you should feel a whole lot better now that I've shoved my hand down your panties and made you sing like the fat lady.* How embarrassing. But, she did feel better now that she'd eaten and . . . uh . . . you know. She closed her eyes. Oh, God, maybe the floor would open up and swallow her whole.

"The djegrali dealt you a mortal blow," Brand continued. "You would have died had I not saved you. In doing so, we merged and you received some of my powers. That is how you banished Ansgar and me beyond your settlement borders, and gave that disagreeable female spots on her rump."

Her eyes flew open. "You think *I* teleported you and Blondy out of town and gave Meredith pizza butt?" She jumped to her feet. "That's mental. Look, bub, I've had a lot to deal with since last night, and your crazy whacked-out ideas aren't helping. Creepy dementors and a new hairdo, and a talking dog and a ten-foot albino deer, not to mention sexy warrior dudes invading my house—"

"Dudes, this is a plural term, is it not?" Brand scowled. "Do you find Ansgar sexually attractive?"

"He's easy on the eyes, I'll give him that. But, I wouldn't let him put his hand down my pants, if that's what you mean."

Whoops, she did it again. Opened her big, fat mouth and said what she was thinking. Talk about diarrhea of the mouth. She had a terminal case of it.

Brand jerked her back onto his lap. "That is exactly what I mean. He is not to touch you. This I cannot allow."

Whew, bossy *and* possessive. "Don't worry, he's not my type. But I don't think you have anything to worry about on that score. I'm pretty sure he's into Evie, in case you haven't noticed."

"I did not notice. You are the only one I see when I am in your presence." He kissed the vee of exposed skin at the top of her silk blouse and nuzzled her neck. "And when we are apart as well." He moved his lips to the sensitive spot beneath her ear.

"I did not like it today when you sent me away. Suppose the djegrali returned to harm you? That is why I will accompany you to this sepulchral service Mistress Evie told me about."

"Sepulchral service?" Addy leaped up and flung open the supply room door. "The Farris funeral! I should have been there twenty minutes ago. I am soooo late!"

"Adara wait, I must accompany you."

She whirled back around. "That's sweet, Brand, but there is no way I'm taking Conan the Barbarian to the Farris funeral. I'll be fine. I'd rather face a hundred demons any day than my mother in one of her snits. And she'll be headed straight for Snitsville if I don't get over there pronto."

She rushed into the front room of the store. "Evie, be a doll and mind things for me, will you? I gotta get over to the body shop."

Snatching up a standing basket of mums, snapdragons, and lilies, she bolted out the front door and down the street in the direction of Corwin's Serenity Chapel and Mortuary.

The storage room door slammed open and the dark-haired hunk Addy had introduced as Brand strode out. Evie eyed him uncertainly. On the surface he looked calm enough, but he radiated suppressed emotion and a raw, animal magnetism that screamed danger. This was not a man you wanted to mess with. She sure hoped she wasn't to blame for his bad mood. She did a quick mental recount. Nope, wasn't her. Addy must have done something to tick him off. Addy sometimes had that effect on people.

He confirmed her suspicion when he bellowed, "Adara Jean, come back here."

His voice rattled the decorative plates and pictures on the wall, but Evie could have told him he was wasting his energy. Addy was long gone. She shot out the door and past the plate glass display window so fast it made Evie blink. Cheese and crackers, it was like Addy was on speed or something. Drugs; that was it. Addy was on drugs. No other explanation for her best friend leaving her alone with two strangers. Two beautiful *male* strangers. Addy knew she suffered from shyness, Evie thought indignantly, especially around men. Men in general made her nervous, and good-looking men gave her the willies. And these two specimens of masculine magnificence shot way past good-looking and into the supernaturally handsome zone. One look at these guys, and the male underwear models of the world would strangle themselves with their own shorts. They were intergalactically gorgeous, especially the blond guy. Ansgar, that was his name. Evie slid him a cautious glance and looked away again. Cripes, he was so gorgeous he glowed.

And he was looking right at her.

Brand growled—he growled!—and turned to glare at Evie. She shrank back from the look in his eyes, a feral gleam like a tiger on the prowl. Or at least that's the gleam she imagined a prowling tiger's eyes might have. She'd never seen a tiger, thank God, except on the National Geographic channel.

"Where did she go?" he demanded.

Evie risked another quick peek at Ansgar. He still watched her, his arms crossed on his broad chest, with an unblinking scrutiny that made her self-conscious. Make that super self-conscious, since plain old ordinary run-of-the-mill self-conscious was normal for her.

Brand growled again, and she stuttered, "T-to the funeral home."

"In Snitsville?"

Evie gaped at him. "Huh?"

For a moment, he looked like his head might explode. "Addy said her mother might be traveling to some place called Snitsville. I must follow Addy there, if that is her destination."

Maybe this guy *was* from outer space. "Addy's mother lives in Snitsville," she said. "It's not a place, it's an expression. It means she stays upset about something or other all the time."

The glittering eyes narrowed. "I see. You are most helpful. Perhaps you also have information about Conan the Barbarian."

Evie was knocked straight back to huh. "Conan?"

"Who is he, and what is he to Addy?"

"Conan?"

"Conan."

Evie struggled to keep up. "I'm sorry, I don't—"

Tiger Man's scowl deepened. "Addy said she could not take Conan the Barbarian to the funeral. What did she mean?"

A bubble of hysterical laughter worked its way up from Evie's belly to her chest. She was going to lose it, going to laugh right in his face. And then Mr. Primeval would kill her, because this was not a guy with a sense of humor. She covered her mouth with both hands and managed to turn her attack of the giggles into a coughing fit instead.

"I'm sorry." She wiped her streaming eyes. "Allergies. Conan the Barbarian is a fictional character, a fantasy warrior. Big guy with black hair and a sword. I think he had blue eyes, though, not green."

"Fictional, you say?"

Evie nodded.

"Good. Then I will not have to kill him." Brand fell silent. After a moment, he said, "She refers to my garb, does she not? Ansgar and I do not dress as other men of your culture."

"Yeah, you could say that. It would be an understatement, but you could say that."

"Ansgar, we must remedy our appearance. We are in violation of the directive against conspicuousness."

"Do not let it trouble you, brother." Evie swallowed a sigh. Ansgar's voice was as cool and soothing as a dip in the creek on a hot summer day. "We have disregarded the warrior code in any number of ways since coming here. One more infraction should not make any difference."

"I have broken our code, not you." Brand's tone was stiff. "Leave lest you suffer the consequences of my actions."

Leave? Evie felt a stab of dismay, which was ridiculous. Why should she care if he left? It wasn't as if Whaley Douglass and Ansgar of the Splendiferous Abs and Ass were going to get it on. Looking at him hurt, for crying out loud, and she was . . .

She was plain old Evie.

"No, I think I will stay," Ansgar said. Evie darted a glance at him and froze, trapped by his unblinking silver gaze. "I find I'm in the mood to break a few rules myself."

"Very well," Brand said. "Is there a reputable tailor in this town, Mistress Evie? My friend and I need new attire."

With an effort, Evie broke eye contact with Ansgar and looked at Brand. "Uh, yeah, there's a men's store right down the street. They carry some big and tall stuff for the Wilson brothers."

"You have my thanks." Brand strode toward the door. Hand on the doorknob, he turned and looked back at Ansgar. "Brother?"

"I will follow in a moment. You go ahead."

The bell on the door clanged in protest as Brand slammed out of the store, leaving Evie alone with Ansgar. She flashed him a tremulous smile. Boy, oh boy, he made her jumpy. Picking up the cardboard box she'd brought with her that morning, she scurried over to her display table. Her hands shook as she unloaded the carton and rearranged the rows of soap. She tried her best to ignore the hunk on the other side of the room as she replenished her stock of almond and honey bath bars. She was adding her latest concoction to her men's line—a soap for hunters made with olive oil, oak bark, dandelion root, and cedar wood oil—when her skin prickled with awareness. Somehow, without making a sound, *he* was behind her. She could *feel* him. She spun around. He was right on top of her. God, he was beautiful. His pale blond hair and his strange eyes seemed to radiate light. No human man had a shine to him like that. It was hypnotic, mesmerizing. She could not move. He was a wolf and she was a rabbit, and he was going to gobble her up unless she did something to break the spell.

"Your friend seems a-a little intense," she stammered.

"He is a hunter and single-minded in his pursuit of what he wants . . . as am I."

She jumped when he reached out and removed her floppy gardening hat. Her hair tumbled down around her shoulders. She stared up at him, feeling self-conscious and nervous. This guy was so perfect, and she was so . . . *not*. She was a big blob, an awkward, ugly thing compared to his shining perfection. Why was he paying attention to her? It was some kind of cruel trick.

He lifted a long, red curl, and examined it. "Why do you conceal your fire with an ugly cap and your beauty beneath a shapeless gown, Evangeline? You cannot hide your true self from me."

Evie gasped. "Who told you my name? Nobody has called me Evangeline since my mama died."

"Evie is the name of a frightened, lonely girl. Evangeline is a beautiful, strong woman. You are Evangeline."

"Yeah, right, this coming from a guy like you."

Ansgar's brows drew together. "What does this mean, 'a guy like me'?"

"Oh, come on, don't make me say it. You've seen yourself in the mirror."

He smiled, and Evie thought the top of her head would blow off. Wow, this guy was something else.

"You find me attractive in a physical sense?"

Attractive, who was he kidding? He had to know he was drop-dead gorgeous. He'd probably heard it a thousand times before from a thousand other women. Did he need another female to tell him so? Did he need *Whaley Douglass* to stroke his ego?

No.

No, she did not think so.

She looked him square in the eye—a very un–Evie-like thing to do—but for some reason around this guy she was something else, too. "Let's say you don't exactly suck in the looks department."

He tilted his head, as though considering her words. "Not to suck is a good thing in your culture, is it not? You use sarcasm. It shows spirit. You are not at all the meek, timid mouse you pretend to be."

Taking her by the arm, he pulled her toward the door.

"Wait, where are we going?"

He gave her another bone-melting smile. "You will accompany

me to the tailor's to purchase a new suit of clothes so that I am not conspicuous."

"Mister, you're six-foot-four if you're an inch, and you look like a cross between Thor and an escapee from Rivendell. The clothes don't exist that would make you inconspicuous. Besides, I told Addy I'd mind the shop."

"Then you will close the shop. At the tailor's, we will select what you like. I want to please you."

Evie stared up at him in confusion. "Why? Why on earth do you care what I think? I'm nobody, and you just met me." With a sinking feeling in her stomach, she looked around for the hidden camera. "This is a joke, isn't it? Meredith put you up to this. It's some kind of sick reality show. That's great, really great. Well, you're going to have to get yourself another stooge, 'cause I'm not going anywhere with you."

She spun around and marched behind the counter.

Ansgar followed her. "Evangeline, I do not jest with you. I do not know how. What has Adara told you about me and Brand?"

"She didn't tell me anything. She started to tell me and Meredith came in. You and Brand came in right after that. So, see, I don't know anything. Innocent as a lamb, that's me. You can go out of here knowing your secret is safe, whatever it is."

"I see." He sighed, as if reaching a decision. "I said I was going to break the rules, did I not? Telling you the truth will be my first transgression."

Evie prided herself on her intuition, and her instincts were on high alert. She was not going to like what Ansgar was about to tell her. She held up her hand to ward him off. "Look, mister, don't bend any rules on my account. Sometimes ignorance is bliss, you know what I mean?"

"But I want you to know." Ansgar stepped closer. Evie sidled back, and he stopped. "Brand and I are Dalvahni."

"What's that, like Italian?"

"No. The Dalvahni are a tribe of immortal warriors. We hunt demons called the djegrali through space and time. We came to this place in pursuit of them. Several of them, in fact."

"Demons."

"That is correct."

"Uh huh."

Crazy as a Betsy bug. She might have known. Bitterness burned the back of her throat. No man in his right mind would think she was beautiful. Oh, well, it was nice for the milli-second it lasted.

A man wearing a cheap blue suit with a boutonniere pinned to the lapel stopped in front of the plate glass window and looked in. Evie recognized him at once, in spite of his waxy, unnatural pallor and frozen features. He looked at her with glassy, unmoving eyes for an instant, and turned and shambled down the street in the direction of the funeral home.

Evie stared out the window in shock. "Demon hunters, you say?"

"I have told you so, have I not?"

"You sure did, and I believe you. Dwight Farris just looked in the shop window, and he's dead."

Chapter Six

There was scarcely time for Evie to activate the alarm system and grab her purse before Ansgar dragged her out of the flower shop.

"Wait, wait!" she protested. "Give a girl a minute to catch her breath, will you? I just saw my first zombie."

Ansgar looked down at her, a gleam of amusement in his silver eyes. "What you saw, in all likelihood, was a ghoul, a corpse made animate by a demon. Humans are so imprecise."

Evie pushed the hair out of her face. Nine o'clock, and already the heat and humidity were suffocating. It was like breathing under water, not that Ansgar the Magnificent seemed affected. Cool as a cucumber, he was.

"Ghoul smoul, call it what you want," she said, "but there's a dead guy walking around Hannah."

"Do not concern yourself. The matter will be dealt with. Where is this tailor?"

She pointed. "On the corner at the end of the block."

Ansgar pulled her down the street, his long stride forcing her to break into a trot to keep up. The businesses along Main Street were beginning to stir to life. Two familiar wrinkled figures perched on a bench outside the Sweet Shop Café and Grill. Herbert Duffey's moose-like countenance was hidden behind the morning paper. Beside him, Jefferson Davis Willis puffed on his pipe and watched passersby.

"Good morning, Mr. Duffey, Mr. Willis." Evie smiled at the octogenarians. "Warm day, isn't it?"

"Herbert, get your long snoot outta that paper and tell me who that is with Evie Douglass," Mr. Willis said.

Evie smothered a laugh and promptly tripped over a crack in the sidewalk.

Ansgar's grip tightened on her arm. "Have a care."

Her face burned. Why, oh, why did she have to be such a klutz? "Sorry. The—uh—tailor's is on the corner at the end of the block."

There were three clothing stores in Hannah: Tompkins's for men, the Greater Fair for women, and Toodles for children. They reached Tompkin's and pushed open the front door. The shop was empty except for Brand and the sales clerk, Tweedy Gibbs. Tweedy, a slim wisp of a man in his early thirties with thinning red hair, stood toe to toe with Brand in front of the counter.

"I'm telling you, I'm slap out of anything that will fit a man of your size." Tweedy glared up at Brand like a Chihuahua squaring off against a Great Dane. "Dean Wilson bought the last tall suit I had in the shop two weeks ago. Or maybe it was David." He frowned and shook his head. "Hard to keep all those Wilsons straight. Every last one of 'em built like a tank, and all of 'em with names that start with 'd.' Darryl and Daniel, Dalton and David, Dean and Del." He gave a disgusted snort. "It's like trying to name Santa's reindeer or the seven dwarves. What was their mama thinking? There are twenty-five other letters in the alphabet she could have used. Duh-duh-duh-duh-dee. I feel like Porky Pig every time one of 'em comes in." Shrugging aside his irritation at the Wilson matriarch, he said, "I could maybe get you something in a week, but that's the best I can do."

Brand frowned at the smaller man. "I cannot wait a week. I need appropriate clothing now."

"I tell you nothing I have will fit." Tweedy eyed Brand up and down. "What are you, six and a half feet? I put you in a thirty-inch inseam and we're talking high waders."

"Is there a problem, brother?" Ansgar asked.

"There will not be once I ascertain the appropriate garb for this realm." Evie's stomach lurched as Brand turned his cold gaze on her. "I see you have brought Mistress Evie. Good. She can help us select clothing."

Tweedy whipped around, his eyes widening when he spied Ansgar's tall form. "Good Lord, there's two of 'em!"

Out of the corner of her eye, Evie saw Ansgar stiffen. She smiled at Tweedy. "Morning, George," she said, calling Tweedy by his given name to soothe his ruffled feathers. She shot Ansgar a meaningful look. "I'm sure Mr. Brand and Mr. Ansgar don't mean to be any trouble."

Ansgar lifted his brows, but remained silent.

Tweedy unbent a little. "Oh, you know these gentlemen, Evie?"

"They're here for the Farris funeral."

Tweedy pulled her aside. "What's with the getup?" He cut his eyes toward the two big men and back again. "Are they in some kind of cult?"

"They're actors." Evie felt a twinge of conscience at the lie, but somehow she didn't think Tweedy was ready to add CLOTHIERS TO INTERDIMENSIONAL DEMON HUNTERS EVERYWHERE to the sign outside the store.

"Oh." Tweedy seemed to digest this for a moment. He raised his voice for the benefit of the other two men. "And both of them are looking for suits? Like I said, I don't have their size."

"They don't have to have a suit," Evie said. Lord, give her patience. The very idea of Whaley Douglass giving anybody fashion advice was laughable. "What about a nice pair of slacks and a dress shirt? Something more conservative than they're wearing now."

"Show up at a funeral sans jacket?" Tweedy shuddered. "Tacky. Still, when you live in a town where camouflage is considered haute couture, I don't suppose it matters, especially since they're not from here."

"As long as the apparel is not something Conan would wear, it will suffice," Brand said.

Tweedy gave Evie a look of confusion. "Conan? Who's Conan?"

"A new designer." Boy, she was getting scary good at this lying stuff. "Really out there. Lots of leather, but too avant-garde for a small-town funeral. They're looking for something—uh— a little more traditional."

Traditional for medieval transrealm warrior types. Granny Moses. Addy owed her big time.

"I've got a pair of summer-weight wool dress pants on hold for one of the Wilsons," Tweedy said. He looked Brand and Ansgar up and down. "They'll probably be too short and too big in the waist, but it's all I got."

He disappeared in the back of the store and returned with two pairs of trousers draped over one arm.

"You're in luck. I found another pair." He held a pair of slacks against Brand's waist. "Like I thought, too big and too short in the inseam. The Wilsons aren't quite as tall as y'all and softer in the middle. The beer diet, you know."

Brand took one pair of pants from Tweedy and tossed the other pair to Ansgar. "These will suffice. Is there a place where we may withdraw to don them?"

"The dressing rooms are this way." Shaking his head, Tweedy led Brand and Ansgar to the back of the store. "I'll bring y'all a couple belts and some shirts to try. Will you gentlemen be needing shoes?"

"No, we will wear our boots," Brand said.

Evie dropped into a chair in the shoe section of the store to wait. Tweedy muttered to himself as he selected three or four dress shirts and neckties to match, and handed them into the changing rooms.

"What is this?" Brand stuck a heavily muscled arm through the opening at the top of latticed dressing room door. A necktie dangled from his fingertips.

"It's a necktie." Tweedy rolled his eyes at Evie.

"Hmm," Brand said. "What is its purpose?"

"Purpose?" Tweedy rubbed his temples. Evie sympathized with him. She had the beginnings of a headache too. "Heck, I don't think it has a purpose. It just looks good."

"Ah," Brand said. "It is decorative. No neckties."

The neckties flew over the top of the dressing room doors and settled in a bright pool at Tweedy's feet.

Tweedy gave her an incredulous look. "Who *are* these people and what planet are they from? I thought you said they were looking for something conservative to wear to the funeral, but they don't know what a *necktie* is?"

Oh, crap, she wasn't such a good liar, after all. "Conservative in an—uh— out there kind of way." Tweedy stared at her, and she lifted her hands in a helpless gesture. "You know how unconventional these big-city artsy-fartsy types can be."

"Big city? You mean they're from Mobile?"

"Farther away."

Tweedy's eyes grew round. "Atlanta?"

The dressing room doors opened, and Brand and Ansgar stepped out. Evie gaped at them, feeling a little lightheaded. The super fine wool trousers fit the two men as though tailor-made, and the cotton shirts they wore molded themselves to a pair of wide, muscled chests.

Wow. Double wow. Great googly mooglies.

"Well, I declare." Looking befuddled, Tweedy fiddled with the tribble of hair at the top of his forehead. "I'd have bet my bottom dollar those trousers wouldn't fit, but they're perfect. Must have been sized wrong or something."

He shook his head and hurried into the dressing room to get their discarded tags.

Brand came to a halt in front of her. "What do you think, Mistress Evie? Will we do?"

Evie realized she was staring and flushed. "Yeah, you'll do."

"Good." Brand strode toward the front of the store. "Ansgar, settle our bill with the Tweedy human. I must find Adara."

"Of course, brother. Evangeline and I will join you shortly." Ansgar straightened his cuffs. "Oh, I almost forgot. Evangeline may have sighted one of the djegrali on the street a few moments ago."

Brand halted, his broad shoulders stiff. "What did you say?"

The undercurrent of violence in the softly spoken words sent a warning bell jangling in Evie's head. Tiger, tiger burning bright.

She cut her eyes at Ansgar. He was either unfazed by Brand's ill temper, or he was channeling Captain Oblivious.

"Evangeline thinks she saw the dead man Dwight Farris standing outside the shop," Ansgar said in his calm, detached way. "Since dead men do not typically walk about in the light of day, I assume it was one of the djegrali."

Brand turned. His eyes burned with a predatory glow. "Why did you not tell me this sooner?"

Ansgar shrugged. "I did not see the creature myself, so I could not be sure."

"For your sake, you had better hope Mistress Evie was mistaken," Brand said through his teeth.

The door slammed, and he was gone.

Evie jumped to her feet. "He thinks that thing is after Addy, doesn't he? We've got to warn her!"

"Do not be alarmed, Evangeline. Brand will take care of the djegrali and your friend. Adara is safe, I promise you."

"But—"

She swallowed her protest as Tweedy bustled out of the dressing rooms. "I thought I'd put your other clothes in a bag," he said, looking puzzled, "but they aren't there."

"We took care of them," Ansgar said. "Do not trouble yourself."

"But I didn't see—" Tweedy took a deep breath. "Forget it. I'll ring you up."

Ansgar stepped in front of her, blocking her view of the cash register and Tweedy. "What passes for coin in this plane?" he asked in a low voice.

"Huh?"

"Recompense, payment, currency."

"Oh, you mean money. I'm afraid all I have is a twenty."

"I do not expect you to pay for my clothes, Evangeline. Show me this twenty of yours."

Confused, Evie pulled her wallet out of her purse and handed him the bill.

Ansgar took the twenty from her and studied it carefully,

front and back. "It is flimsy and somewhat fragile, but much easier to carry than gold or jewels, is it not?"

"Yeah, I guess it is."

A flat leather pouch appeared in his hand as if by magic.

Evie blinked. "Whoa, how'd you do that?"

"What, this?" The pouch vanished, then reappeared in his hand. "I keep it hidden in plain sight, as I do my quiver and bow."

"Q-quiver and bow?"

"Brand and I use a concealing charm to shield our weapons from humans so as not to cause undue alarm. You did not notice Uriel, Brand's flaming sword?"

Addy *did* say something to Meredith in the flower shop about weapons, but Evie thought she was kidding. "Uh, no, can't say as I did."

Ansgar chuckled. "Humans. They see what they want to see."

He opened the pouch and slipped her twenty-dollar bill inside. The pouch glowed briefly, bright as a Christmas tree, and grew thick. Ansgar reached inside the swollen purse and handed Evie a twenty-dollar bill. Curious, she peeked inside the pouch. The leather purse bulged with good old American greenbacks.

"Holy smokes, you really are from another planet!"

"Not another planet, Evangeline, another dimension. I know you are puzzled, and that you must have many questions."

"Yeah. Oh, yeah. But, right now only one comes to mind."

"What is it? Tell me what troubles you. I will do my best to answer you."

She raised her eyes to his. "Where can I get me a purse like that?"

Chapter Seven

The town of Hannah nestled in a cluster of rolling hills created during the Cretaceous period when a chunk of rock tired of spinning through space and crashed into Behr County, rumpling the earth like an unmade bed. Hannah's business section was situated at the south end of Main Street, a frayed gray ribbon of asphalt that ran past the flower shop and other stores and the Methodist and Baptist churches, and chugged up a steep hill to the town square. At the top of the ridge, Main Street split into a round-about that circled the park and rolled down the hill on the other side, spilling into North Florida where it became Highway 97. The funeral home was located at the north end of Main Street past the river bridge and near the edge of town.

Addy flew down the street, her thoughts focused on avoiding a tongue-lashing from her mother. She skidded to a stop at the employee's entrance of Corwin's and paused to finger-comb her hair and smooth her twisted skirt. She smelled something burning and looked down. Good grief, her shoes were smoking and she'd blown a heel. She limped inside and hurried down the hall to State Room A or the "Camellia Room" as Mama liked to call it.

Mr. Farris's casket stood open against the right wall. Her gaze skittered past the burial box and moved on. She did *not* want to see Mr. Dead Dude. Death was good business. Death was money. Death was dependable. The flower shop wouldn't survive without dead people. Sooner or later, everybody took the old dirt nap. But the simple truth was Addy hated dead people. She despised the Southern ritual of mumbling over the body. *Don't he look natural,* people would say. What did they *mean?* Her brother Shep was an excellent mortician, took pride in his work, but she'd never seen a dead person she thought looked good. How could anybody look natural with their cheeks jammed full of cotton balls and their lips superglued shut?

She looked around. No sign of Mama. Thank God. Maybe she could finish what she had to do and slip back out without getting caught. So she was a major league weenie. But, she did not want to face her mother, not yet. Setting down the basket of flowers, she headed for the knot of memorial sprays clustered in one corner of the room and grabbed a standing arrangement of gladiolas and carnations. A familiar ladylike Southern drawl drew her up short.

"Adara Jean Corwin, what have you done to your hair?"

Startled, Addy dropped the flower arrangement. Elegantly coiffed and dressed in a tasteful linen suit and matching heels, Bitsy Corwin glared at her from the doorway.

"God, Mama, you scared the pea turkey out of me."

"Don't take the Lord's name in vain, young lady, and answer my question. What on earth have you done to your hair?"

Addy lifted the wire frame with care and placed the arrangement at one end of the casket. She whirled and trotted across the room for another. Always make yourself a moving target. That much she'd learned. Stand still and you were dead meat. "Nothing, Mama, it was like this when I woke up this morning."

Addy felt her mother's laser vision bore into her back and picked up the pace. It was no use, she was done for. She felt her liver curl and her lungs shrivel to husks under the heat of that maternal stare. The woman should be requisitioned by the government as a weapon of mass destruction, for Pete's sake. She was a thermonuclear device. Point her at the enemy, and *wham! Summa exstinctio maternus.* Total extinction by the mama.

"Uh huh," her mother said. "If you think I'm stupid enough to swallow that line, you got another think coming. Hair doesn't turn white overnight unless you're a mother—put those two sprays of roses over there . . . no, not there, further to the right . . . and we both know you're not that. Don't even have a boyfriend, though Lord knows I've introduced you to every eligible bachelor in town. You're too picky, Adara Jean, and that's the truth. I despair of having grandchildren."

Oh, dear Gussie, her mother had whipped out the grandchildren card. Next came the wilting ovaries speech. Addy's, of course. At fifty-five her mother had long since sailed down the menopausal highway. Holding a peace lily in front of her like a shield, Addy turned. "You have two beautiful grandchildren, Mama, or are you forgetting about Shep?"

"You two talking about me again? You can't help yourselves, can you?" Addy's big brother Shep stood in the doorway dressed in the somber hues of the professional undertaker. Shep's perma-pressed blond hair was as neat and crisply starched as the spotless white shirt he wore. He smiled and walked over to Addy. "Hey, Cotton Top, what's with the new do? You look kind of like that Tempest chick from *X-Men*."

"You mean Storm," Addy murmured.

"Yeah, that's it, Storm."

"It's dreadful." Mama shuddered. "Peroxide blonde. I can't imagine what possessed her. The roots are going to be a nightmare."

"Hello, I can hear you." Addy waved a hand at them. "Remember me, the Invisible Woman? I'm standing right here."

It was a waste of time. Her two nearest and dearest went on talking about her like she wasn't in the room. Nothing new about that. Shep was Mama's right-hand man, had been for fifteen years since Daddy died. Mama always went to Shep when she had a "problem" with Addy. Translation: Addy wouldn't do what Mama wanted. Good old Shep, he always went to bat for her. Calmed Mama down and got her off Addy's case. Nothing fazed Shep, not even Mama. And that was saying something, 'cause Mama could piss off the Pope. Shep was as laid back as a rat in a quaalude factory. Shep, the Teflon Man, the perfect son; the one who stayed to run the family business. Unlike Addy, who'd hauled boogie out of Dead Folks Be Us as soon as she could.

"Relax, Mama, it's a wig," Shep said. "You know Addy wouldn't bleach her hair."

"Oh, thank heavens. I don't know why I didn't think of that myself. I was so upset. You're right, son. Of course it's a wig."

Oh, so she believed Shep, but not her? Peachy. Still, it was her way out. Keep her mouth shut and let Mama think she wore a wig. No scenes, no recriminations, no long-suffering looks. Be quiet and go with the flow.

Addy set the peace lily down with the other potted plants in front of the casket.

"It's not a wig," she heard herself say. What was the matter with her? Was she *nuts*? "It's my hair and, no, Mama, I did not bleach it. And I'm sorry if you don't like it, because it's going to stay this way. I'm not sure I could change it if I wanted to."

Shep chuckled. "She's kidding, Mama, pulling your leg. Hair doesn't grow six inches overnight."

Her mother's lips thinned. "Stop kidding around, young lady, and take that wig off right this minute before folks start to arrive. You want people to think you're cheap?"

"Cheap? That's not fair, Mama," Shep said. "I think Sis looks gorgeous. That pale blond hair with her brown eyes is a killer combination."

Her mother's expression softened. "Well, of course she's gorgeous. She'd look good with a chicken on her head, but that's beside the point. Everybody will be looking at that wig. We don't want to take away from Dwight's Big Day."

"Big day?" Addy stared at her mother. "The man's not having a party, Mama. He's *dead*. And you can be darn sure he won't care what color my hair is!"

"But his family might, Adara. It's our job to make a painful time easier for them. So, for the last time, take off that wig."

Something snapped inside Addy. She danced up and down in front of the casket. More of a lopsided jig thanks to her broken shoe. "And for the last time, I'm telling *you* it's not a wig!" She grabbed her hair in both hands and yanked. "See, it won't come off. Here, Mama, pull on it yourself, since you don't believe me."

She knew she must look like a crazy person with her wild hair and her raggedy shoes. The very least she expected was a lecture from the Mom-i-nator. Never mind that she wasn't using her inside voice. She was dancing right smack dab in front of Old Man Farris's bone bucket, and he was a good Southern Baptist. Well, maybe *good* was a bit of a stretch. The man was a serial adulterer, after all. His tally whacker had been handled more than a FedEx package. But Dwight Farris never *danced,* unless you counted the horizontal mambo, so doing the funeral home bop in front of his casket was definitely uncool.

But, to her surprise Mama and Shep did not say a word. Her first real hissy fit since the age of thirteen when Mama made her go to the country club Christmas dance with Pootie Jones— dubbed Pootie by folks because of the dooky-scented cloud of effluvium that hovered around him like rush hour smog over Mexico City—and neither one of them paid her any mind. They stared at the casket behind her, their faces all waxy and funny. Shep looked rattled, and that in and of itself scared Addy. Nothing rattled Shep. Shep was so cool his boxer shorts were refrigerated. Something was wrong. Something was very wrong. She should look. She knew she should look. *She did not want to look.* Look and she'd get dead man cooties on her eyeballs. Gross.

She looked anyway.

The casket was empty. The white satin lining bore the imprint of the body, but Dwight Farris was gone.

"Where'd he go?" Shep sounded stunned.

Her mother turned an accusing glare on her. "Addy, did you do something with Mr. Farris?"

"Sure, Mama, I got him right here in my back pocket. Of course I didn't do anything with him! What do you think I would do with him?"

"I've never lost a body before." Shep's tone was conversational. "Oh, sure, one or two have hit the floor while I was working on them. But I figure bodies are like Oreos and the ten-second rule applies. No big deal. But this . . ." He shook his head. "I don't know what to do about this."

"Maybe it's somebody's idea of a prank," Addy suggested, desperate to help Poor Shep. He looked so forlorn. "You know, like when the seniors roll the mayor's yard at homecoming."

"You think somebody *stole* Old Man Farris?" Shep groaned. "Oh, Lord, I wonder if Corwin's is liable. I'd better call Sammy Gordon down at Bama Farms and check on our coverage."

Great, she'd made things worse. Way to go, Addy.

Her mother shot her a basilisk glare. "Don't you worry about it, son. We'll find him. He can't have gone far."

"Find who?"

The three of them jumped like they'd been shot, and spun around. Shirley Farris, Dwight's wife, stood in the doorway. Everything about Shirley was round, her face, her bright blue eyes, her melon-shaped breasts and wide hips. She was a round little blueberry of a woman in a belted Sunday dress and orthopedic shoes. Her gray hair was round, too, worn in tightly permed sausage curls that bounced when she walked. She was as soft and plump as a newly risen yeast roll, a cherubic Southern Mrs. Santa Claus with rosy cheeks, a double chin, and a tiny pink bow of a mouth. If the Teletubbies had a mom, it would be Shirley Farris. Addy could see her tripping across the sterile, green golf course Tinky Winky, Dipsy, Laa-Laa, and Po called home.

"Find who?" Shirley repeated. She tilted her head and widened her baby doll eyes at them. "Is something wrong?"

Mama's mouth worked, but nothing came out. Beside her, Shep made strangling noises. Great, both of them down for the count. Addy took a deep breath and gave Mrs. Farris a bright smile.

"Wrong is maybe too harsh a word, but we do have the teensiest, little situation here with Mr. Farris."

A tiny, adorable wrinkle formed in the space between Shirley's brows. "Oh, dear, was the blue suit too small? He has put on a few pounds in the last few years. Maybe we should have gone with the gray."

"No, ma'am, the suit is not the problem." Addy looked past Shirley's plump figure. The rest of the family was gathered in the hall for the visitation . . . visitation for a dead man who'd taken a powder. Oh, Lord, things were about to get ugly. Addy waited, hoping—no, *expecting*—her take-charge mom to leap in and take over. But, for once, Bitsy seemed content to let her daughter do all the talking. Huh? Who would've guessed that all it took to shut Mama up was an itinerant corpse? Either that or she'd had a stroke. Addy forged ahead. "It's—uh—like this. Mr. Farris is not exactly where we want him to be."

"Where would you like him to be, dear?"

"In the casket, for starters."

Plink, plink. Shirley blinked her doll-like eyes at them. "I don't understand."

"Neither do we. Mr. Farris is gone."

"Gone?"

"Yes, ma'am, gone, as in 'he ain't here no more.' "

Shirley Farris clutched her pocketbook to her generous bosom. "Praise the Lord, he's been raptured."

Good grief.

"I don't think so, Mrs. Farris. 'Course, I'm Episcopalian, and I'm pretty sure we don't get raptured. But, Baptists get raptured, don't they? So, I guess Mr. Farris could have been raptured, but we're thinking it's more likely someone took the body. Can you think of anybody who might have *borrowed* Mr. Farris for some reason?"

"No, I can't thi—" The furrow in Shirley's brow deepened. "Unless . . . No, no, she wouldn't."

Shep seemed to wake from his stupor. "She?" he said eagerly. "If you have any idea who did this, Mrs. Farris, you need to tell us. It's a violation of state health law to be toting around a dead body, not to mention disrespectful to the dearly departed."

"Oh, my goodness, I can't believe I didn't think of it before! We should call the police," Bitsy said.

"Not yet, Mama," Shep said. "Let's see what Mrs. Farris has to say first." With an effort, he seemed to shake off his shock and became, once again, the consummate professional. "Mrs. Farris, what were you going to tell us?"

"We-l-l." Shirley leaned closer. "You may not be aware of this, but Mr. Farris had a wandering eye."

Wandering eye? With a struggle, Addy kept her face straight. All of Dwight's parts wandered, especially his doodle. He had the wandering-est doodle in three states. His doodle had its own set of legs. His doodle was hardly at home. Heck, according to rumor Dwight Farris's doodle was hardly ever in his *pants.*

"Course, now that he's in heaven with Jesus, all his earthly sins are forgiven," Shirley added.

"Yes, ma'am," Addy said, "but Mr. Farris's body isn't in heaven. In fact, we don't know where the Sam Hill he is, and that's the problem. There's a funeral scheduled in less than two hours, and we got no body. Do you have any idea where he might be?"

"That's what I'm trying to tell you, dear." Shirley's pink mouth trembled. "My husband had a girlfriend, a painted hussy by the name of Bessie Mae Brown. Maybe *she* can tell you where Dwight is."

"Did somebody say my name?" A middle-aged woman with Elvis Presley shoe-polish-black hair pushed her way into the room. She wore a lavender dress that strained across her generous breasts and thighs, and spiked purple heels. Rhinestones glittered on her long, manicured nails, and on the barrette she wore perched at a random angle on her stiffly teased and sprayed hair. She propped one hand on her hip and winked at Shep, then turned to address Mrs. Farris. "Hello, Shirley. Sorry for your loss."

Show up at her married boyfriend's funeral and offer condolences to the grieving widow as cool as you please. Wow, the woman had a major set. This was the funeral parlor version of a twenty-car pileup, and they were all caught in the twisted, metal wreckage. Fascinated and horrified, Addy looked over at Mrs. Farris. The widow looked like she wanted to blow groceries all over Bessie Mae Brown. Of course, being the Teletubbies' mom, she'd probably blow marshmallows or Skittles. Addy's stomach rumbled at the thought. Rainbow Skittles, or maybe Lucky Charms with all those little pink hearts and green clovers . . .

"What have you done with my husband, you Jezebel?" Shirley's shrill voice recalled Addy to the nightmare.

"Me?" Bessie Mae's heavily mascaraed eyes widened. "What are you talking about?"

People in the hall heard the commotion and wandered into the room. A low, murmuring buzz began and grew as folks noticed the empty satin-lined box.

Shirley pointed a fat finger toward the casket. "I'm talking about the fact that my husband is missing. I want to know what you did with him."

Bessie Mae teetered across the room on her four-inch heels. "Sugar Scrotum," she cried. She flung herself on top of the metal box. "What have they done with you?"

Sugar Scrotum? Eww.

"Please, Ms. Brown." Addy hurried over to the wailing woman. "This is highly inappropriate, not to mention downright tacky."

She put her arms around Bessie Mae and tried to peel her off the casket.

"No!" Bessie Mae screeched and hung on tighter, kicking her purple heels. "I won't go. Not until somebody tells me what happened to my sugar."

"Oh, Lord have mercy, Jesus," Shep groaned, relapsing. "What else?"

"I can't take any more." Addy's mother toddled over to a chair. "Somebody tell me when it's over."

Shirley waved her pocketbook. "I got your sugar right here, Bessie Mae Brown," she quavered in her Aunt Bea voice, "or at least the only part you cared about."

A shiver of dread shot down Addy's spine. She let go of Bessie Mae—the damn woman was stuck like a tick to the casket, anyway—and turned to look at Mrs. Farris.

"Uh oh," she said when she saw the triumphant gleam in the widow's china-blue eyes.

Bessie Mae must have had a premonition, too, because she unsuckered herself from the casket and turned around. "What have you done, Shirley?" she hiccupped.

Mrs. Farris opened her pocketbook and pulled out a ziplock baggie. Some kind of watery fluid smeared the inside of the see-through plastic. Formaldehyde, maybe. Addy tried not to think about the particulars of her brother's work. At rest in the bottom of the bag like an abandoned hotdog was Dwight Farris's one-eyed monster. Or, at least Addy *hoped* it was Old Man Farris's one-eyed monster. She'd never met this particular monster . . . until now, thank goodness. As Addy stared, she could have sworn the thing winked at her.

"Your sugar's not here, and even if we find him, he won't be the same," Shirley said. "What's more, you won't be diddling my husband in the afterlife. Nobody will, 'cause I got his winky right here. This winky is finally all mine, and it's going to stay that a-way. I'm going to have it buried with me. I'm going to hold it in my cold dead hand. I'm taking this winky with me through the Pearly Gates. Not even Saint Peter's prying this cold dead winky out of my hand. But maybe—if Dwight asks me real nice, mind you—I might let him have his winky back in the hereafter. But only on special occasions and only if he plays tiddley winks with me, and nobody else."

"You crazy bitch!" Bessie Mae launched herself at Mrs. Farris.

Growling like a pack of dogs after a meat wagon, the two women hit the floor and wallowed around. The family gathered in a circle to watch the catfight. Shirley's dress rolled up like a window shade, exposing her chubby behind. The moon was full, and it wore support hose and flowery granny panties.

"My eyes, my eyes." Shep staggered back and collapsed into a chair beside his mother.

"Shep, don't just sit there," Addy cried. "Do something!"

"I can't. All I can see is Shirley's big flowery butt. I think my retinas may be permanently scarred."

"Well, somebody has to do something. They're going to murder each other."

"Give me that weenie," Bessie Mae screeched, making a grab for the baggie in Shirley's hand.

Shirley slammed her fist into the side of Bessie Mae's head. "You stay away from this weenie, Bessie Mae Brown. This weenie's been Fabreezed and Cloroxed. I like to never got your coochie juice off it."

"Mercy," Bitsy Corwin moaned, and slid off the chair and onto the floor.

"Mama!" Addy rushed over. "Shep, what's the matter with her?"

Shep's shoulders shook. He lifted his head. Tears streamed down his face. "Fainted," he gasped. "I think it was hearing the words 'coochie' and 'juice' in the same sentence."

Bessie and Shirley crashed into the flowers in front of the casket.

"My flowers!" Addy cried. "Shep, call the police before they wreck the whole place over Dwight Farris's ding dong."

Shep whooped and fell out of his chair.

Addy grabbed a vase of cut flowers off the lacquered chinoiserie table by the door. She was standing over Shep and Mama pouring water on them when Brand stalked into the room.

Chapter Eight

Addy stared at Brand in shock. He'd traded his black leather warrior garb for a crisp white cotton shirt and a pair of silk and wool blend dress slacks. The new clothes fit him to perfection. If anything, modern apparel showed his magnificent physique to greater advantage. Talk about your sartorial splendor. Wowza. Conan meets *GQ*. Good God, it ought to be illegal for anyone to look so good. If he looked this yummy in dress duds, she couldn't wait to see him in a pair of jeans . . . or better yet, out of them. She'd like to—

"Adara, is it your intent to drown those two unfortunate humans?" Brand said, bringing her lustful, little fantasy to a screeching halt.

"Uh, no." Addy tilted the vase upright.

"Then why are you watering them?"

"I had to do something. Mama fainted and Shep was in hysterics."

"I'm all right." Shep got to his feet. He wiped the water out of his eyes and squinted at the two women rolling around on the floor. "Looks like Shirley has Bessie Mae in a camel-clutch sleeper hold. This could get ugly. Guess I'd better call the police. Addy, you take care of Mama."

"Sure."

Shep turned to leave. He stopped in front of Brand and held out his hand. "I don't believe we've met. I'm Shep Corwin, Addy's older brother. And you are?"

"Well met, brother of Adara. I am Brand."

"Nice to meet you." Shep eyed the bigger man up and down. "You play any ball, Brand?"

"No."

"Shame. Brand your first name, or your last?"

"Just Brand."

"Just Brand, is it? What are you, one of those West Coast celebrities with only one name?"

Uh oh, the West Coast, synonymous in Shep's conservative Southern mind with pot smoking, free love, liberals, and worst of all—*gasp*—tofu burgers. No self-respecting Southern male would be caught dead eating tofu. Eating tofu led to all kinds of degenerate practices, like yoga and meditation, and God forbid, art appreciation. She'd better do something fast, before Shep classified Brand as a girly man. Not that she cared what her brother thought about the big galoot. But it seemed like the nice thing to do.

"He's teasing, Shep," she said. "His name is Brand . . . uh . . . uh . . ." Her brain raced like a hamster on a wheel. "Dalvahni. Yeah, that's it, Brand Dalvahni. He's here for the Farris funeral."

"Delmonte, like Viola's husband at the Sweet Shop?"

"No, Dal-vah-ni."

"Don't believe I know any Dalvahnis. Knew a Dalboski once, but they weren't from around here. Think they were Lithuanian, or something. You Lithuanian, Mr. Dalvahni?"

"No."

"You know any Lithuanians?"

"No."

"Me, neither, 'cept for the Dalboskis, and I'm not sure about them."

A loud whoop from the circle of mourners surrounding Shirley and Bessie Mae recalled Shep's attention to the wrestling match across the room.

"Well, I guess I'd best make that call before the Farris boys crack open a keg and start taking bets," he said. "Looks to me like Bessie Mae's the Alpo in this fight. Shirley's giving her a beat-down, and still ain't let go of Dwight's trouser snake."

Shaking his head, Shep left the room.

Bitsy sputtered and sat up. "What's happening?" She blinked up at Brand in confusion. "Who are you?"

"This is Brand Dalvahni, Mama," Addy said. "Brand, this is my mother, Bitsy Corwin. He's here for the Farris funeral."

Amazing how the lie slipped off her tongue with ease the more times she said it. Before very long, she'd believe it herself.

Bitsy groaned and covered her face with her hands. "Oh, Lord help us, the Farris funeral. What on earth could have happened to Dwight?"

Looking at Mama nearly gave Addy a heart attack. Mama was always put together, her hair done and her makeup flawless. She was Donna Reed doing housework in a chic frock, high heels, and pearls, a gardening goddess in a red and white Malia sundress and matching flats. But not anymore. Mascara ran down her powdered cheeks, and her stylish champagne-blond tresses lay in a sodden wad against her scalp. A big wet spot and a sprinkling of wilted lily petals marred the front of her once pristine linen suit. It was wrong. It was John Wayne in a pink tutu and tights. It was a preacher farting in church. A work of art had been despoiled, and Addy was the desecrator who'd drawn the big, black mustache on the *Mona Lisa*.

Mama was going to kill her.

"Your mother seems disturbed, Adara. Is there a problem?" Brand asked.

"Yeah, there's a problem. Dwight Farris is missing in action, and he's the dead guy. I don't know how things work where you're from, but around here, we don't usually have a funeral without a body, not without the police and the district attorney being involved." She pointed a finger at Shirley and Bessie Mae. "Those two are the wife and girlfriend of the deceased. Shirley's the one on top with her dress up around her waist. She's Dwight's wife. The other one is the girlfriend, Bessie Mae. The *latest* girlfriend, I should say. Dwight believed in spreading the love, if you know what I mean. Anyway, we get here this morning and Dwight is nowhere to be found. Shirley thinks

Bessie Mae stole him, maybe to have one for the road." Addy shrugged. "And that's not the worst part. Turns out Shirley already removed Dwight's pocket rocket. Seems she has ideas of keeping Dwight all to herself in the hereafter."

Bitsy stiffened. "Adara Jean, do not refer to that particular part of Mr. Farris's anatomy as a *pocket rocket*. It's vulgar."

Addy felt her cheeks grow warm. "Sorry, Mama."

Brand frowned. "Pocket rocket? He was armed?"

"No," Addy said. "I was talking about his . . . his, you know."

"I do not know."

"For crying out loud, don't make me say it in front of my mama! She'll have a fit."

"Adara, I am not being purposefully obtuse, I don't—" He stopped, his expression growing pained. "Oh. I see. She unmanned him. Not a common mourning ritual in this realm, I hope?"

"Certainly not." Bitsy straightened her skirt. "Corwin's has been in business for more than fifty years, and nothing, *nothing* like this has happened before."

"Tramp!" Shirley yelled, pounding Bessie Mae's head into the floor.

"Sicko weenie whacker," Bessie Mae flung back.

Hooked together like a couple of love bugs, they rolled into a standing spray of snapdragons, Queen Anne's lace, and asparagus ferns, and sent it crashing into the floor.

Addy winced. "There goes another one."

"I will handle this," Brand said.

He strode across the room to the two snarling, spitting women, and touched each of them on the neck. They stiffened and went limp. Bessie Mae rolled off Shirley and flopped onto her back. She stared up at Brand like a gigged fish. Shirley stared at him, too. Her tiny pink mouth formed a perfect "o."

"Guck," Bessie Mae said, gaping at Brand.

Plink, plink. Shirley's Kewpie doll eyes opened and closed. She seemed oblivious to the fact that her dress was wadded up under her armpits, her Playtex 18-hour bra showed, she'd lost a shoe and there was a big hole in one of her support stockings.

"Am I dead?" She gazed up at Brand with a worshipful expression on her plump, pink face.

"No."

He helped Shirley to her feet. Gravity kicked in, and her dress slid down, but even the forces of nature could only do so much. The garment caught on her hips and hung there.

"You sure? 'Cause you look like an angel to me. I was thinking maybe I'd done been raptured like Dwight, praise the Lord."

Brand helped Bessie Mae wobble upright on her purple stiletto heels. Her rhinestone barrette dangled over one bruised eye. "Raptured?" she said. "What are you on about, Shirley? Dwight ain't been raptured."

"Then where is he, you slut monkey? Did you take him?"

"I didn't take him, you crazy old bat. Tell you what happened though. Dwight probably got up and left when he saw what kind of cheap-ass casket you plan on burying him in. You always were a tightwad. I'm surprised you didn't dig a hole and stick him in the backyard. Spring for something better than a shoe box and some tissue paper, and maybe he'll come back."

"Cheap?" Shirley screeched.

"Please, ladies, no more." Bitsy looked close to tears. The chief of police and a second officer stepped through the door with Shep at their heels. Bitsy's expression eased. "Carl, thank goodness you're here." She hurried over. "I've been at my wits' end."

Chief Carl E. Davis smiled at her. "Don't get your bowels in an uproar, Hibiscus, we'll get this all sorted out."

Addy blinked. Hibiscus? Nobody called Mama by her given name, not even Daddy. What was going on here? Did Bitsy have a boyfriend? The very concept was mind blowing.

"Oh, Car-lee," Bitsy said, "it's been awful. First we find out Dwight's body is missing, and then these two start fighting and nearly destroy the place. I am so upset."

Car-lee? It wasn't Sugar Scrotum, but in the Bitsy universe it was close.

The chief patted Bitsy on the hand. "There, there, Hibiscus, you let me take care of this. Everybody stay put, until Officer Curtis and I sort this thing out." He pointed to a man sporting a powder-blue tuxedo jacket and a mullet who was trying to ooze out of the room. "That means you, too, Dinky Farris. I want to talk to everyone here."

Bitsy gave him a misty smile. "Thank you, Car-lee. I know I can count on you."

He motioned to the other officer. "Dan, you stay here with these good folks while I talk to Ms. Brown and Mrs. Farris in another room."

"Right, Chief."

"The Magnolia Room is available, if you like," Bitsy said quickly.

"That will be fine." He gave Bitsy a conspiratorial wink and ushered Shirley and Bessie Mae out into the hall.

Bitsy turned back to them. "Well, this has certainly been an interesting morning. You handled that rather well, Mr. Davinci."

Addy's stomach lurched. There was a speculative gleam in Mama's eyes when she looked at Brand. "Dalvahni, Mama."

"Of course, Mr. Dalvahni. What is it you do for a living?"

Oh, Lord, the interrogation had begun. "He's in the military, Mama. Special Forces."

"I knew it. That's where he learned that Jedi nerve pinch thing, isn't it? My, that was impressive."

"It's a *Vulcan* nerve pinch, Mama, and a *Jedi* mind trick."

Bitsy waved her hand. "Whatever. I'm sure Mr. Dalvahni knows what I mean." Her lips settled in a determined line. "I want to know all about you, Mr. Dalvahni. Where are you from? Who are your folks?"

"I told you, Mama, he's here for the Farris funeral."

"Oh, yes, that's right." Some of the sparkle left Bitsy's eyes. "Kin to the Farrises are you?"

"No."

The sparkle sprang back to life. "Of course you aren't related to them. Silly old me to even ask," she said. "Are you a friend of the family, then?"

"No."

Bitsy tapped her foot. "Not a big talker, are you, Mr. Dalvahni."

"No."

"He's on assignment, Mama."

"Assignment?" Bitsy's eyes widened. "It's that Dinky Farris, isn't it? Did you see that hair and that awful coat he was wearing? Powder-blue crushed velvet. In the summer. To a funeral." She shuddered. "Tacky. What's he into, drugs?"

"Drugs" became the longest word in the English language when Bitsy said it. *Druuuugs.*

"I do not know this Dinky Farris. I hunt the djegrali."

"Jah-bally?"

"It's a . . . a drug, Mama, made out of cow pie mushrooms. The government is looking into it."

Brand gave her a look of reproach. "Adara, this is absurd. I do not think—"

"I know you don't want people knowing your business, Brand, but Mama won't tell anybody. Isn't that right, Mama?"

"Hmm." Bitsy considered Brand. "So you're working under-cover trying to bust a bunch of cow pie drug dealers in the big city of Hannah. Glad to see my tax dollars at work. Tell me, Mr. Dalvahni, how does my daughter, the florist, fit into all of this?"

Crap, busted. Time to try a diversionary tactic.

"Mama, you look different. Have you changed salons?"

"What? No, I—" Bitsy gave her hair a perfunctory pat. Her hand stilled. "What in the world?"

Spinning on her heels, she trotted over to the gold and umber beveled mirror that hung by the door. She stiffened in horror.

"Incoming. Duck," Addy said.

"What?"

"Cover your ears, Brand."

"Merciful heavens, my *hair,*" Bitsy shrieked. "And look at my makeup! I look like somebody melted a clown. Car-lee saw me like this? Adara Jean Corwin, how could you?"

The Mom-i-nator whirled about. Flames and lightning bolts and promises of retribution shot from her eyes.

"Run," Addy said. "Run like the wind."

She grabbed Brand by the hand and pulled him out the door.

Chapter Nine

The moment Adara slipped her hand in his the tightness in Brand's chest eased. What was it about this one female that set his universe on end? She had him tied up in knots, crazy with lust and consumed with worry about her safety. Never again did he want to experience the sheer mind-numbing terror that coursed through him when he thought the djegrali stalked her and he was not there to protect her. He could have killed Ansgar for not telling him sooner. If something had happened to Adara, he *would* have killed him, the consequences be damned. He should not have let her out of his sight. He would not do so again, not until the djegrali was slain or banished from this realm. Adara was in danger, and she must be made to understand.

"Adara, wait, I have something to tell you."

She tugged him down the hall. "Sure, sure, tell me anything you like, but let's get out of here first."

"You are in danger."

"You're telling me. Did you see the look on Mama's face? One more second, and we'd have been nuked."

"Am I to glean from this untoward haste that you are afraid of your mother?"

Adara stopped at the door, her hands on her hips. "Didn't you *see* her? She was about to detonate. Five more seconds, and we'd have both been pillars of ash."

There it was again, that annoying feeling of lightness that rose in his chest when he was around her. His lips twitched. He clamped them together to keep from smiling. This excess of levity was becoming bothersome.

"Your fear is illogical. Your mother is a mortal woman, and a diminutive one at that."

"Do you *have* a mother?"

"No."

"Are you Southern?"

"No."

"Then shut up. You don't know what you're talking about." She pushed open the door and started outside. "Wait." He put his hand on her shoulder. "I will go first."

She frowned but allowed him to step in front of her. "It's broad open daylight and hot as a fox outside, and you're worried about demons?"

"The djegrali are unaffected by heat or cold, or time of day. They can strike you from a blizzard or the burning heart of the desert, at any hour." A slight movement at the corner of the building caught his eye, a blur of motion that could have been the flutter of cloth or his imagination. He looked around. Nothing moved. His desire to protect the woman had him on edge. "You can come out, but stay close to me."

She brushed past him and hobbled down the sidewalk. "There you go again, trying to be the boss. Thing is, I don't remember promoting you to that position. Seems like last time I looked, I was a free—"

"Adara, you are limping. What happened to your shoe?"

"—woman, and that means I don't have to do what you—"

He caught up to her in two strides and scooped her up in his arms.

"Brand, put me down. People will talk."

"No."

"Brand, please, I'm too heavy. You'll hurt yourself or have a stroke in this heat."

"Do not be ridiculous. You hardly weigh more than a child. In any event, it does not matter. I have carried injured brothers off the battlefield on more than one occasion. You are as a feather next to them. Besides, I am unaffected by the heat."

"You have a brother?"

"A brother warrior, Adara. The Dalvahni do not know family as you do."

"Oh." She sighed and rested her head against his shoulder. "Sometimes, that can be a good thing."

"Are you thinking about the mama again?"

"No, I was thinking about the Farrises. Poor Shirley, her husband ran around on her all over town. Her oldest son, Dwight Junior, is almost as bad. Cats around on his wife something terrible. And then there's Dinky. He always seems to be in one kind of trouble or another. His mama is always having to bail him out of jail."

"Ah, yes, Dinky Farris, the man whose garb so offended your mother. I am sorry for his deformity. Human males often define themselves in comparison to other men. It must be difficult to know you have been measured and found wanting. To be dubbed according to one's inadequacy, and to have others remind you of your shortcomings each time they address you, must be unbearable."

Adara giggled. "He's got a deformity, all right, but not the one you're thinking."

"I do not understand."

"He's called Dinky because his mister is so big."

"His mister?"

"Brand, you're the guy here. I can't believe I have to spell it out for you." She motioned with her hands. "He's got a big hose, all right? A trunk like an elephant. He has to roll it up to put his pants on. People call him Dinky to be funny. His real name is Rod, which is just as bad when you think about it. Me, I'd have changed my name. But I guess after all these years, he's gotten used to it."

Brand halted in the shade of one of the big live oaks that lined the sidewalk. A swinging sign on a black iron post proclaimed the avenue they strolled along to be Main Street. Adara's shop was a block or so farther down, but Brand could hardly see for the red haze that obscured his vision. "I see." He kept his tone even with an effort. "It is ironic, is it not, that he is called Dinky when he is, in fact, quite the opposite?"

"Uh yep, you could say that." Adara waved at a woman on the sidewalk. "Oh, hey, Miss Mamie, how you doing?"

An elderly woman with white hair waved back. "Fine as frog hair, Addy. I like your new hairdo. You hurt your ankle?"

"No, ma'am, I broke a heel, and this nice gentleman is giving me a lift to the shop." To Brand, in an undertone, she said, "That's Mamie Hall, the biggest gossip in three counties. By sundown, this will be all over town and she'll have us canoodling right here on Main Street."

"Well, bye, Addy." Eying Brand curiously, Miss Mamie moved on down the street.

He tried to control his simmering rage. It should not matter that Adara had seen this Dinky's manhood. She was a woman full grown. Over the eons, he had been with other females hundreds of times, albeit all of them thralls. Why, then, this fire in his gut and brain, and the unreasoning desire to permanently separate Dinky Farris from his mister?

"Is something wrong, Brand?"

He dragged his unfocused gaze off the street and looked down at Adara. Her pale hair curled in a tangled halo around her lovely face. A rose blush tinted the delicate curves of her cheeks and stained her lush mouth. She gazed up at him, her brown eyes luminous.

"You have lain with this Dinky?"

Her eyes widened. "Me with Dinky Farris? Not no, but hell no. Major yuck."

"Then how do you know how he puts it in his pants?"

"I don't! It was a joke. For Pete's sake, Dinky is my brother's age."

"Many women find older men attractive."

"Well, sure, but not Dinky. I mean, did you see him? He's got about as much meat on him as a chicken wing, and then there's the mullet from hell. Billy Ray Cyrus on Rogaine and acid." She looked at him under her lashes. "I do like older men.

Much older men. Men who've been around the block a few thousand year—"

"You did not lie with him?"

"*No.*" She kicked her heels in an adorable fashion. "Put me down. You've gone and made me mad."

"Good. I am glad I make you mad. *I* think I have been a little mad since first I saw you."

He kissed her. She tasted like honey and spices. He forgot about the djegrali and his duty as a warrior, and the directive against fraternization with mortals. He forgot they stood on a street corner in full view of everyone that passed. He forgot everything except the blissful heat of her mouth. He was shaking with need by the time he ended the kiss, and cognizant of one fact. If he did not have this woman and soon, he would go stark staring mad.

"Mama, what's that man doing to that lady?"

"She's got something stuck in her throat, Little Will. He's trying to get it out."

Brand raised his head. A small crowd had gathered around them. A woman and her little boy stood closest to them, gawking.

"With his tongue? Yuck, grown-ups are weird." The boy looked up at his mother. "You ever get something caught in your mouth like that, Mama?"

" 'Course not, Little Will. Don't be silly."

"Then how come I saw Mr. Lucas sticking his tongue in your mouth down at the hardware store last Saturday? You want me to tell Daddy? Maybe he can help you get it out."

The woman turned scarlet and jerked the little boy down the street.

Bemused, Brand watched the woman hurry off.

"Well, at least that will give them something else to talk about," Adara said. She waved her hand at the cluster of onlookers. "Hey, how y'all doing?"

"That you, Addy?" An elderly man with a long, saggy face squinted up at them. "You all right, or is this feller bothering you?"

"I'm fine, thank you, Mr. Duffey."

"Saw your gal friend Evie a while ago. She was with another long, tall drink of water. Great big blond feller."

"Really?" Adara murmured.

"Yep." The old man's gaze shifted to Brand. "Your mama know where you are, Addy?"

"Yes, sir, she knows."

Brand looked around. "The mama has supernatural powers of sight in addition to being an incendiary device?"

"No."

"Then that is an untruth, Adara. The mama does not know where you are."

"She might not know *exactly* where I am right this minute, but she knows I'm in town and that I'm with you."

"That is not what you told this human. Your speech is most imprecise."

The old man slapped his leg. "He's a funny one, ain't he? I take it from the way you two was a-smooching that he's your beau."

Adara flushed. "Uh, well . . . I don't . . ."

Brand processed this bit of conversation. *Beau,* a term signifying a man who was a young woman's lover. He and Adara were not lovers yet. Not in the strictest sense of the word. But they would be. Soon. This was an immutable fact.

"Yes," he told the Duffey human. "I am Adara's beau."

Mr. Duffey looked him up and down. "That so?"

"And you fussed at me?" Adara said. "Talk about telling a whopper. Liar, liar pants on fire."

Brand felt her quiver with indignation. "A rhythmically pleasing but ambiguous expression, Adara," he said. "Are you implying that I am such a horrible liar that my pants have recently, or are about to, burst into flame? Or do you mean to say that hearing me lie is comparable to donning blazing garb?"

"I'm saying you told Mr. Duffey a big old *lie.* Is that clear enough for you, bub? You are not my beau. We met yesterday."

Brand looked her in the eye. Some of the seething mixture of lust and frustration that churned within him must have shown in his expression, because she went still.

"We may have met yesterday, but we have exchanged essences. And we *will* be sexual partners, Adara. It is only a matter of time."

Adara gasped. "Are you out of your mind?"

"Exchanged essences?" The lines around Mr. Duffey's eyes crinkled in delight. "That's not what they called it in my day, but I reckon the gist is the same."

The old man chuckled and moved off down the street.

Chapter Ten

For a moment Addy gaped at Brand, too stunned and embarrassed to say anything. No Southern lady aired her business in public, and Brand had done everything short of parading down Main Street wearing her panties on the top of his perfectly formed head. Exchanged essences, indeed. He might as well have put an ad in the *Hannah Herald* saying they'd boinked. She went to church with Herbert Duffey. How was she supposed to look him in the eye the next time they passed the peace, for goodness' sake? He'd be thinking of a different kind of piece from now on, wouldn't he? That sweet old man thought that she and Brand had . . . had . . . That she would . . .

Okay, so maybe she would—in a heartbeat—but that was beside the point. A gentleman did not do anything to call a lady's honor and virtue into question. Her virtue had been laid out on Main Street and rolled over by a Mack truck. Her virtue was flatter than a flitter and had big, black tire marks all over it.

"Put me down, you jerk." Equal parts hurt and humiliated, she thumped him on the chest with both hands. "Right now."

"No."

"I said put me *down*."

Addy's skin tingled. The next moment she was sitting in the tree looking down at Brand.

"Adara, come down."

"Very funny. Like you didn't put me up here in the first place."

"I did not put you in the tree. Such a thing would be illogical. It would serve no purpose." His voice deepened. "Why would I put you up there, little one, when I would much rather have you here in my arms?"

Man, oh man, he was good! She was mad enough to spit nails, and he still had her melting into a puddle with his sexy voice.

Something moved, distracting her. She turned her head. Miss Mamie slunk back down the sidewalk toward them like a CIA operative disguised in a baggy skin suit and a gray wig. The nosy old lady was a bloodhound hot on the trail of fresh gossip. Great, Addy thought bitterly. First, Brand toted her down the street like a marauding Viking carrying plunder, and then he kissed her on the street corner in full view of half the town. If Miss Mamie found *that* titillating, she'd have a field day when she heard about Brand's little announcement. *We will be sexual partners, Adara. It is only a matter of time.* She closed her eyes. She was up a tree. Literally.

She knew the exact moment the old snoop spied her sitting on the limb, because Miss Mamie sucked in enough air to fill the Goodyear blimp. Addy opened her eyes and looked around. Brand was gone. Fine. Who needed him?

Miss Mamie peered up at her. "That you, Addy? What in the world are you doing up there? Pull your skirt down, girl. I can see all the way to Christmas."

Addy jerked her skirt over her thighs, her mind spinning as she groped for a logical explanation. What *was* she doing in the tree? What would a normal person say in her situation? Who was she kidding? A normal person wouldn't *be* in her situation.

"Say something, dodo," Addy muttered under her breath, "before she has it all over town you're crazier than a run-over dog."

Brand materialized on the branch next to her. "Why do you care what this human thinks?"

Addy glared at him. "You wouldn't understand. Go away. It's a great big planet with lots of foliage. Go find your own tree."

"No."

"What's that, dear?"

"I-uh-said I'm rescuing a kitten, Miss Mamie."

No sooner had the words left her mouth than Addy heard a soft mewl. A fluffy white kitten with blue eyes and orange markings scrabbled down the tree and crawled into her lap. The kitten purred and began to make biscuits, punching holes in Addy's skirt with its sharp little claws.

She stared at the fur ball in her lap. She said "kitten" and one showed up. How freakazoid was that?

"That so?" Miss Mamie sounded disappointed. No doubt she expected something a bit more out of left field from the Flying Cat Lady's great niece. "Shall I call the fire department?"

"N-no. I think I can handle it."

"You've got your young man with you. I'm sure *he* knows how to handle it."

With an irritating titter, the old lady shuffled away.

"You are angry with me," Brand said.

Addy stroked the velvety top of the kitten's head with the tip of her finger. Still purring, the kitten curled up in her lap and went to sleep. "No, you think?"

"What have I done to make you wroth with me?"

"You wouldn't understand."

"Certainly I will not understand if you do not explain it to me."

Addy sighed. "Look, bub, let's say we're from different worlds and leave it at that. Go away. This tree ain't big enough for the both of us."

"I will not leave you, so it would be more logical if you told me what I have done to distress you."

"This is my home. You let people think that we . . . that I . . ." Her face went hot. She waved her arms around. "And we haven't. If we *had* . . . um, you know what I mean, that's not something to share with anybody and everybody. I sure as shoot don't talk about my sex life on the street! I own a business in this town. I have roots here. I have to live here after you sail off to Valhalla or Hunky Warriorsville or wherever it is you live. And I have my family to think of. I don't want them hurt by idle gossip."

Admit it Addy, she scolded herself, *you* don't want to be hurt. You've never felt this way before, and it scares the crap out of you.

"I am sorry if I hurt you, Adara. I assure you it was not my intention. It is not my nature to dissemble, particularly when it comes to my desire for you. I want you. I have lived a long time—a *very* long time—and I have never wanted anyone the way I want you."

"You see, that's part of the problem. You're a ten-thousand-year-old demon hunter, and I'm a small-town girl with a flower shop. We have nothing in common. We're apples and oranges on a great big galactic scale, which makes us *big* apples and oranges. Planet-sized apples and oranges, with our own moons and—"

"Adara, you digress."

"Yeah, I digress." She felt like crying. "So I think it would be better for both of us if we said toodle-loo."

"I do not understand this toodle-loo."

"It means good-bye, so long, see you later, pal."

"You do not want me?"

"No."

"Little liar." He jerked her into his arms. With a meow of protest, the kitten slid into Brand's lap. "I can feel your heat."

He kissed her. Again. The guy sure needed to work on his conflict resolution skills . . . or maybe not.

Addy sighed and gave herself up to the hot ecstasy of his mouth. He had a little heat of his own. Sort of like a supernova. Maybe she was the teensiest bit of a liar. She wanted him. Big time. She was royally ticked off with the guy, and she *still* wanted him. She'd known him less than a day, and she wanted to monkey hump him in a tree—*on Main Street, for Pete's sake*—that's how much she wanted him. If she was a superhero, she'd be Super Slut Puppy able to leap a guy's bones in a single bound, wearing a cape and nothing else, 'cause Super Slut Puppy was *always* ready for action.

He dragged his mouth away from hers. Tangling his hands in her hair, he bent her head back. "You want me, Adara. Look me in the eye and say it. Tell me you want me. Tell me I do not burn alone."

"I won't! Because this is going nowhere, and I refuse to have my heart smashed into itty bitty pieces by Conan the Demon-Chaser dude."

"Conan is a fictional character. Mistress Evie told me. I am quite real, I promise you."

"But what else can you promise me? Can you promise if I sleep with you it won't be wham bam, thank you, ma'am?"

"Are you asking me in your somewhat perplexing fashion if I will stay with you?"

Yeah, that's what she was asking. She'd known the guy less than a day, and already she was making demands. She ought to laugh the whole thing off, pretend it was a joke. That would be the cool thing to do. But she was a small-town girl, not sophisticated or worldly. She wanted Brand with an intensity that frightened her. It all happened so fast. It had to be hormones, right? What else could it be? The scary four-letter "L" word flashed through her mind. No way. Still, one night of passion with Brand or a few precious stolen moments weren't going to be enough. Addy knew it in her bones. If she gave herself to this man, she would never be the same.

Pride urged her to pretend she didn't care. She raised her chin. She would not play games. "Yeah, I guess that's what I'm asking."

"I will not lie to you, Adara. I do not know if I can stay. Sexual congress with humans is forbidden the Dalvahni. For ten thousand years, the way of the warrior is all I have known. I do not know the consequences if I break my vows. To my knowledge, it has not been done." He raised her hand and brushed her palm with his lips. A shiver of longing danced down her spine. "Yet break them I will, for given the choice of forsaking my warrior's vows and not knowing your sweetness, I choose you. For however long we have together, I choose you." His voice darkened to that smoky timbre that melted her bones and left her a panting little mess. "Choose me, little one. I beg you, choose me."

Addy sighed. The man had her at *such* a disadvantage. Sign her up for a room at Heart Break Hotel, 'cause here she came barreling down Ruination Highway at breakneck speed.

"How can I possibly stay mad at you when you talk like that?"

Brand's eyes darkened. Wowza, talk about your hot looks. And she thought Mama was a thermonuclear device. Oh, Lord, she was a goner.

"Adara," Brand said. He reached for her. "I—"

"Climbing trees at your age, brother?" A familiar and annoying voice came from below.

Addy almost fell off the branch. Brand draped an arm across her shoulders to steady her. "I do what I have to in pursuit of the djegrali, Ansgar."

"I see no demons." Ansgar arched a brow at them, an affectation Addy was starting to hate. "All I see is a certain bothersome female dangling from a branch of this rather impressive woody perennial."

Bothersome? Of all the nerve.

"I have a name, Blondy. It's Addy. Wear yourself out using it, why don't you?"

Evie stepped in front of Ansgar, an anxious expression on her face. "Addy, are you all right? We went to the funeral home, but you were gone. I've been so worried about you."

Good old Evie, Addy thought warmly. She found Addy playing patty-cake in a tree with Captain Orgasm, and no odd looks or smart-ass remarks, nothing but genuine concern for Addy's well-being. What a keeper.

Addy leaped out of the tree and onto the sidewalk. Brand landed beside her, the kitten clinging to his shoulder.

"I'm fine, Evie, though it has been a strange morning. I guess you heard about Mr. Farris? Somebody took his body. Mrs. Farris and Bessie Mae had a throwdown at Corwin's. I thought Mama and Shep were going to die. Mrs. Farris seems to think Bessie Mae snatched ol' Dwight for a little farewell hokeypokey, but I don't know. If you ask me, Shirley's the one gone round the bend. She cut off Mr. Farris's mister and put it in a Ziploc, like it was last night's meat loaf. Eww, forget I said that. Bad analogy. Waved it around at the funeral home, hollering about de-germing the thing. Sca-ary."

Addy didn't know what she expected, but she sure as heck expected *something*. Life in Hannah proceeded at a pace roughly that of a snail on sticky fly paper. Orin Schneider's two-headed calf and Lorraine Bradberry's prize-winning squash casserole were big news in Hannah. On the juicy tidbit scale, the scene at the funeral parlor was a ten. It darn sure wasn't every day a widow sliced off her husband's cock-a-doodle-doo and stuffed it in a press-and-seal. But, Evie didn't say anything. She stared at Addy all googly-eyed, like she'd grown another head or something.

"Something wrong, Evie?"

"Addy, you jumped out of the tree."

"Yeah, well a dress and heels are not what I call climbing clothes."

"You were twenty feet up."

"What? No way."

She turned and looked at the tree. There, that mossy branch high above with the crook in it, like a giant's elbow. That was where she and Brand were sitting. Addy blinked in confusion. Twenty feet, at least, maybe more. She'd jumped from a height of a two-story building onto pavement, and the bottoms of her feet didn't even sting. She should be dead or at the very least have a broken bone. Several, in fact. The day's bizarre events played through her head. The platinum-blond hair she'd mysteriously acquired above and below deck, the rapid and remarkable improvement in her vision, and the disappearance of decades-old scars, along with the instantaneous healing of her slightest boo-boo. The timely and glorious pimply retribution visited upon the Death Starr's munchkin-size ass, not to mention the F-22 Raptor fighter jet trip she'd taken that morning from the flower shop to the funeral home. She tried to process it all, but her brain seemed to have turned to mush and her legs felt noodly. She swayed.

Brand caught her. "Easy, little one."

"Brand, what have you done to me?"

"I told you, Adara. We exchanged essences."

"You keep saying that, but what does it *mean*?"

"I will tell you what it means." Ansgar's usually cool, unruffled voice held a note of irritation, or anger, perhaps. "It means my brother has done the forbidden. Broken his vows and called down untold retribution upon his head to save *you*. I hope you are worth it, human, although, to be precise, the term 'human' no longer applies to you."

Addy bristled. Boy, Prince Flaxen Fart got under her skin with his sneering manner and condescending "I am so much better than you my poop don't stink" tone. "Spit it out, Blondy. What are you trying to say?"

"It means that in saving your miserable hide Brand has given you a portion of his powers and immortality," Ansgar said. "It means, Adara Jean Corwin, you are no longer human."

Chapter Eleven

Addy chuckled. "Not human? You on something, Blondy?" She looked at Brand. "Hear that? Your buddy thinks I'm not human. What a maroon. Reckon he got him some of Dinky's cow pie mushrooms?"

Brand's impassive expression did not change. Jeez, the guy was a real heartbreaker, but he seriously needed to develop a sense of humor.

"Ansgar is not intoxicated," he said. "The Dalvahni are impervious to the effects of alcohol and drugs. We cannot get drunk like lesser species. To answer your question, Ansgar is not under the influence of a mind-altering substance. And I must remind you, Adara, that you fabricated the entire 'bovine dung fungi' story to appease the mama."

"Yeah, well, I—"

"Ansgar is correct. Strictly speaking, you are no longer human."

Addy snorted. "Yeah, right."

"If you will remember, I told you this morning when I pleasured you—"

Whoosh, all the blood rushed to Addy's face. Pleasured her? Stuck his hand up her skirt and made her sing notes only dogs could hear, that's what he did. "Hold it right there," she said. "Not another word, or so help me . . ."

"—that we merged and that you received some of my powers," Brand finished.

"Yeah, but I thought it was temporary," she wailed. "Like a rash or something."

"No, Adara, the change is permanent. You are part Dalvahni and part human. We have already discussed this."

"And you thought I believed you? Who could believe something like that? That's nuts."

Brand seemed to contemplate this statement. After a moment, he nodded. "I think I understand. This is an expression of your confusion with the situation, and not a reference to a large, hard-shelled seed or the ancient Egyptian goddess of the sky."

"Huh?"

"The circumstances are unusual, Adara." His patient tone set Addy's teeth on edge. "Naturally, you are somewhat bewildered."

"Bewildered? You've turned me into some kind of mutant freak, and you tell me it's okay if I'm *bewildered*? You've got a talent for understatement, bub." Addy pointed to her face. "Do you see this? This is not a bewildered face. Oh, no. This is a seriously pissed-off face." She poked Brand in his broad, muscled chest. "Kind of goes with the rest of me that would love to kick your gorgeous Dalvahni ass all the way from here to Canada."

Evie gave a little gasp. "Addy, lower your voice. You said the 'a' word on the street. If your mama finds out you been cussing in public, you'll never hear the end of it."

"What do you think Mama's going to do when she finds out I've gone and changed *species* without her permission? Talk about a hissy fit!"

"Calm yourself, Adara," Brand said. "You are upset."

"You bet your bippy I'm upset." Addy's voice rose. "I'm Mount Vesuvius, and I'm fixing to go Pompeii on your ass."

"*Addy.*" Evie's whisper was anguished. "You said it again."

"Ass, ass, ass! Double ass, triple ass, horse's ass. I don't care. You hear me, Evie?" She was losing it, but she couldn't seem to help herself. Suddenly, all the steam went out of her, and she groaned and dropped her face in her hands. "Oh, my God, did you hear what I said?"

"Sure, Addy, I heard you." Evie darted a worried look over

her shoulder. "I'm pretty sure folks clear down to the Baptist church heard you. You said ass. Like a bunch of times."

Addy lifted her head. "Not that, Evie. I said bippy. Nobody says bippy anymore except Bitsy. It's bad enough I'm a mutant. Now I'm channeling my mother."

Evie put her arms around her and gave her a quick hug. "Get a grip, Addy. I know you're upset, but you've got bigger problems."

Addy raised her head to stare at her friend. "Evie, I just found out we're not the same species. What could be worse than that?"

"I saw Dwight Farris this morning."

"You did? Where?"

"At the shop."

Addy wrinkled her nose. "Gross, somebody left a corpse at the shop? That's great. I'll have to de-cootie the whole place. And how am I going to explain this to the police?" Her eyes widened. "Or my mother? She'll think I had something to do with it. Oh, man, I am so dead."

Evie put her hands on Addy's shoulders and gave her a little shake. "You've got to listen to me, Addy. Mr. Farris wasn't *in* the shop. He was *at* the shop. I saw him standing on the sidewalk peering through the front window. You hear me, Addy? There's a dead guy running around town, and I'm pretty sure he's looking for you."

Addy's mouth dropped open. Guck, to borrow one from Bessie Mae. Double guck.

Brand turned to Evie. "Mistress Evie, you are certain the creature you saw was the Farris human?"

"It was him," Evie said. "I'm sure of it. Eyeballed me right through the shop window." She shuddered. "He looked real bad, Addy. All pasty and stiff and creepy, like something out of a movie."

"WHA-A-A-T?" Addy screeched, regaining the use of her tongue. "THERE'S A DEAD GUY LOOKING FOR ME? I *HATE* DEAD GUYS!"

Brand and Ansgar winced, and Evie covered her ears. *Pop, pop.* Two nearby street lamps exploded in a shower of frosted glass. Addy heard an ominous crack as the glazed plate glass windows along the front of the Hannah Pharmacy cracked down the middle.

There went another of Mama's rules, busted all to hell and back. A lady did not raise her voice in public. A lady's voice should be a soft, dulcet caress upon the ear, as languid and cool as a slow-winding stream, as pleasing to the senses as the sound of the wind playing through the blossom-heavy branches of a dogwood in spring. A lady did not yowl like a cat in heat or wail like a busted firehouse siren.

"Why would Old Man Farris be looking for me?" She lowered her voice with an effort. "If he's mad about . . . you know . . . he needs to take it up with Shirley. *I* don't have his weenie."

"Calm yourself, Adara, the being you knew as Dwight Farris is no more," Brand said. "In all likelihood, the creature Mistress Evie saw was a demon, the same djegrali, no doubt, that marked you."

Ansgar nodded. "My thoughts exactly, brother."

"Is that your way of trying to make me feel better? 'Cause if it is, I got to tell you it sucks." Addy raised her hand to her forehead. "Whew, I feel lightheaded. Probably has something to do with finding out I've got a starring role in *Night of the Living De-weenered Dead*."

"You need to eat." Brand took her by the arm. "You are not fully recovered from the djegrali attack or the transmutation you have undergone, and you have further weakened yourself by engaging your new powers. Where is the nearest pub or hostel where we can obtain sustenance?"

Evie pointed down the street. "The Sweet Shop is down the block that a-ways. They serve the best BBQ in town and fried chicken that'll make you want to slap yo' mama."

Brand raised his brows. "A strange custom, especially in view of the apprehension with which Adara views the matriarchal vessel."

"She doesn't mean *my* mother, Brand," Addy said. "God, that would be like suicidal."

"Ah, I see." Brand gave a nod of understanding. "Mistress Evie peppers her speech with strange sayings and colorful phrases in the same manner you do. Tell me, what is the meaning of this BBQ?"

Ansgar cleared his throat. "Allow me to offer a supposition, brother. I believe BBQ may be a shortened term for meat that has been cooked over an open fire. My hunter's nose has detected the tempting aroma of roasted meat wafting southward this past hour and more. If that be the case, I would not be averse to partaking of sustenance myself. Evangeline and I will accompany you."

"Which in warrior speak, means let's eat," Evie whispered in Addy's ear. "Whew, he talks funny, but he's way cute."

"Blondy? He's a gigantic pain in the butt. I can't believe you're attracted to him."

"Believe it. I mean, *look* at him! He's gorgeous."

"Hmm, I suppose so, if you're into the 'fair haired Viking prince surfer boy' type."

"Surfer boy? No, no, Adds, you got it all wrong. He's the *Legolas* type, only taller and way brawnier than the dude in the movie." Evie gave a soulful sigh. "He can munch on my lembas any day."

"Eww, is that some kind of euphemism? 'Cause if it is, Tolkien just rolled over in his grave."

Evie giggled. "I'm just saying . . ."

"Well, stop saying. I'm getting a mental picture of you and Blondy doing the wild thing, and it's giving me a full body huzz."

Evie giggled again. "You are so funny. Where'd you find the kitten?"

"Duh, in the tree. Don't kittens grow there, or something? Cute little thing, isn't he?"

"How do you know it's a he?"

Addy shrugged. "I assumed. I didn't check his engine, if that's what you mean. We just met."

"Are you talking about Brand or the cat?"

"Very funny. I was talking about Mr. Fluffy."

"Mr. Fluffy? Uh oh, you've already named the cat."

"Yep. His full name is Mr. Fluffy Fauntleroy Corwin," Addy said. "What do you think?"

The world shifted as Brand lifted her in his arms. "I think it a remarkably silly name. I greatly fear for your future progeny."

"Hey, put me down. I can walk."

Brand strode down the sidewalk in the direction of the Sweet Shop. "No, you are lightheaded and those ridiculously flimsy things you wear on your feet have been damaged. You will sprain an ankle and not be able to flee should the djegrali attack."

"Sweet, big guy, but I broke a heel. No big deal. You don't have to carry me around like a sack of flour." She gave him a shove to the chest. "Put me down, Brand. I mean it. If you're so all-fired worried about my shoes, then break off the other heel so they match. Problem solved."

"A surprisingly sensible solution and one I should have thought of myself." Brand lowered Addy to the sidewalk. "I must be in need of nourishment also. My thought processes seem somewhat muddled."

"Your thought processes have been muddled since making the acquaintance of a certain female," Ansgar said with a knowing smirk.

Addy rolled her eyes. "Oooh, careful, Brand. Looks like Blondy's had a humor chip added to his hard drive. Too bad it's a dud."

Brand held out his hand. "Hand me your sandal, Adara, and stop tormenting Ansgar." He snapped off the heel with ease and handed her back the shoe. "I would consider it a personal favor if you two would cease this incessant bickering. Should it continue, I might have a—what did you call it?—ah, yes, a *hissy* fit myself."

"Fun sucker." Addy looked up at Brand. "I think it might be kind of interesting to see you lose that cool of yours, Ice Man. You're wound way too tight, if you ask me."

She gave a startled yelp as Brand jerked her into his arms and kissed her.

"Do not tempt me, Adara." He released her with a growl. "Lest I demonstrate exactly how I would like to relieve my tension."

"Please, brother, not on an empty stomach," Ansgar said.

Addy stiffened. "Oh, why don't you go—"

Brand took her by the arm and pulled her down the street. "Ansgar is right. We need to eat."

"Wait, what about Mr. Fluffy?" Addy dragged her feet. "We can't take a cat in a restaurant. It's a health code violation."

Brand halted. Reaching up, he plucked the kitten from his shoulder. "In truth, I had forgotten about the creature. I would advise you to put the troublesome flea bag back in the tree and walk away."

"I can't do that! Something might happen to him. He's so cute and helpless. I'm going to keep him."

Brand sighed. "Of course you are. Already the creature has ensorcelled you. You are too soft-hearted, Adara." Looking the kitten in the eye, he said sternly, "You will stay where I put you. Is that understood?"

"*Meow*," the kitten said, and disappeared.

Chapter Twelve

Addy looked between Brand's feet and all around for the missing cat. "Hey, where'd Mr. Fluffy go?"

"Do not be troubled." Brand strode down the sidewalk. "Mr. Fluffy is quite safe."

Addy hurried after him. "But, Brand I—"

"Adara, he is in a safe place. Do you want me to explain the particulars to you?"

"You did something freaky, didn't you?"

"I do not consider it freakish. It is quite simple. There are pockets of space between dimensions, and I have placed the creature there—"

"Stop!" She clapped her hands over her ears. "Don't say any more. It makes my head want to explode. Promise me you can find him again."

"I can find him."

Evie and Ansgar caught up with them. "Hey, what's the big hurry?" Evie sounded out of breath. "It's ninety-five degrees in the shade, and you two are running a race."

Addy felt a pang of guilt. She hadn't noticed the heat. It didn't seem to affect Brand or Blondy, either, but poor Evie looked done in. Her pale face was flushed and her damp curls clung to her brow.

"I think Brand's hungry," Addy said.

"Yeah, I'm getting that idea." Evie glanced around. "Where's the kitty?"

"Don't ask." Addy hooked her arm through Evie's. "Come on, sweat ball. Let's get you inside."

"Ladies don't sweat. They glow," Evie said primly.

"Well then, you must be radioactive."

They halted at the entrance to the Sweet Shop. A neon sign in the window blinked the words AIR CONDITIONED. The air conditioner was sacred in the South, right up there with duct tape.

They pushed open the door and stepped inside. A bell jingled overhead, announcing their arrival. Addy looked around with satisfaction. The Sweet Shop was a constant in an inconstant world. The building that housed the restaurant had once been a warehouse, and the scarred plank walls and metal ceiling remained. Worn wooden booths lined the walls along both sides of the rectangular dining space, and round laminated tables filled the remaining space. On the walls, tin signs advertised everything from cigarettes to soda pop and filling stations. The signs competed with folksy sayings, the backend of an old car, outdated calendars, and ancient rusted farm implements that looked like medieval torture devices.

It was early, the start of the lunch hour. The restaurant was empty except for a scattering of breakfast holdovers and a lean, gray-haired man in a back booth. The man hunched over the remains of his meal, muttering to himself.

"Amasa John Collier," Addy murmured in response to Brand's raised eyebrow. "The town drunk and crazy as a loon besides."

They seated themselves at one of the big round tables and waited. Before long the kitchen door swung open and Viola Williams, the Rubenesque owner of the Sweet Shop, hurried over.

Her smooth, brown cheeks split in a warm smile. "Morning, folks, welcome to the Sweet Shop." Her smile widened when she saw Evie sitting between Ansgar and Brand. "Oh, hey, Evie, I didn't see you sitting between these two big fellows. You look like a lost ball in high weeds." She shifted her curious gaze back to Brand and Ansgar. "You gentlemen hungry? If so, you've come to the right place. Best food in town. What can I get you folks to drink?"

"We'll have sweet tea all around, Miss Viola," Addy said.

Viola started in surprise. "Lord have mercy, that you, Addy? I didn't recognize you. What on earth have you done to yo' hair?"

"I changed it up a little, Miss Viola. That's all."

"Hmm, I expect you did at that. What's yo' mama think about it?"

"Oh, well, you know . . ."

"Uh huh," Viola said. "I know yo' mama. Well, today we got fried chicken, hamburger steak, or baked catfish, and, of course, barbecue. Slow-cooked pork ribs, Del's specialty, or you can have a chopped pork sandwich, if you've a mind. Lunch special is a meat and three. The sides today are mashed potatoes and gravy, fried corn, collards, sweet potatoes, field peas, cabbage, fried okra, baby limas, fried green tomatoes, sliced tomatoes, cole slaw, pear salad, and deviled eggs. Chocolate pie and banana pudding for dessert." She leveled her dark gaze at Brand and Ansgar. "Addy and Evie already know this—Lord, they been eating here since they was in pull-ups—but this being your first time and all—and, I know it's your first time, 'cause I'd have remembered two fine-looking gentlemen like you— I'll tell you flat out everything is made from scratch. None o' them boxed taters or tasteless canned veggies or powdery box macaroni and cheese served at the Sweet Shop. Del and I do all the cooking, and we make it fresh. I drive over to the farmer's market in Paulsberg twice a week and buy my produce there. Hand picked and Bama grown, every bit of it. Might as well warn you, I cook with bacon fat and real butter, and you can't make good biscuits and dumplings without using a little lard. Why put that fake stuff in yo' body anyway? Did you know you can set oleo out in the yard and the ants won't touch it? Why anybody would put something in their body the ants won't eat is beyond me. No, when it comes to eatin', it ought to be God-made, homemade, and man-made, in that order, I always say. Well, y'all think about what you want while I get your tea."

She bustled over to the drink counter, returning with four

jumbo-size brown plastic tumblers filled to the brim with iced tea and garnished with a lemon wedge. "Four sweet teas with lemon." She plunked the glasses down on the table and removed an order pad from her apron pocket. "What'll you folks have?"

"I will sample a generous portion of your roasted meat, without the accompanying herbs," Ansgar said in his silken voice.

"The same for me," Brand rumbled. "A very *large* portion of roasted meat, Mistress Viola. My friend and I have not partaken of sustenance in some days, and our appetite is sharp."

"You don't say." Viola gave Addy a questioning look. "Ain't from around here, are they? What's he talking about, herbs?"

"I think Blondy's talking about the sides, Vi. Something tells me these guys don't eat a lot of vegetables. Bring on the animal flesh and maybe something to sop up the sauce with."

Viola nodded. "Hog wild, high on the hog, or whole hog?"

"I do not understand," Brand said.

"She's asking you how much barbecue you want." Addy looked down at the menu. "Hog wild is a slab of ribs, high on the hog is two slabs, and whole hog is four slabs. Feeds four to six people. That's a lot of meat, big guy." She indicated a group of pictures hanging over the register. "Anyone that scarfs down a whole hog gets their picture on the wall. See that guy on the end there covered in sauce looks like he wants to hurl? That's Skeeter Johnson. Had him a heart attack right after he finished a whole hog. Took him out of here on a gurney. All that protein in one sitting is bad on the old ticker. Better start off with a hog wild or a high on the hog. You can always order more."

"I will take a whole hog," Brand said without hesitation.

"I also," Ansgar added.

"Or you could ignore me, and go with the coronary bypass special." Addy slid the menu back behind the napkin holder. "You heard them, Viola. Mr. Cholesterol and his twin brother, Clogged Arteries, will each have a whole hog. I'll have the fried chicken, mixed, mashed potatoes, collards, and fried green tomatoes. You, Evie?"

"Sounds to me like you're working on your own arteries, Addy." Evie studied the menu for a moment. "A veggie plate for me, Viola. Sweet potatoes, cabbage, and . . . Oh, heck, can't let my friends here go to Heart Attack land alone, bring me the fried okra and fried green tomatoes."

Viola scribbled some notes on her pad. "Got it. Y'all be sure and save room for dessert." The door jingled, and four men wearing farmers' tans and overalls entered the restaurant. "Oh, Lordy, the lunch crowd's started," she said. "I'd best get Pauline out here to wait tables and go help Del. He gets bent outta shape when things get busy."

She shooed the four men toward a table and disappeared into the kitchen. A short while later, the door swung back open and Pauline, the Sweet Shop's rawboned, harried-looking waitress, brought them their food. Pauline had worked at the Sweet Shop as long as Addy could remember. In all that time, the woman had not changed her hairstyle, scraped back in a bun so tight her eyebrows met her hairline. Lifting their plates in her gnarled, blue-veined hands, Pauline handed Addy and Evie their food, and set a huge platter of smoking ribs in front of the men. She slammed two rolls of paper towels on the table. Blowing a stray wisp of graying hair out of her face, she glared at Brand and Ansgar. "You want regular or drunk sauce with that?"

"Give 'em the drunk sauce, Pauline," Addy said.

Pauline's gimlet stare shifted from Brand to Addy. "You want pepper sauce with them greens?"

"Yes, ma'am."

"Rolls or cornbread?"

"Both, please."

"Huh." Pauline thumped a bottle of pepper sauce and two Jim Beam bottles of Del's special drunk sauce on the table and left.

"Whew, she's been ticked off since the house fell on her sister," Evie said.

Brand grabbed a smoking hot rib off the platter and tore off a chunk of meat with his teeth. "I can understand how such a tragedy would sour your outlook on life. Was the house deposited on the female's unfortunate sister by an act of nature, or an angry behemoth?"

"Dude, it was a joke," Addy said. "Pauline doesn't have a sister. It's from a movie called *The Wizard of Oz.*"

"I am relieved." Brand chewed thoughtfully. "A movie is a form of human entertainment that enacts a story through a series of images that give the illusion of movement, is it not?"

Addy shook a few drops of pepper sauce on her greens. "I guess that's one way of putting it, but it sure sucks all the fun out of it."

Brand picked up a Jim Beam bottle and dumped some drunk sauce on his mound of ribs. He took a bite of rib. His eyes widened. "I must say, this sauce is most pleasing to the palate. What is in it?"

"Oh, that's Del's secret recipe. Nobody knows everything that's in it, not even Viola," Addy said. "But, the secret ingredient is whiskey. Not a whole lot, mind you, just enough to give it that extra little kick."

"You are frowning, Evangeline," Ansgar said around a mouthful of pork. "Is your food not to your liking?"

"No, dang it, I forgot to ask Pauline for hot sauce. I don't dare ask that old grump pot for it. She'll bite my head off and hand it to me."

Ansgar slathered his ribs with drunk sauce. "You require this hot sauce to enjoy your repast?"

Evie sighed. "Yeah, I'm a real nut about it. I eat Texas Pete on just about everything, eggs, toast, pizza, greens. They usually have it on the tables, but I guess they forgot. It's all right. I'll live."

Ansgar stilled, a half-eaten rib in one hand. There was a look of abstraction on his face. "Ah, I think I see it. Is it a red liquid in a slender glass bottle with a picture on the front of it depicting an odd creature brandishing some kind of rope?"

Evie gave him a look of surprise. "Yeah, that's it. How'd you—"

"There are a number of such bottles on a shelf in the cooking area of this establishment. I will procure one for you."

"Oh, no, I don't want to be any trouble."

"No trouble at all."

Ansgar went back to his food.

Evie made a *what the?* gesture to Addy, who shrugged. There was a startled shriek from the kitchen. The door swung open, and a bottle of hot sauce floated through the air and made a wobbly landing on the table beside Evie's plate. Evie stared at the bottle of Texas Pete like it was a snake. Viola flew out of the kitchen, her husband Del at her heels.

"Call the pastor, Del, and tell him to get over here double quick," Viola said. "We got us a haint."

Del, a big, handsome man with graying hair and the beefy physique of a former football player, seemed baffled by his wife's outburst. "Vi, I don't know what you think you saw—"

"I don't *think* I saw. I *know* I saw, Delmonte Lorenzo Williams. I saw a bottle of hot sauce fly through the air."

"Honey, we been in this building for thirty years. Why would a ghost decide to haunt us now and pick a bottle of hot sauce to do it with? Why not pepper sauce or drunk sauce, or plain old ketchup, for that matter? It don't make sense."

"You mean you didn't see it?"

"I had my eyes on that fryer. I didn't see no hot sauce fly through the air." Del looked around the room. "Anybody else see it?"

To Addy's relief, the rest of the customers shook their heads. Thank God the restaurant wasn't crowded yet and the food at the Sweet Shop was so delicious. All the other diners must have been too busy stuffing their faces to notice the floating bottle of hot sauce.

"I know what I saw, Delmonte Williams." Viola's voice rose. "And I saw that bottle of hot sauce float off the kitchen shelf and go right out the door like it had wings or something."

"Vi," Del pleaded. "Think about what you're saying."

"I don't have to think. I saw what I saw." Wild eyed, Viola looked around the room. She marched up to them like an avenging fury and pointed to the bottle of Texas Pete. "Where'd you get that hot sauce?"

"Uh," Addy said. Great, brain freeze. Again. "I uh—"

"I got it for them, Miss Vi. Used my contrabulator." Amasa

Collier slid out of the back booth and ambled up to their table. Eyes lowered, he pulled his hand from behind his back. He held a contraption made out of two coat hangers straightened and twisted together. "I heard Miss Evie say she'd like some hot sauce, so I took the liberty of getting it for her. Sorry if I startled you." He bobbed the wire up and down. "See, it's got this handy little loop at one end for grabbing things. I opened the door a crack and snagged a bottle of Texas Pete right off the shelf. Guess you didn't see me. From a distance, you probably couldn't see the wire, either, and thought the bottle was levitating. I'm sorry if I frightened you. I was trying to help."

"Well, ain't that nice." Viola looked relieved and a little put out. "Next time, Amasa, wave at me so as I can see you. You like to give me a stroke."

"Yes, ma'am. I'm real sorry."

Shaking her head, Viola shooed Del back into the kitchen.

"Nice—uh—contrabulator, Mr. Collier," Addy said. "What's it for?"

"It's a kind of divining rod, I guess you might say. I tinker around with wire sculpture, and I recently started using coat hangers as a medium. Makes some interesting pieces, and reusing coat hangers is Earth-friendly. No sense relegating a perfectly good coat hanger to the dump yard when I can make something out of it. You still staying in your aunt's house?"

"Yes, sir."

Brand gave her a curious look. "The dwelling you occupy belongs to someone else?"

She nodded. "I keep an eye on things while my Aunt Muddy is away. Muddy likes to travel. It's been a good arrangement for us both."

"You think she's coming home anytime soon?" Mr. Collier sounded wistful. "She's been gone almost a year. I miss her."

"You know Muddy. She could blow into town any time, or get a hankering to see New Zealand."

Mr. Collier scuffed his foot on the linoleum. "Yeah, you never know what she'll do. Well, you and your aunt come by the house sometime if you like, and I'll show you gals my work."

"Sure thing, Mr. C. I'd like that. Soon as Muddy gets back, we'll drop by." She waved a hand at Brand and Ansgar, who were once again demolishing ribs with single-minded devotion. "Mr. Collier, allow me to introduce my friends, Brand and Ansgar." She nudged Brand with her elbow. "Brand, this is Amasa Collier. He and my Aunt Muddy are old friends. Went to high school together, in fact."

Brand wiped his hands on a paper towel and shook Mr. Collier's hand. "Well met, Amasa Collier. Adara says you are the town drunk and crazy as a loon."

Evie spewed her corn muffin all over Addy.

Red faced, Addy brushed the crumbs off her blouse. "Brand, what a thing to say! Mr. Collier, my *friend* here has a warped sense of humor. I didn't say any such thing."

"Adara, that is an untruth and you know it," Brand said. "Why do you dissemble?"

Addy flashed Mr. Collier a nervous smile. "Brand, you're embarrassing me. We'll talk about it later."

To Addy's surprise, Amasa chuckled. "It's all right, Addy, I *am* the town drunk, and you aren't the first person to call me crazy."

Addy felt terrible. "I'm sorry, Mr. Collier," she said in a rush, her face flaming hotter. When would she learn to keep her big mouth shut? Please, God, let the floor open and swallow her up. "I don't know what else to say. I didn't mean to—"

"Always kind of figured I was crazy myself, until now," Amasa cut her off. "I was in a car wreck when I was a few years older than you, Addy. Had a concussion and spent a few days in the hospital. After the accident, I started seeing things, things normal people don't see. Figured folks were right and I was crazy. Started drinking, and my law practice dried up. Didn't care about that. I wanted the visions to stop. The drinking helped, so I drank more. You see, when I drink, I don't see things. Been drinking nigh on thirty years." He took a deep breath. "Not drunk this morning, though. As a general rule, I don't start drinking before noon. I may be a drunk, but I got my standards. Saw that bottle of hot sauce float across the room, and figured it was another hallucination. Then I saw the expression on your face, Addy. Evie's, too. You both saw that bottle fly. I know it." He looked at Brand and Ansgar. "Since both of these girls looked plum flummoxed, I figure one of you fellows did it. That right?"

Ansgar nodded, his expression wary. "I am responsible. I am in your debt, Friend Collier."

"No, no, quite the opposite, Mr. Ansgar. I owe you. All these years, I been sure I'm crazy, but for the first time I'm thinking . . . maybe not." He beamed at them. "Figure something big must be in the wind to bring the Dalvahni to Hannah."

Addy felt Brand go still beside her, like a predator ready to pounce. She stole a glance at him. The hard, ruthless expression on his beautiful face sent a chill down her spine. Whew, make that a large, very ticked-off predator.

"How do you know of the Dalvahni, Mr. Collier?" he asked softly.

Amasa chuckled. "How do you think? A demon told me, that's how." His gaze shifted to a spot behind Brand. "That's a real nice sword you got there. Your friend's longbow is a real beaut, too. Don't see workmanship like that anymore. Well, nice to meet you, gentlemen. I'm sure I'll see you around. 'Spect you'll be real busy, you being demon hunters and all. Whole dad-blame town is crawling with the nasty critters."

He stepped away from the table and looked back with a grin. "By the way, Addy, nice hair. It suits you, though I'm sure yo' mama's going to have something to say about it. You know how she is."

Swinging his contrabulator, he sauntered out the door.

Chapter Thirteen

The door closed behind Mr. Collier with a jingle. Looking out the window, Addy saw him pause on the sidewalk. He waved his contrabulator back and forth in front of him. She smothered a giggle. No doubt about it, Amasa was an odd duck. She glanced at Brand and Ansgar and stifled a gasp. Yikes! The two warriors watched the gray-haired man through the plate glass window with the unblinking, hungry intensity of a polar bear eying a baby seal.

"Guys, guys, take a chill pill," she said. "Mr. Collier is harmless."

"He is not harmless. He could see our weapons, and he knows we are Dalvahni," Brand said. "He also admits to consorting with demons. He is dangerous."

"Mr. Collier, consort with demons?" Addy picked up a drumstick. "Didn't you hear a thing the poor man said? The demons have been pestering him. All these years he's been drinking so he *won't* see them. That's so sad."

She took a bite of the drumstick, and the delicious taste of fried chicken walloped her senses. The golden-brown skin was crisp and seasoned to perfection, the dark meat tender and juicy. Her mouth had a little orgasm right then and there, in front of God and everybody. God, she loved fried chicken. Loved the smell of it, loved it hot or cold, summer or winter, any time of day. If the scent of fried chicken could be bottled, she'd wear it. *Bouquet de poulet frit.* So what if every dog in town followed her around? She'd smell like a little slice of heaven.

With an effort, she recalled her thoughts from her culinary orgy and handed the bread basket to Evie. "Here, have another corn muffin. I'm still wearing most of your first one."

"Thanks." Evie took another corn muffin and shook hot sauce on it. "Addy is right about Mr. Collier. He's a sweetheart."

Addy gave Brand a stern look. "Seems to me, you big, bad demon hunters ought to think about enlisting Mr. Collier's help. Maybe he can tell you where the creepy dudes hang out. How many demons are we talking here, anyway? Two? Three?"

"I do not know," Brand said. "At first, this seemed like any other mission, but it has turned out to be anything but ordinary, in more ways than one." He gave Addy such a smoldering look it was a blue wonder she didn't burst into flames on the spot. "If this is, indeed, Han-nah-a-lah," he continued, just as if he hadn't raised her internal temperature by a few degrees, "we may be dealing with an infestation. If that is the case, we may need reinforcements."

Evie looked up, the bottle of Texas Pete in her hand. "Hannah-a-lah? What's that?"

Addy snorted. "These two think Hannah is some kind of demon magnet, a kind of metaphysical morass that attracts paranormal phenomena. *Hannah.* Is that messed up, or what?"

Evie looked down at her plate. "I don't think it's so messed up."

Addy stared at her in surprise. "You don't?"

Evie's hand tightened around the Texas Pete bottle. "Mr. Collier's not the only one in Hannah who sees things."

"What is this?" Ansgar demanded. "Do you have the sight, Evangeline?"

"No-o-o-o, I don't see demons, if that's what you mean."

Ansgar's tense expression eased. "That is good, very good."

"I see fairies."

Addy's mouth dropped open. It seemed to be doing that a lot today. Maybe the damn thing had a busted hinge or something. "Say what?"

Evie lifted her chin. "I said I see fairies."

Ansgar frowned. "By fairies, do you mean small supernatural beings that are human in form and possess magical powers?"

"Yes."

"How long?" Addy blurted out.

"Well, they vary in size . . ."

"I'm not asking you how big they are, Evie. How long have you been able to see them?"

"Like always. My mother saw them, too. Guess it's genetic." A black hole opened at Addy's feet. Her best friend saw fairies—had *always* been able to see fairies—and she was clueless until now.

"Why didn't you tell me?"

"Addy, I've heard the way you talk about your aunt Etheline and Mr. Collier. I didn't want you thinking I'm crazy, too."

"Evie, for crying out loud, a few minutes ago you found out I'm not *human,* and you didn't kick me to the curb. That's a pretty darn good friend, if you ask me. I think I can handle a little Tinker Bell."

"Oh, Addy." Evie flung her napkin over her face and burst into tears.

Ansgar put his arm around Evie and scowled at Addy. "See what you have done, you pestilential female. She is leaking."

"Me? I didn't do anything to her!"

Evie lowered her napkin. She was smiling through her tears. "It's all right. I'm so happy to be able to talk about it, that's all. You don't know how many times I wanted to tell you, Addy, but I couldn't. Mama made me promise. She was afraid of how people would react." She gave Addy a watery smile. "But, we're both different now, so I guess it's okay."

"Oh, Evie." Addy started to cry, too. "You are such a nut."

Laughing and crying, they clasped hands across the table.

"Now they are both leaking," Ansgar said in a tone of disgust.

"Females are most peculiar." Brand looked down at the pile of bones on his platter. "Perhaps we should order another round of roasted meat?"

"You can't be serious!" Addy sat back in her chair. "You've eaten enough to feed a small army."

"I never jest about food, Adara. The fare here is exceptional, but I am still hungry." He eyed Addy's plate. "On second thought, brother, we should sample the fried poultry. The scent is tantalizing."

"Like cows in red clover," Addy told Evie with a shake of her head.

She caught Pauline's attention, gave the waitress the order, and sat back to wait for the explosion. Sure enough, a few moments later Viola slammed out of the kitchen.

"What's this about you two wanting fried chicken?" she said. "Something wrong with them ribs?"

She stared at the heap of bones in front of the two warriors. "You ate a whole hog in less than fifteen minutes and you want chicken? Lord have mercy. Del! *Del,* get the camera and get out here. You gotta see this."

"What is it now, woman?" Delmonte entered the dining room from the back. "A napkin dispenser grow legs and do a tap dance or something?"

"Very funny." Viola pointed to the stack of bones. "Them two ate a whole hog *each,* and they're wantin' chicken. Have you seen anything to beat it?"

"'Course I have," Del scoffed. "Ate like that myself when I was a younger man. Can't do it no more, 'cause I gots to watch my figure. Well, don't stand there, Vi. Take their picture and then bring these gentlemen some chicken."

Del gave Brand and Ansgar a conspiratorial wink and disappeared back into the kitchen. Brand and Ansgar posed on either side of the huge pile of decimated pork ribs. Their picture was snapped, the table cleared, and a platter with a dozen pieces of hot fried chicken placed in front of them. They attacked the chicken with the same ruthless ferocity they'd devoted to the ribs. In no time at all, the fried chicken was gone.

Brand sat back and wiped his hands on his napkin. "That was most enjoyable. Quite splendid. I would not be averse to finishing off such an excellent meal with a dish of sweetmeats."

"Sweetmeats? You mean *dessert* on top of what you ate?" Addy shuddered. "I think I'm going to be sick."

Brand looked concerned. "You feel ill, little one? We will leave at once."

"No, no, I was kidding." Addy motioned to the waitress and pointed to Brand. "He wants dessert, Pauline. Can you stand it?"

"Ain't that something?" Pauline said in an almost pleasant tone, eyeing Brand up and down. "Glad I ain't yo' mama. You musta et that poor woman out of house and home. We got 'nanner puddin' and chocolate pie. Them's yer choices." At a startled yelp from another table, Pauline barked over her shoulder, "Hold your horses, Jim Bob. I'm coming." She turned back to them. " 'Scuse me a sec. That's the second glass of sweet tea Jim Bob's done tumped over this morning. Man's an accident waiting to happen. Think about what you want, and I'll be right back."

"I am not familiar with either dish," Brand said as Pauline hurried off.

"Whoa, you mean, you've never had *chocolate?*" Addy was horrified. "Chocolate is a *necessity.* How could you live ten thousand years without chocolate? That's harsh."

Evie paled. "Wait a minute. Did you say *ten thousand years?*"

"Do not let the difference in our ages trouble you, Evangeline," Ansgar murmured. He brushed the back of Evie's hand with his lips. She blushed. "I merely existed until I met you."

"Why, Blondy, that was actually nice!" Addy said. "Maybe you're not a complete hemorrhoid after all."

"You cannot imagine how relieved I am that you approve."

"Hah, you'd better want my approval, Slick. That's my best friend you're slobbering all over."

"My name is Ansgar, not Blondy or Slick, and I do not slob—"

They were still bickering when Pauline came back to their table. She gave Brand a sympathetic look. "Them two sound like a couple of cats in a croaker sack. They go at it like this all the time?"

Brand sighed. "I am afraid so."

"Kind of like being nibbled to death by ducks, ain't it?"

"An apt description, Mistress Pauline."

"Sorry about that, mister. You seem like a nice feller. And you're easy on the eyes, that's for sure. Kinda remind me of my third husband. 'Course he was shorter 'n you and bow-legged, and bald and ugly as a mud fence daubed with lizards, but you remind me of him all the same. Had them same bedroom eyes. Give me that come-hither look and that was all she wrote, 'til I caught him cheating on me. In *my* bed, mind you. Bumping nasties with another woman on my sheets. Sicced the dogs on the both of them. They was my dogs, see, and they never did cotton to Fred Frank—Fredrick Franklin Bowden, that was his proper name. Real pretty, ain't it? Kept the name and dumped the skunk. Last time I seen him, he was running down the road naked with the dogs nipping at his giblets. I laid into his girl-friend with the broom handle, and she took off out the win-dow shrieking like a Howler monkey." She sighed. "Well, that's enough of that. I don't get paid to stand here and look at you, much as I'd like to. You want dessert, or what?"

"He'll take the chocolate," Addy said. "Heck, Pauline, better make it a whole pie."

Pauline grunted and vanished into the kitchen. She returned a short while later with the pie. She plopped it down on the table along with two dessert plates and forks. Taking a knife out of her apron pocket, she deftly sliced the pie into four large sec-tions. She flipped the knife on its side, scooped a five-inch thick slice of chocolate heaven out of the plate, and dumped it on one of the saucers. A frothy white swirl of lightly toasted meringue crowned the sinfully rich chocolate base, jiggling in sugary invitation.

She slid the piece of pie and a fork in front of Brand. "Don't go for sweets much, myself, but that there's better'n cake."

"Thank you, Mistress Pauline." Brand picked up his fork and took a large bite of pie. His eyes widened with pleasure. "I must say, this is quite tasty."

Pauline made a sound like a startled hen. "Told you it was good."

She shoved their empty dishes onto a plastic tray and hurried off.

Addy stared after the waitress in surprise. "I'm not sure, but I think Pauline laughed."

"Either that or she laid an egg," Evie said.

"I cannot allow you to ridicule Mistress Pauline." Brand slid a second piece of pie onto his plate. "She brought pie."

Addy rolled her eyes. "Mr. I Cannot Allow. Pauline's his new best friend all because she brought him pie. Wonder if he realizes Miss Vi made it?"

Brand took another bite of pie. "I hold Mistress Viola in the highest esteem. She is a jewel among jewels, a goddess of the hearth, a treasure to be protected at all costs." He waved his fork at Ansgar. "Brother, you must try this . . . this chocolate." He took another bite and closed his eyes as if savoring the flavor. "It sends pleasure straight from the tongue to the brain. It is quite unlike anything I have had before."

"If you insist."

"I do."

Ansgar shrugged and forked a chunk of pie into his mouth straight out of the pie plate. Watching him, Addy knew the exact moment the chocolate registered with his brain. The bored expression on his lean face vanished, and his silver eyes glowed with pleasure.

"Most unusual," he said, scooping up another bite.

Evie pulled the aluminum pie plate away from him. "For goodness' sake, don't eat out of the dish like a dog." She put the last piece of pie on a saucer. "Use a plate."

Ansgar finished the pie in three bites. "I do not see what difference it makes what kind of dish the sweetmeat is served upon, Evangeline. The taste is the same."

"It's tacky," Evie said firmly.

"Careful, Ansgar," Brand said. Addy glanced at him in surprise. His dark voice vibrated with suppressed amusement. Good Lord, the big guy had sprung a leak in his humor valve. She'd have thought that thing was locked down tight, but the chocolate pie seemed to have loosened him up. "The mama used the same term of censure in reference to one Dinky Farris. I fear it is a serious charge."

"You're darn right it's serious," Addy said. "Few things are more unforgiveable in the South than being tacky. Mama could give a whole lecture series on the subject. Why, I could spot tacky by the time I was five years old."

"Me, too," Evie chimed in. "And don't get tacky and trashy confused. There's a big difference between the two."

"I do not understand," Brand said.

"W-e-l-l." Addy considered how best to explain. "Tacky is wearing white dress shoes to church before Easter, and trashy is—"

"—going to church on Palm Sunday wearing white dress shoes and no underwear, and sitting on the front pew so the preacher can see your vertical smile," Evie finished.

Addy and Evie looked at each other and burst out laughing.

"Easter and Palm Sunday are religious holy days, are they not?" Brand said once the women had managed to stop giggling. "And vertical smile is, I take it, a reference to the female sexual organs."

Evie turned beet red. "Uh, yeah."

Brand nodded. "And it is considered inappropriate to visit a place of worship without girding your loins?"

"None of the best people go commando to church," Addy assured him.

"Thank you for that useful bit of information. I will endeavor to remember it." He leaned back and draped a muscular arm around Addy's shoulders. "When we are alone, we will discuss this further, Adara. The subject of female anatomy—your anatomy in particular—greatly interests me."

Addy choked and looked up at him through her lashes. He seemed . . . relaxed, mellow almost. Usually, he radiated a sense of barely leashed power. But, she could have sworn the tiniest of smiles tugged at the edges of his beautiful mouth.

"I believe I will have more dessert." He slammed his hand down on the table. "Two more of your excellent chocolate pies, Mistress Pauline, Oh Loveliest of Serving Wenches," he boomed. "One for me, and the other for my brother."

"You got it, Sweet Cheeks." Pauline batted her sparse eyelashes at Brand and scurried through the swinging door.

"Sweet Cheeks?" Addy said, regaining her composure in the

wake of The Look. "Watch your giblets, Brand. I think Pauline has you tagged as Husband Number Four."

The corners of Brand's mouth kicked up again, and Addy's heart rate went into overdrive. Fight or flight; that was the biological response of animals under acute stress, wasn't it? Well, her instincts were in working order, because she . . . because she—

—was going to sit here like a bedazzled lust-drunk female fascinated by the slightest movement of his sensuous lips, waiting to see if he—

Oh, crappy doodle, he was going to do it. *Run away. Run away,* Smart Addy screamed. But Dumbass Addy didn't listen. Oh, no. Dumbass Addy sat there and stared at him, transfixed. She was Eve reaching for the apple. Pandora opening the box because she just *had* to see what was inside. She was a big fat bug drawn to the irresistible glowing radiance of Brand, the Dalvahni bug zapper.

"I am glad you are worried about my giblets, little one," he said.

His rich, smoky baritone sent an electrical shiver down her spine. And then the dirty, low-down bastard did it. *Zzzzt,* he zapped her with a smile. Smiled right at her, too, so she took the full blast.

The busted hinge on her jaw gave way, and her mouth dropped open. Again. She needed to see about getting that thing fixed, she thought dimly through the roaring in her head. The guy showed his pearly whites and the whole freaking room lit up. Little birdies sang, and silvery sparkles danced at the edge of her vision. It was like a freaking Disney movie. She gaped at him, as dizzy and punch drunk as a raccoon in a beer barrel. It was *so* unfair, she thought, gazing in dazed bemusement at his perfect teeth and killer dimples. A smile like that was a thing of power. It ought to be registered as a lethal weapon. It was terrifying, mesmerizing.

It made her want to drop trow right then and there.

She wouldn't. No, no, of *course* she wouldn't. She had better raising. Why, a moment ago, she'd been going on about the difference between tacky and trashy. Having sex in public with Conan the Stud Muffin would be majorly trashy, at the top of the trash-o-meter with Evie's hypothetical floozie airing her fluff bunny in the Lord's temple . . . only without the divine retribution part. Maybe the Big G wouldn't tap-dance on her head for having sex in public, but Mama sure as shoot would. It would also probably get her banned for life from the Sweet Shop, and that was a bad thing. No more Miss Vi's fried chicken. No more greens cooked with ham hocks, Tony Chachere's Creole Seasoning, and a splash of cider vinegar for that little extra punch. No more buttery corn muffins, fragrant and moist on the inside and golden brown and crusty on the outside. No more crunchy, tangy fried green tomatoes. She would not have sex in public. She would not.

No, no, *no*.

The ladies' room in the back of the Sweet Shop . . . that was a different story. Not public at all. All right, maybe technically it *was* public. But, Miss Vi kept a clean restroom, and the door locked.

Holy mackerel, she was seriously contemplating having sex in a restaurant bathroom because the guy *smiled* at her.

She was in big trouble.

Chapter Fourteen

Blondy, of all people, saved her by bursting into song. He had a great set of pipes, Addy would give him that. A pure tenor that darkened and deepened as he caressed the lower notes and soared bright and clear on the top notes of the cheerful little ditty he sang. Or at least it *sounded* cheerful. She couldn't understand a word he said, probably because he wasn't speaking English . . . or any language she recognized. Not that it mattered. The guy could sing right out of the phone book and nobody would care. He was that good.

Evie gazed at Blondy all limp and dewy eyed. It made Addy want to slap her. But then she'd have to slap herself, too, wouldn't she, because hadn't she looked at Brand the same dopey way a few seconds ago? Truth was she owed Blondy one. If he hadn't started wailing she might have forgotten who and where she was and dragged Brand off to the ladies' room, and there would have been wailing of a different kind. And Mama would have found out—'cause Mama *always* found out—and all her years of being a good little girl and a rule-follower would have been for nothing, 'cause it would be all over town that she had sex in the Sweet Shop bathroom with a man she'd known less than twenty-four hours.

Her secret identity would be revealed once and for all, and everyone in Hannah would know that boring Adara Jean Corwin was Super Slut Puppy in disguise.

Addy glanced around the restaurant. None of the other diners seemed to mind the impromptu karaoke. In fact, they seemed spellbound, gazing at Ansgar in rapt adoration. The farmers at the next table clapped and stomped their booted feet in time to the music. Things shot into hyper-weird when Pauline spun out of the kitchen like a jewelry box ballerina. She twirled across the black-and-white checkerboard floor, set two chocolate pies in front of Brand and Ansgar, and pirouetted away, Anna Pavlova in sensible, slip-resistant rubber-soled waitress shoes.

She floated up to the table of farmers, executed a graceful *attitude en pointe,* and refilled their tea glasses.

"Uh, is it me, or is Pauline acting a little strange?" Addy said.

Brand helped himself to half a pie. "It is Ansgar's singing. It has that effect on some humans."

"Look at Evie, for crying out loud. She's practically a puddle."

Brand glared at her over his plate. "What about you, Adara Jean? Does Ansgar's singing make you puddle?"

Addy wrinkled her nose. "Jeez, dude, leave a girl a little mystery, won't you? That's kind of personal."

His scowl deepened. "That is not an answer."

The room became dark and airless. A deafening clap of thunder rattled the tin roof overhead. Startled, Addy looked out the window. The blue sky had darkened to an ominous gray, and a stiff wind bent the heavy branches of the live oaks on Main Street. A sudden change of weather in the summertime wasn't unusual in steamy, sultry Hannah, but even for the Deep South this was freaky. Almost as if . . . She took a quick peek at Brand. Nah, couldn't be. That would be too bizarre. What was she *saying*? Like everything in her life right now wasn't bizarre.

"Relax, big guy," she said. "Blondy doesn't do it for me."

Brand's expression cleared. "Good," he said, returning his attention to his pie.

At once, the heavy sense of oppression lifted from the room. Addy looked back out the window. The heavy, black thunderclouds thinned to ragged wisps and blew away, and the trees stopped whipping around. Note to self. New boyfriend's moods may affect weather.

Ansgar launched into another verse.

"What's he singing?" she asked. "I mean, it's not English."

"A Gorthian folk song. Ansgar has a fondness for the place." Brand shrugged and slid the rest of the pie onto his plate. "Why, I do not know. Gorth is an inhospitable clime, beautiful but harsh. A land of treacherous mountains and raging seas, infested with dwithmorgers and other dangerous beasts."

"Dwith—" Addy shook her head. "Never mind, I'm not going to play your silly little game."

Ansgar stopped singing and reached for the other pie. Beside him, Evie stirred, like Sleeping Beauty waking from a century-long nap.

Her eyelids fluttered. "My goodness, that was wonderful."

"Huh," Addy said. "While you were making goo-goo eyes at Blondy you missed Pauline *grand jeté*-ing through the kitchen door."

"What?"

"Pauline was dancing. On her tippy-toes."

Evie gave a deep sigh. "It's Ansgar's voice. It does things to you."

"Didn't do a thing for me. And a good thing, too. Somebody has to keep a level head around here, what with you mooning over Blondy, Pauline dancing Swan Lake, and Jim Bob and Clyde over there doing the River Dance."

Evie giggled. "Now who's being the fun sucker?"

Addy stiffened. "I am not—"

"Good pie." Brand pushed aside the empty plate. He watched with an expression of dreamy indulgence as Ansgar devoured his dessert. "Is it not excellent, brother?"

"In truth, I have not tasted anything like it." Ansgar scraped the last bit of chocolate off the plate. "Quite extraordinary."

Brand grinned. "I knew you would like it."

To Addy's astonishment, a mini jungle of thorny, green vines sprang from the wall next to their table. The vines produced buds and burst into full bloom, perfuming the air with the fragrant scent of tea roses. On the other side of the dining room, cracks opened in the rough wooden panels and thick ropes of wisteria slithered out, festooning the wall and rafters with purple clumps of sweet-smelling blossoms. The scents of jasmine, honeysuckle, and gardenia filled the room. The black-and-white tile floor erupted in a profusion of poppies, buttercups, daisies, blue bonnets and foxgloves, transforming the interior of the Sweet Shop into a garden wonderland and a living hell for allergy sufferers.

Jeez, the guy smiled . . . and jungle city.

"Pretty," Evie said with a rapturous smile.

Evie was slack faced, her pupils dilated. Great, best-est buddy was stoned out of her gourd. Whether from the intoxicating floral miasma that hung over the room or the happy hormones Brand and Ansgar shed like a St. Bernard in Miami, Addy did not know. Evie was smashed, pickled . . . loaded to the gills. She looked around the room. Clyde and Jim Bob were making daisy chains. Over in the corner, Edith and Mildred Judson, the prim retired twins who'd taught Addy and Evie math and science in high school, held hands and danced in a circle. Their cousin, Myrtle Glenn, pranced around the room on a pretend pony, her spray-starched, lavender-tinted beehive hairdo bobbing up and down as she galumphed. Miss Vi, Del, and Pauline came out of the kitchen and joined the Judson twins in a noisy game of ring-around-the-rosy.

"This is nuts," Addy said. "Where am I supposed to get fried chicken now that you've turned the Sweet Shop into the Dalvahni freaking botanical gardens?"

Brand gave her a lopsided grin. "You worry too much, little one. Have some pie. Pie is good."

Ansgar nodded. "Pie. Good."

Addy gave them a narrow-eyed glare. "You're drunk."

Brand sat up straight in his chair. "You are mistaken. The Dalvahni are not affected by stimulants of any kind."

"Hey, I was a sorority girl at Alabama. I know a drunk male when I see one. You're loaded."

"Inconceivable." Brand waved his hand at Ansgar. "Ansgar, another song."

"Yes, brother." Ansgar pulled a giggling Evie onto his lap. Taking a deep breath, Ansgar launched into a bawdy English chantey that made Brand grin and slap his thigh in time with the beat. Vi and Del broke into a vigorous jig. Blondy reached the third verse about a farmer's daughter and a tin peddler, and Brand threw back his head and laughed.

The sound left Addy feeling breathless and wobbly. Or maybe it was the earthquake. The building shook, and a white tree shot out of the floor and grew to the ceiling. Bright silver leaves formed on the branches and unfurled in a glistening canopy. Miss Vi and Del giggled and ran to dance under the tree.

"Way to go, Miracle Grow." Addy scowled at Brand. "You've gotten my friends high on Dalvahni pheromones and destroyed the only decent place in town to eat."

"Do not distress yourself, Adara." Brand tried to prop his elbow on the table and missed. "Once we abandon this place, all will be as it was. Ansgar and I would not dream of doing anything to cause Mistress Vi or her excellent spouse a moment's distress. She gave us pie."

Addy smacked her forehead. How could she be so stupid? "It's the pie, of course! You said you'd never had chocolate before, right?"

Brand's eyes crossed in thought. "That is correct," he said at last. "It has been some ten or eleven centuries since last I visited this realm. What about you, brother?"

Ansgar still held a starry-eyed Evie in his lap. His glacial hauteur was gone. He blinked sleepily, but did not answer.

"Ho, Ansgar!" Brand waved his hand in the other warrior's face. "How long since last you hunted the djegrali in this place?"

Ansgar stared at him, uncomprehending.

"Toasted." Addy shook her head in disgust. "Whacked out on chocolate. A thirteen-year-old girl with PMS could eat both of you under the table in M&M'S." She got to her feet. "Come on, big guy, let's get you out of here before you have a fit of the giggles and throw a rain forest or something."

"Dalvahni warriors do not 'giggle,'" Brand said with great dignity. "It is not manly."

She pulled him out of his chair. He was very heavy. "Sorry, I don't know what I was thinking."

He swayed and almost fell.

"Hey now, none of that." Addy grabbed him and placed both of his hands on the table. If he crashed and burned, she'd never get him out of here. "Hold on to this while I get Evie and Blondy up and moving."

Keeping one eye on Brand, she walked around the table and tugged Evie out of Ansgar's lap, ignoring the blond warrior's protests.

"Pretty," Evie mumbled, giving Addy a glassy-eyed stare.

"Right. You're hammered, sweetie. Let's get you some fresh air."

Addy guided the unresisting Evie through the flower-strewn restaurant and outside to a wrought-iron bench.

"Deep breaths," she ordered.

Evie obeyed. After a moment, some of the stupor faded from her expression. Addy was relieved. Zombie Evie was scary.

Evie put her hand to her head. "I feel funny. What happened?"

"Don't you remember?"

"Uh uh."

"Oh, boy. Well, uh . . . Blondy started singing and you went stupid on me."

"Addy!"

"Sorry, but it's the truth. The smell from all the flowers was pretty intense, and Brand's smiling didn't help, but I think it was mostly Blondy's singing that fried your brain."

"Flowers? Brand smiling? Addy, you're not making any sense."

Addy sighed. "You do remember Ansgar and Brand?"

Evie gave Addy an *as if* look. "Two guys. Big. Beautiful. Musk-cally."

"I think 'muscular' is the word you're looking for."

"That, too. Who could forget a couple of hotties like that?"

"Do you remember coming to the Sweet Shop for lunch?"

Evie frowned. "Yes, but after that things get fuzzy."

"Long story short, Ansgar started singing, and you lost your beady little mind, and Brand got happy on chocolate pie and smiled the place into the Hanging Gardens of Hannah."

"Addy, what *are* you talking about?"

"No time, Evie. Got to get back in there before Brand and Ansgar hit the sauce again. The chocolate sauce, I mean, not the drunk sauce. If you don't believe me about the flowers, take a gander through the window. And don't leave. I'm going to need your help."

Addy hurried back inside. To her relief, Brand and Ansgar were right where she'd left them. She hesitated, unsure which one to tackle first.

Ansgar lifted his head, his eyes bleary. Poor Blondy, Addy thought with a reluctant pang of sympathy. Drunk on chocolate pie. So much for the mighty Dalvahni warriors. Felled by a simple bean.

"Whersh Evangeline?" he mumbled.

"Outside." Addy pointed to the window framed by wisteria and climbing roses.

With an obvious effort, Ansgar turned his head. Evie blinked at them in astonishment from the other side of the window.

Ansgar's expression darkened. "Evangeline, wharsh you doing out thersh?"

"She can't hear you," Addy said. "Come on. I'll take you to her."

Brand pushed off from the table. "Allow me."

He reeled, and Addy leaped around the table to catch him. She guided him to the wall. "Don't move."

"Feisty." Brand closed his eyes. "I like it."

"Uh huh." She returned to Ansgar's side and took him by the arm. "Come on, Blondy, you first."

Brand opened his eyes and pushed upright. "No, Adara, this I cannot allow." He removed her hand from the other warrior's arm. "I will take him."

Brand ignored her protests and helped Ansgar to his feet. The two warriors lurched toward the entrance. Addy darted ahead of them. She held open the door, and they reeled outside.

Ansgar grinned and waved at Evie. "Greetings, fair one."

Evie's frowning gaze moved from the blond warrior to Addy. "He's plastered."

"Told you," Addy said. "So's the other one."

Brand swayed but managed to keep a grip on Ansgar. "The other one is right here, and he can hear you."

"And they got this way on *chocolate*?" Evie asked.

"Yep," Addy said.

Evie shook her head. "Unbelievable. Addy, did you know there's a tree in the middle of the Sweet Shop? A great big *silver* tree."

"Yeah, I know, Eves. I'm not a happy camper about it, either. How in the world are we going to explain this to people?"

"Do not be troubled," Brand said. "The tree is no more."

"But I saw—" Evie looked back through the window. "It's gone," she gasped. "It's all gone, the flowers, the trees. All of it."

"Thank God," Addy said. "That's one problem solved."

Brand gave her a crooked grin, and the sidewalk at her feet exploded with flowers. "I told you all would be as it was. You worry too much."

"For goodness' sake, stop smiling!" Addy scolded. "When you smile, something sprouts. What about Vi and Del and the others? They'll think they've had a mass hallucination. How you going to fix that?"

"Peace, little one. They will remember nothing but a sense of contentment and well-being."

Addy gave him a black look. "You mean you messed with their brains."

"I altered their memories."

"I don't like it, but I guess it can't be helped." She turned to Evie. "Come on. Let's get them out of here before something else happens."

"We could go to my house," Evie suggested. "It's not far."

"Good idea." Addy patted Brand on the shoulder. "Come on, big guy. Bring Blondy. We gotta walk off some of that pie."

Brand's handsome features assumed a blissful expression. "Pie."

"P-i-e," Ansgar echoed.

"Oh, no you don't." Addy caught them at the door to the Sweet Shop and turned them around. "No more chocolate for

you. Not so much as a Milk Dud. You're quitting, cold turkey."
She gave Evie a pleading look. "Help. Blondy likes you. Talk
to him."

"Sure, Addy, sure." Evie hurried up and took Ansgar by the
arm. "Would you like to see where I live?"

Ansgar gazed down at her, his silver eyes unfocused. After a
moment, recognition seemed to dawn.

"Evangeline," he said.

With a drunken grin he burst into song. Evie's face went
slack.

She mooned up at Ansgar. "Pretty."

"Good grief," Addy said.

Chapter Fifteen

Somehow, Addy coaxed Brand, the still-singing Ansgar, and a stupefied Evie past the drug store, the hardware store, and Toodles, then around the corner onto Church Street without anybody seeing them. Evie trailed after Blondy like an eager little puppy. She was flotsam drifting on the mesmeric tide of Blondy's alluring voice, a leaf helplessly swirling in the seductive eddy of Ansgar's song. He was a male siren, and poor Evie's ship had been lured from the safety of deep water and dashed upon the rocks.

With Addy in the lead, they left the small cluster of businesses that constituted downtown Hannah and entered the quiet neighborhood that Addy and Evie had grown up in and Evie still called home.

Addy loved this part of town with its hodgepodge of cozy 1920s arts-and-crafts-style homes, rambling two-story Victorians, and occasional Tudor dwelling. A few blocks over, the older homes disappeared, choked out by the drab, uniform ranch-style houses that sprang up in the 1960s like crabgrass and dandelion weeds bespoiling a once well-tended garden. But, on Magnolia Street, magnificent towering oaks shaded the deep, narrow lots, and dignified magnolias splayed limbs studded with broad, glossy leaves. In spring, dogwood, redbud, pear, and crabapple trees festooned the yards with a lacy profusion of pink and white petals, and banks of pink, orange, and white azaleas lifted their skirts to show off their colorful bloomers.

Alas, spring was gone, and the dogwoods, redbuds, and azaleas had shed their bright petals for a more sedate garb of summer green.

Evie lived down the block from Bitsy's house in a brown Craftsman bungalow with stone accents and a deep, square-columned front porch. Addy looked anxiously up and down the street. What if Ansgar's seductive crooning ensorcelled the entire neighborhood? She envisioned a zombified stream of blue-haired old ladies, old men tipsy on Dalvahni happy hormones, and bedazzled young housewives shuffling mindlessly after them. She was exhausted and running on raw nerve by the time they reached Evie's house and climbed the steps to the porch.

"Put him over there." Addy pointed Brand toward the porch swing that hung from one of the rafters.

Brand heaved Ansgar into the swing. Ansgar sighed and stretched out his long legs. He closed his eyes and lapsed into quiet humming. From the top of the steps, Evie gazed down at him, her expression adoring but not quite so befuddled as before. Huh. Seemed like Ansgar's humming only *addled* Evie's brains, instead of scrambling them the way his singing did.

"Your turn." Taking Brand by the hand, Addy led him to a large wicker arm chair and gave him a little push. He dropped into the chair. "You sit here while I talk to Evie about something."

"Where are you going?"

"Just around the corner of the house. I need to get Evie away from Blondy so I can detox her. He's like Dalvahni crack or something. His singing messes with her head."

It seemed to take Brand a moment to process this. "You refer to a drug, and not a narrow opening or a witty remark."

"Uh yeah."

"Very well." Brand put his head against the back of the chair and closed his eyes. "Do not wander any farther. The dje-grali . . ."

His words trailed off as he fell asleep. Taking Evie by the hand, Addy eased off the porch to the side yard.

"Evie. *Evie.*" Addy patted her on the cheek. "Snap out of it. I need your help."

"Huh? Wha—" Evie blinked at Addy. Gradually, her eyes

cleared. "He did it again, didn't he?" She sounded disgusted with herself. "Whammied me with that si-reen voice of his."

"'Fraid so. Listen, I need to run, and check on the shop. Think you can handle both of them for a few minutes? I'll be right back."

"Sure." Evie made a face. "I've had plenty of practice, re-member?"

Addy felt a rush of sympathy for her friend. Evie's father had been a weekend drunk. At his job at the feed store clean and sober Monday through Friday, week in and week out. But come five o'clock Friday, he started drinking and wouldn't quit until he passed out Sunday night. Poor Evie had poured him into bed, cleaned up after him, and been his caregiver until his death two years earlier. Drunks Evie knew about.

"I won't be gone long," Addy said, "but I need to close the register and check my messages and that kind of stuff. You set the alarm when you left the store, right?"

"'Course I did."

"Good. Don't tell Brand. He's asleep. With any luck he'll stay that way until I get back."

"But, Addy, what about the demons? Suppose something hap-pens to you? Suppose . . ." She shuddered. "Suppose *Old Man Farris* happens on to you? I saw him, Addy. He's out there."

"I'll be fine. It's broad daylight. What are the chances he'll show up at the flower shop while I'm there? I'll pop over and right back, I promise. If I see him, I'll run like hell. How fast can a dead guy be, right?"

Evie shook her head. "Think what you're doing. You're act-ing like those dumb people in the horror movies we make fun of. *You're going to the flower shop alone, and there's a creepy dead guy out there looking for you!* If this were a movie, we'd give you the Darwin award for being colossally stupid."

"I'll be fine." Addy assured her again. "Trust me. I wouldn't go if I didn't feel like I had to. You know I hate dead guys. But the thermostat on one of the new coolers is acting up, and I can't afford to lose a whole shipment of roses. I'll check on it and be back in a flash."

Addy peeked around the edge of the porch at Brand. He was still sitting in the wicker chair asleep. She hesitated, captivated by the beauty of his chiseled features in repose. Hot damn, he was gorgeous. Why did guys always have the longest eyelashes? It was so unfair. Women gooped their pitiful little eye hairs with mascara, and guys hit the planet naturally follically enhanced.

The corners of Brand's finely shaped lips curled, and she stepped back with a little gasp. Cripes, if he smiled she was done for, as loopy and brain dead as Evie high on Blondy's yodeling. Taking a steadying breath, she tiptoed into the neighbor's yard, slinking from tree to tree so Brand could not see her if he happened to open his eyes. She felt ridiculous, a grown woman playing hide-and-seek from a man she hardly knew. The back of her neck tingled, and she was as jumpy as a frog in a frying pan. The feeling did not subside until she reached the next yard over.

Shaking off the jitters, she set out at a trot for Main Street. In what seemed like two steps, she was standing at the front door of the flower shop. She looked down. Smoke curled from the bottom of her shoes. She'd done the Speedy Gonzales thing again. At this rate, she'd blow through half a dozen pairs of shoes a week. She put her hand on the door. It swung open. The alarm was off. Evie said she set it, didn't she? The hair on the back of her neck stood up and saluted, and she got an unpleasant crawly sensation along her spine.

"Get a grip, Addy," she muttered.

She stepped into the shop and looked around. Nothing seemed out of place. She was greeted by the low hum of the coolers and the familiar sweet smell of blooms and greenery mixed with the herbal scent of Evie's soaps. Then why did she have that creepy, itchy feeling, like someone was watching her? She was overreacting, that was all. She hurried over to the troublesome cooler and checked the thermostat. Thirty-nine degrees, plenty cool enough to keep the roses at optimum freshness.

She stepped behind the counter to turn off the computer and close out the cash register. The answering machine light was on. She was trying to decide whether to check the messages or leave them until first thing Monday morning when she heard the storeroom door creak open. She whirled around expecting to see Dwight Farris's waxen figure standing behind her, but the doorway was empty. Probably a draft, she thought, relaxing a little. She wrinkled her nose as she was assailed by the rancid buttery smell of microwave popcorn. The odor was coming from the back room. She started for the storeroom door and stopped. What was she doing? Evie was right. She was acting like those stupid bimbos in the horror movies, the ones who went into the darkened basement without a flashlight or walked down a deserted alley alone in the dead of night.

The shop lights flickered and went out. Addy froze at a scuffling noise in the back room. In her mind, she was up and running, survival instinct in full gear. She raced around the counter and fumbled for the front door. But, in reality, terror glued her feet to the floor, the legs that ran her more than thirty miles a week as useless as the palsied limbs of a paralytic. It was the old childhood nightmare of being rooted in place, petrified with fear as the monster under the bed crept out to gobble her up.

A low groan sounded from the inky well of the storeroom. Her skin did a strange, shivery dance like thousands of invisible insects were running a road race up and down her body.

"Ad-d-d-y." Her name was a whispered moan from the other side of the door. She heard the slow drag of feet on the concrete floor. This was no dream. The monster was here, and it was coming for her.

"A-a-d-d--y."

Crappy doodle, where was a flamey sword–carrying–demon–chasing guy when you needed one?

Asleep on Evie's front porch sloshed on chocolate pie, that's where.

Perfect.

Chapter Sixteen

The ghoul moaned her name again from the darkened recesses of the storeroom. Not "the ghoul," she corrected. Mr. Farris. This ghoul had a name, and somehow that made it worse. Or at least she *assumed* it was Ghouly Farris, unless her storage room was infested with some other supernatural icky thing that knew her by name.

"*Ad-d-d-y,*" it called again.

Actually, it sounded more like "*Humm-humm.*" But Addy heard it loud and clear *inside her head,* a sibilant hiss that slithered through her mind, full of hate and an evil hunger that made her shiver. There was a humming ghoul in the back of her flower shop. How did these things happen to her? And why was the damn thing *humming*? Humming was annoying under the best of circumstances. Was it trying to freak her out before it finished her off? If so, it was working. On the freak-out scale, she was past the "heebie-jeebies" and into "pee yourself."

She had but a moment to ponder this question before Mr. Farris shuffled out of the storeroom. As animate corpses went, he looked pretty good. The hair and makeup job Jeannine, down at the Kut 'N' Kurl, had done on him looked fresh, and his shirt and tie were still neatly pressed and starched. His eyes, though . . . His eyes were horrible bits of grape jelly, liquid and wobbly, like pudding that hadn't set. He smiled at her, a slow sinister smile that made her feel faint. Correction. He *tried* to smile. The most he could manage was a slight upward tilt of his lips, which were tightly pressed together. That explained the humming. It's hard to talk when your lips are superglued shut.

For some reason, that made her feel better. Out of a whole town of live ones, this demon picked a dead man to possess. How bright could he be?

"Having a little trouble with the old chops, are we?" she said, taking refuge in smarminess to disguise her fear. The sound of her voice steadied her. Heck, she'd been dealing with her mother for twenty-seven years. A demon ought to be a piece of cake. "It's that whole lip-glue thing you got going on there. You can't enunciate properly if you can't open your mouth, and so 'Addy' comes out "humm-humm.' The cotton balls probably don't help. Bet you got that dry, tickly feeling in the back of your throat. Don't you hate when that happens?"

There was a wet tearing sound as Ghouly Farris opened his mouth. The superglue held. Part of his bottom lip stuck to the top, and the flesh tore in a ragged line, leaving a tattered open-ing that exposed the corpse's bottom teeth and gums. The ghoul hawked, spitting out the wad of cotton balls that puffed his cheeks. The gooey mess landed on the floor.

"That's nasty," Addy said. "Do you have any idea how dirty the human mouth is? Dirtier than a dog's, and a dog will lick his butt." Along with her smart-ass mouth, her muscles had started to work again. She eased away from the ghoul. "I imag-ine your mouth is dirtier, you being dead and all. I'll have to scrub that floor with hot water and Pine-Sol to get the dead cooties off it. May even have to rent a steam cleaner. Did I mention I hate dead guys? I know it's narrow minded and prej-udiced of me, but there it is."

"You talk too much," the ghoul said. The raspy voice re-minded Addy of the whir of insect wings or wind-rattled husks of dead roaches in an abandoned shed. "I wonder if you'll have so much to say when I crack you open and eat your liver while you're still alive."

"Hmm," Addy said, pretending to consider this. "Tempting, but no thanks."

She turned and made a dash for the front door. Something dark and foul smelling whooshed past her. A smoky shape formed and solidified between her and the exit. Ghouly Farris; so much for her theory about no-pecker dead guys being slow. This guy moved faster than poop through a goose.

The ghoul's mangled mouth widened in a horrible, toothy smile. "Come to me."

"Sorry, dude. You're not my type."

The ghoul raised its arm and pointed. Addy cried out in pain as the black mark on her breast seared and burned.

"But you are *my* type." The ghoul smacked his torn lips. "I have marked you, and you are mine. I will feed upon you and grow stronger."

A triumphant gleam shone in the ghoul's watery eyes. So, Dead Dude planned to make a Happy Meal of her and thought she'd meekly comply. Dead Dude had a lot to learn. She sensed the power behind the command. Oh, yeah, the compulsion was there, plain as the nose on her face, but she wasn't the teensiest bit inclined to play along. Oh, no. The scar on her chest hurt like a son-of-a-bitch, but that was all. Something, maybe the infusion of Dalvahni DNA Brand had given her when he saved her, gave her the ability to resist.

Addy pressed her hand to the throbbing mark and shook her head. "Sorry, Ghouly, no can do."

For a moment, the ghoul looked puzzled by her resistance. Then it sprang at her with a snarl, knocking her to the floor. She hit her head on the counter edge on the way down. Dazed, Addy looked up at the nightmare crouching on her chest. The mark on her breast ached, and her head hurt. The smell of burned powdered butter pummeled her senses, making her gag. Man, this guy *stank.*

The ghoul wrapped its fingers around her throat and squeezed. Black spots danced in front of her eyes. Breathe. She had to breathe. She grabbed the ghoul's wrists and pulled. To her surprise, the demon's steely hold broke.

The ghoul seemed surprised, too. "You are very strong." Addy flinched as the ghoul touched her cheek with the tip of one clammy, ossified thumb. "And yet so very soft. I am going to enjoy feasting upon your tender flesh, Addy Corwin."

Eww. A dead guy was touching her, getting his own special brand of dead guy germs all over her. It should have been her worst nightmare. Addy hardly noticed. She was too busy dragging in a lungful of air through her bruised windpipe, an act she regretted an instant later when another puff of the thing's moldering breath hit her in the face.

"Dude, have a mint, why don't you?" she gasped. "You could knock a buzzard off a shit wagon with that breath."

The ghoul chuckled. "You have spirit. That is good. The stronger you are, the stronger I become." He grabbed Addy's breast, the one with the mark, and squeezed. She screamed as blinding pain shot through her. "No, no, don't pass out," the ghoul said. "I want you awake when I begin to feed."

The ghoul opened its horrible, gaping mouth and lunged for her throat. Addy got a flashing impression of crooked, yellow teeth and pus-filled gums, and then the ghoul was gone. A deafening roar shook the room followed by a loud crash. Somehow a wounded lion had gotten inside her shop. Huh. Which was worse? she wondered. Being eaten alive by an enraged lion or a creepy dead guy with halitosis and serious gum issues? It was an old game, one she and Shep used to play. *Which would you rather have happen to you—and you have to choose one!—be eaten alive by a Great White shark or chewed up in the blades of a tractor combine?* Before she had time to decide, Ghouly Farris flew past. Dead Dude hit the wall across the room with a satisfying splat and slid to the floor. The ghoul jumped up, a look of terror on its frozen features.

The lion roared again. The roaring coalesced into a word: her name. More craziness. How could a lion know her name?

Addy blinked and sat up. There was no lion. A glowing figure limned in fire stalked the ghoul around the room. The fire creature roared and reached for the ghoul with blazing arms. The ghoul shrieked and scuttled away. The fire creature followed, pulsing with a horrible rage. Addy could *feel* the thing's anger and hate. It wanted the ghoul, wanted to destroy it, to burn it to ash leaving nothing. She smelled burning linoleum. With each menacing step, the fire creature left a melted footprint in the floor. At this rate the whole place would go up in flames. Addy got to her feet. She had to get out of here. Her breast ached and her head hurt. There was blood on her silk blouse and blood on the floor, but whose? She touched the throbbing knot on the back of her head. Her fingers came away wet. The blood was hers.

Other than feeling a little woozy, she seemed to be all right. Head wounds always bled a lot, didn't they? Time to leave, before the fire demon finished off the ghoul and came after her. That fire critter was *not* something she wanted to deal with. She almost felt sorry for poor old Ghouly.

Almost, but not quite. If not for the timely intervention of the other fiend, the ghoul would have eaten her alive.

Holding on to the edge of the counter, she eased away from the battle. Not that it was much of a battle. Mostly, it consisted of Ghouly Farris shrieking like a girl and running around the room as he tried to avoid the other demon. Ghouly was fast, but the fire demon was faster. And relentless, driven by that all-consuming rage that was a palpable presence in the room. She could *feel* the fire demon's rage and . . . and grief? No, that didn't make any sense.

The fire demon caught the ghoul by the neck. A horrible stench rose up, the smell of burning flesh and embalming chemicals. Mr. Farris's clothes burst into flames. With a roar, the fire demon tore off the ghoul's head and tossed it aside. The body hit the floor with a sickening thud. Something dark flew out of the ragged neck of the smoldering corpse and streaked toward Addy. She shrieked and ran behind the counter, flattening herself against the wall. The dark shape flew past her and into the storage room. She heard a loud crash and a lot of thumping and bumping as the terrified demon wraith thrashed about the supply room like a sparrow in a chimney, trying to find its way out. The security alarm on the back door beeped and the metal door slammed shut, leaving her alone with the fire demon.

The fiery head turned in her direction. The fiend saw her. No way could she outrun the thing. It was much too fast. The trick was not to panic. Move slowly and maybe it wouldn't notice.

Forget it. She was getting the hell out of here.

She lunged for the door.

"Adara? You are *alive?*"

Something in the hoarse cry stopped her. Addy turned. The blazing halo around the fire demon wavered and went out. A man stood in the wreckage of her flower shop, his back to the sunlit display window. She knew him. She'd seen him like this before, his broad shoulders outlined by the light-filled portal behind him, his handsome features in shadow.

Brand.

The fire demon was Brand.

Chapter Seventeen

Addy wavered, torn between her desire to run screaming out the door and the desperate urge to fling her arms around Brand and comfort him. He looked so shaken, so . . . so *desolate*. But, a minute ago he'd been ablaze, a demon of fiery retribution, a flaming Nemesis. Why couldn't she fall for a normal guy, a nice Southern boy who loved God and country, football and hunting, his mama and her, not necessarily in that order? Oh, no, not her. She had to go for Mr. Complicated. An alpha male bounty hunter from another dimension who carried a big sword and burst into flames when he got provoked.

"Adara?" Brand fell to his knees.

"Brand!" Addy dropped to the floor and threw her arms around him. "I'm all right. I'm all right."

"I saw blood. I thought you were dead." He wrapped her in a crushing embrace. "I thought I was too late." He ran his hands over her body as if to reassure himself that she was real. "I don't remember anything else, only darkness and a terrible rage. I think I went mad."

"Berserk," Ansgar said, materializing beside them. He looked a little pale, and his eyes were bloodshot, but he otherwise seemed clearheaded. Chalk one up for the Dalvahni constitution. Dead-drunk and then sober again in a matter of minutes. He surveyed the damage to the shop, his cool, dispassionate expression back in place. "It happens sometimes in the heat of battle or when emotions run too high. Your emotions have been in extremis since we arrived here, brother. I warned you, did I not? You need a thrall."

Addy scowled at him. Boy, he rubbed her the wrong way. So supercilious . . . so *annoying.* "What's this junk about thralls, Blondy?"

"The Dalvahni's sole purpose is to hunt the djegrali and return them to their proper plane of existence lest they wreak havoc on unsuspecting mortals," Ansgar said.

"Yeah, yeah, I've heard the 'we are the Dalvahni' speech before. You're super dudes sent to kick demon butt. Navy SEALS on acid. If the Terminator and Predator had a baby, it would be a Dalvahni warrior. I get it, so spare me. What's that got to do with thralls?"

"The thralls serve the Dalvahni." Ansgar spoke with that air of exaggerated patience that made her want to scream. "They rid us of excess emotion so we may better serve our purpose."

"You mean they suck all the feelings out of you, like some kind of emotional vacuum cleaner? That's horrible. What kind of way to live is that?"

"It is our way. Until you came along, Brand was very good at what he did. The best, a legend among legends. The Dalvahni are not mere warriors. We are the undying, the immortalis, created to maintain order and the delicate balance between good and evil. You have diverted Brand from his divine purpose."

Brand stirred. "That is enough, Ansgar. This was not her doing."

Ansgar raised his brows. "You seek to protect her, but she needs to know what we are, brother." He looked at Addy with his usual arrogance and a hint of something else—fear? uncertainty? *Blondy?*—in his eyes. "The thralls do more than rid us of excess spleen. They serve as a receptacle for our lust. You have noticed our enormous appetite for food. Our appetite for other pleasures—*carnal* pleasures—is equally voracious, particularly in the wake of battle."

An image of her and Brand making love, their damp bodies entwined, flashed through her mind. The thought made her heartbeat speed up and her skin tingle.

"So you get a little het up after a fight." She shrugged, trying to act blasé when she was anything but. Then the import of
Ansgar's words sank in. "Wait a minute. Are you saying these
'thralls' are *sex slaves*? That's disgusting."

"Not slaves, Adara," Brand said. He sounded weary, drained.
"Thralls require emotion to survive. They give us the emptiness we seek so we may be better suited to our task. Emotion
in combat is a dangerous thing. It is a fair exchange."

He described a symbiotic relationship between the studly
demon-chasing Dalvahni and a cosmic race of hoochie mamas.
Two dissimilar organisms locked in an intimate association for
survival. Allow some over-sexed female leech to get her suckers into Brand? No. Way. The very thought made Addy see red.

"Over my dead body," she said.

Ansgar's gaze sharpened. "What?"

She stood and pulled Brand to his feet. "Come on, big guy.
I'm taking you home." She felt a moment's anxiety when Brand
swayed. "Do you think you can make it?"

"Yes."

"He needs to eat," Ansgar said. "The berserker rage has
depleted his strength."

"Of course he needs to eat. It's been thirty minutes since he
ate a hog and a whole flock of chickens. Don't worry. I'll fix
him something at my place. I'm no Miss Vi, but I make a heck
of a grilled cheese."

"Are you sure you want to do this?" Ansgar asked. "You
could get hurt."

"Making a grilled cheese sandwich? If it makes you feel any
better, I promise not to use a sharp knife."

"You are a most annoying female, Adara. You know that is
not what I meant."

Yeah, she knew what he meant. He wasn't talking about
physical injury. If she gave herself to Brand, she'd be stepping
off a cliff and into the great unknown. Hadn't she been
wrestling with that very dilemma all day, telling herself to run
the other way? She was going to get her heart broken before
this was over. She knew it, and Ansgar knew it. With a sudden

flash of insight, she realized the source of the odd disquiet she sensed in him. She'd seen the way he looked at Evie, like he wanted to whisk her away to some desert island and keep her all to himself. Sweet little Evie rocked his world. Calm, cool, collected, ain't-no-flies-on-me Ansgar was afraid of getting his heart broken, too.

"What choice do we have, Blondy? Are you going to cut and run because things might get a little rough?"

For a moment, he blinked at her, and then he gave her a slow, dazzling smile. "That is not the Dalvahni way."

"It's not the Corwin way, either." She gave him a warning look. "By the way, Slick, that's my best friend you're messing with. Hurt her, and you'll have *me* to deal with."

"I would cut off my own arm before I hurt Evangeline."

"It's not your arm you should be worrying about."

Taking Brand by the arm, Addy started toward the back door. He pulled away from her and staggered back.

"The corpse, your shop," he said, panting with the effort. "We cannot leave things as they are. There will be questions."

Questions? That was the understatement of the year. Good God, she'd been so concerned about Brand that she'd forgotten all about the dead guy in her shop. The flambéed decapitated dead guy. The dead guy with a wacky wife, a floozy girlfriend, and a whole passel of mullet-wearing relatives waiting to stick him in the ground, mumble a few words over him, and get pounded. And then there was her mother's new boyfriend, the chief of police. She tried to picture herself explaining this to Carl E. Davis, and gave up.

"Shep can fix Mr. Farris. He's a genius at that sort of thing," she said, thinking quickly. "If we can keep the widow and the girlfriend from getting too cozy with the stiff once he's back in the casket . . ." She glanced at the hunk of meat that had been Mr. Farris, and shuddered. "No one will know."

"Who is this Shep?" Ansgar said.

"My brother. He runs the local funeral home." At Ansgar's look of confusion, she added, "Prepares the dead for burial."

Ansgar's expression became distant. "Ah, yes, I see him. He

is in some sort of building, pacing the floor. He seems . . . agitated."

"He's normally a pretty cool guy. Not in permanent deep freeze like you, but it usually takes a lot to rattle him. But he's had a bad day. First time he ever lost a body. It's kind of a big deal in the mortuary business to misplace a client."

"Then no doubt he will be delighted when I return the Farris man to his care. I will take the body to him and explain what happened. When I have arranged matters there, I will come back here and return your shop to its former state."

"That's nice, Blondy, but I don't think—"

He was gone, and so was Dwight.

"Oh, dear, poor Shep," Addy said. "He is so earthbound. He's going to have a hard time with this."

She stumbled as Brand lurched against her. "I regret the distress the djegrali have caused you and your family."

His speech was slurred. Poor guy; he was going to crash and burn any minute. Addy slid her arm around his waist and started for the door. "Forget it. Let's get you to my house and get some food down you. My car is right out back."

"No time. Must rest." He grabbed her, and they reeled into a stand of shelves. A carton split open, showering them with floral foam. His arms tightened around her. "Hold on."

Panic gripped her. He was going to try and teleport them, and in his condition. What if it didn't work? What if they ended up a pile of unrecognizable goo or got splinched?

"Brand, wait, I don't think that's such a good—"

Her ears popped, and she felt a strange stretching sensation. They landed—with all their parts intact and in the proper order, thank God—in the middle of her living room. Brand released her and toppled like a downed pine tree face first onto the couch.

"Brand?"

He did not move.

She shook her head. "Down for the count. Probably won't last long. Guess I'd better make that sandwich before he wakes up."

"Addy, Addy, Addy!"

Startled, Addy spun around. Dooley had her nose pressed to the French doors that opened onto the back lawn. She wagged her tail when Addy looked at her.

"Dooley in. Dooley in NOW!"

"Shh." Addy hurried to open the door. "Do you want the neighbors to hear? How am I supposed to explain Dooley the Remarkable Talking Dog?"

A talking dog was strange, but no stranger than anything else that had happened since last night. She figured she had two choices. Accept the reality of what was happening or end up in a rubber room.

Dooley rushed inside, tail wagging. *"Addy home! Dooley love A—"*

The Lab spied Brand's supine form on the couch and sprang across the room to investigate. Her tail thumped against the coffee table.

"Brand man! Dooley like Brand man." She gave Brand a curious sniff. *"Asleep? Brand man asleep?"* She nudged the back of his neck with her nose. *"Wake up. Dooley play, Brand man."*

Brand moaned and turned over on his back. Tongue out, Dooley went for his face.

"No, Dooley, leave him alone." Addy grabbed the dog by the collar and dragged her away from the couch. "Brand man doesn't feel well."

She kicked off her ruined sandals and threw them in the trash. Looking down at her blood-splattered blouse, she wrinkled her nose in disgust. She remembered the bump on the head and gingerly felt her scalp. The bump was gone, but her hair was matted with blood. Gross. She tiptoed back into the living room to check on Brand. Out like a light. Good. Maybe she had time for a quick shower and a change of clothes.

She shook her finger at the dog. "You leave him alone, young lady. I mean it. Be a good dog and I will give you cheese when I get out of the shower."

"Cheese? Dooley get dog cheese?"

"Only if you're good."

"Dooley be good. Watch Brand man. No lick."

Addy showered in record time and threw on a pair of loose shorts and a T-shirt. After towel-drying her hair, she padded barefoot back into the kitchen. Dooley's eyes lit up when she saw her.

"Cheese? Dooley get dog cheese?"

"Oh, good grief. Yes, Dooley can have dog cheese."

Dooley danced around Addy's feet. *"Dooley like cheese! Cheese. Cheese. Cheese!"*

"All right, all right, calm down."

Muddy's house had an airy, open floor plan. All that separated the kitchen from the living room were a couple of decorative columns and a big island that served as a combination work space and table, with chairs along one side. Addy kept one eye on Brand as she retrieved the block of cheddar cheese from the refrigerator door. She sliced off a hunk and broke it into pieces in the dog's bowl. "There, desist already."

Dooley slurped up the cheese and rolled her brown eyes at Addy. *"More?"*

"No, ma'am. You'll ruin your supper." She dumped two cups of dry dog food in Dooley's bowl. "Here, eat."

Dooley gave the bowl a disinterested sniff and sauntered out of the kitchen to flump on the floor next to the couch.

"Brand man?" she whined, nosing Brand on the arm.

"No, Dooley, leave him alone!"

Chastened, Dooley put her head on her paws.

Addy glopped a can of tomato soup into a saucepan and added milk. While the soup warmed, she heated a frying pan and made three grilled cheese sandwiches. Sliding the grilled cheese sandwiches onto a plate, she sliced them in two, then poured the tomato soup into an over-sized mug. She arranged the plate and mug on a wooden tray, and added a glass of milk, salt and pepper shakers, a soup spoon, and a napkin.

Balancing the loaded tray, she went into the living room and set it on the coffee table. She stepped back, eyeing with appreciation the more than six and a half feet of hard-muscled male lying on her couch. She let her gaze roam over the broad chest, past the lean waist, and down the long, muscular legs. Jeez Louise, he was a heartbreaker. There ought to be a law.

"Brand?"

Dooley lifted her head to look at Addy.

Addy cocked her head at the dog. "What do you think, Dooles? Wake him up and feed him, or let sleeping warriors lie?"

Dooley exhaled and dropped her head back onto her paws.

"Thanks, hound doggie. You're a big help."

She leaned over Brand and gently touched him on the shoulder. "Brand? Are you hungry? I've brought you something to eat. But, if you'd rather sleep, I—"

Brand jerked her on top of him and rolled over, pinning her beneath him on the couch. He kissed her. Addy sighed and gave in to the drugging, heated bliss of his mouth. His tongue danced a mad tango with hers, stroking, tasting, sending her spinning closer and closer to the edge of reason. Her breasts tightened. Each velvet brush of his tongue sent an exquisite shock of sensation along her nerves. Her womb clenched, and the flesh between her legs throbbed in response. She heard someone moan, a wanton, keening cry of pure lust, and realized with a little jolt of amazement that someone was her. Something about this guy reduced her to a primal state of raw animal need. But if she was on fire, so was he. Heat came off him in waves. She was amazed he didn't burst into flames and incinerate them both. He wasn't hot, he was highly combustible. He was . . .

Wait a minute, what was she doing? A few minutes ago, this same guy had been a walking, breathing column of fire. Was she insane?

She ended the kiss with a gasp and opened her eyes. Brand crouched over her. His long hair hung about his face, and his sensuous lips were drawn back in a snarl. He looked grim, fierce . . . ferocious. She was prey, a helpless doe trapped in the steely claws of a hungry mountain lion. But it was his eyes that frightened her most, hard as flint and glittering with anger.

His burning gaze drifted over her face and lingered on the

fluttering pulse at her throat. "Good, you are afraid," he said. "Perhaps you possess some modicum of intelligence after all, although I doubt it."

"Are you calling me stupid?"

"YES." His voice rattled the windows. "I AM CALLING YOU STUPID, YOU IDIOTIC, FOOLISH, *INFURIATING* WOMAN! DO YOU NOT REALIZE YOU COULD HAVE DIED BACK THERE?"

Dooley yelped and ran into the laundry room.

"Now look what you've done," Addy said. "You've gone and scared the dog. You ought to be ashamed."

"I ought to be ashamed? *I* ought to be ashamed?" Brand jumped up off the couch and began to pace around the room like he was about to . . . well, like he was about to burst into flames.

He glared at her, chest heaving. "You disobey me and nearly get yourself killed, and you have the audacity, the sheer effrontery to tell me *I* ought to be ashamed. Unbelievable."

Addy leaped to her feet. "Disobey? Look here, buddy boy, I didn't sign up for your stinking Dalvahni army. You aren't the boss of me."

"You are mistaken, Adara Jean." Brand stalked toward her. "For however long I am here, for however long I *choose,* I am very much the boss of you. And you will do as I say, or suffer the consequences."

Addy's heart tripped into a crazy staccato beat. Scared, of him? Maybe a *little.* Not that she'd let him know it. She raised her chin in defiance. "Oh, yeah, like what?"

"I haven't decided." He backed her across the room. "This is a new experience for me, being turned inside out by a mere female. Maybe I'll tie you to my bed and keep you as my thrall for a few thousand years. A few millennia beneath me as my sex slave should teach you your place. But, then again, you are a remarkably stubborn woman."

"Brand, you need to calm down." Addy gave him a coaxing smile and back-pedaled faster. "You're a little wound up, that's all. Going nuclear will do that to a guy."

She turned and made a run for it. He caught her before she reached the kitchen.

"A little wound up, Adara Jean?" He pushed her against one of the columns. *"A little wound up?* You do not know the half of it."

He grabbed her head in both hands and kissed her.

Chapter Eighteen

Just being in the same room with her nearly drove Brand insane. The scent of her, the soft fall of her hair against her neck and shoulders, the slow, sultry sound of her voice made him ache with longing. But, touching her . . . Touching her drove him over the edge. He was on fire, consumed by a driving lust unlike anything he'd ever known. He felt frenzied, unhinged, shaken.

How had this happened? What had he become? He was a warrior, honed by combat, ill-equipped to battle the changeable, maddening welter of *feelings* the woman stirred within him, emotions that a few days ago he would have found unfathomable.

The Dalvahni were created for battle, thrived upon it. Death came seldom to them, for they were unmatched in physical prowess and virtually indestructible. The Dalvahni did not know fear. He had not experienced that particular emotion until he met Adara.

Awaking to find her gone had been a lesson in fear. Not his first such lesson since meeting her, but a lesson well taught nonetheless. Interesting, enlightening, terrifying, and permanently etched in his brain. Then he'd arrived at her shop and found her lying helpless beneath the ravening djegrali, her shirt bespattered with blood and a pool of the stuff around her. That had been another lesson. He had not borne that tutelage so well. Indeed, he remembered little of it, a flash of agonized grief and bitter remorse—too late! too late!—and then darkness and falling into flame. He did not exaggerate when he told Adara he went a little mad. He feared there was no cure for it, this madness in his blood that made him burn for her. Truth be told, he did not want to be cured. He saved her life, infused her with a portion of his power and immortality, and *he* was the one who had been changed in some fundamental way, leaving him a stranger to himself.

It made him angry, made him want to punish her for the anguish he endured when he thought she was dead. He wanted her at his mercy, wanted her to beg for more, to ache for him the way he ached for her.

Tilting her head back, he ended the kiss. Her eyes were closed, her mouth soft and rosy from his kisses. Her hair was damp. The scent of her soap filled his senses. She must have showered and changed her clothes while he slept, because the blood-stained blouse was gone. Fury gripped him anew as he relived that awful moment when he found her bloody and broken on the floor, the ghoul bent over her. Her reckless disregard for her own safety made him want to smash something, anything that threatened her harm. He wanted to carry her off and lock her in some tall, desolate tower, and keep her there safe, for his pleasure and his alone.

"You were injured." His voice sounded hoarse to his own ears. "I saw the blood. Show me where you were hurt."

Her eyelids fluttered open, her eyes drowsy with passion. He felt a surge of triumph. He was once more in control. He would conquer this insanity.

"I hit my head." She relaxed against him. "It's nothing. I'm fine."

"That is for me to decide." He ran his fingers through her hair and examined her scalp. "Here?"

"No, a little higher." She closed her eyes and arched her back. "That feels good."

"Clever little cat." She had no idea she was in danger. "You like that, don't you?"

"Hmm." She leaned into his hands. "There, I think that's the spot."

"You think? You're not sure?"

"It doesn't hurt anymore."

"That's because you are Dalvahni now. We heal quickly. That is good."

Something in his voice must have warned her.

She opened her eyes, her expression wary. "Why?"

"Because if you were still injured, I could not do this." Picking her up, he tossed her over his shoulder and headed for the bedroom.

She squealed and kicked her heels. "Brand, what are you doing? Put me down!"

He smacked her hard on her deliciously rounded bottom. "Be still," he ordered.

"Ouch! I will not be still. I don't have to do what you say."

He strode into the bedroom, dumped her onto the bed, and fell on top of her. He looked down at her with a deliberately sensuous smile. "Perhaps not, but you will want to, little one. Oh, yes, you will want to very much."

She gaped back at him with a dazed expression, her lush mouth forming an "o" of surprise. Good, he thought with a ripple of satisfaction. Let *her* be off balance for a change. He'd been reeling since the moment they met.

He lowered his head and traced the shape of her lips with his tongue. "Kiss me, Adara." He breathed the words of entreaty against her mouth. "Take me in. I'm starved for the taste of you."

She nuzzled him back and caught his bottom lip with her teeth in a gentle nip. The small gesture was almost his undoing, the wave of desire that swept through him so strong he all but forgot his earlier resolve to stay in control. With an effort, he pulled back from the precipice. He was Dalvahni, he reminded himself. He would overcome these puling feelings.

He kissed her, using all his considerable skill. To his delight, she opened for him like a flower. Some of his determination wavered as he lost himself in the sweetness of her mouth.

"That's it, little love." He trailed his lips along her throat. "I want you, Adara. Tell me you want me, too."

"I'll do better than that." Her voice sounded throaty, breathless. "I'll show you."

With a seductive smile, she slid out of his arms. She swung her hips and sauntered to the end of the four-poster bed. Mischief and a hint of shyness gleamed in her sultry brown eyes. Her pale blond hair was mussed and hung in wild curls about her shoulders, her lips still pink from his kisses. She stretched and raised her arms over her head. Her shirt tightened across the fullness of her breasts. He swallowed as the garment rode up and offered him a tantalizing glimpse of her taut belly.

"It's hot in here, don't you think?" She widened her eyes at him. "'Scuse me a sec, won't you?"

She turned her back on him with a swish of her hips. Pulling the shirt over her head, she tossed it aside. Brand stared, mesmerized, by the sharp indention of her waist and the pale, smooth skin of her back. She stood before him clad in some kind of white halter and a pair of loose, short trousers that rode low on her hips. His heart tripped into a gallop as his gaze roamed down the graceful curve of her spine, stopping at the point where it disappeared into the top of her trousers. He stared at her delicious heart-shaped ass and imagined her naked on her knees before him. He would take her from behind, his hands clutching her firm, round bottom as he thrust inside her . . .

He pulled his thoughts away from the heated image. His heartbeat thundered in his ears. By the sword, the woman threatened his willpower. She was not naked and already he weakened.

"Would you like me to turn around?" she asked.

He could do this. He was Dalvahni. He would master these feelings.

"Yes." He cleared his throat. "Yes." There, that sounded better, calmer, more in control. "Turn around."

"*Please,* Adara, turn around."

So, it was not enough that he panted after her like a lovesick boy. She meant to toy with him, too. A warrior did not beg. Still, he reasoned, it was a small enough concession. Let her think for the moment she was in charge.

"Please, Adara, turn around."

The sound of his voice, low and rough, surprised him. He was the hunter, she the hunted, he reminded himself. He would show no weakness. He would not falter.

He . . . would . . . not . . . falter.

She turned around, and he was lost.

The undergarment she wore cupped her breasts like a lover's hands, lifting them so they nearly overflowed the cloth that bound them. Time seemed to slow and then stand still as he stared at her. He felt feverish and lightheaded with desire. With an effort, he reined in his crumbling control.

"Take off your trousers."

Adara smiled and traced the skin of her belly with one hand. He watched in helpless fascination as her fingers toyed with the metal button securing the garment.

"They're called shorts, and I think you mean 'take them off, *please,* Adara.' "

"Call them what you will, take them off, for pity's sake," he said through his teeth.

She unfastened the button. Brand heard a metallic scritch. She wiggled her hips, and the shorts hit the floor. She stood before him clad in the white, lacy contraption that held her breasts up like a sacred offering and . . .

His tortured gaze drifted lower. A scrap of filmy, white material covered her mons, an inconsequential bit of lace all that separated him from heaven.

He drank in the sight of her. His hot gaze drifted over her flat belly and ripe breasts, moved up and lingered for a moment on her full mouth. Their eyes met, and she gasped.

"See how I burn for you? Are you frightened, Adara Jean?" He left the bed in a blur of movement to stand before her. "If not, you should be."

She stepped back with a small sound of surprise.

"No." His voice sounded harsh in the quiet room. "Do not move. I want to look at you."

She stilled. He circled behind her and stopped. His breath caught in his throat at the sight of her. She was beautiful, a creature of fantasy, all lush curves and gleaming, flawless skin. Her legs, sleek and strong, ended in a firm, round rump that was scantily covered by a patch of white cloth.

"So lovely." He ran his fingers down her supple back. To his fierce delight, she shivered in response. "What is this thing you wear?"

"W-what?"

He traced a path along the lacy edge of the garment. "This tempting silk confection that covers your delectably rounded bottom, what is it called?"

"P-panties."

He dropped his hand and stalked around her. "And this thing that displays your bosom to such magnificent advantage?"

She stared at him, wide eyed. "It's called a bra. It supports a woman's—"

"I can see what it does. I *like* what it does very much."

"I'm glad you—"

"Take it off. Slowly."

She reached up and slipped the straps of the bra off her shoulders.

"Stop." He tugged on the straps, freeing her nipples. "Beautiful." He stroked the tips of her breasts. Tilting her chin up, he caressed her full lower lip with his thumb. "Do you like it when I touch you, Adara?"

"You know I do."

"Good. I'm going to kiss you now."

"Yes, Brand, please do." The look in her eyes made his heart pound harder. "I think if you don't kiss me soon, I'll die."

Her entreaty shattered the last vestiges of his resistance, all thoughts of pride and conquest vanquished.

"Adara, you are killing me." He pulled her into his arms. *"Te egeo."*

I need you. The Latin words sprang from his unruly tongue, culled from his memories of a previous trip to Earth more than a thousand years before. Somehow it was easier to say the words in another language, less an admission of weakness.

"Te cupio," he murmured.

I want you.

"*Te adoro,*" he said, throwing caution to the wind.

His restless hands moved down her back. Some instinct guided his hands to the catch beneath her shoulder blades. The bra dropped to the floor, and she was left clad in her panties. He kissed her. His tongue mated with hers in a heady, intoxicating dance. She moaned against his mouth, a breathy sound that went straight to his groin. He tore his mouth from hers at last and lifted her luscious breasts in his hands. The weight and feel of her silken flesh in his hands was glorious. Murmuring her name, he took first one nipple and then the other into his mouth, stroking, suckling, savoring her small shrieks of pleasure. He trailed his fingers down her flat stomach and touched her between her legs, teasing her through her panties.

"*Brand.*" She arched against his questing hand.

He gave a ragged laugh. "I wanted to take this slow, little one, but I don't think I can."

She opened her eyes to glare at him. "Well, who asked you to?"

With another shaky laugh, he removed his shirt.

"Oh, my God," she said. Her gaze on him was like a physical touch. "You are so damn beautiful."

He shook his head. "I am not the beautiful one, you are."

"No way. You're like a freaking god or something."

He unbuckled his belt and dropped his trousers to the floor.

Her eyes widened. "Oh, my damn. That's quite a mister you got there, Mister."

The way she looked at him, all breathless appreciation, nervous anticipation and wonder, made him want to throw back his head and howl.

"I am glad you approve, Adara. But if you do not stop staring at me like that, I am going to explode."

"That would be a shame, now wouldn't it?"

She came to him then, temptation itself wearing a knowing smile. His breath stilled in his lungs as he felt the cool, exquisite brush of her fingers against his cock.

"So, maybe you'd better put this somewhere before you lose it," she said.

The familiar lightness rose up in his chest, and he almost laughed. Then her fingers closed around him, and he tumbled headlong into the fire.

"*Adara.*"

He swept her into his arms and lowered her to the edge of the bed. Shoving her knees apart, he ripped the crotch of her panties with a muttered curse and pushed aside the tattered lace. He looked down at her, spread before him like a sumptuous pink and cream feast, and thought he would lose his mind. He wanted to kiss and lick her all over, from the blush-colored tips of her lovely breasts to the deep rosy flesh between her legs. She had ruined him for other women. No thrall could satisfy the raw hunger he felt for her. Once with her would not be enough, could not assuage this burning need. He would crave her again and again. He would never get his fill of her.

"*Ril ak ilgan straalf,*" he said in Gorthian. My heart's undoing, he called her.

He positioned himself above her and hesitated. She would be exquisitely tight, fit him like a glove. Being inside her would drive him wild with pleasure, but what about her? She was so small. What if he hurt her? He was a brute to think of coupling with her.

"Do it, Brand. Do it now, please." Her expression was fierce. "I need you inside me."

"No, I'm too big. I—"

His breath expelled in a sharp hiss as she wrapped her hand around him. She lifted her hips and rubbed against him. The sweet torment made him shudder, and he clenched his teeth to keep from shouting.

She looked up at him and tangled her fingers in his hair. "I want this, Brand. I think I've wanted it forever. Please don't make me wait any longer."

His skin was on fire. The blood pounded through his body.

"Adara, little one, I did not dream it could be so . . . I've got to—"

He thrust inside her. She was wet and warm and oh-so-tight that he thought he might die from the pleasure—from the *rightness*—of it. He moved again and again, unable to stop himself. Each desperate plunge drove him deeper, closer to something wonderful just beyond his reach. She pulled him down on top of her. Wrapping her legs around him, she matched him stroke for stroke.

"Adara." Her name was like a prayer on his lips. "Adara, I—"

"Don't stop." She panted beneath him, her skin damp and flushed with passion and her pale hair spread in a glorious tangle on the bed. "Please. Don't. Sto—"

She arched her back and went still, her beautiful mouth slack with surprise. She pulsed around him. The sweet pull of her flesh catapulted him into space. A thousand stars exploded around him, white hot shards of rapture unlike anything he had imagined. With a roar, he spilled himself into her. He lay over her, exhausted by the most shattering sexual experience of his very long existence. He waited for the familiar emptiness to take him.

The numbness did not come. His chest ached and his eyes burned, and he shook like a green sapling in a high wind, but the numbness eluded him. Something cool tickled his cheeks. He reached up and touched his face. Bemused, he stared at his tear-damp fingers.

He wept.

Chapter Nineteen

Addy drifted back to awareness, two hundred plus pounds of solid, muscular, unbelievably spectacular sex-spent male resting on top of her and *in* her. She blushed when she thought of how she'd acted. She stripped for him, bold as you please—*so* unlike her—touched him, caressed him, begged him to take her, driven by a raw, frenzied need unlike anything she'd felt before. When he thrust inside her, she knew a moment of doubt. The Big Guy was *big*. But then he began to move, and she forgot to be nervous and moved with him. Each delicious stroke sent her higher and higher until she'd reached the top and shattered into a million fragments. She'd fallen back to herself, her cheeks wet with tears of joy and gratitude that she'd met this amazing, maddening, infuriating man and had the most splendid sex of her, admittedly, limited-in-experience, sex-starved life. She'd suspected all along that it would be like this, sensed at some primal level that having sex with Brand would change her.

She was ruined. She was worse than ruined. She was rurnt, as Pauline would say, destroyed beyond recognition. She would never be the same. How on earth would she bear it when he left? Where did a girl go after she'd had perfection?

Something wet splashed against her skin, and she opened her eyes. Brand posed above her, weight braced on his elbows, his head lowered. His face was hidden by his long, black hair. Something about his rigid stillness alarmed her. Gently, she smoothed his hair back. There were tears on his cheeks, and the strained expression on his beautiful face startled her. Something had happened to her stoic, implacable warrior. She wanted Mr. Freeze to thaw out, but this . . . He looked so vulnerable . . . so *bewildered*. It made her heart ache.

"Hey, you all right?" she whispered.

"No."

He rolled over, taking her with him. He settled against the head of the bed with her on top, somehow without disengaging the—uh—crucial parts that connected them. She rested quietly against his broad chest. Not much of a chore, when you got right down to it. It was wonderful to lie next to him, skin to skin, heartbeat to heartbeat, her legs draped over his, the scent of hot, sex-damp male teasing her senses. He made her feel feminine, Woman to his Much-a-Man.

She gasped as he moved inside her. His palms slid down her back and grasped her bottom.

"See what you do to me?" Lazily, he stroked her backside. "Already, I would couple with you again, without a care for your tender body. My rod has no conscience, it would seem."

She wrinkled her nose. "Eww, don't say 'rod.' That's Dinky's name."

"What would you prefer I call it?"

"I don't know. All the slang terms for the—uh—male and female parts are either vulgar or gross or just plain silly, if you ask me. And, 'penis' is such a wimpy, whiny little word."

She sat up and moved her legs to either side of his waist so that she rested on her knees.

"Adara," he said through his teeth, "I am trying to do the right thing. That is not helping."

"I'm not trying to help." She rocked tentatively against him and heard his breath catch. Joy surged through her. Tomorrow was uncertain, but he was hers for the moment. She vowed to enjoy their time together. Emboldened, she lifted her hips. "You won't hurt me, I promise. I'm a big girl and I—" Slowly, she slid back down. Being with him like this was drugging, addictive. Her breasts tightened, and the now-familiar giddy fluttering began in her stomach and spread to her womb. She shuddered and lifted her hips again. "I'm tired of doing the right thing."

With a muttered curse, he grasped her by the waist and began to move, urging her on with rough words of entreaty. The dark, passion-drunk sound of his voice added to her delirious pleasure and sent her whirling closer to oblivion. He made her feel reckless and sensuous, awakened something—*someone*—inside her, the wild, red-hot sex goddess she had not known existed. She wanted to give him pleasure and take it in return. She threw her head back and took him deeper.

"Oh, Adara, my love, that is so—"

He groaned and said something guttural. Then in English, *"Mine,"* he growled. His warm palms slid up to cup her aching breasts possessively. "Only mine."

Moving his hands from her breasts to her hips, he withdrew and plunged back inside her, burying himself to the hilt. Jagged streaks of pleasure pulsed through her.

"Brand," she said.

"Say it. I want to hear you say it."

"Yours," she gasped. "Only yours."

Somehow, she was on her back and he was driving into her. The delicious tension built to a crescendo of sweet release as he took her with him once more into that heady place of aching, soul-shattering joy.

She floated back to consciousness in his arms. Her head rested on his chest. The steady sound of his heartbeat drummed in her ears. She felt limp, weak as a kitten.

Kitten?

"Mr. Fluffy!"

Brand opened one eye. "Adara, I cannot allow you to refer to any part of my anatomy as 'fluffy.' It is not manly."

"Not you, silly, the cat! I forgot all about him. He's probably scared and lonely and *hungry* in Never Never Land or wherever it is you put him."

"In truth, I had forgotten about the creature." He sighed and opened the other eye. "But clearly, you have not. You will not be still until you see him, will you?"

She shook her head.

"Very well."

The kitten appeared on Brand's chest. Addy picked him up and cuddled him.

"He is *so* cute, isn't he, Brand?"

Brand eyed the orange and white fluff ball with a sour expression. "Adorable. Have you considered how the other animal might react?"

"Dooley has a few unresolved cat issues, but she'll be fine. If not, there's always doggie therapy."

She plopped the kitten on a pillow and jumped off the bed. Bending over, she retrieved Brand's discarded shirt. She heard a muffled groan behind her and straightened, the shirt dangling from one hand. She looked over her shoulder. Brand sprawled across her bed. His black hair swirled about his shoulders and his heavily muscled body was laid out for her perusal. God, he was beautiful, like something out of a dream with his big, powerful body and lazy grace. She saw the look on his face, and her eyes widened. Oh, my damn. He watched her with the same ravenous, intent expression a starving lion might give a tender, young gazelle. Surely, he couldn't be thinking of—

Her gaze drifted lower. Yeah. Oh, hell yeah, he could.

"Put the shirt on, Adara," he said softly. "Or you will find yourself flat on your back with me inside you again. There is only so much temptation a warrior can withstand."

She slipped on his shirt and buttoned it. The garment hung to her knees, the sleeves six inches too long. It smelled deliciously of Brand, spicy, intoxicating. *Male.*

"You need to eat." Rising from the bed, he swept her into his arms and carried her into the kitchen. "You are weak."

"Me? What about you? You did the whole man-on-fire thing. And you didn't eat the sandwiches I made."

He sat her down in one of the high-backed chairs that lined one side of the center island and looked into the living room.

"No, but judging from the scattered remains, someone or something ate them."

Addy whirled around. The plate of sandwiches was gone, the mug overturned. Splashes of congealed tomato soup stained the wooden tray.

"Dooley Anne Corwin!"

Dooley jumped up from her place by the couch and wagged her tail. *"Addy, Addy!"*

Addy pointed to the coffee table. "Did you eat Brand's sandwiches?"

Dooley's ears drooped. *"Dooley like cheese."*

"You know better than to eat food off the table, young lady. Bad dog."

Dooley hung her head. *"Dooley like cheese."*

"That is no excuse. There's somebody I want you to meet, and I want you to promise to behave yourself."

Dooley's ears perked. *"Dooley promise. Dooley love Addy. Love, love lo—"*

The kitten wobbled out of the bedroom and into the kitchen.

Dooley charged the tiny animal. *"Cat! Cat! CAT."*

Addy shrieked in alarm. "Dooley Anne, you promised!"

Dooley screeched to a halt and sniffed the startled kitten. *"Dooley hate cats."*

"His name is Mr. Fluffy Fauntleroy," Addy said. "You don't have to like him, but you can't eat him."

Dooley gave her a look full of reproach. *"No like cat. Bad Addy."*

"Meow." The kitten rubbed against Dooley's legs.

"See, Dooley, he wants to be friends."

Dooley stalked out of the kitchen, stiff legged. The kitten wobbled drunkenly after her.

"Adara, where do you keep your comestibles?"

Addy swiveled around in the chair. Brand padded around her kitchen in the altogether. He seemed comfortable with his nakedness, but she found it . . . distracting to say the least. Like having a Greek statue come to life in front of you, she thought, admiring his broad shoulders and the corded muscles of his back and arms. His long, powerful legs made her mouth water, and you could eat off his butt. *There* was an all-day buffet she'd like to try. Or would it be butt-fet? A muncheon? A smorg-ass-borg?

She giggled, and he turned and caught her staring. "Adara, if you do not stop looking at me like that, I will not be responsible for what happens."

"Dude, put some clothes on, or *I* won't be responsible for what happens."

His grin nearly melted her in the chair. "You like my body?"

"Like it? I'm contemplating using that perfect butt of yours as a dining table, what do you think?"

He took a step toward her and stopped. "No. You are temptation itself, but I *will* resist you, if only for your own good." He vanished and reappeared a second later wearing his trousers. "There, perhaps you can control your carnal urges long enough for us to eat. Where do I find food?"

She jumped down from the chair. "Here, let me do it."

Going to the refrigerator, she took out lettuce, cheese, turkey, ham, sliced chicken, mayonnaise, and mustard, then quickly constructed four thick sandwiches, one for her and the other three for Brand. She poured two glasses of milk and set a bowl of fruit on the island.

She motioned for Brand to sit down. "Soup's on."

He picked up a sandwich and examined it. "I do not understand. Soup is a liquid food, is it not?"

"Dude, it's an expression."

"So, this is not soup?"

"No."

"Then it is a stupid expression. To say 'soup's on' in reference to a concoction of bread and meat—"

"It's called a sandwich."

"—does not make the slightest sense. Nor does the term 'sandwich,' for that matter. Why would you name a foodstuff after a female being with malefic powers fashioned from sedimentary material?"

Sand Witch. Oh, brother. Talk about your communication gaps. "Look, go with the flow. If you try and make 'sense' out of the English language, you'll drive both of us crazy."

She ate her sandwich and drank her milk under his watchful eye. He made short work of his three sandwiches and helped himself to a pear and a bunch of grapes out of the bowl.

Addy rinsed their plates and glasses and put them in the dishwasher and then went in search of a litter box and something to eat for Mr. Fluffy. She found the things she needed in the pantry. A can of chicken and an unused litter box, a bag of kitty litter and cat bowls that Muddy had saved after her cat died. Since the kitten was new to the household, she decided to put him in the laundry room for the night and arranged things there, including a pillow and blanket in one corner for the kitten to sleep on. She fetched fresh water in one of the cat bowls and scooped a generous spoonful of the chicken into the other. She stepped back and waited for the kitten to pounce on the treat. To her surprise, Mr. Fluffy sniffed the bowl and walked away, tail twitching.

"Huh. What kind of cat doesn't like chicken?"

The Lab came into the laundry room to investigate. Nose quivering, Dooley did the doggie "feed me" dance, her nails clicking on the tile floor. *"Dooley like chicken."*

"Dooley like everything, except cats. How can you eat Mr. Fluffy's food, when you say you hate cats?"

Dooley snuffled in disgust. *"DOOLEY LIKE CHICKEN."*

"A subtle but distinct difference," Brand said. "Let her have it, Adara. The other creature does not want it."

Addy gave the dog a nod, and the chicken disappeared in two bites. Dooley sniffed around for more.

"Out, greedy gut." She shooed Dooley out the door and shut the kitten in the laundry room. "Do you think Mr. Fluffy will be lonely by himself?"

"Adara, the creature will be fine."

He picked her up in his arms and headed for the bedroom.

"Brand, put me down."

"No."

"But, what about Mr. Fluffy? I'm worried about him. He needs to eat."

"Adara, my patience with the subject of Mr. Fluffy is at an end. I do not want to hear another word about that ridiculous creature or his even more ridiculous name."

"Oh, yeah? What *do* you want to talk about then?"

He pushed the bathroom door open with his foot and set her down inside the large walk-in shower.

"This," he said, pulling her into his arms and kissing her. "I like seeing you in my shirt." He unfastened the top three buttons and pushed the shirt off her shoulders, exposing the tops of her breasts. Tracing the curve of her bosom with his fingertips, he slowly undid the rest of the buttons. "Better yet, I like seeing you out of it."

The shirt sailed over the shower door, followed by his trousers. He stared at the chrome shower valve in obvious puzzlement for a moment and waved his hand. Warm water poured out of the double shower heads mounted at both ends of the stall. Addy hardly noticed. She was too busy gawking at the six- foot six-inches of naked, glorious male standing in her shower. The water coursed over his taut, gleaming skin and down the firm ridges of his muscles in fascinating rivulets.

"Adara." Brand's tone held a note of warning. "I told you not to look at me like that."

"Like what?"

"Like you are a she wolf, and I am a-a—"

She stepped closer. "Baby deer? Fuzzy wuzzy bunny rabbit?"

"That is hardly the image I was searching for. I was thinking of something more—"

"Manly? Macho? Mister-ish?"

As she spoke, she followed the winding streamlets of water with her tongue, licking a path down his unyielding chest, over the fascinating bumps and ridges of his six-pack abs and lower to his . . .

"*Adara.*" He yanked her to her feet, his chest heaving. "I only have so much self-control, and you push it to the limit."

"So lose control."

"No, you have been injured. You must rest. I would not treat you as I would a thrall . . . slake my unseemly lust upon you again and again without a care for your well-being—"

She traced a circle around one flat nipple with the tip of her finger. To her delight, he shivered in response. "That's sweet, big guy. But there are a couple of things I think you might not have considered. First, as you pointed out, I'm Dalvahni now, thanks to you, and that means I heal quickly." She waggled her brows at him. "Everywhere. Get it?"

"I think I grasp your meaning. Your head wound seems to have healed satisfactorily."

She dragged her lips across his chest in a lingering open-mouthed kiss. "Uh huh, all better."

Beneath her fingers, she felt his heart give an uneven thud. She hid her smile against his chest and flicked her tongue across his nipple.

He grasped her bottom and lifted her, pressing her back against the shower wall. "And the other thing I might have not considered?" he said through his teeth.

She wrapped her legs around his waist and smiled. "That I might have a little unseemly lust of my own. And since you're the fellow responsible, I think it's your duty to do something about it."

She felt the head of his shaft nudge her entrance. Her heartbeat quickened in anticipation.

"You've come to the right place then, milady," he said. "A Dalvahni warrior always does his duty."

He entered her and withdrew. Clasping her hips, he drove into her again, setting a steady, rocking rhythm that careened her once more into the white-hot heart of the storm where they merged and she forgot where he began and she ended, and they were one.

Chapter Twenty

With a grateful sigh, Shep ushered the last of the Farris family out of Corwin's Serenity Chapel and closed the door behind them. Not that there'd been much "serene" about the place in the last few hours. Not with bodies missing, and Shirley Farris and Bessie Mae Brown rolling around on the floor of the Camellia Room like it was Mud Tussle night down at the Do Drop In. Poor Daddy was probably spinning in his grave. Wouldn't surprise him a bit if Daddy up and haunted his ass. Lord knows if anything could bring William Shepton Corwin from the Great Beyond it was the ruination of the business that had been in the Corwin family since the Great Depression.

Maybe "ruination" was a bit strong. Still, Shep felt sure things would have gone differently if Daddy were alive. Daddy was the consummate professional, smooth and faultless, as unemotional as the corpses he worked on, devoted to the dead and their grieving families. Nothing like this would have happened with Daddy at the helm.

Nope, he was not the man his daddy had been, a fact immediately confirmed by Mama.

"Lord have mercy, I'm glad your daddy didn't live to see this." She tottered down the hall supported on Carl Davis's arm. "A body gone missing at Corwin's! And those horrible women. What on earth are we going to do, Shep? Something like this could ruin us."

"We're the only funeral parlor for thirty miles, Mama. What they going to do, bury 'em in the backyard?"

"Shepton, this is serious!"

Chief Davis patted her on the arm. "Let him alone, Hibiscus. We'll sort this thing out." He gave Shep his best chief of police stare. "Where'd your sister and that tall fellow go in such an all-fired hurry? I didn't get a statement from them."

"You can mark her off your list of suspects, Carl," Shep said. "Addy wouldn't touch a corpse with a ten-foot pole. As for that Brand fellow, he ain't from around here, but I don't think he's responsible."

"Don't say 'ain't,' Shep," Bitsy said. "People will think you're a hick."

"I *am* a hick, Mama. And, what's wrong with being a hick, anyhow?" Anger and resentment stirred to his surprise. "How you going to be anything else in Hannah?"

The chief gave him an uneasy sideways glance. "It's been a stressful day, Little Bit. Let's get a bite to eat and let Shep regroup."

Mama sighed and leaned against him. "That sounds wonderful." Her hand stole to her mangled hair. "But first, I need to run by the house and do something with my hair. I must look a mess."

"You look beautiful, Hibiscus. I don't recall seeing you look anything less."

Mama sighed like a young girl. "Oh, Carl, you say the sweetest things. Let me get my purse and I'll be with you in two shakes of a lamb's tail."

She bustled off, leaving Shep and Carl Davis standing in the elegantly appointed foyer of the funeral home.

The chief cleared his throat. "Reckon where I might catch up with that sister of yours?"

Shep glanced at his watch. "It's past noon, so the flower shop's closed. You'd best try her at home."

"I'll do that. Before your mother comes back, Shep, there's something I've been meaning to talk to you about."

The back of Shep's neck prickled. He eyed the older man warily. What now? Lord, hadn't he had enough awkward scenes to deal with for one day? His instincts told him to run like hell. Good manners, however, made him say, "What's that, Carl?"

"It's your mother. We have a sort of an understanding. Hell, if it was up to me, I'd marry her tomorrow. Been in love with the woman since high school, but she's still kind of skittish, so I'm trying to take things slow. Thought you ought to know, you being the head of the family and all. Wanted to assure you my intentions are honorable."

"I appreciate that, Carl, but Mama has a mind of her own. If she decides to marry you, nothing I say will make any difference."

"You're wrong, Shep. Your mama loves you and Addy better 'n snuff. She wouldn't do anything to hurt either of you, especially you. You're her right-hand man." He shifted and looked away. "I know she's a woman who likes nice things. I may not be rich, but I got a little set aside. I want you to know I'll be able to provide for your mama, if she'll have me."

Lord Jesus, where did Mama leave her purse anyway, Alaska? He did *not* want to have this conversation. "I appreciate that, Carl. Tell you what. Why don't we talk about this again, if you and Mama decide to get married?"

Shep squelched a snort. Carl E. Davis was a fine man. Hells bells, Shep *liked* Carl, but Mama . . . Mama was all about the social scene, always had been. Somehow Shep didn't see Mama marrying the chief of police of podunk Hannah. Carl was hardly a member of the country club set, a life that suited Mama down to her pedicured toenails. And Carl was nothing like Daddy. Not necessarily a bad thing, mind you, but there it was.

"Here I am." Mama hurried back down the hall. "I'm ready to go, Car-lee."

Shep's head was pounding by the time he saw Mama and the chief out the door. He retreated to his office and sank into the leather executive chair behind his desk. He dropped his head in his hands. It was a terrible thing for a man to be staring forty in the face and realize the life he'd carefully constructed for himself, the life he thought he wanted, the life he'd been raised to think he *ought* to want, was nothing but shit. A big old pile of—

A loud pop drew Shep's attention from his dark thoughts. He lifted his head. A huge, blond-haired man stood on the other side of his desk. In his arms he held—

The Goliath dropped the dismembered corpse onto the floor with a loud thunk. The severed head rolled under Shep's desk. Shep scrambled to his feet. "Who the hell are you, and how'd you get in here?"

He glared up at the stranger. He played football in high school, measured six-foot-one in his stocking feet and worked out, but this guy towered over him. What was it, circus freak day in Hannah or something? First, that black-haired fellow his sister had been with, and now this guy. They made him feel like a shrimp. And plug ugly. Not that Shep normally noticed the way other guys looked. No damn way. But, crap on a Christmas tree, these two guys were frigging perfect. It was enough to give a fellow a complex.

"I am Ansgar." The blond guy's cultured, musical voice crawled all over Shep. Jesus, with a voice like that broads probably ate this guy up with a spoon. "I bring greetings from your sister Adara and my brother, Brand, and return to you the corpse of the human called Farris."

"Holy mother of God, don't tell me that thing is Dwight Farris?"

Shep rushed around the desk and stared at the headless corpse. His startled gaze shifted to the head under his desk. Dwight Farris stared back at him. Dwight looked bad, real bad. Not that the dick-whittling son-of-a-bitch had been much to look at to begin with, but jeez, he looked terrible. For one thing, his head had been ripped off and the skin on his neck looked like somebody had taken a blowtorch to it. As for the blue suit, it was history.

He pointed a shaking finger at the corpse. "What the hell do you expect me to do with that?"

The blond guy shrugged. "Your sister assured me you were up to the task. I have delivered the corpse as promised. The rest I leave to you. I bid you farewell."

The blond guy vanished. Poof, pop, gone, like he'd been beamed up or something.

Only this was real life, and things like this did not happen in real life, especially in Hannah. Hell, the most exciting thing to happen around here had been last week, when the mayor—the dumbass—left a case of Co-Cola in his car and the cans exploded from the heat. Sounded like guns going off, *pop, pop, pop!* Mayor Tunstall screamed like a girl and crawled under his desk, hollering for his secretary to call the police because somebody was trying to assassinate him. As if anyone would waste a bullet on such a cheese dick monkey turd. The police had showed up, and the fire department and the sheriff. They searched city hall and the surrounding block for the evil mayor-killing terrorists before somebody noticed the brown foam covering the interior of the mayor's car. Warm, sticky Coke dripped down the windows and the windshield, and covered the mayor's fancy leather seats in brown goo. It even coated the inside of the air-conditioning vents. The story made the front page of the paper. COKE BOMB TARGETS MAYOR, the headline read.

No, nothing exciting happened in Hannah, and people did not get beamed up.

Shep staggered to the edge of the desk and sat down, his mind reeling. It was the shock. He'd had a lot to deal with lately, and it had caught up with him. There hadn't been a blond guy, or a beheaded corpse. No, he was—

He looked down. Dwight's severed head stared back at him. Oh, God, it was real. Old Man Farris was back, but he looked like something the dogs drug up. And he was supposed to make this right? No damn way. Even Daddy couldn't fix this one.

He raked his hands through his hair. What to do first? The suit, replace the suit. Worry about the damage to the body later.

He picked up the phone and dialed the number to Tompkin's. "Tweedy? Shep. Do you have Dwight Farris's size on file?" Tweedy answered in the affirmative, and Shep's choke hold on the receiver loosened. "Good. Listen, I need you to bring me a new suit in Mr. Farris's size, new shirt and tie, too. Bring 'em to the funeral home right away. Put it on my bill. What? No, don't worry about the cost, make it something nice. Yeah, he's turned up. No, still don't know who took him." He ran his hand through his hair again, not caring about the damage to his carefully combed locks. "Look, I haven't told the chief yet, so I'd appreciate it if you kept this to yourself. Thanks, Tweedy. I owe you."

Five and a half hours later, wringing wet with sweat and exhausted from wrestling with the ossified corpse, he was putting the final touches on Mr. Farris in the casket. He'd used a combination of staples, stitches, and superglue to reattach the head to the body, no easy feat when the flesh on Mr. Farris's neck had been toasted to a crisp. Fortunately, the high collar of the dress shirt Tweedy brought covered most of the damage. Shep had to admit the new wool suit was an improvement on the original polyester blend. Too bad he had to cut it up the back to get it on the stiff. He restuffed the corpse's cheeks with cotton balls and repaired Mr. Farris's mangled mouth the best he could with more superglue and a thick layer of makeup—how the hell did that happen, anyway?—and retouched the corpse's frazzled hair. He was no Jeannine, but he didn't dare trust anyone else with the task. Half a dozen tree-shaped car air fresheners tucked discreetly beneath the body and he was done. Old Man Farris smelled like a combination of new car scent and a giant pine fart, but the air fresheners disguised the odor of burned flesh and formaldehyde.

He stepped back, surveying the body dispassionately. Not bad. Not bad at all, if he did say so himself. He doubted Shep Senior could have done any better.

A high-pitched humming noise disrupted his all-too-brief moment of self-satisfaction. He turned, his eyes widening in shock as a woman materialized before him. Woman, hell, more like a freaking *goddess.* She was mostly naked—thank you, Lord Jesus!—and perfectly formed, with high, generous breasts, a tiny waist, and flaring hips. Her lush body was draped in ribbons of filmy cloth that clung and flowed across her satin flesh, blown by some invisible breeze. The same unseen current lifted her long, black hair and whirled the silken strands about her shoulders and breasts.

Black brows lifted above eyes that were icy blue. "You are not Dalvahni."

Christ, she had a sexy voice, throaty, alluring . . . The slightly stilted accent, like English was a second language, sounded vaguely familiar, but it was hard to think with all the blood draining out of his big head and into his little one.

"Uh, no." He swallowed heavily. Her words slowly percolated through the haze of lust. "I met a Brand Dalvahni this morning, but he's not here. Who are you?"

"I am Lenora. Conall sent me to service the Dalvahni. They linger overlong at their task. I must find them."

Shep's brain whirled. It was hard to think when he was as horny as a three-peckered goat. "S-service them? What exactly does that mean?"

"I am thrall. I empty them so they may better perform their task."

"Task?" He found it harder and harder to think. "What task?"

"The Dalvahni hunt the djegrali. Demons, I think you humans would call them." She tilted her head, considering him. "You are human?"

"Oh, yeah."

"I thought so. I have not met a member of your species before, but I have heard stories . . ." She stepped closer. Her delicate nostrils quivered. "Do all humans reek so deliciously of emotion, or are you special?"

"I don't know what you're talking about. I'm not—"

She circled him. The strands of her flowing gown curled around him, the scent of her hair and skin enfolding him in her spell. "Do not be ashamed." He shivered as she ran her fingers lightly down his arm. "I find it delightful, intoxicating. A heady mixture of feelings I did not dream existed, so much more than blood lust and sexual excitement. Quite . . . irresistible."

She paused in front of him and twined her arms around him. "Let me help you." She pressed a trail of hot kisses down his throat. "Empty yourself into me."

"Look, I don't—"

"Your wife left you for another man," she said. The sensuous purr made his dick stand up and pay attention. "She has already filed some sort of document ending your union. You feel emasculated, bewildered. Anger, so much delicious anger. It makes me quite giddy. What did you do wrong? you wonder. Were you not lover enough for her? Did she find satisfaction in your arms?"

"How the hell did you—"

Her hands moved over him. Somehow, his shirt was gone and his pants and shoes. She caressed his chest. Her hands moved lower, and then her luscious mouth—

"You are concerned what others will think, that you will be an object of ridicule. Shame, sharp, stinging like a knife. Your offspring, too, you worry about. You have sent them away to protect them, but what heartache will they discover upon their return? They are young and will not understand. The anguish you feel on their behalf is . . . delectable."

Half-heartedly, he tried to free himself. But, the relief of having it all out there, of being able to open up to another was impossible to resist. He'd bottled it up inside for so long, tried to be a good son, father, husband—*oh, God, Marilee, I tried*—done what was expected of him for so many years. Married the right girl, buried himself in a business he detested, become what others wanted. Not what he wanted. Never what he wanted.

She pulled him to the floor and somehow he was inside her, pouring himself into her.

Ah, the relief . . . the sweet, blessed relief.

Chapter Twenty-one

Dooley nuzzled Addy's arm. She opened her eyes to find the Lab smiling at her.

"Addy up! Addy up!" Dooley whined happily.

"In a minute, Doodle Bug. You know I'm not a morning person."

Addy stretched and sat up. Brand sprawled face down on the bed beside her, one corner of the sheet thrown carelessly over his body. Lord, he was something else, golden skinned, sleek and smoothly muscled. She itched to touch him again. She'd been something else in the past few hours as well, a woman she hardly recognized. The things she'd done with him, the things she still wanted to do. She couldn't get enough of him, had lost track of the times they made love during the night.

And what a night, the best night of her life.

She'd been afraid of this, that being with Brand would become an obsession. The guy ought to come with a warning label. *Caution, this Brand may be habit-forming.*

She slowly peeled the sheet back so she could admire his world-class ass. God, he was gorgeous. Like a child fascinated by the spinning blades of a fan, she reached out to touch him, knowing the danger and drawn to it all the same.

His deep, rumbling voice drew her up short.

"Woman, you are insatiable."

He rolled over and gave her a lazy, heart-stopping grin. *Thwack!* The smile hit her right between the eyes. Her mouth dropped open. She knew she probably looked like a mooning idiot, gaping at him love struck and starry eyed and—

Wait a darn minute, *love struck*? No. No way. She would not have her heart broken. She was Super Slut Puppy, able to leap a guy's bones in a single bound. She would enjoy this thing while it lasted. *Oh, God, oh, God, oh, God, what would she do when he left her?* She would be calm, cool, and collected. She could do this. She *would* do this. She—

—reached out and touched his beautiful, archangel's face with her fingertips, unable to resist, the moth to the flame, and smoothed the palms of her hands down his chest and arms. There it was, the familiar tingling, the building tension . . . the *heat* she felt at the slightest contact with him . . . and without it.

"Stop me, Brand," she whispered. "I can't help myself."

He pulled her beneath him. "I don't want you to stop." He moved over her, in her. She cried out as he rocked his body within hers, driving, plunging. "Don't stop," he groaned. "Don't ever stop."

Some time later, she rolled over and looked at the clock. Good grief, it was after eight. She'd overslept. She jumped out of bed and slipped on her housecoat.

"Where are you going?" Brand said from the bed.

"I've got to let the dog out." She felt his gaze on her back like a physical touch. "Poor Dooley's eyeballs are probably floating."

"A turn of phrase, I hope, and nothing more." His deep voice sent a shiver of longing down her spine. Mercy, she had it bad. "I assume you mean the creature needs to empty her bladder?"

"Uh, yeah, and I need to check on Mr. Fluffy."

She hurried toward the bedroom door.

"Adara."

She slowed her steps, but did not turn.

"Look at me," he said softly.

"I can't."

"Why not? Have I displeased you in some manner?"

She laughed shakily. "Hardly. If I were any more pleased, I couldn't stand it."

"Then why won't you look at me?"

She put one hand on the door frame for support. "Because if I look at you, I'll come back to bed, and we'll pick up where we left off. And one thing will lead to another, and then another, and before you know it hours, no days, will go by, maybe even *weeks,* and they'll find the dead, desiccated husks of our bodies in the bed, and people will be mumbling over our corpses. *'Ain't it a shame?'* they will say, and *'Reckon why they forgot to eat?'* and *'Too bad they let the dog and cat starve, too,'* and Mama and Shep will be heartbroken and Aunt Muddy and Evie, too, all because I'm pitiful and weak and can't resist you."

Suddenly, he was there behind her, his warm, hard, naked body pressed against hers. "If you are pitiful and weak, then what does that make me?" He slid his hands beneath the folds of her housecoat, his warm palms cupping her breasts. She sighed and leaned back, closing her eyes. A shiver of delight coursed through her as he laid a trail of hot kisses along her neck. "All I have to do is look at you, and I lose my mind. The mighty Dalvahni warrior brought to his knees by a woman. How much more pathetic a creature am I?"

A soft, Southern drawl from the other part of the house interrupted them. "Addy, this is all very interesting, I'm sure, but I'm starting to feel like a pervert. Tell that young man of yours to put on some clothes and come on out here so I can meet him."

Addy's eyes flew open. "*Muddy?*"

Addy started out the bedroom door, and Brand stopped her. "Wait." He stood still, his expression distant for a moment before he nodded. "It is safe. You may go. It is not the djegrali."

"Of course it's not the djegrali. It's Aunt Muddy."

Fumbling with the edges of her housecoat, Addy stepped into the kitchen and peered into the living room. Her great-aunt sat on the couch looking as cool and elegantly beautiful as ever, her stylishly cropped silver hair in place, her makeup flawless. She wore a black and white cotton skirt and a matching summer weight sweater set. Silver earrings dangled from the lobes of her delicately shaped ears, and a heavy, silver bracelet

encircled one wrist. From all appearances, she was the quintes-
sential Southern lady. But, Addy knew better. That demure,
country-club chic exterior concealed a wild woman underneath. Aunt Muddy was, in the local vernacular, "a mess," an
affectionate term used to describe someone, usually female,
whose character and personality defied succinct description.
Someone who often set social and cultural dictates on their ear,
like as not causing, in equal measure, chagrin and delight to
those around them. She was funny and wise and interesting and
unpredictable, and Addy loved her to distraction.

Dooley pranced up. *"Addy, cat bad—"*

"Shh! No talking. You want to freak Muddy out?"

"Addy, cat—"

"Not now, Dooley."

"Did you say something, Addy?" her aunt called from the
next room.

"I said I'll be there in a sec, as soon as I let Dooley out."

She opened the French doors and shooed Dooley into the
backyard. Pasting a smile on her face, she turned around. "Aunt
Muddy, what a wonderful surprise."

"You're something of a surprise yourself. How splendid you
look, child! Not many people could pull off that pale blond
hair, but I must say, it suits you. Ravishing with those brown
eyes of yours."

"Thanks. Have you been here long?"

"Long enough."

Long enough, as in long enough to hear her and Brand in the
next room? Had the bedroom door been open or closed?
Open, Addy realized with dismay. She flushed.

Brand, oh, Brand, oh . . .

Oh, *God*, Muddy heard her wailing like an air raid siren. It
was all Brand's fault, she thought darkly. He turned her into
some kind of uninhibited sex maniac. She was pretty sure she'd
hit notes a lyric soprano would envy. Lord have mercy Jesus,
she'd never be able to look her aunt in the face again. Look at
her? She might have to move to another *continent*.

"I got here about six o'clock," Muddy said. "Let myself in

with the spare key under the turtle in the flower bed. I would have called first if I'd *dreamed* you were entertaining a young man, but how was I to know? You've never done anything like this before."

"I am very glad to hear it," Brand said, joining them. "Otherwise, I would have to kill someone."

He was dressed, and he looked downright perfect. His long hair was smooth and untangled, his slacks and shirt miraculously wrinkle-free. She, on the other hand, was a rumpled mess. How the heck did he do it? Dalvahni woo-woo, like with the shower head and the killer smiles, and the teleporting from place to place.

Muddy looked Brand up and down, a calculating gleam in her eyes. "Addy, why don't you introduce me to your young man?"

"Uh, Brand, this is my great aunt, Edmuntina Fairfax," Addy said.

Her stomach fluttered. What if Muddy didn't like him? He wasn't Southern, and Muddy would probably hate the long hair. What if—

Brand gave Muddy a slow smile. "I am honored to meet you, Edmuntina."

Thwack! The smile hit Muddy right between the eyes.

To Muddy's credit, she recovered quickly. "Granny Moses, what a smile! Like being hit upside the head with a two-by-four. Where on earth did you find him, Addy?"

"Oh, you know, we kind of ran in to one another one night."

"I didn't just fall off the turnip truck, gal. You don't run into a man like him, especially in Hannah." Muddy gave Brand a measuring look. "You aren't from around here, are you, Mr. . . . ?"

"Dalvahni, Aunt Muddy. He's in town for the Farris—"

"It is no use, Adara," Brand said. "Your aunt is much too perceptive to buy that feeble story about the Farris funeral. We had better tell her the truth."

"T-the truth?" Addy stuttered. *She* found it hard to believe the truth. How was she supposed to explain it to anybody else? Demons and talking dogs, and ghouls and—

"Edmuntina from the Old English 'Edmund,' meaning 'protector,' is it not?" Brand continued smoothly. "It is a lovely name."

"It's a god-awful name, so you can stop trying to butter me up. What brings you to Hannah and what are you up to with my niece?"

Addy rolled her eyes. "I'm a grown woman, Muddy."

"Your aunt has a right to be concerned about you, Adara. She is your family." He slipped his arm around Addy's waist. "I am in town on business, very important business. As for what I am 'up to' with your niece, as you so charmingly put it, I assure you my intentions are honorable. More than that, I cannot say."

"Honorable, huh?" Muddy sighed. "Shucks, and here I was hoping you were in it for the poontang. Nobody needs a good old-fashioned dose of balls-to-the-wall sex like our Addy."

"Muddy!" Addy thought her face might catch fire. "I am not having this conversation. If you'll excuse me, I'll see about breakfast."

She flounced off, ignoring her aunt's chuckles. She was almost to the kitchen when the doorbell rang.

She started for the door, and Brand appeared at her side.

"You will let me go first," he said in a low voice. "By some lucky chance the djegrali did not attack last night. I was so bewitched by you that I forgot to put the customary protective spells in place, leaving us vulnerable. I have been remiss in my duty, but no more."

"Don't beat yourself up about it, dude. After yesterday, I have a feeling Mr. Nasty went somewhere to lick his wounds. You scared the dickens out of him with that flamethrower routine of yours."

"Who is Mr. Nasty?"

"The demon."

"There is more than one demon in Hannah, Adara."

"Yeah, but they can't all want a date with me."

She reached for the doorknob, but he got there first.

"You are a remarkably stubborn woman," he said. "Stay behind me in case there is trouble."

"This is silly. Like a demon's going to ring the doorbell."

"It might if it has possessed a human. Someone you know and trust, perhaps."

"Oh, I didn't think of that."

The doorbell rang again.

"What are you two whispering about?" Muddy hollered from the couch. "Answer the door. It's Amasa Collier and the chief of police."

"Yes, ma'am," Addy said. "Hey, wait a minute, how do you know who's—"

Brand opened the door. Amasa Collier and Chief Davis stood on the doorstep.

"Your aunt is a perceptive woman." Brand looked at the two men without smiling. "Gentlemen."

"Oh, for goodness' sake, don't stand there glowering at them, Mr. Grumpy Pants. Ask them in." Addy gave them a bright smile. "Good morning, Mr. Collier, Chief. I was about to put on a pot of coffee."

Mr. Collier stepped inside. "Sorry to bother you so early, Addy. But I need to talk to Mr. Dalvahni." He glanced at the chief. "A little *birdy* told me he was here."

Chief Davis stayed on the porch. "I can't stay. I was in the neighborhood and thought I'd stick my head in and give you the latest on Mr. Farris. Your brother called last night and said somebody brought the body back. Visitation is this afternoon, and the funeral will be first thing in the morning."

"Oh, good," Addy said, not meeting his eyes. "I know Shep is relieved. He was so upset."

The chief frowned. "I'd still like to know who took that body. I don't like that kind of prank."

"Addy, have them come in," Muddy called. "Tell the chief there's pound cake to go with that coffee. I'll get it out of the freezer, and we can toast it with a little butter. It'll be yummy."

Mr. Collier's face lit up. "That you, Edmuntina? I thought you were still scooter-pooting around the world. I had no idea you were back."

"I'm back."

The chief removed his hat and came inside. "I am a sucker for sweets. Maybe I will stay for a minute."

Addy heard her aunt puttering around in the kitchen. "How did she know I have a pound cake in the freezer?" she muttered, hurrying to help. "Here, Muddy, let me do that. You go talk to Mr. Collier and the chief, tell them all about your world travels while I fix the coffee."

"If you insist, dear."

Muddy glided into the living room to greet the two men. Satisfied her aunt had things under control, Addy put on the coffee and sliced and arranged the pound cake on a cookie sheet.

"All I have to do is slather a little butter on the cake," she said, getting a table knife from the drawer.

Brand took the knife from her. "I will do that. You go and get dressed. I find it too distracting knowing you are naked under that robe."

"Think you can handle it?"

"I think I *have* handled it. Several times, as I recall."

Addy blushed. "Not that, the cake."

"Adara, I am ten thousand years old. In all that time, do you think I never learned to cook?"

She fluttered her lashes at him. "Eye candy and the man knows his way around a kitchen. Be still my beating heart."

Brand pointed the knife at the bedroom door. "Out."

She flew into the bedroom to dress. Casting a longing look in the direction of the bathroom—she'd dearly love a shower, but that would have to wait—she threw on panties and a bra, a pair of jean capris and a linen top, and slipped a pair of polka-dot canvas flip-flops on her feet. She dashed into the bathroom to brush her hair and halted in front of the mirror. Good grief, her hair was a disaster. It had grown another two inches overnight and hung below her shoulders in loose platinum curls. At the rate it was growing, she'd have to cut it every two weeks or she'd be sitting on it. She secured it at the nape of her neck and quickly washed her face and brushed her teeth.

She scrutinized her reflection in the mirror. One good thing about Dalvahni DNA, makeup was superfluous. Her skin glowed, and her cheeks and lips were bright with color. The hair was a mess, though. She had no idea what to do with it. She ran a brush through her curls and wadded them on top of her head in a loose knot. A few stray tendrils dangled around her face. A couple of swipes of mascara and she was done. Primped and dressed in under five minutes. Not bad.

In the kitchen, she found Brand putting the finishing touches on the slices of pound cake. The rich aroma of coffee filled the air.

"Thanks." She took the loaded cookie sheet from the counter. "I'll stick this under the broiler. It'll be ready in a jiffy."

She put the pan in the oven and turned on the broiler. She was reaching into the cabinet for the coffee cups and plates when she felt Brand come up behind her. A warm shiver went through her that had nothing to do with the heat from the oven.

"I thought you were going to get dressed," he murmured, caressing her bottom.

"What are you talking about? I am dressed."

He caught her earlobe in his teeth. "This garment you wear shows the delectable curves of your, of your, oh-so-delectable rump. It makes me want to undress you."

She turned and thumped him playfully on the chest. "Down, boy, I am *not* having hot monkey sex with you in the kitchen. There are people in the next room."

He nuzzled her neck. "We could repair to that smallish space over there."

"You mean the pantry? You want to have sex in the pantry?"

"It has a door that closes." He lifted his head. The look in his eyes made her breathless. "We could be very quiet."

She pictured them, grappling in the dark, her legs around his waist as he moved inside her, taking her with him to—

No, not going to happen. He'd have her screeching like a flock of toucans. Still, the idea was tempting. Maybe if she . . .

The smell of melted butter and toasted sugar brought her to her senses.

"Forget it." She pushed him away. "I'm not having sex with you in the pantry."

Brand sighed. "I suppose I will have to console myself with food instead." He sniffed appreciatively as she set the cookie sheet on top of the stove. "That smells good."

"It is good. It's an old family recipe, butter, sugar, flour, eggs, and vanilla extract. You start the cake off in a cold oven. That's what makes it crusty and delicious." As she reached into the cabinet for a cake plate, she noticed the top was off one of her canisters. Sugar was all over the counter.

"What in the world?" She ran the tip of her finger through the spilled granules. "Muddy must have knocked over the sugar jar when she was looking for the coffee." She shook her head. "It's not like her to leave a mess. Oh, well, I'll clean it up later. Let's get this coffee and cake out there while they're hot."

Twenty minutes later, the pot of coffee was gone and all that remained of the pound cake was a few crumbs.

Chief Davis put down his cup and stood up. "Thank you, ladies, for the cake and coffee, but I reckon I'd better be off if I hope to make church."

"My stars, I forgot today is Sunday," Addy said. "Looks like I'll miss church."

"I think God will understand, my dear." Mischief gleamed in Muddy's eyes. "You've had a busy weekend."

Addy's cheeks burned. "Yes, well, I'll see you to the door, Chief."

The doorbell chimed.

"Don't get up, Addy." Chief Davis started for the door. "Let me get that for you on my way out."

"Thanks, Chief," Addy said. "I'll bet that's Shep come to tell me about Mr. Farris," she told Muddy. "I'm surprised I haven't heard from him by now."

"What the hell?" the chief bellowed.

Addy jumped up. "What is it?"

Somehow, Brand was at her side by the time she reached the door and looked outside.

"Holy happy horse shit!" she squeaked, forgetting that a lady doesn't cuss and never refers to a body function, thereby committing a double violation of the Rules of Lady-tude that Bitsy had drummed into her head since infancy.

Fortunately, Bitsy wasn't here. But Addy felt sure even Mama would cut her a little slack under the circumstances. She was looking at the four-ton bronze statue of Jebediah Gordon Hannah, Spanish-American War hero, champion of the lowly peanut as the cash crop that saved Behr County farmers during the devastating cotton blight of 1915, and all-round swell guy.

For more than eighty years, Jeb had held his two-foot-high peanut aloft in the town square, a symbol of the enduring spirit of the American farmer and a beacon to peanut butter lovers everywhere.

But not anymore. Somebody had planted Jeb and his giant peanut on Muddy's front lawn. Somebody had also decapitated poor Jeb and left the severed head at the statue's feet.

Correction: *something*. A jagged black mark marred the front of Jebediah's Cavalry uniform, a mark that matched the scar on Addy's right breast.

The demon had left a calling card, a great big headless four-ton calling card.

Addy was no expert on demons, but she knew a challenge when she saw one.

This was a declaration of war, demon-style.

Chapter Twenty-two

The chief stomped out to his patrol car. Addy followed him outside, her ever-constant Dalvahni shadow at her heels.

"I gotta call this in. The mayor needs to be notified. And the town council," he said.

The chief's face was bright red. Addy had looked like that once after a day at the beach. But, the chief wasn't sunburned. Nope, the chief was about to blow a gasket.

"How the hell did somebody move this thing all the way from downtown?" he fumed. "It 'ud take a forklift to move the son-of-a-bitch. Don't matter. If I find out who did this, I'm gonna bury 'em under the jail. Stealing a corpse is one thing, but this here is desecration of a war hero. It's like shooting the pope a bird. These suckers have crossed the line."

"Who shot the pope a bird?" Muddy stepped out onto the porch. She gave a startled yelp when she saw Old Jeb. "Why is there a decapitated Civil War hero sitting in my yard?"

"Spanish-American war hero, Muddy," Addy said. "Jeb was a Rough Rider, remember? Saved Behr County from the pernicious boll weevil by convincing local farmers to stop planting cotton and go nuts. That's why he has the big peanut in his hands."

"Is that a peanut? I always thought it was a pickle."

"What in the world gave you that idea?"

"Lots of folks around here grow cucumbers, Addy. Pickles are big in the food industry. Think about it. There are bread-and-butter pickles and sweet pickles, and kosher dills and hamburger chips, not to mention gherkins and pickle relish." She peered at the statue. "It's not a very good peanut, if you ask me. Otherwise, I wouldn't have thought it was a pickle."

"Don't look so much like a pickle to me as a cat turd," Mr. Collier said, eyeing the statue. "I had this cat once that made the oddest-shaped poop. Kinda like that pickle there."

"I remember that cat." Muddy cocked her head. "'Course, looking at it from this angle, it could be a dildo."

Oh, good Lord. Like the City Fathers would commission a statue of Hannah's favorite son holding up a two-foot dildo.

"Got me a notion about that statue." Mr. Collier lowered his voice. "But I'd better wait until the chief leaves. Wouldn't want him to think I'm crazy."

Addy rolled her eyes. Everybody in Hannah thought Amasa Collier was crazier than a sack of weasels.

As it turned out, the chief didn't leave until after noon. Not until the mayor, the town council, the whole police department, the fire and sheriff departments, and half the town had traipsed through Muddy's yard gawking at Headless Jeb and scratching their collective heads over such a peculiar thing as a migrating statue. Robyn James showed up from the *Hannah Herald* to take pictures and interview the rubberneckers, since the chief would say no more than, "The matter is under investigation." To be exact, what the chief said was, "You bet your *beeping* ass the *beeping* matter is under investigation," and then he stomped off.

"But, Chief, I can't put that in the paper!" Robyn wailed, whereupon the chief promptly told Robyn where he could stick the *Herald*.

"I've never seen the chief so upset," Addy later confided to Evie. "Good thing Mama didn't hear Mr. Potty Mouth. She'd a-gone all Bit-zoid on his butt."

Various opinions were espoused by the gawkers as to how Jeb got himself in such a predicament. Payback by the Paulsberg football team was the most popular theory. It was no secret the Wildcats, Hannah's longtime sports rival, still nursed a grudge over a prank the Hannah Blue Devils had pulled three years earlier involving the Paulsberg mascot. Neb the Billy Goat was kidnapped, dipped in a vat of purple dye, outfitted with a black hooded mask, and attached to a dozen large weather balloons, the idea being to float Neb over the football field at halftime. The pranksters miscalculated Neb's weight, and he drifted over the grandstands and into the wild blue yonder, never to be seen again.

A Bolo went out for a purple flying goat, and animal rights activists and volunteers from five surrounding counties turned out to look for the missing mascot. Crop dusters and pilots from Montgomery to Mobile scanned the skies to no avail. Neb had vanished. The story made the Mobile paper and was picked up by the national press. Neb's picture appeared on the front of the *National Globe*, under the headline FLYING PURPLE GOAT ALIEN TERRORIZES REDNECKS.

Last fall all hell broke loose at the Paulsberg/Hannah football game when the Blue Devil fans started chanting *"Spa-a-a-ce Go-o-at"* There was talk of ceasing competition between the two teams until things cooled off. Like in a few hundred years.

Some folks reckoned Jeb's statue was beamed up by space aliens and deposited in Muddy's yard after the ETs had their wicked way with him, although sunspots, earth vortices, a message from Elvis, electromagnetism, a diabolical communist plot, and the pull of the full moon were also popular theories. Mamie Hall reckoned as how the town witch was responsible, but nobody paid her much mind. Miss Mamie blamed everything from her sciatica to the weather and the ping in her Ford Taurus engine on Cassandra Ferguson.

It was a hot day. Addy fixed a pitcher of lemonade and carried it outside to offer the chief and the others a cold drink. Brand went with her.

She stopped on the porch. Brand stopped, too.

"Dude, the 'me and my shadow routine' is getting on my nerves. Stay here."

"No."

She set the pitcher down and put her hands on her hips. "I'll be right over there offering those nice officers something to drink. Notice the big crowd of people? I'll be fine."

"The djegrali are masters of dissemblance. They could be secreted within any of these humans."

She looked at the crowd milling around the front yard. They all looked pretty normal to her. Well, normal for Hannah. "So, how do you tell if someone has been possessed?"

He shrugged. "It is difficult, especially if the demon is very clever. The djegrali crave human sensation and physical pleasure. Those possessed will often overindulge in food, drink, drugs, or sex. Some will become violent, if the demon or the human they possess has a taste for bloodshed. Sometimes, the victim acts out of character, or displays some other sort of eccentricity that gives the demon away."

"Hate to break it to you, but this is the South. We pride ourselves on being eccentric. You've got your job cut out for you."

"Adara, I was trying to explain how one human can tell if another human is possessed. The Dalvahni have other ways."

"Like what?"

"The djegrali give off an odor when they are excited or angry."

"You mean they stink?"

"Exactly."

"Eww. What do they smell like?"

"It is most unpleasant, like rancid fat or something burning. I do not know how to describe the scent. Once you smell it, you will know it. It is unforgettable." He paused. "But that is not the only means the Dalvahni have at their disposal."

"Ooh, Mr. Mysterious. Do tell."

His lips twitched. "I believe you would call it 'woo-woo.'"

"Say no more. You know that stuff gives me the creeps."

"My objective is to keep you safe, Adara. By any means possible. It is not my intent to annoy you or present you with the creeps. I will make myself inconspicuous."

He vanished.

Addy blinked. "Brand?"

"See? Inconspicuous," he said in her ear, making her jump. "I will not get on your nerve, and you can go about your business."

"Nerve-*zah*, dude. And don't think about copping a feel because I can't see you."

Addy and her unseen escort approached the police officers. The area around Headless Jeb had been cordoned off by three-inch-wide yellow crime scene tape. Officer Curtis stood outside the line of tape contemplating the statue.

"Maybe it moved on its own," he offered at last.

The chief gave him a scathing look. "Moved on its own *how*, Dan? You think the damn thing grew legs and walked here?"

"I saw something on the Discovery channel last weekend about sliding rocks in Death Valley," Officer Curtis said. "These rocks are on a dry lake bed, see, but they move. Leave long trails in the dirt behind them like a snail. Real creepy stuff, rocks moving on their own. I'm not talking little rocks, either. These rocks weigh like a hundred pounds. Got them brainiac scientists stumped, I can tell you that." He shook his head. "Rocks ought not move. It ain't natural. But it's a known fact them rocks in Death Valley move. Look it up, if you don't believe me. Maybe Jeb moved on his own."

Chief Davis's face went from tomato red to a deep, eggplant purple. "And how, exactly, do you propose he did that?"

"Wind. Wind's a mighty powerful force."

"The wind." Chief Davis took off his hat and ran his hand through his hair so that it stuck up in all directions. "You think the *wind* moved a four-ton statue."

"Or an ice sheet like that Agassiz glacier that flattened North Dakota like a pancake. Saw that on the Discovery channel, too."

"It's a hundred degrees in the shade, Dan," the chief said. "You could fry an egg on the sidewalk, and you think a giant sheet of ice moved into town and deposited Jeb Hannah on Miss Muddy's front lawn and then crept back out again while I was inside her house having cake and coffee. Great Jumping Jehosephat."

Officer Curtis looked stubborn. "I'm just saying."

"And *I'm* just saying you're an idiot."

Uh oh. Time to run interference before two of Hannah's Finest had a smackdown in Muddy's front yard.

"Lemonade, Chief?" Addy asked with a bright smile. She handed the chief a glass and turned to Dan Curtis. "Dan, would you like something to drink?"

"Thanks, Addy."

He took the glass without looking at her. He was too busy eyeballing the chief. Jeez, talk about your testosterone overload. The two men eyed one another like a couple of banty roosters in a barnyard. Addy was contemplating turning the garden hose on them when Brand whispered a warning in her ear.

"Despair all ye mortals," he said in a voice of doom. "The mama approacheth."

For a man with no sense of humor, he sure was turning into a wiseass.

Less than a minute later, Mama's car pulled up.

"Car-lee, I brought lunch." Mama didn't say the chief's name, she *sang* it, making it four syllables instead of two. "*Car-rah-lee-hee,*" she said.

Toting an oversized picnic basket, Mama picked her way across the lawn. She still wore her Sunday clothes, Addy noticed with a pang of guilt. She'd blown church off, what with the sexual marathon of the night before, and Muddy and Headless Jeb showing up, but maybe God wouldn't tap her on the head too badly for last night's carnal sin. Make that sins *plural*. More like a whole night of uninhibited, full-blown, out-and-out debauchery. Bad Girl Addy had opened up a can of Behr County whoopass on Good Girl Addy. And she didn't regret it one little bit. No sir-ree bobtail, not a smidge. Given a choice, she'd do it all over again. And again . . . and again.

She was officially a sex addict when it came to a certain guy. Thank goodness her God wasn't one of those fire-and-brimstone-hellfire-and-damnation-type Supreme Beings. Her God was a laid-back kind of fellow with a sense of humor. He created the duckbilled platypus, and he let the bishop get away with wearing that funny hat. An omnipotent being with a sense of humor, if ever there was one.

And, a good thing, too. Otherwise she'd be in deep doo-doo in the lust-as-a-sin department. Along with anger, pride, gluttony, envy, greed, and sloth, lust was one of the seven deadly sins, right? One out of seven wasn't bad. Oh, very well. Maybe she'd been guilty of envy and anger a couple of times. She'd sure envied Ruthie Bowab that pair of neon pink roller blades Santa brought her in the fifth grade. And just looking at the Death Starr made her mad, so add anger to the list. But all in all she hadn't done too badly in the sin department.

Whoops, was that pride? That left gluttony, greed, and sloth. Crap, she forgot about her and Evie's biannual mint chocolate chip ice cream binges. Six out of seven. Yikes. The jaws of hell yawned before her.

Mama handed the picnic basket to the chief and turned her lasers on Addy. "You still wearing that wig, Addy?"

"I told you, Mama. It's not a wig."

"Hmm." Which in Mama-speak meant *We'll talk more about this later, young lady.* "Why weren't you in church?"

"Muddy came home, and then things got a little crazy when Old Jeb showed up."

Bitsy blanched. "Muddy's here?"

Hah, that had her on the run. Muddy did and said what she darn well pleased. Drove Mama nuts.

"You heard from your brother this morning?" Mama tried to act casual, but Addy could see her looking out of the corner of her eye for Muddy. "He wasn't at church, either."

"No, ma'am. He's probably busy getting ready for the visitation this afternoon. I hear the Farris funeral is tomorrow morning."

"That's right." Mama returned her attention to the chief. "As awful as this must be for you, Car-lee, I can't help but be glad about Jebediah. People at church were talking about it, and not You-Know-What."

"What's that, Little Bit?" The chief sounded distracted.

"You know . . . the unfortunate incident at Corwin's." Bitsy fanned herself. "I am so relieved that body showed back up and people have something else to talk about. Anyway, I figured you'd be busy at the crime scene and forget to eat, so I brought you a bite."

"That's real thoughtful of you, Hibiscus." Chief Davis took Bitsy by the arm. "Why don't we go sit under a tree and have us a real picnic."

They left, and Addy turned to Officer Curtis with a smile. "More lemonade, Dan?"

"Guck," Officer Curtis said, staring at her.

Addy took a step back. "You all right, Dan? Your face looks all funny."

He gave her a goofy grin. "You sure are pretty, Addy. Want to go out sometime? We could drive over to Namath Springs and have dinner at that I-talian restaurant there."

Awkward. She'd known Dan Curtis since middle school. They were friends, nothing more.

"Thanks, Dan, but I—"

"Hey, good looking." Dinky Farris swaggered up. A wife-beater T-shirt exposed his stringy arms. He grinned and adjusted the bulge in his jeans. "What say you and me go for a ride in my new four-wheel-drive truck? I'll throw a cooler of beer in the back and we can have us a par-tay."

Eww. Dinky Farris and his jumbo mister had asked her out.

"Thanks, Dinky, but I'm not much of a partier."

Addy turned and ran like hell for the house.

She slammed the front door and leaned against it. "Whoa, that was majorly freaky."

Muddy came out of the kitchen. "What's that, dear?"

"Dan Curtis and Dinky Farris came on to me. *Dinky Farris!* Gross." She collapsed onto the couch. "And I've known Dan since seventh grade."

Muddy went to the window. "They're gone. Is that Bitsy with Chief Davis under the tree?"

"Yes, ma'am."

"They sure look cozy."

"I think they're dating."

"Good," Muddy said. "Your daddy was a hard worker and a good provider, but I'd bet money that Chief is a stem winder in the sack."

"Muddy, puh-leeze. Do not put that image in my head."

Brand materialized in the middle of the living room. "The Dinky human and the other one decided to take a trip."

Muddy turned away from the window. "Oh, Mr. Dalvahni, I didn't hear you come in. Amasa's in the backyard playing with Dooley. He wanted to talk to you. I'll go get him."

She hurried past Addy and out the French doors.

"What do you mean Dinky and Officer Curtis took a trip?" Addy eyed him suspiciously. "A trip where?"

"I did not like the way they looked at you. They seemed overheated. I decided a dip in the river might cool them off."

"Brand, you can't go around dumping people in the river."

He raised his brows. "I cannot?"

"No. For starters, what if they don't know how to swim? And don't you think they're going to wonder how they got there and start asking questions?"

"I do not care what they do, as long as they do not look at you like that."

"Oh, brother," Addy said.

Muddy came back inside with Dooley at her heels. Dooley gave Addy a questioning look. Addy shook her head and put her finger to her lips, signaling silence. Looking slightly put out, the Lab slunk into the kitchen and flopped on the tile.

"He's not out there," Muddy said. "He must have gone around to the front." She opened the front door and looked out. "There he is by Jeb's statue. What on earth is he doing with that wire thingy?"

Addy got up and went to the door. "That's his contrabulator, Muddy."

"Looks like a divining rod. What do you think he's doing?"

"No telling." Mr. Collier looked up, and Addy waved. "Here he comes."

Mr. Collier hurried into the house. He seemed relieved to see Brand.

"I'm glad you're still here, Mr. . . . uh . . ."

"Call me Brand."

Mr. Collier gave him a nervous smile. "Well, uh, Brand, I never did get a chance to talk to you this morning, what with all the excitement over Old Jeb. Been afraid you wouldn't believe me, but now I'm sure of it."

"Sure of what, Amasa?" Muddy said.

Mr. Collier fiddled with his contrabulator. "Try and keep an open mind, Edmuntina. This is going to sound crazy."

"Of course, Amasa. Go on."

He took a deep breath. "I see demons. Been seeing them since I hit my head in that car accident thirty-five years ago. That's why I started drinking."

"I know."

Mr. Collier stared at Muddy in surprise. "You do?"

"Lord, yes. You told me about it years ago when you were on one of your three-day benders."

"I did?"

"Yes, you did."

"Did you believe me?"

"'Course I believed you," Muddy said. "Why would you lie about a thing like that?"

He frowned. "You aren't saying that to be nice, are you, 'cause you think I'm crazy?"

"I don't think you're crazy, Amasa. I'd have married you years ago if that was all. But I refuse to marry a drunk."

Mr. Collier's lean face creased in a grin that made him look years younger. "I've quit drinking, Edmuntina. I've quit for good."

"I know."

"You do?"

"I see things, too," Muddy said. "Oh, not demons. Sometimes I know things before they happen. Like with your drinking. I knew you were going to quit. That's why I came home early."

"I'm glad you came home. I missed you."

"I've missed you, too, Amasa. I love you, you know."

Mr. Collier's grin widened. "You do?"

"Yes, you old fool. I've loved you these thirty years and more."

"I've wasted a lot of time."

"Yes, you have."

"I don't want to waste any more. Will you marry me, Miss Fairfax?"

Muddy gave him a radiant smile. "I thought you'd never ask."

Chapter Twenty-three

M uddy was in love with Amasa Collier, had been for more than thirty years. It boggled Addy's mind, made her want to weep. Her sweet, lunatic great-aunt had waited a lifetime for a man, would be waiting for him still if not for Blondy and a bottle of Texas Pete. That floating bottle of hot sauce had changed everything, given poor Mr. Collier his first glimmer of hope in decades that he might not be crazy after all. The only one who'd believed in him was Muddy, dear, sweet, unpredictable Muddy.

She'd had no idea her aunt was in love with Amasa Collier. So much for her female intuition. Since she was a little girl, she and Muddy had paid frequent visits to Mr. Collier at his house outside of town, a grand plantation-style home built around 1900 with the Collier timber money. While she played along the winding driveway that led to the old home and swung in the branches of the oak trees, Muddy and Mr. Collier sat on the columned porch enjoying frosty glasses of iced tea. All the while they laughed and talked and argued about art and literature and politics, Addy didn't have a clue that beneath the surface of their friendship ran a current of regret and longing and shattered dreams. Dreams that, thanks to a certain blond horse's ass, were coming true. She owed Blondy a great, big thank-you. And somehow she'd tell him, too, in spite of the hairball of pride that clogged her throat at the thought.

"Addy, you'll be my maid of honor, won't you?" Muddy glowed with happiness. "And Shep can give me away. Nothing elaborate, a simple wedding with a few family and friends. Trinity's such a beautiful, old church. I've always wanted to be married there. If that's all right with you, Amasa."

"Anything you want, Edmuntina."

"I'd love to be your maid of honor, Muddy." Addy gave her aunt a tearful hug. "You're going to be a beautiful bride. We'll go wedding dress shopping in Pensacola and Mobile."

"Nothing too foo-foo," Muddy said. "Something elegant and tasteful, maybe in tea length. And no virginal white." She looked at Amasa, her eyes twinkling. "There have been one or two revenge affairs through the years while I waited for someone to come to his senses."

He squeezed her hand. "I've come to my senses, so there won't be any more of that." He turned to Brand. "About what I wanted to tell you. I'm sure you know there are demons, and then there are *demons*. What I mean to say is, in my experience some of the critters are mischievous, but otherwise not half bad. They rattle on about anything from the number of raindrops in a thunderstorm to the song the tree frog sings on a warm summer night, but they aren't evil."

"The creatures you refer to are, I believe, elementals," Brand said. "Nature spirits indigenous to this world, benign or harmful, depending upon their mood. The djegrali are not of this world. They are nearly always bent on mischief of the worst kind."

"Call 'em what you want. They gossip like a bunch of old biddies about humans . . . and other demons, too. Seems these demons plan to take over the town. Showdown at the O.K. Corral, Hannah style. Mean to kill anyone that gets in their way." Mr. Collier looked at Addy, his eyes full of concern. "And here's the worst part. Their ringleader is one of the bad ones, the worst of them all, so the talk goes. And he's got it in for you, Addy."

"Oh, this is terrible, just terrible." Muddy wrung her hands. "But what can Mr. Dalvahni do to stop these awful creatures, Amasa?"

Addy nudged Brand. "I think it's time you showed Muddy your big sword."

Her aunt perked up. "Is that a euphemism for the male part like they use in those bosom-heaver romance novels? Like 'his magnificent scepter' or 'his throbbing love muscle'? 'Cause if it is, I'm an engaged woman. Not that I'm not interested, academically speaking, but I don't think I should be looking at another man's sword. Maybe you could tell me about it. Or Addy could draw me a picture."

"Get a grip, Muddy. I'm talking about a real sword. Show her, Brand."

Brand reached behind him. "Behold Uriel," he said in ringing tones, holding the burning blade aloft. "Flaming nemesis of evil and scourge of the djegrali."

"Dude, a simple 'here's my sword' would have sufficed."

Muddy clasped her hands to her bosom. "My, that *is* a big sword, Mr. Dalvahni. What do you use it for?"

"Brand is a Dalvahni demon hunter, my dear," Mr. Collier said.

Muddy looked perplexed. "I thought Dalvahni was your last name."

Brand shook his head. "No, Dalvahni is what I *am*. We are warriors. It is our task to find the djegrali and return them to their proper plane of existence, kill them if necessary, before they wreak havoc on unsuspecting folk and disrupt the balance of the universe. Be assured that Ansgar and I will meet and deal with this threat to your town." He looked at Addy. "Do not worry about your niece. She is under my protection."

"Who is Ansgar?" Muddy said.

"Another Dalvahni warrior, Muddy," Addy said. "A real—" She bit her tongue. She'd been about to say "a real pain in the butt," but she owed Blondy. "What I mean to say is, he and Brand are like brothers."

"I see." Addy felt her aunt's worried gaze upon her. "And after you take care of these demons, what then, Mr. Dalvahni? Will you stay on in Hannah?"

A giant hand squeezed Addy's heart. Here it was: The Bottom Line, the Big Unanswered Question, the future and whether she and Brand had one. She looked at him, and her heart sank. The strained, unhappy expression in his eyes told her everything. He would do what he came here to do and leave. He might not be happy about it, but he would do it all the same, big, bad demon hunter that he was. There was no future for them, no happily ever after.

What had happened to all the air in the room? She couldn't breathe. She had to do something, move before it all came down, crushing her beneath a mountain of pain and sorrow and loss. She turned away, unable to bear the sadness in his eyes. If she could get outside, maybe she could breathe again.

"Adara, wait," Brand said.

She shook her head. Stumbling blindly across the room, she opened the back door. Dooley barreled inside, almost knocking her over.

"Addy, cat. Stupid cat . . ." Dooley panted.

"Mr. Fluffy!" Addy blinked back her tears. "Oh, my goodness, that poor little kitten has been shut up in the laundry room all this time. I feel horrible! He's probably hungry and lonely."

"Adara, you worry needlessly about that creature," Brand said. "He is—"

Addy ignored him. Rushing past a stunned Mr. Collier and her gaping aunt, she flung open the laundry room door. The litter box was undisturbed, the food and water bowls untouched. Mr. Fluffy was nowhere to be seen.

"Mr. Fluffy? Here, kitty, kitty." She looked behind the washer and dryer for the kitten. "He's gone. I don't understand. Where could he be?"

Dooley followed her into the laundry room, her entire backend wriggling with excitement. *"Ooh, Dooley know! Stupid cat! Dooley know! Show Addy!"*

"Yes, Dooley, if you know where Mr. Fluffy is, show me."

"Dooley show Addy stupid cat!"

Addy was starting to detect a recurrent theme in the dog's conversation. Clearly, dog/cat relations remained somewhat strained. Dooley pranced ahead of Addy into the living room.

"Dooley show Addy. Show Addy stupid cat."

"You hear the dog talking, Edmuntina, or am I having delirium tremens?" Mr. Collier said as Dooley galumped by.

"You're not hallucinating, Amasa. I hear it, too. That dog talks."

Mr. Collier wiped his brow with a linen handkerchief. "Thank the Lord."

Dooley bounded up to the French door that stood ajar. *"There cat! See, Addy?"*

Addy looked through the glass. The perimeter of Muddy's backyard was shaded by trees, but at the sunny center of the lot was a sparkling fountain surrounded by fragrant, blooming rose bushes. Flitting from flower to flower on gossamer, diamond-dusted wings like a furry overgrown demented butterfly was Mr. Fluffy Fauntleroy.

Muddy walked up behind Addy. "A flying cat! I haven't seen one of those in years. Not since Etheline died."

"Ack," Addy croaked. Her vocal chords seemed to be frozen and her brain right along with them. The world tilted crazily as Brand swept her up and carried her over to the couch. Twisting in his arms, she pointed over his shoulder at the winged feline. "C-cat."

"Yes, dear, I know it's a shock," Muddy said. "The first time I saw one, I fainted dead away. Etheline threw water on me. Ruined my best silk blouse. I was so mad at her I wouldn't speak to her for a week." She sighed. "I'd give every silk blouse I ever owned to be able to talk to Ethie again. Lord, I miss her."

Dooley barked and charged out the door to chase the cat away from the rose bushes. Mr. Fluffy buzzed around the dog's head, an orange and white horsefly with gauzy wings.

It drove Dooley crazy. *"Cat! Cat! Cat!"*

Mr. Fluffy flitted off with the Lab in pursuit.

"Isn't that sweet?" Muddy closed the door behind Dooley. "They're playing." She slid her arm through Mr. Collier's. "I think we could all use a bite to eat. Let's you and me go in the kitchen and leave these youngsters alone so they can talk."

"Sure thing, Edmuntina."

Mr. Collier gave the frolicking pair of animals a last lingering look and followed Muddy into the kitchen.

Brand lowered Addy to the couch.

"You knew, didn't you?" Addy scowled up at him. "You knew Mr. Fluffy was not an ordinary cat."

"I suspected he was one of the fae," Brand admitted. "A fairy cat, Adara. That is why he refused the meat you offered him last night. The fae have a weakness for sweet things, like nectar and honey."

"The sugar! Mr. Fluffy must have knocked the top off the canister and gotten into the sugar jar." She frowned. "But how did he get out of the laundry room with the door closed?"

"Doors and walls are no barrier to the fae."

As if on cue, Mr. Fluffy flew through the outside wall and into the living room, proving Brand's point. Dooley bounded up to the French doors and pressed her nose to the glass.

"Cat in?" Dooley pawed at the door. *"Dooley IN!"*

Mr. Fluffy sailed back and forth through the wall, taunting the barking dog.

Brand sighed. "Did I not tell you the creature would be troublesome?"

He waved his hand, and the door swung open. Dooley scrambled inside and trotted up to Addy.

Mr. Fluffy hovered around Dooley's head like a hummingbird at a feeder. "Meow."

"Addy, stupid cat?"

"I see him, Dooley."

"Company's coming," Muddy said from the kitchen.

Ansgar materialized.

"How does she do that?" Addy muttered. "It's creepy."

The dress slacks and shirt Ansgar wore the day before had been exchanged for a pair of jeans and a pin-stripe button-down shirt worn open at the neck. He was not her type, but Addy had to admit he looked good. The sleeves of the shirt were rolled up, exposing his muscular forearms.

"Greetings, brother."

"Well met, Ansgar," Brand said.

Muddy popped into the living room. "Mercy, are they all so big and handsome? I'd better make more sandwiches."

She disappeared back into the kitchen.

Ansgar arched a pale brow at Brand. "Is it wise, brother, to alert so many humans to our presence?"

"She is a most unusual human, brother. Her name is Edmuntina, and she is Adara's maternal aunt. She has the sight. She is also handfasted to the Collier human."

"Ah," Ansgar said. "The man who sees demons."

Addy took a deep breath. She wasn't one to put off unpleasantness. And as unpleasantness went having to make nice to Blondy was clear off the icky scale.

"Uh, Blondy . . . I mean, Ansgar, I wanted to say thank you. That thing you did in the Sweet Shop with the hot sauce yesterday helped convince Mr. Collier that he's not crazy. He quit drinking, and he and my aunt are getting married. She's happy and that makes me happy, and we owe it all to you."

"You owe me nothing," Ansgar said with chilly hauteur. "What I did was a violation of the directive against conspicuousness. I could have jeopardized our entire mission."

Jeez, talk about your giant frozen hemorrhoids. Well, she tried.

"Still," Ansgar continued stiffly, "if some good came of my imprudence I am glad of it. I wish your aunt and the Collier human much happiness."

"Uh, thanks," Addy said. Okay, maybe he was a *medium*-size hemorrhoid.

"Addy," Muddy called, "Tweedy's here. You might as well ask him to stay for lunch."

The doorbell rang. Addy jumped off the couch. "I'll get it." Brand beat her to the door.

"Dude, that is so annoying," she said.

Tweedy Gibbs stood on the front porch, his hands filled with Tompkin's shopping bags. The tribble of red hair at the top of his forehead stood on end. He looked thoroughly confused.

"I brought you the clothes you ordered. Even though it's a Sunday, and the store is closed and I don't work on Sunday, and though, to save my soul, I don't remember you ordering them or where they came from." He eyed Brand up and down, a glimmer of hostility in his befuddled gaze. "Like I said yesterday, we don't have anything that will fit a man of your size, but there was nothing doing but for me to bring 'em. Couldn't relax until I did. Couldn't seem to help myself."

Ansgar stepped to the door. "Thank you, Master Gibbs. Your services are sorely needed. If you will but observe, my brother still wears the raiment he purchased yesterday at your establishment."

"The same clothes he wore yesterday?" Tweedy's mouth sagged open in shock. "I'm just in time. This here is what you call your fashion emergency."

Chapter Twenty-four

Sunday afternoon the City tried to move Jebediah Hannah by borrowing a forklift from Fred Schneider at the Hannah Feed and Seed, and a flatbed truck from farmer Boyd Sigafoose. A crowd gathered in the street to watch Jeb lifted onto the truck under the supervision of the fire and police departments. The mayor and several members of the town council stood nervously nearby. Muddy, claiming jet lag, stayed inside to nap. Addy and Brand surveyed the proceedings from the relative cool of the front porch swing.

Addy peeked sideways at Brand. He wore some of the new duds Tweedy had brought, a pair of blue jeans and a T-shirt. She sighed. He looked as fine in jeans as she'd thought he would. All lean, hard muscle, he radiated an aura of barely suppressed animal power. The guy was a total babe.

Dan Curtis, still slightly damp around the edges from his impromptu swim, eased around the edge of the porch. He gave her a moony-eyed look. "Hey, Addy."

Good grief, Dan Curtis had a crush on her.

She gave him a little finger wave. "Afternoon, Dan."

Brand rumbled deep in his chest.

"Easy, boy," she muttered.

Brand glared at Dan until the younger man got the message and slunk away. "I do not like the way he looks at you. It is pitifully easy to read his thoughts. I think it is time the Curtis human paid another trip to the river."

"Don't you dare! Poor Dan had a hard enough time explaining it the first time."

"He did not explain. He lied. He said he had a suspect under surveillance and fell in the river when the other human fled."

"Well, what did you expect him to say? *'I fell in the river, Chief, but I have no idea how I got there'*?" She pointed to the people gathered across the road. "There's a whole gaggle of females over there ogling you like you're the last drink of water between here and the Mojave Desert. I can practically hear them salivating from fifty yards away. You don't see me throwing *them* in the river."

"That is different."

"It most certainly is not. I'd like to scratch their eyes out."

Brand grinned. *Thwack!* The grin left the porch, floated across the yard, and hit Brand's admirers right between the eyes. There was an audible sigh of ecstasy. Addy was pretty sure several of them peed themselves.

"You are jealous?" he asked.

"Green as goose poop."

"I am glad," he said, and kissed her in full view of the crowd of gawkers.

It was, Addy realized once she'd recovered from that mind-blowing kiss, Brand's way of staking his claim. Primitive and medieval, perhaps, but thrilling all the same. And dangerous. She already had a crazed demon after her, and now Brand's groupies were glaring at her like they'd like to snatch her bald headed. Myrtle Glenn Hollingsworth looked like she wanted to take her shoe off and beat Addy to death with it. And Myrtle Glenn was *married*. Too bad, she thought, resisting the urge to stick her tongue out at the older woman. Myrtle Glenn and the rest of those women would have to get their own "inter dimensional demon hunter smack your lips he was so gorgeous" dude. This one was hers, at least for now.

The forklift rattled across Muddy's lawn and stopped in front of the statue. Wilton Miller, the city attorney, pulled up and rolled down his window.

"Mayor Tunstall, Mayor Tunstall," Wilton hollered, waving at the mayor through the open window. Slamming the car in park, he jumped out. Miller was on the shady side of forty, with a balding pate and very hairy legs that hung out of a pair of cargo shorts like two skinny, hirsute caterpillars. He hurried to the mayor's side. "I'm glad I got here in time. I've been out of pocket and just heard what happened." He took a swipe at his glistening head and brow with a handkerchief. "As city attorney, I advise you not to allow anyone but the State or the County to move this statue. If someone was to get hurt, the city might be held liable."

"Lawyers," Chief Davis said in disgust. "You can't turn around without one of the blood suckers trying to sue you."

"I'm trying to *prevent* a lawsuit, Chief Davis," Wilton protested. "Did anybody check the weight limit capacity on that forklift? Suppose you manage to get that statue on the truck and have an accident on the way downtown, and Jeb ends up in somebody's lap? The City gets sued, that's what."

Mayor Tunstall blanched. "Wilton has a point. We'd better leave Jebediah here until we get this thing sorted out."

"In the meantime, I would advise you to post an officer to watch the statue," Wilton added. "You don't want a bunch of kids to get hurt trying to steal Jeb's head."

"Oh, for the love of—" Chief Davis took off his hat, ran his hand through his hair, and then slammed the hat back on his head. "You're right, Wilt, that's the kind of thing a bunch of stupid kids would do. I'll make sure the damn thing's guarded."

The flatbed and the forklift were removed, and an officer posted across the street to keep an eye on Jeb. Bitsy went home but came back later that evening to visit with Muddy.

"Addy, your mama's coming up the sidewalk," Muddy said from the back bedroom.

"For crying in the beer." Addy ran to put Dooley and Mr. Fluffy in her bedroom. She *did not* want to try to explain a talking dog or a flying cat to her mama.

"Not a word," she warned Dooley. She shook her finger at the cat. "And you stay put. I mean it."

She hurried back into the living room.

Bitsy buzzed through the front door like a bluebottle fly in her turquoise linen walking shorts and matching top. "Oh, Mr. Dalvahni, I didn't realize you were here," she said. Addy could have sworn the barometric pressure dropped. Mama was a force of nature that caused atmospheric disturbances wherever she went. "What a pleasant surprise to see you again. How long did you say you plan on being in town?"

Mama had that "I'm looking for a husband for my poor old maid daughter, and tag you're it" look in her eyes. Poor Brand might be a ten-thousand-year-old demon hunter, but Mama was a matchmaking succubus from hell.

"Never mind about that, Bitsy," Muddy said, charging to the rescue. She'd showered and changed clothes after her nap and wore a pair of casual slacks and a top. Addy flashed her great-aunt a grateful smile. If there was one person who could take the wind out of Mama's sails, it was Muddy. "I want to know what's going on between you and Carl E. Davis. I saw you two canoodling under the tree at lunch."

Bitsy flushed. "I'm sure I don't know what you're talking about, Aunt Muddy. Carl and I are friends."

"Too bad for you then. That Chief strikes me as a man with lead in his pencil."

"Lord, Muddy, the things you say!" Bitsy looked ready to die from embarrassment. "What will Mr. Dalvahni think of us? He's not used to your sense of humor."

Muddy gave Addy a sly glance. "Oh, if I were a betting woman, I'd bet Mr. Dalvahni has canoodled a time or two. What about you, Addy? You think Mr. Dalvahni has done any canoodling recently?"

Whoosh, Addy felt her face grow hot. If Bitsy was a force of nature, Muddy was that times ten. Unpredictable as lightning and as dangerous. Muddy had saved her from Bitsy, but who would save her from Muddy?

"Muddy, why don't you tell Mama your big news?" Addy said, grasping for a lifeline. Life was like that with Bitsy and Muddy. Great White shark or combine, take your pick.

Bitsy perked up like a hound dog on the scent. "What news?"

Twenty minutes later, Bitsy rose to take her leave, her attention diverted for the moment from her favorite game of Find A Man For Addy, and firmly focused on Muddy's upcoming nuptials. Addy had expected Mama to be horrified that Muddy was marrying the town drunk and, according to popular opinion (and Mama's), a bona fide nutter. But the groom came from old money, and that cured all ills.

"Addy, of course, will take care of the flowers," Bitsy said, "and I will host a bridal luncheon in your honor at the club. I must remember to call tomorrow and book a room, and then see about invitations . . . oh, and have you thought about registering?"

"Amasa's all the gift I need," Muddy said firmly.

To Addy's surprise, her mother's expression softened. "Are you sure you know what you're doing, Muddy? I know Mr. Collier has money and is from a fine family and all, but sometimes that isn't enough. He's . . . well, he is a bit *eccentric,* and then there's his drinking."

Mama putting Muddy's happiness before social position? What was the world coming to? And, what did she mean "sometimes that isn't enough"? Had Mama been unhappy with Daddy? Her parents' marriage was something Addy had taken for granted. She'd been barely twelve when her father died. She remembered him as a kind but remote man, his attention focused on his business, no hobbies, and no outside interests except Corwin's. Didn't hunt, didn't fish, and didn't play golf. Death had been his life, so to speak, and his obsession with work had, undoubtedly, shortened his life. But had it also killed his marriage? Viewing her parents' union through adult eyes, Addy realized that Mama must have been lonely at times. Maybe that's why she threw herself into the social whirl, to fill the void. The realization that she might not know her mother at all was an uncomfortable one.

"Go ahead and say what you're thinking," Muddy said. "You think Amasa's a fruitcake and drinks too much. Truth be told, we're all a little crazy. Some of us just hide it better." She gave Bitsy a swift hug. "As for the drinking, Amasa says he's quit, and that's good enough for me."

Bitsy wiped her eyes. "I'm real glad to hear it." She picked up her purse and noticed Brand leaning against a wall on the other side of the room. "You didn't answer my question, Mr. Dalvahni. How long you plan on being in town?"

"I do not know."

"Hmm," Bitsy said. "The strong, silent type, aren't you?" Addy could almost hear the wheels turning. "Where are you staying?"

"I stay near Adara."

"Hmm," Bitsy said again. "Got you a room at the Hannah Inn, have you?"

"That's right, Mama," Addy said quickly before Brand could answer.

"Well, Mr. Dalvahni, have Addy bring you by the house one night and we'll have supper."

Brand bowed. "I am honored to be invited to your domicile."

"My goodness!" Bitsy said. "Well, you've got good manners, even if you are a Yankee."

"Brand's not a Yankee, Mama."

"Of course he's a Yankee, Adara Jean. It's plain from his accent he's not from the South."

Addy opened her mouth to argue and shut it again. People fell into two categories in Mama's reality. They were either from the South or they were not. If you weren't from the South, you were a Yankee. Or maybe European. That was as exotic as Mama got. Her world vision ended there. Neat, tidy, and easy to manage.

"Brand's European, Mama," Addy heard herself say.

She saw Brand's eyebrows shoot up and shook her head in warning.

"That right?" Bitsy said. "Well, I knew he wasn't from around here."

And with that, she sailed back out of the house taking most of the air and half the electricity with her. Addy could have sworn every lightbulb in the house dimmed when Mama left.

The bedroom door flew open.

"Addy, Addy, Addy!" Dooley bounded up to Addy like Argos greeting Odysseus after a twenty-year absence.

"Hey, Dooley. Who let you and Mr. Fluffy out of the bedroom?"

"Stupid cat open door, Addy."

Muddy came back from seeing Bitsy to the door. "Addy, why'd you let your mama think Mr. Dalvahni is staying at the Hannah Inn?" She swatted half-heartedly at the kitten flying around the room.

"What else could I say? It's the only place in town."

"That place is a flea bag. There are pubic patterns on the sheets."

"How would you know?"

"That's where they caught Francine Deason with that new dentist from Namath Springs. He was filling a different sort of cavity, if you know what I mean."

"Please," Addy said. "Francine Deason taught me third grade. You'll give me nightmares."

"Where *are* you staying tonight, Mr. Dalvahni?" Muddy asked.

"I stay with Adara to protect her from the djegrali."

"That's real nice of you, Mr. Dalvahni."

"I do not stay to be nice. I stay because it is my duty—"

"But, Mama can't find out, Muddy," Addy cautioned, interrupting him. "She'd have a heart attack."

"—and because Adara has promised me hot monkey sex," Brand finished.

"Hot diggity dog," Muddy said.

Chapter Twenty-five

As promised, Chief Davis put a man on duty across the street from Muddy's to keep an eye on the statue. Dan Curtis volunteered for the six-to-midnight shift and made a nuisance of himself by "checking" on them every half hour.

"Next time the doorbell rings, let Addy answer it," Muddy said after her fourth trip to the door. "That Curtis boy has the hots for her."

"What is this 'hots'?" Brand asked.

"He wants to do it with her."

"Do what?"

"You know, the mama and daddy dance."

Brand's expression remained blank.

"Oh, for goodness' sake." Muddy made a circle with the thumb and forefinger of one hand, stuck her finger in the hole and moved it in and out. "Get it?"

Brand scowled. "You mean he wants to have sexual congress with Adara."

Muddy gave him a thumbs-up. "Bingo."

Addy heard a deep rumble in the distance. Lightning flashed, and a deafening clap of thunder shook the house. Dooley yelped and tried to ram her eighty-five-pound body under the couch.

"No," Brand said.

Addy patted him on the chest. "Relax, big guy. Congress is not in session."

"I do not understand."

"She means she's not having sex with you tonight, not as

long as I'm in the house." Muddy's eyes twinkled. "Addy's a bit of a fuddy duddy. She's embarrassed because I heard y'all going at it this morning."

Addy's cheeks burned. "Please, Muddy, don't remind me. I'm thinking of moving to New Zealand so I don't have to look at you again." She turned to Brand. "Relax. I don't want to have sex with Dan Curtis or anyone else but you. Why would I? Next to you, every other guy on the planet is dog poop."

Brand's eyes darkened. *"Adara."*

Addy backed away. "Uh uh. You're gorgeous and irresistible and you make me crazy, but I am *not* having sex with you tonight. Muddy is right. I can't have sex with you while my great-aunt is in the house, not when you make me sing like the Morman Tabernacle Choir." She shrugged. "Maybe it's because I *am* a fuddy duddy like Muddy says, or maybe I don't want to share what we have together with anyone else."

Brand looked thoughtful. "I see."

"That is so sweet," Muddy said, wrinkling her nose. "I think I'm going to puke."

Later that night, Addy left Brand on the couch and retired to her bedroom alone. Dooley flumped on the floor beside the bed and went to sleep. Dogs could do that, Addy reflected, listening with envy to Dooley's gentle snoring. Turn the switch and sail off to Dreamland. Mr. Fluffy buzzed around the room for a little while and settled on the floor next to Dooley. Folding his wings, the kitten curled in a ball between the Lab's legs and went to sleep.

The door down the hall clicked shut, the signal that Muddy had gone to bed for the night. Quiet settled around the house. Turning on her side, Addy stared into the darkness. For some strange reason, her eyes burned. Must be allergies, she thought, snuffling. She sure as heck wasn't crying over that big jerk sleeping in the living room. He was respecting her wishes, damn him. She was disappointed and sad and lonely, and angry at herself for being such an emotional wreck. She said no to sex, and she meant no . . . didn't she? A tear trickled down her nose and landed on the pillow. Who knew how much time they had left together? One day soon, maybe tomorrow, he would leave her. She sniffed angrily and wiped her eyes. Maybe he didn't want her anymore. Maybe he . . .

"Adara, why are you crying?"

She was so wrapped up in her little pity party she hadn't heard him come in. He stood by the bed looking down at her with a perplexed expression. He was shirtless and barefoot. His jeans were unbuttoned and rode low on his lean hips. Her befuddled gaze drifted from his heavily muscled chest to the sculpted plane of his abdomen. God Almighty, he was beautiful. And ripped. He didn't have a six-pack. He had a whole freaking case. She followed the narrow strip of dark hair that trailed down his taut stomach and disappeared into the top of his jeans. Her eyes widened when she saw the thick bulge that strained against the denim. Somebody was glad to see her.

"Oh, no you don't, bub!" She shot upright in bed. "Super Slut Puppy has turned in her cape for the night."

"Who is Super Slut Puppy?"

"I am, when I'm around you. You turn me into some kind of sex maniac. I can't help myself." She glared at him. "It's not like me, I'll have you know. I don't act this way. I don't understand it."

"I am very glad to hear it." He gave her a sexy grin, and she was done for, fried to a crispy, crackly crunch, too stunned to protest when he stretched out on the bed beside her. She gaped at him, hardly noticing when he pulled the covers back, baring her to his gaze. "I do not like to think of you with other men," he said. "The very thought fills me with rage and sets my brain on fire. And then you know what happens."

"Y-you burst into flame?"

He traced a pattern along her thigh, and slipped her T-shirt up, exposing her stomach. "Yes, Adara Jean." He leaned closer. "You set me on fire. I have the—how did your aunt put it?— ah, yes, the *hots* for you."

"You do?"

"Most definitely." He hooked his hand in the waistband of her panties and slid them off. "All day I have burned for you, wanted to be inside you. I was close to despair when you told me you would not have sex with me tonight. I need you, Adara." He brushed his lips against hers. "I want you. Let me in."

Her resistance crumbled beneath the tender onslaught. "My aunt," she gasped as he slipped his finger inside her. "She'll hear. I can't—"

"Shh." Lowering his head, he nuzzled her breast through the cotton T-shirt. The combination of his finger inside her and the damp heat of his mouth on her breast was almost too much to bear. She clenched around him, shuddering. "No one will hear," he said. "I have placed a shield around us."

"A-a shield?"

He sat up and knelt between her legs. Pushing her thighs apart, he looked down at her. She should have been embarrassed, should have felt exposed, vulnerable. She did not. How could she when he looked at her that way, all hot and hungry, like she was the most beautiful thing he'd seen? He made her *feel* beautiful, sexy . . . seductive. He made her ache for him.

"Pull your shirt up, Adara." His deep voice made her shiver. "I want to see your breasts."

She obeyed, dragging the T-shirt over her breasts.

"Put your hands over your head."

Again, she obeyed, offering herself to him, legs wide, breasts bare, and arms above her head like the shameless wanton she was. But only for him. Only *with* him.

He looked down at her spread out before him, his expression intense, strained. "I'm going to kiss you, Adara Jean." Slowly, he trailed his fingers through the thatch of blond hair between her legs. "Here."

He bent his head and put his mouth on her, licking, suckling, stroking the sensitive flesh first with the tip and then with the flat of his tongue, driving her out of her mind, sending her spiraling out of control, making her forget everything but the exquisite pleasure of his touch. Super Slut Puppy took her cape out of mothballs and sighed. She moaned, she begged, she pleaded. And, when she reached the top and went over the edge, she screamed, brazen hussy that she was.

With a muttered curse, Brand shoved his jeans down and thrust inside her, moving his hips in a rocking motion that sent her spiraling into another climax. He came a moment later with a hoarse shout.

Their cries of ecstasy echoed around them loud enough to wake the dead.

Or a dog.

Or a flying cat.

Certainly loud enough to wake a certain bawdy old lady.

But the shield held. The quiet of the house remained unbroken by the scuffle of paws, the flap of wings, or a single *huzza huzza* from Muddy.

Thank God for Dalvahni woo-woo.

Monday morning Jeb Hannah still sat on the lawn in all his headless glory. The migrating statue had become something of a local sensation and a tourist attraction for folks as far as Montgomery. The mayor had contacted the state highway department about moving Jeb, but it would be two weeks before the heavy equipment arrived. In the meantime, the Hannah police were hard-pressed to keep the gawkers out of Muddy's front yard. People walked through the flower beds, picnicked on the lawn, and rang the doorbell to offer advice on the proper way to move Jeb or to volunteer their theories on Jeb's mysterious un-statue-like behavior. Everything from giant earthworms and the shifting of the Earth on its axis was suggested. Addy's personal favorites involved inebriated leprechauns and radioactive mice.

Addy waved at the family of four who stood on the sidewalk taking pictures of Headless Jeb when she left for the flower shop early Monday morning. Brand went with her, of course. She hadn't suggested otherwise. The thought of going to the shop alone gave her the creeps. She'd worked hard to make her little business a success. Now, thanks to a supernatural thug with an attitude, she was scared to go to her own shop. That ticked her off and made her want to kick some demon booty.

On the other hand, although the demon thing was getting

on her nerves, if the demon went, then so did Brand. And that thought was unbearable. So maybe her best hope was that things did not get resolved. That way, Brand would stay in Hannah, and they'd live happily ever after and have hot monkey sex forever and ever, amen.

Yeah, right. Like that would happen.

Maybe they didn't have forever, but they had last night. They made love all night, and without an audience, thanks to Brand's magic. Muddy had seemed kind of disappointed, to tell the truth.

"You sleep well, Mr. Dalvahni?" she asked that morning.

Addy cringed, but all Brand said was, "I slept a little, Edmuntina."

True, strictly speaking. They'd fallen asleep in each other's arms near daybreak.

"Me, too. Quiet as a graveyard around here." Muddy eyed Addy. "What about you, girl? You sleep well?"

"Like a rock."

The moment she said it, Addy knew she was in trouble. She felt Mr. Literal's gaze upon her and tensed. Didn't she know better than to fib around him? She was so busted.

"I do not understand the reference, Adara," he said. "Why do you say you slept like a rock? Rocks do not sleep."

"It's an idiom, Brand. A figure of speech."

"I see," he said. "You use a rock for comparison, because they do not meet the scientific definition of a living thing in this reality as they do not move, think, grow, consume or react to stimuli. This lack of interaction with the environment, I take it, is interpreted as being in a very deep sleep."

"Uh, yeah."

"But, Adara, you did not sleep like a rock. You—"

"Oh, no you don't! No, sir!" she shrieked. "Do not go there, bub. So help me, I mean it."

"Don't go where?" Muddy suddenly looked very interested. "Did I miss something?"

"As I was about to say, before I was so rudely interrupted," Brand said, an expression of bland innocence on his face, "I do not think Adara slept like a rock, because she got up early this morning and prepared a sumptuous repast of scrambled eggs and strawberry Poop Tarts."

"Pop tarts," Addy muttered. "I haven't been to the store. It's all we had."

Muddy looked disappointed. "Well, I guess I'd better get busy. I've got a wedding to plan."

Leaving Muddy to her own devices, Addy and Brand went to the flower shop. Addy punched in the security code on the back door and entered the supply room behind Brand. She looked around in surprise. From the way the panic-stricken demon had bumped and thrashed around on his way out Saturday night, she expected the supply closet to be a mess. But nothing seemed out of place. The front room would be a different story, thanks to Ghouly Farris and the Human Torch trashing the place. She worried her bottom lip. She'd have to call Ned Farnsworth down at Bama Farms and check her coverage. Maybe she should call the police first to report the damage. But what would she tell them? Not the truth, that was for sure. Vandalism? Nah, nobody in Hannah would vandalize her shop. Opossums? But what about the holes in the floor? A passel of rabid flame-throwing opossums from outer space? Yeah, that was more like it.

So much for calling the police.

Bracing herself, she stepped into the show room. She gazed about in stunned disbelief. No mess, no blood, no broken vases or display racks, no icky stench of cooked dead dude hanging about the place. And no holes in the linoleum floor. Everything in order.

"How?" she asked, unable to manage anything more coherent.

Brand, bless him, seemed to understand. "Ansgar."

"Blondy did this?"

He nodded. Great, she thought with an inward groan. She owed the frozen hemorrhoid another one. Her cup runneth over.

She flipped the CLOSED sign to open, booted up the computer, and checked her messages. She was working on the flower arrangements for the upcoming monthly meeting of the Purple Hoo-Hah Club, a supper club of rowdy, cigar-smoking whiskey-slugging older women who Chief Davis proclaimed a "frigging nuisance," when the bell chimed and Evie and Ansgar strolled in. Evie looked different. She looked . . .

She knew that look, that dewy, glowing, multiple-orgasm look. She'd seen it this morning when she looked in the mirror. Blondy and her best friend had been canoodling.

Addy stiffened. "Oh, no he didn't."

Brand put his hand on her shoulder. "Leave it alone, Adara. It is not your affair."

"She's my best *friend*."

"And he is my brother. I believe Ansgar has strong feelings for Mistress Evangeline. I have not known him to act thus before with a human."

"So help me, if he hurts her—"

"Morning," Evie said, not looking at Addy. "We thought we'd check and see how you two were doing." She glanced shyly at Brand. "Ansgar said you weren't feeling like yourself last night, Mr. Dalvahni. Are you all right?"

"I am fully recovered, Mistress Evangeline. And call me Brand."

Evie blushed. "All right, but only if you call me Evie."

Brand smiled at her. "Very well, Evie."

"I'm starving," Addy announced. "Why don't you two guys slide on down to the Sweet Shop and get us something to eat?"

"Adara, you have already broken your fast," Brand said.

"I'm hungry again. So sue me."

"I will not leave you unaccompanied. It is too dangerous with the djegrali about."

"Ahem," Ansgar said. "Brother, I believe the females would like to converse alone. The usual protective spells and a guardian should suffice for the short time we will be gone."

"I do not like it," Brand said. "Trouble has a way of finding Adara."

"Oh, for Pete's sake, leave the stupid guardian and go," Addy said. "Blondy's right for once. Girlfriend and I need to talk."

"Very well." Brand's expression grew distant. "Stop aggravating that poor creature and make yourself useful," he said, speaking to someone unseen.

Mr. Fluffy materialized with a sharp metallic *ping!* The kitten meowed and fluttered around Brand's head.

Evie squealed in delight. "A fairy cat! I haven't seen one of those since your Aunt Etheline died."

"Mr. Fluffy is your idea of a *guardian?*" Addy said. "You've got to be kidding."

"The fae have many talents," Brand said. "But if you feel unsafe with Mr. Fluffy . . ."

"No, no, that's all right." Addy watched the kitten make a circuit around the shop. "Mr. Fluffy will be fine."

"Very well." Brand held out his arm, and Mr. Fluffy landed on his wrist. He addressed the cat sternly. "Ansgar and I have to leave for a short time. You will remain here and guard Adara and Evangeline while we are gone. Understood?"

"Meow."

"Good. You will alert us at the first hint of trouble. Do not attempt to engage the djegrali on your own. If other humans arrive, disguise yourself. Is that clear?"

"Meow."

Brand put the cat down on the counter. He leaned over and gave Addy a hard kiss. "We will return shortly. You should be safe here for the time being. Do not leave this place."

He strode to the door and looked at Ansgar over his shoulder. "Brother?"

Ansgar nodded. He tugged Evie into his arms and kissed her. "To hold the taste of you in my memory until I return," he murmured, releasing her.

Evie watched him leave, a goofy grin on her face.

"Hello, Earth to Evie." Addy waved her hand in Evie's face. "Spill it, girl. What's going on with you and Blondy?"

"He has a name, Addy. It's Ansgar."

Addy rolled her eyes. "Oh, all right. What's up with you and Ansgar?"

Evie blushed rosily. "Oh, Addy, I'm so happy!"

"You and Blondy had sex, didn't you?"

"Addy!"

"Well, didn't you? Sorry to be so blunt, but I don't have time to beat around the bush, if you'll excuse the pun. Brand is Mr. Over Protective. He won't stay gone long."

Evie walked over to her display table and made a business of straightening her soaps. "Yes, to answer your question, and it was wonderful. More wonderful than I could have imagined." She whirled around, her lips trembling. "I didn't expect to feel this way. I'm so happy and . . . and, at the same time, *terrified*. What am I going to do, Addy?"

Addy hurried across the room and gave Evie a quick hug. "I know how you feel. It's been a crazy couple of days."

Evie chuckled and wiped her eyes. "You can say that again. Remember how we used to moan and groan about nothing happening in Hannah? We sure can't say that anymore." She gave Addy a curious look. "What about you? Have you and Brand . . . uh, you know?"

"Yep, we have definitely 'you know-ed.' And, that's all I'm going to say about it, except that I'm crazy about the big jerk and I don't know how I'm going to stand it when he leaves."

Evie sighed. "I know what you mean."

"Evie, I have so much to tell you. Muddy's back in town. And you were absolutely right. I shouldn't have gone off alone. Ghouly Farris was waiting for me, and Brand turned into a fire monster and there was a big fight and he pulled Dwight's head off, and the two of them wrecked the shop."

Evie blinked. "Slow down, Addy. Dwight Farris was waiting for you? Here?"

Addy nodded and launched into a condensed version of all that had happened since Saturday afternoon, telling Evie about the demon attack and Brand going berserk, and Ansgar repairing the damage to her shop.

"And when I got up yesterday morning, Muddy was sitting in the living room and Mr. Fluffy was a flying cat, and Jebediah Hannah was on the front lawn," she said, winding things up. "The demon cut Jeb's head off and left him as some kind of sick-o demon message that he's not through with me." Addy shivered. "The police are at Muddy's guarding Old Jeb until the folks downtown can figure out how to move him. Oh, and Dan Curtis has a crush on me—how weird is that?—and Muddy and Mr. Collier have secretly been in love with each other for thirty years, and Mr. C has quit drinking because he knows the demons are real and he's not crazy, and he and Muddy are getting married." She took a deep breath and blew it out again. "There. I think that's about it."

Evie stared at her openmouthed. "Wow that was some weekend."

"Meow." Crossing his front paws, the fairy cat assumed a wide, fake grin and turned into a figurine.

"How 'bout that? Mr. Fluffy has made himself a bobble head. What do you think it means?" Evie's eyes grew round, and she grabbed Addy by the arm. "Oh, my goodness, Addy, what if it's the *demon*. What do we do?"

Addy looked out the window with a feeling of dread. "It's a demon, all right," she said.

The bell on the front door jingled angrily, and the Death Starr walked in.

Chapter Twenty-six

Meredith waddled up and slammed her purse down on the counter. Mr. Fluffy's head bobbed up and down.

"Hey, watch what you're doing." Addy laid a protective hand over the kitten. "This is a very special bobble head, I'll have you know."

"I don't give a hoot in Hades about your tacky little bobble head, Addy Jean Corwin. You take this curse off me."

"No idea what you're talking about, Meredith." Addy looked her up and down. "Nice muu-muu, by the way. Living on the edge though, aren't we? I mean, going around town in a housecoat. You know how big Trey is on appearances."

"Don't you dare make fun of me!" Meredith fidgeted with the front of the hot pink terrycloth bag she wore. "I hate you! It's all your fault I have to wear this ugly old thing. Nothing else is comfortable, because of the . . . the . . ."

"Gi-normous bumps on your butt?" Addy widened her eyes at Meredith. "Humongous boils on your backside?"

Meredith pounded her fist on the counter, and Mr. Fluffy's head moved crazily up and down. "I can't stand it! I can't sleep. I can't sit down. Make it go away, or I'll ruin you. So help me, I will, if it's the last thing I do."

Addy raised her brows. "Listen to what you're saying, Meredith. You're blaming me because you got pimples on your butt. That's crazy."

"You did this because you're jealous."

"Jealous? Of what?"

"Of *me*. That I married Trey and you didn't. You've hated me since I took him away from you in high school."

Addy laughed. "That's funny. Sorry to burst your bubble, Meredith, but I don't want Trey. I lost interest in him when I caught the two of you boning in the backseat of his car. What I *do* want is an apology. Tell Evie you're sorry you were so rude to her, and I'll bet your little—er—dermatological problem goes away."

Meredith slid Evie a venomous look. "Apologize to that disgusting pig? I'd sooner eat roadkill."

Addy shrugged. "Suit yourself. But I think I should warn you that spite is a very negative emotion. Poisons the whole system. Why, there's no telling where you might break out next."

Meredith's eyes narrowed. "Don't you threaten me, Addy Corwin. You fix this, or I'll make you sorry you were born."

"Sorry, no can do." Addy propped her elbows on the counter. "Say, Meredith, what's that on your face? You getting your period? 'Cause it looks like Zit City from here."

Meredith's hands flew to her face. "No! What have you done?"

Hobbling over to a mirror, she stared at her reflection in horror. Dozens of angry-looking red pimples erupted on her once flawless skin. A huge ugly bump swelled on the end of her nose and burst.

"Eww, that's gross." Addy shook her head. "Negativity is a very destructive emotion. Gosh, wouldn't it be terrible if you got a zit on your face for every time you've been ugly to Evie? Why, that would mean hundreds of zits, maybe thousands! I'd work on that negativity if I were you. Try and find your happy place."

"I'll get you for this, Addy Corwin!" Meredith raged. "And you, too, Whaley Douglass." She looked around the room and spied Evie's neatly arranged wares on a nearby display table. Stomping over, she swept her arm across the tabletop, scattering soaps and lotions and scented oils onto the floor. "I'll get you both for this, if it's the last thing I do."

Turning on her heel, she stalked across the room. She

snatched Mr. Fluffy off the counter and hurled him against the wall. He bounced off with a muted squeak and took flight. Spreading his wings, the furious kitten dive-bombed her like a crazed mockingbird protecting its nest.

"What is that thing? Go away!" Meredith shrieked and batted at the flying cat. "Make it go away!"

"I told you not to mess with the merchandise," Addy said.

Mr. Fluffy made another swoop, and the Death Starr ran screaming out the door.

The enemy routed, the outraged kitten spit and burbled like a kettle, then settled back down on the counter.

Addy gently stroked his fur. "Mr. Fluffy, I owe you an apology. You are a magnificent guardian."

"Meow," Mr. Fluffy said, and vanished.

The air shimmered and Ansgar and Brand appeared, weapons drawn.

Brand looked around. "I heard a noise. Is something amiss?"

"Addy put the whammy on the Death Starr," Evie said in tones of awe. "It was so cool."

Brand frowned. "I do not understand. Explain."

"Meredith came in acting all ugly and stuff and Addy gave her what for." Evie giggled. "You should have seen the way Meredith walked."

"Like a constipated duck," Addy said.

"Quack, quack." Evie's eyes brimmed with laughter. "Oh, I know it's mean of me to laugh, but it was *so* funny."

Brand visibly relaxed. "Ah, I see. The unpleasant female with the viperous tongue was here. Adara, it does not behoove you to use your abilities to torment humans."

Addy snorted. "Meredith isn't *human*. Besides, she had it coming. She's been hateful to Evie since the seventh grade."

"Do not be too hard on Adara, brother." Ansgar put his arm around Evie. "I remember the creature. She is most unpleasant."

"Unpleasant?" Addy repeated. "That's an understatement. She's a giant, moon-size carbuncle on the ass end of mankind, that's what she is. Now, where's my food?"

Brand re-sheathed his sword. "I regret to say that in our haste to return we did not obtain sustenance."

"Damn," Addy said. "Whammying the Death Starr gives me the munchies."

Evie and Ansgar stayed behind to mind the flower shop while Addy attended the Farris funeral at 10:30 Monday morning. Generally, she avoided such things like the plague, but this was one dead guy she wanted to personally see put in the ground. And she was nervous about the whole mutilated corpse thing. What if Shep hadn't been able to reattach Dwight's head? She imagined Shirley running around Corwin's, her husband's severed head dangling from one plump, pink hand, and his . . .

She shivered, her mind balking at the terrible image.

Brand accompanied her to the funeral home, looking disgustingly gorgeous in his blue dress shirt and black slacks. The guy was a major hunk, no matter what he wore, but in dress duds he was a killer. Every time Addy looked at him, her eyeballs did a little happy dance in their sockets and her hormones went into overload. To her disgust, all the females at Corwin's had a similar reaction. And a few *males,* too, she noticed, taking mental notes about who was and was *not* out of the closet in Hannah. In fact, she suspected there might have been a stampede if they'd been anywhere other than a funeral home.

Addy went straight to the chapel, a two-hundred-fifty-seat space decorated in traditional funeral home blah. Canned music floated out of the speakers mounted in the four corners of the room. The blond paneling on the walls gleamed softly in the muted light from the arched windows. The flowers had been moved from the viewing room and lined up on one side of the pulpit in anticipation of the service. Working quickly, Addy made a few last-minute repairs to the arrangements and hurried to take a seat beside Brand on a cushioned pew in the back of the room. The casket was rolled past the Farris family members and placed in front of the wall of flowers. Shep came in bearing a large, framed picture of Dwight Farris. He placed the picture on an easel and stepped back. Addy studied the likeness. Young Dwight looked a lot like Dinky, sans mullet. There was one gene pool she wouldn't want to take a dip in.

Shep turned, and Addy stifled a gasp. Although he was dressed with his customary care, his hair smooth and polished, something about him seemed *different*. The expression on his face startled Addy. He looked beatific . . . serene. Heck, Big Bro looked *stoned*. Shep wasn't into drugs or a big boozer. Still, it had been a stressful forty-eight hours, what with Dwight disappearing and showing back up decapitated. Who could blame Shep if he had a little something before the funeral? Poor guy was probably petrified Dwight would lose his head again.

Shep's weird behavior increased Addy's anxiety. She needed to *know* that Dwight was dead. She wanted to see the head. Shirley was bound to notice if Dwight didn't have a head. Sure, *she* cut things off the poor guy. Important things, Dwight's *favorite* thing, rumor had it. But that didn't mean anyone else was allowed to do it. So, when the eerie wailing from the phantom organ overhead intensified and, one by one, people began to drift out of the pews to file past the dearly departed and pay their respects, Addy got up and got in line.

Shirley stood at the head of the casket accepting condolences. Dressed in a powder-blue, double-knit dress with a belt and shoes to match, she clasped a shiny patent leather blue purse in one hand and a white lace hanky in the other. Addy couldn't help but wonder if Shirley had *it* in the bag. Knowing Shirley, the answer was probably yes.

With a combination of morbid curiosity and dread, Addy shuffled closer to the body. Reaching the deceased at last, she sent up a prayer that the dead guy cooties wouldn't jump out of the casket and permanently stick to her eyeballs and looked down. Dead dude's head was right where it ought to be. Dwight's eyes were closed, thank you, Lord Jesus. One of the worst things about Ghouly Farris had been that horrible wet, purple-black gaze, like liquid evil. As she gazed upon Dwight's waxen features, she realized something. She was nose to nose with a dead guy, and she hadn't fainted or run screaming out of the room or thrown up. Her fear of dead people was gone. She still wasn't crazy about the living-impaired, but she could deal. Huh. How about that? Her little run-in with Ghouly Farris probably had something to do with it. Nothing like rolling around on the floor with a flesh-eating dead guy to cure a girl of necrophobia. Immersion therapy at its best.

She inspected the corpse critically. For a guy who'd been emasculated, demonically possessed, beheaded, and barbecued, Old Man Farris didn't look half bad. The gray suit was a definite improvement over the cheap polyester nightmare Widow Farris had put him in. His cheeks had been restuffed and the damage to his mouth repaired. Super-glue was good stuff. Her big brother was some kind of freaking funeral home genius, because the only evidence of the ugly gash between Dwight's lower lip and chin was a single thin line that looked like a scar. The collar hid Dwight's neck, so Addy couldn't tell how Shep had reattached the head. She suspected duct tape was involved. Southerners use duct tape for everything from patching mufflers and hemming pants to wart removal. There were rumors floating around town that Darryl Wilson had once used Saran Wrap and duct tape to create a super condom. The duct tape stuck to his skin, so the story went, and Darryl and the Silver Surfer ended up at the ER in Paulsberg.

Various family members and friends had left little offerings in the casket with Dwight, a kind of Great Beyond travel kit. There was a pack of apple-flavored Skoal, a pair of nail clippers, a fountain pen—Wha? Did they think the guy was going to *write?*—a bag of circus peanuts, a box of Good & Plenty, a girlie magazine, and a jar of spiced peaches. The edge of a photograph peeked out of Dwight's lapel pocket. Addy bent over for a better look. It was a picture of Dwight standing next to Bessie Mae. In the photo, Bessie Mae wore black, leather-look, spandex leggings, a leopard print tube top, and five-inch black stilettos. A cheetah print headband separated the front of her jet-black, cotton-candy hair from the high poof of sprayed and teased hair in the back. Dwight had a death grip on one of

Bessie Mae's boobs. Like he was afraid it might escape or something. Girlfriend had a terminal case of camel toe. Addy could practically read the woman's lips.

Addy glanced over at Shirley. Clueless, bless her heart. Bessie Mae was like the Stealth Bomber of girlfriends, able to penetrate the enemy's defenses, nuke 'em, and glide back out again without being seen.

Mama appeared out of nowhere at Addy's elbow. Mama was a Stealth Bomber, too. Real sneaky like Bessie Mae, only without the camel toe, thank God. Mama's genitalia would never betray her in such an uncouth manner. Growing up, Addy was certain Mama was a smoothie, like Barbie. No hootie at all.

"Move along, Addy," Mama said. "You're holding up the line. You want to make a scene?"

A scene at the Farris funeral? Heaven forbid. Addy gave Shirley a sympathetic smile and sat back down.

Three preachers, two yowling soloists, and an hour and a half later, Addy and Brand waited at River Oaks Cemetery for Old Dwight to be interred. Located at the edge of the older part of town, the cemetery had been built at the turn of the twentieth century on the slopes of a gentle hill. Hundred-year-old oaks shaded the lots. The Farris plot was one of the newer ones situated at the front of the cemetery on a small rise. Shep stood to one side of the prepared grave, his expression unnaturally placid. The sarcophagus was removed from the hearse by eight deacons from the Cleansing Waters Baptist Church—referred to by the irreverent as Massengill Baptist—and placed in the center of the tent that covered the gravesite. The pallbearers stood sharply at attention as the family members exited their vehicles and seated themselves in fabric-covered chairs under the awning and out of the heat. Everyone else was allowed to bake.

Addy looked around. It was past noon on a blistering Alabama summer day. The heat index was one hundred and ten in the shade and the humidity was so thick the air was breathed in chunks. Everybody was sweating buckets except her and Brand. Score another one for Dalvahni DNA. She looked back at Shep and frowned. It was one thing to adopt a funereal demeanor as part of his job as funeral director, but Shep didn't look solemn. He looked like nobody was home.

She made a mental note to check on her big brother as yet another preacher mumbled something over the body. At last, Shirley and the rest of the Farrises got up to leave. Someone pushed past Addy. It was Bessie Mae Brown. She'd gone all out for the funeral, pouring herself into a hot pink bustier that displayed an acre of tanned, wrinkled cleavage, a clingy midriff-length short-sleeve sweater in bright lemon yellow, a tight, short black skirt, and open-toed pink pumps. The pleather on the four-inch plastic heels had started to peel. Her signature barrette roosted at the back of her nest of black hair.

Bessie Mae tottered onto the white gravel walkway and right into Shirley's path.

"Uh oh," Addy muttered. "It's fixing to hit the fan."

Dinky and his brothers took one look at the two women and darted off like startled rabbits. Clumps of sweating funeralgoers hesitated, their fascination with the imminent outbreak of hostilities clearly at odds with their desire to escape the brutal heat.

Shirley's china doll eyes narrowed. "What do you want, Delilah?"

"Between the two of us, you're the one who's scissor happy, not me. What else did you cut off the poor man before you buried him? Serve you right if he haunts your ass."

Shirley's grip tightened on the blue purse. "I got the only part you were interested in, you trollop. That's all you need to know."

"That right?" Bessie Mae gave Shirley an evil smile. "Checked that deep freeze in your garage lately?"

Shirley stiffened. "What do you mean?"

"Oh, I don't know, thought you might have missed *this.*" Bessie Mae plucked a neatly wrapped brown paper package out of her pink and yellow purse. "It says, 'Dwight's weenie. Do not microwave,' on it. That's real thoughtful, Shirley. Wouldn't want anyone to mistake poor Dwight's manhood for a leftover hotdog or an old pork chop, would you?"

"Give me that weenie."

"I don't think so."

Shirley swung her purse at Bessie Mae's head. "You give me that weenie, Bessie Mae Brown."

Bessie Mae waved the package at Shirley. "Wiener, wiener, who's got the wiener? Ooh, whadda yah know? Looks like *I* do!"

It was like waving a red cape in front of a bull. Shirley lowered her gray, sausage-curled head and charged. Bessie Mae took off at a wobbly run with Shirley hard on her heels. Shep gave them a bland smile and stepped smoothly to one side. Bessie Mae darted past him and under the tent. She made a lap around the casket with Shirley in hot pursuit.

"Tramp!" Shirley screeched as they made a second loop. Her pink bow mouth was drawn back in a snarl. "White trash bimbo!"

"Call me all the names you want, you crazy old heifer," Bessie Mae panted. "I got my Sugar Scrotum's lollipop, and I ain't giving it back!"

"Stop this, both of you. Stop this unseemly behavior at once." Deacon Forrest Hewlett pointed his finger at Bessie Mae as she rounded the bend. "Mend your wanton ways, Jezebel. Lest the dogs lap at thy flesh."

"Oh, blow it out your ass, you old fart," Bessie Mae said.

She pancaked him as she went by with a hard thrust of her elbow. He plowed into Deacon Samford, who fell into the man behind him. *Boom, boom, boom.* Eight deacons toppled like dominoes. Shirley caught up with Bessie Mae, grabbed the back of her bright yellow sweater, and yanked. Bessie Mae pitched backward into Shirley. Shirley made a grab for the package.

Bessie Mae held the package out of Shirley's reach. "Oh, hell no you don't."

Shirley squealed in frustration and wrapped her arms around Bessie Mae's neck. Bessie Mae grabbed hold of Shirley's ample waist. The two women careened drunkenly around the tent, clinging to one another like a couple of winded boxers in the tenth round. Shirley slammed Bessie Mae into a support pole. Bessie Mae grabbed Shirley by the hair. They staggered back,

snapping and snarling. Bessie Mae caught her heel on the rumpled carpet and crashed on top of the casket, taking Shirley with
her. Dwight's casket tilted sideways and slid to the ground. The
weakened support pole buckled, and the tent collapsed.

Muffled squeaks and grunts and more than one un-deacon-
like swear word were heard from those trapped under the tent.
Smiling sweetly, Shep threw back his head back and sang.

We are one in the Spirit,
We are one in the Lord.
And we pray that all unity may one day be restored.

His rich baritone floated down the hill, swelling as he reached
the chorus.

And they'll know we are Christians
By our love, by our love,
Yes, they'll know we are Christians by our love.

"Tart," Shirley wheezed from beneath the folds of the fallen
tent.

"Fat ass," Bessie Mae said.

Chapter Twenty-seven

Addy and Brand made their way down the graveled path behind the flow of mourners streaming back to their cars. She'd parked the delivery van, a Pepto-Bismol pink monstrosity that came with the shop, under a tree so the vehicle wouldn't overheat. A blistering steering wheel and a car seat like molten lava were not her idea of comfort.

Herbert Duffey and Jefferson Davis Willis trailed at the back of the departing crowd. Addy and Brand soon caught up with them. Addy slowed her pace. The last time she'd seen Mr. Duffey, Brand had announced to anyone within earshot that she and Brand were going to have sex. Like that, twenty-seven years of staying on the down low gone faster than a green bean casserole at a Methodist covered-dish dinner.

She and Brand did have sex, but that was beside the point. The point was she was crazy about Brand. She didn't regret having sex with him one minute, but she couldn't face Mr. Duffey without her face catching on fire. Muddy was right. She was a hopeless fuddy duddy, so small town it was pathetic. What hope did a girl like her have of maintaining the interest of a man like Brand? The guy was ten thousand years old, for Pete's sake. He probably had so many notches on his bed post the damn thing was a toothpick.

Mr. Duffey, thank God, hadn't seen them yet. The path was uneven, and he kept his eyes and his cane on the ground. Mr. Willis did likewise. With any luck, maybe they wouldn't notice her. Maybe they—

Brand stepped forward and took the two old men by the elbow. "The path is rough, gentlemen. Allow me to assist you down the hill."

Mr. Duffey peered up at Brand. "Thank you, young man. Jefferson, this is Addy's beau, the one I told you about."

Translation: This is the guy Addy's humping. Oh, God, maybe she would move to New Zealand. Maybe she'd join the Peace Corps, become a missionary in the Congo, or join the circus. She'd become a rodeo clown. Yeah. Nobody would recognize her under all that makeup. Too bad there really wasn't a cow pie mushroom drug cartel in Hannah. She could turn government snitch and join the witness protection program. Move to North Dakota and never have to look at Herbert Duffey again. Uff da.

"Nice to meet you," Mr. Willis said.

Mr. Duffey peered over his shoulder. "That you, Addy?"

Busted. Oh, well, might as well get it over with.

She hurried to Mr. Duffey's side. "Yes, sir. It's me." She took him by the arm. "How you holding up in this heat?"

"I'm making it. That was some funeral, wasn't it?"

"Yes, sir, it sure was."

"When I die, I want them same three preachers at my funeral," Mr. Willis announced.

Mr. Duffey gave him a startled sideways look. "Why in tarnation would you want to do that, Jefferson?"

" 'Cause if I ain't dead, I'll climb right out of that coffin and kick them Sunday jawers in the ass." Mr. Willis slammed his cane on the ground for emphasis. "Never seen such a windy bunch of fellers. And if the sermonizing wasn't bad enough, every one of 'em prayed at the end. I counted thirty-seven 'Jesus-We-Justs.' "

Mr. Duffey shook his head. "Remind me not to outlive you. I ain't sitting through another one like that, not without the Shirley and Bessie Mae show. Funniest damn thing I've seen since Beau Shackleford's wife caught him with another woman. You remember that, Jefferson?"

Mr. Willis snorted. "Reckon I do. She knocked him out

with a frying pan, painted him red, and rode him naked through town on the back of a mule."

"Nekked," Mr. Duffey corrected. He blinked at Brand through his thick glasses. "You know the difference between 'naked' and 'nekked,' young man?"

"No."

"When you're naked you ain't got no clothes on," Mr. Duffey said. "When you're 'nekked' you ain't got no clothes on and you up to something."

"I see," Brand said, although it was obvious he did *not*.

"Dude, it's a Southern-ism," Addy said.

Brand's expression grew distant, like he was cross-referencing Mr. Willis's comment against his Dalvahni translator.

And maybe he was, because a moment later he nodded. "I see. 'Up to something,' as in 'unclad and engaged in lascivious and/or questionable behavior.' It is quite humorous, is it not?"

"A real stitch," Addy said. "Especially when you put it that way."

Mr. Willis eyed Brand. "How 'bout you? You up to something with our Addy?"

"If he ain't, I sure would like to be." Darryl Wilson sauntered up with his brothers Dean and Del. Darryl nudged Del. "Told you she was fine, didn't I? Uh uh uh, I'd like to get me some of that."

"Hint for the future, Darryl," Addy said dryly. " 'I'd like to get me some of that' almost never works with women. Neither does, 'Yo, sweet thang, wanna ride my baloney pony?' "

"Ooh, she knows all your lines, baby brother," Dean said. "You got burned."

Darryl scowled. "Shut up, D."

All the Wilson brothers called each other "D," maybe because they had as hard a time keeping their names straight as everybody else. The Wilson brothers were long on beef and short on brains.

Del made a rude noise. "You're a dumbass, D. Raeleene catches you with another woman she'll have your ass for lunch. She's meaner than a snake in heat."

Darryl scowled. "Who you calling dumbass, dumbass?"

Addy heard a low rumbling sound in the distance. She glanced at Brand. Uh oh. He had that pissed-off predator look. The Wilson brothers had stepped in it for sure.

"Go away," Brand said.

The Wilsons forgot their differences and turned their attention to him.

Dean, the biggest of the three brothers, frowned at Brand. "Biggest" being a relative term, of course. All the Wilson boys were built like bulldozers.

"What did you say, pretty boy?" Dean said, hiking his britches up over his belly.

"Go away," Brand said again.

Dean advanced on Brand. "Why don't you try and make me, Hollywood."

"Very well."

Brand released Mr. Willis's arm and took Dean down hard and fast. One moment Dean stood in front of Brand, three hundred fifty pounds of hulking testosterone and bubba menace, and the next he was out like a light. Afterward, Addy could hardly say how it happened. The same could be said of Dean. He never saw it coming. Even with her new and improved vision, all Addy saw was a blur of movement followed by the solid, meaty sound of flesh on flesh, and Dean hit the ground.

Darryl and Del stared at their brother in shock, then threw themselves at Brand. Brand stepped in front of Mr. Willis. Grabbing Darryl and Del by the hair, he slammed their heads together and tossed them to the ground like a couple of rag dolls.

Darryl and Del groaned and rolled to a sitting position.

Brand towered over them. "Apologize to Adara and the old ones for your behavior." Brand gave the unconscious Dean a scathing glance. "Your brother, I will excuse this once."

Darryl and Del mumbled something that sounded like "sorry."

Addy hurried over to the fallen brothers. "You boys all right?"

She checked Dean and was relieved to find him breathing.

Darryl held his head in his hands. "No, I think I got me a concussion. Shit, my head hurts. Jesus H. Christ, who is this guy, Addy?"

"You watch your language, Darryl Wilson, or I'll tell your mama," Mr. Duffey said.

"Sorry," Darryl muttered a little clearer.

Brand picked Addy up and set her down away from Darryl. "Do not touch the cur, Adara. I saw his thoughts. He wants to fornicate with you." He pointed to Del. "This one also."

Del squinted painfully at Brand. "Hate to break it to you, Mister, but anybody with a dick that don't bat for the other team will want to do her. She's a real hottie." He dropped his head in his hands again. "No offense, Addy."

"None taken, Del."

"It offends me." Brand gave Darryl and Del a death glare. "Adara is under my protection. Stay away from her, or the consequences will be most unpleasant. Do I make myself plain?"

Darryl and Del gaped at him.

"Answer me, louts," Brand said. "Do you understand?"

They nodded.

"Good. Adara, we are leaving."

Addy glared at him. "Way to mark your territory, dude. Next time, why don't you pee on me and be done with it?"

Brand ignored her and helped the two old men to Mr. Duffey's land yacht, an emerald-green 1976 Cadillac Fleetwood in mint condition.

Mr. Duffey gingerly lowered himself into the driver's seat and waited as Mr. Willis climbed in on the other side. The engine rumbled to life. He rolled down his window. "I like the way you handled yourself back there, young man," he said to Brand. "All in all, this has been one peach of a funeral. Ain't had this much fun since the pigs ate my little brother."

Mr. Willis stuck a bony arm out the passenger-side window and waved. "Me, neither."

Mr. Duffey made a wide circle in the grass and motored off. Brand watched them leave with a puzzled expression.

Taking him by the hand, Addy led him over to the van. "The pigs didn't really eat his brother, Brand. He was being funny. Mr. Duffey has four sisters."

"Yes, *now* that the swine has eaten—"

"*Ever*, Brand. He was an only son."

"Humans are most strange. They rarely say what they mean, or mean what they say."

"You can say that again."

"Very well, although I do not see the point. Humans are most—"

She pushed him against the van and shushed him with her mouth. "That whole 'I am warrior, hear me roar' thing you did back there got me going. You ever had sex in the back of a van, big guy?"

"No."

"Ooh, a virgin. What say we pop your van cherry? I know a place down by the river that's cool and quiet. I can have my wicked way with you before we go back to the shop."

He tugged her closer and nuzzled her neck. "I like your wicked way. Is popping a van cherry anything like hot monkey sex?"

"If you want to know, get in the van."

By the time they got back to the shop it was close to one thirty. Evie was writing something down on an order pad while Ansgar slouched lazily on a nearby stool. He watched Evie as if she was the most fascinating creature in the world. Wow, poor Blondy had it bad. She almost felt sorry for him.

Almost.

Evie looked up. " 'Bout time you two got back. I was getting worried. That must have been some funeral."

Addy flashed her a smile. "Oh, you know how it is. These things always take longer than you expect."

"You look flushed. You get overheated?"

"Noooo . . . Well, maybe a little."

"Uh huh."

Oh, God, Evie knew. Probably the multiorgasm glow on her face gave her away. She might as well have a neon sign on her forehead that blinked: ATTENTION. ADDY GOT LAID. She'd never look at that old van the same way again. She and Brand almost broke the back axel. It was the Van of the Sacred Hump, the Scream Machine, the Pink Passion Pit, a palace of love on four wheels.

Might as well brazen it out.

"Anything exciting happen at the shop while we were gone?" she asked.

A tell-tale blush crept up Evie's neck and spread to her cheeks. "Oh, you know, the usual."

"The usual" her hind foot. Girlfriend and Blondy had been having sex, too.

"So, Brand," Evie said brightly. "What did you think of your first Southern funeral?"

"Most enlightening. I found the sepulchral speeches a bit tedious, but the part at the end where the two females chased one another around the burial ground was quite interesting."

Evie's eyes widened. "Who—"

"But, my favorite part was when Adara took me down to the river and popped my van cherry."

Note to self: Explain the meaning of TMI to new boyfriend. If Evie had any doubts about what she and Brand had been doing, the Dalvahni blabber mouth dispelled them. Thank goodness it was only Blondy and Evie. Evie was her BFF and Blondy merely looked confused. Now, if Brand had said it in front of Mama that would be a different story. She'd get lecture number 238 from the Mama Handbook about the cow and the milk and giving it away for free, and how all things come to those who wait but she hadn't waited, so she'd get bupkis.

As if on cue, the front bell jingled and Muddy and Bitsy walked in.

"Mr. Dalvahni, fancy meeting you here," Bitsy said, turning on the charm. Uh oh, Mama was up to something. "You and my daughter seem to be joined at the hip these days. Everybody in town is talking about what a beautiful couple you two make."

She gave a tinkling little laugh. "Why, I wouldn't be one bit surprised if I'm planning another wedding in the near future."

Of course. Matchmaking, that's what she was up to. Mama was on a mission from God to get her hitched.

"Mama, Brand and I only met three days ago."

Three days. Had it really only been three days?

"Oh, well, I believe in being prepared." Bitsy turned to Ansgar. "And who might you be, young man?"

He stood and made a little bow. "I am Ansgar. I am Dalvahni."

Bitsy's eyes widened. "Dalvahni? Oh, you must be Mr. Dalvahni's brother. My goodness, you don't look a thing alike, do you? Are you staying at the Hannah Inn, too?"

"I stay with Evangeline."

"Really, Evie dear, is that wise?" Bitsy lifted her finely arched brows. "You know how people talk. A reputation is a delicate thing."

Hah, lecture number 239. More of a codicil, really, than a separate lesson, a clarification of lecture number 238.

Poor Evie turned red and began to stutter.

"The Hannah Inn was full, Mama, so Ansgar is renting a room at Evie's," Addy said, coming to the rescue.

"Adara, I do not think—"

Addy held up her hand. "I know, I know, Brand. You don't think Evie's charging him enough for the room. But, that's between *the two of them*." She emphasized each word. "*Their* business, not Mama's, if you know what I mean."

"I understand," he said. But there was disapproval in his eyes.

Addy swallowed a sigh. They were so unalike. He was Mr.-I-Cannot-Tell-A-Lie, and she was the Mistress-Of-Little-Fibs. But, he didn't know her mama. Let him live a few thousand years with Bitsy, and he'd be lying like a rug. As far as she was concerned, white lies were a matter of survival when it came to dealing with Mama. He could get over it.

"I had no idea you were running a bed-and-breakfast, Evie," Bitsy said.

Evie looked more flustered. "Well, I'm not exactly—"

"But I'm delighted to hear it." Bitsy bulldozed right over Evie. "I'm sure Addy has told you that Muddy and Amasa Collier are getting married. We might need to book a room or two, depending on who comes into town for the wedding."

"Land's sake, Bitsy, who in the world you think is coming to this wedding?" Muddy asked.

"Scads of people. No one will want to miss this." Bitsy set her purse down. "Now, let's talk flowers for the bridal luncheon and the wedding."

"Ansgar and I will wait outside while you converse," Brand said.

He scooted out the door with Ansgar hard on his heels. He was such a guy. The merest mention of girly stuff, and he bolted.

"Oh, but the heat—" Bitsy protested.

Addy put her hand on Mama's arm. "Let them go, Mama. I don't think they want to listen to a bunch of women talk about flowers."

Bitsy wrinkled her brow. "Too frou-frou?"

"Definitely," Addy said.

Thirty minutes later, they were winding things up when Brand tapped on the front window and pointed down the street. A minute later, Meredith Peterson walked through the door looking like Death eating a cracker. She'd exchanged the pink terrycloth housecoat for a loose shift of pale blue linen. A heavy layer of makeup covered the mass of pimples on her face. The Queen of the Hannah social scene looked like the Joker.

Bitsy's mouth fell open when she saw Meredith, but she quickly schooled her features into an expression of bland welcome. "Meredith, what a pleasant surprise," she said. "How are you doing?"

"I look like something out of a horror movie. How do you think I'm doing?"

"Now that you mention it, you do seem to have some sort of rash," Bitsy said. "Have you tried Calamine lotion?"

Muddy inspected Meredith. "That's no ordinary rash. Looks like impetigo to me. You'd best get yourself down to Old Doc Dunn and get an antibiotic, girl."

"It's not a rash." Meredith glared at Addy. "It's a curse your witch of a daughter put on me, Bitsy Corwin."

"Addy, a witch?" Bitsy tittered. "You must be joking."

"Mad as a hatter," Muddy declared. "She probably has syphilis. That philandering husband of hers probably gave it to her."

"I do *not* have syphilis," Meredith shrieked.

Addy held up her finger in warning. "Inside voice, Mer."

Meredith gritted her teeth and tried to smile, which did scary things to the pancake makeup on her face. "I've come to apologize, Addy, and to ask you to take this curse off me."

"I don't believe I heard the magic word."

Meredith reddened under her thick makeup. "Please."

"Very nice, Meredith, but you're talking to the wrong person. It's Evie you owe an apology."

Meredith's face got redder. "I'm sorry I was ugly to Evie."

Addy considered this. "Nope, doesn't do it for me." She turned to Evie, who was staring at Meredith in fascinated horror. "What about you, Eves? That do it for you?"

Evie started. "Oh, well, I guess it—"

"Nope," Addy said. "Doesn't do it for Evie, either. You're going to have to do better than that, Meredith."

"Perhaps you should give me some idea what it is you want me to say, Addy."

Addy thought about this. "Okay, I guess that's only fair. And fun. Listen carefully, Meredith, and repeat after me. 'I'm sorry, Evie, that I've been such a poisonous bitch to you since we were twelve years old.'" She gave Meredith an encouraging nod. "Go on. Give it a try."

Meredith's expression was wooden, but she repeated the words.

"'And I'm sorry for all the hideous things I've said to you, especially the times I called you Lard Ass or Whaley Douglass or some other version of fat,'" Addy said. "'And I promise not to be mean or unkind to you again, and if I am, may the boils on my behind and on my face come back three times as bad.'"

Meredith's lip curled. She opened her mouth and Addy stopped her.

"Look at Evie when you say it, Mer," she said gently.

Meredith looked like she was trying to swallow her own head, but she did it.

Addy beamed at her. "Very good. Buy half a dozen bars of Evie's complexion soap and a jar of her special bath salts, and go home and have yourself a nice long soak. That should fix you right up. Make sure you use Evie's soap, or it won't work."

Evie scrambled over to her display table and quickly shoved the soaps and the bath salts into a bag. Meredith flung some money in Evie's direction and stalked out.

Bitsy looked thoughtful. "You know, Addy dear, I don't think Meredith likes you."

"No? You think?"

"I feel sorry for her."

Addy stared at her mother in surprise. "You do? Why? She always gets what she wants, including Trey."

"Sometimes you get what you think you want, and you find out too late it wasn't what you wanted at all," Bitsy said. "I think Meredith is very unhappy, in spite of being Mrs. Trey Peterson." She paused. "Or maybe *because* she's Mrs. Trey Peterson."

"He's got little ears and a skinny mouth," Muddy said. "My mama always said don't marry a man with little ears or a skinny mouth, 'cause he'll be mean. I'll bet that Trey Peterson is mean."

Bitsy nodded. "Could be."

"And I'll bet he's got a little dick," Muddy added.

Bitsy gasped. "Muddy! Such language!"

Muddy gave Addy a hopeful look. "Addy dated him in high school. Does he have a little penis?"

"Sorry to disappoint you, Muddy, but Trey and I never slept together."

Which, in fairness to Trey, was probably why he ended up banging Meredith. As a general rule, teenage boys were walking sperm banks looking for a place to deposit.

"You sure?" Muddy persisted. "You might not have noticed."

Addy rolled her eyes. "I'd have noticed. It never happened."

"Huh," Muddy said. "Well, if he's got a little dick that might have something to do with why Meredith is such a sour puss. Think about it. You'd be ornery, too, if you went to bed with a Vienna Sausage."

"Mercy." Bitsy fanned herself. "I'll never be able to look at Trey Peterson again."

"Forget that," Addy said. "I'll never be able to eat another Vienna Sausage."

Chapter Twenty-eight

Before Bitsy left the flower shop, she confided to Addy that she was worried about Shep. "He didn't come back to Corwin's after the funeral," she said. "And that's not like him."

"I'll go by the house and check on him after I close the shop, Mama," Addy promised.

Bitsy's worried expression eased. "Would you, dear? I'd go, but I don't want him to think I'm hovering. You know I try not to stick my nose into my children's business."

Oh, yeah, since when?

Mama was right, though, Addy thought as she went about the business of closing up for the day. It was not like Shep to blow off work. He was the consummate professional, always Mr. Cool. Today at Old Man Farris's funeral, however, he'd seemed distant, mechanical, like he was going through the motions.

Then there was the spontaneous singing thing. The Shep Corwin she knew didn't burst into song in public. Yet today he'd belted out a hymn like it was the most natural thing in the world. Something was going on with him, and Addy meant to find out what.

Shep and Marilee lived on the river outside of town about two miles from the gated community that Muddy called home. Addy and Brand bumped down the long, gravel drive in the pink van and pulled up to the house, a sprawling one-story cottage with a tin roof, triangular-shaped dormer windows in the front and back, and a wrap-around porch. She got out of the van and looked around. Shep's car was there, but the house showed no other signs of life. The wind blew through the trees and scattered a few dry leaves across the driveway. The air was fragrant with the scent of pine. From nearby, she heard the river's rough music, water over stone. She clunked up the steps to the porch. Brand followed silently behind her, his expression watchful. The shuttered windows were dark, empty eyes in the skull of the house. The porch swing creaked gently in the breeze.

"Shep?"

"'Round back," he hollered.

Breathing a sigh of relief, Addy moved toward the sound of Shep's voice, but Brand got in front of her.

"Wait. There is something amiss here. I sense a presence . . ." He shook his head. "I do not like it. I will go first in case there is trouble."

She grabbed his arm. "This is my brother we're talking about. Don't you even *think* about sticking him with that sword of yours. If he's infested with something nasty, deal with it some other way. Call the exterminator or hold a séance, but you're not—I repeat, *not*—shish-kabobbing Shep with that sword."

"I will do what I must to protect you."

Ignoring her sputtering protests, he strode off down the porch. She scurried after him. He rounded the corner and stopped abruptly, blocking her path.

"Lenora." There was surprise and unease in Brand's deep voice. "What brings you here?"

"Sol' Van," a sultry female voice murmured. "You and Ansgar did not report in as is customary."

Addy stiffened. Something about that low, sensual voice grated on her nerves. And what the heck was a soul van? Who was this woman, anyway? Addy disliked her, sight unseen. The fact that Brand and the sexpot were acquainted had nothing to do with it.

Okay, maybe it had *everything* to do with it, but that was beside the point.

"There were signs of an enemy engagement but no word from either of you," the woman continued. "Conall was otherwise occupied, and I was bored, so I volunteered my services. I found myself delightfully detained by this human."

Addy had heard enough. She stepped around Brand. A voluptuous woman with long, flowing black hair reclined on the back porch swing against a bank of chintz pillows. She was clad in one of Shep's white dress shirts . . . and from the looks of it, nothing else. Her left leg was draped along the back of the swing and her right leg was stretched out in front of her. She didn't strike Addy as the kind of woman who'd bother with a trifling thing like underwear. If Shep's shirttail had not hung between her legs, Addy suspected the woman's business would have been out there for God and everybody else to see. Her gaze shifted to the stranger's face, and she found herself pinned by a pair of cold, blue eyes. Talk about your glacial bitches. This gal was the Ice Queen.

Addy saw Shep and forgot about the woman. He stood in front of a large easel, shirtless and barefoot and covered in paint. There was an expression of utter joy on his face as he moved his brush across the canvas. The only time she'd seen him that happy was when his children were born.

"Shep?"

"One second, Addy." Shep's brow furrowed in concentration. "I'm al . . . most finished." A few more flourishes of his brush, and he stepped back. "There. What do you think, Nora?"

The woman called Lenora stretched like a cat and got to her feet. She was tall, nearly as tall as Shep, and she screamed sex from her red, pouty lips to the curtain of dark hair that swung about her hips. She stared at the canvas for a moment, and turned and wrapped her arms around Shep's neck.

"It is beautiful, my love." Her husky voice made Addy want to smack her. "So earthy and sensuous. Teeming with dark, swirling energy like the river that flows past your home."

"It's you," Shep stammered. "You're the river, full of mystery and promise, a slinky, curving enigma I can lose myself in."

Eww. Shep Corwin had him a demon, no bones about it. Maybe two or three. Her big brother would never talk that way unless he was possessed.

"You see me as the river?" Lenora's voice was a smooth whisper of invitation. "That is so sweet."

She pulled his head down and kissed him. And Shep kissed her back. Right in front of his little sister. Another minute and they'd be hunching like bunnies on the back porch steps. Shep, Mr. Conservative, a two-term member of the vestry at the Trinity Episcopal church, the perfect son, brother, father and husband . . .

"William Shepton Junior, have you lost your mind?" Addy shrieked. "Who *is* this woman, and where the hell is Marilee?"

Lenora released Shep and stepped back. "I am Lenora," she said. "Your brother has told me much about you, Adara Corwin. I am thrall. I serve the Dalvahni."

A red film blurred Addy's vision. A thrall, a sex slave indentured to the Dalvahni, created to serve them sexually and suck all the feelings out of them so they could return to battle unhampered by emotion.

And Brand knew her by name, which meant she'd serviced him in the past, would do so again once he left Earth.

Addy's brain felt like it was on fire. She wanted to scratch the other woman's eyes out. She wanted to tear her apart. So, this was jealousy, this great big snarling beast that consumed her from the inside out.

"Adara?" Brand said.

She took a deep breath. She needed to get a grip, set aside her own feelings and concentrate on the issue at hand. Her married big brother was screwing a sex machine from another dimension. Shep. Mr. Perfect, the good child.

Un-freaking-believable.

Shep seemed to wake from the spell the thrall had woven. "Addy, calm down. It's not what you think."

"Shep, where is Marilee?"

"She's gone, Addy." He picked up a clean cloth and wiped his hands. "Ran off three weeks ago with that tennis instructor from the club. She's filed for divorce. I got served with the papers last week."

"What?"

Brand cleared his throat. "Lenora, why don't you and I walk down to the river?"

Lenora lifted her shoulders in a gesture of cool indifference. "Very well, Sol' Van, if you insist."

Brand and the sexy thrall left the porch and walked down the sloping lawn to the shallow bluff that overlooked the river. Addy watched them leave with mixed feelings. Desperate as she was to talk to her brother in private, she didn't want Vampira anywhere near Brand.

Shep chuckled. "Relax, Addy, she's not going to eat him."

Addy scowled. "Damn straight she's not." With an effort, she dragged her attention back to Shep. "Now, what's this about Marilee leaving? I thought she was at the beach with her mother and the kids."

"Marilee's gone. She dropped the kids off at the beach house with Janice and took off. No one's heard from her since." He grimaced. "Unless you count the divorce papers."

Her brain scrambled to process the stunning news. "Lily and William?"

Shep shook his head. "They think their mama's here. They keep calling to talk to her and I keep making excuses. It's been a bad couple of weeks."

Addy sank into one of the rocking chairs that were scattered around the porch. "I had no idea you and Marilee were having problems."

"That makes two of us. I never saw it coming. Apparently, she's been carrying on with this guy for months." He laughed harshly. "When I think about all the money I spent on her stupid tennis lessons . . . I was paying the guy to screw my wife." He wadded up the cloth and threw it aside. "I tell you what, I get my hands on him, I'm gonna pound some sand up his ass."

"Are we talking about the new guy, the one the club brought over from Namath Springs? Curly hair and a tattoo on his arm?"

"Yep, that's the one."

"But Shep, he's younger than I am," Addy said. "He's—"

"Twenty-four. Ten years younger that Marilee." His expression was bitter. "But who's counting."

Addy couldn't think, couldn't focus. Shep and Marilee had been happily married for more than ten years. Marilee adored Shep. She was like a sister to Addy. It was hard to believe she had left Shep and the children to run off with another man. Was nothing what it seemed to be? The past few days, she'd been hammered by one shock after another, but this last one . . . She couldn't take this one in. Shep and Marilee divorced.

She jumped to her feet and paced up and down the porch, thinking. "Does Janice know? Did Marilee tell her mother where she was going, or did she dump Lily and William with her mom and leave?"

"She told Janice we needed some alone time and took off. Janice thought Marilee was here with me. I had to work late the night they left. I came in and went straight to bed. Didn't find the note until the next morning. I called Janice and told her what was up. She didn't believe me, not until Marilee called and told her mama she wasn't coming home. Janice and I talked about it and decided to keep quiet about it, not let the children know, in case . . ."

"In case she changed her mind?"

Shep blew out a breath. "Yeah, just in case. She didn't. Things were really bad for a while there, but then Nora showed up." His gaze drifted to Lenora and Brand down by the water. "Things are much better now. Clearer. I know what I want to do with my life."

"What do you mean 'do with your life'? You've got Corwin's."

"Corwin's has *me,* Addy. I didn't want it, but Daddy died and I didn't seem to have a choice. Then I got married and Lily and William were born, and it was easier to go with the flow. What I wanted didn't seem to matter, seemed . . . irresponsible, a pipe dream."

Addy stared at him in bewilderment. "What on earth are you talking about, Shep?"

His eyes lit up. "I want to paint, Addy."

"Paint?" She couldn't have been more surprised if he'd said he wanted to join the circus.

He rushed on. "Oh, I know I can't walk away from Corwin's

right now, but maybe someday, when I've established myself as an artist, I can sell the funeral home and open up a little studio."

"Sell Corwin's? Are you crazy?"

His jaw hardened. "You got to do what you wanted, Addy. It's my turn. You're not the only one who hates dead people, only I couldn't run down the street to Aunt Muddy. I had to stay. Somebody had to stay. I've given fifteen years of my life and my marriage to the business. Do I have to give it the rest of my life, too?"

"No, of course not." Addy felt sick with guilt and remorse. Shep was not quite twenty-one when Daddy died, she not quite twelve. She'd been so hell-bent on getting away from Corwin's she didn't stop to consider what Shep wanted. "I don't know what to say. I had no idea you were so miserable."

She flung herself in Shep's arms and burst into tears.

"There, there, sis, don't cry." He patted her awkwardly on the back. "You're getting my shirt all wet."

She gave a watery chuckle. "You're not wearing a shirt, smartass." Wiping her eyes, she straightened with a sniff. "So about this painting of yours. Are you any good?"

"Hell, sis, I don't know. You tell me."

He turned her around.

The canvas was a swirl of color, browns and greens and blue, the river in high summer set against a cloudless sky. Addy stared at the painting in shock. She was no expert, knew nothing about color, composition, technique, or brush strokes, but Shep's painting called to her, stirred her. The river on the canvas was a living thing, a gleaming, sinuous snake that coiled through the trees, a siren that lured men from their homes with the promise of wonders around the next bend.

"Wow," Addy said. "I am so embarrassed."

Shep's eyes twinkled. "That bad, huh? Gee, thanks, brat."

Addy shook her head. "I'm embarrassed because I didn't know you could draw stick people, much less paint something so wonderful. My own brother, and I'm clueless." She glared at Shep. "About a lot of things, apparently. How did you get mixed up with that—that *woman?*"

"Lenora?" Shep grinned like a jackass eating briars. "She showed up at Corwin's Saturday night. She's something else, isn't she?"

"She's a barracuda with legs, that's what she is. You be careful."

Lenora and Brand came back up the porch steps.

"What is this barracuda?" Lenora asked.

The thrall's silky voice crawled all over Addy. "It's a voracious fish with lots of sharp pointy teeth," she snapped, not bothering to be polite.

Lenora slithered up to Shep. "Your sister does not trust me. She thinks I mean you harm."

"I know what you are, what you *do*," Addy said. "You've turned him into some kind of zombie."

"Nonsense." Lenora pointed to the canvas. "Could a zombie paint something so passionate, so fierce and full of life? Your brother is quite good, is he not?"

It stuck in Addy's craw to admit it, but the thrall was right. "Yes, he is," she said gruffly. "So good, I mean to hang that painting in the shop, if he'll let me."

Shep's expression grew alarmed. "Slow down, sis. That's a big step. I don't know if I'm ready for that."

"Get ready." She hurried on, excited by the idea and eager to do something, *anything* to make up for her selfishness. "You haven't signed it. No one will know who did it. You said you wanted to open a studio some day. Lots of people come into the flower shop, people with money. I do business with folks from out in the county, and from Paulsberg and Namath Springs, and I go to market in Atlanta. Here's your chance to see if anyone will buy your work." She frowned impatiently when Shep remained silent. "Well, don't stand there like a knot on a log. You're the one who wants to be a painter. Put your money where your mouth is, Big Shot."

"Adara," Brand said.

Shep laughed. "Don't worry about it. It's just her way."

"Well?" Addy put her hands on her hips. "Are you a man or a mouse, bro? Come on, I dare you. I double-dog-dare you."

Shep rubbed his jaw thinking. "Nothing's dry yet, but in a week or two you can have your pick." He looked down and scuffed his bare foot against the porch floor. "That is, if you like any of them."

"There are more?" Addy said. "I want to see them now."

Lenora sank down on the swing, reclining once more against the cushions, all languid grace and sensuality. "I will wait here for you, Shep, my love. I find the river so peaceful."

Yeah, right. More like the succubus was lounging in the swing planning her next meal.

Addy followed Shep and Brand through the back door and into the den. Canvases in assorted shapes and sizes lined the wall and leaned up against the furniture.

Addy looked around the room in astonishment. "Shep, there must be ten or fifteen paintings here."

"I've been busy."

"Busy? You did all of this in the past few days?"

Shep nodded

"Impossible," Addy said.

"I was inspired."

Addy moved about the room, examining the paintings. They were all nudes of Lenora. There was *Lenora Reclining, Lenora at the Window, Lenora Looking Over Her Shoulder, Lenora*— yikes! Holy cow, that one must be called *Lenora the Explorer.*

"I can see that. They all seem to have a—er—recurring theme."

Shep blushed. "I was a little hyperfocused on Lenora at first, but she's encouraging me to move on. I told you she is my muse." He looked anxious. "You can take what you like when they're dry. That is, *if* you like any of them."

Addy heard the uncertainty in his voice and was touched. Her got-it-all-together big brother didn't have it all together any more than she did, and he was insecure about his painting. She considered the nudes, trying to set aside her natural dislike of the subject matter. Lenora might be a siren from hell, but she had to admit Shep was good. He'd captured Lenora's bewitching beauty and allure. And something else as well, the essence of the thrall. The pouting red lips and curvaceous body promised untold carnal delights, but the world-weary blue eyes held the shadow of loneliness.

"I'll take the landscape and these to start." She pointed to three of the nudes. "You better come up with a pseudonym, bro. Mama finds out you been painting dirty pictures, she'll scob your knob."

"Thanks, sis." Shep grinned. "I owe you one. Say, you going to the Grand Goober tomorrow night?"

Addy groaned. "Oh, Lord. I completely forgot about it. Yes, I'm going."

"What is this Grand Goober?" Brand demanded.

"It's a formal ball, *the* social event of the year. Kicks off the Hannah Peanut Festival," Shep said. "The Grand Goober is our biggest fund-raiser. Everybody will be there. Who you going with, sis?"

Addy mumbled something under her breath.

Shep put his hand to his ear. "I'm sorry. Could you say that a little louder?"

"You heard me, Shepton Corwin. I'm going to the ball with Bruce Jones."

Shep crowed. "Pootie Jones? You've got a date with Pootie Jones?"

"Poo—er—I mean Bruce is lactose intolerant, a problem he fortunately now has under control," Addy said loftily.

Brand scowled. "Is not 'date' a term used by humans to signify a social engagement with another person, often one for whom you feel romantic interest?"

"Yep." Shep was still laughing. It made Addy want to slug him. "I wasn't planning on going to the ball," he said, "but now I might. Addy has a date with Pootie Jones. Hoo boy, that's rich."

"No," Brand said.

The air grew heavy and thick and hard to breathe. A wall of swift-moving dark clouds rolled over the river from the east.

Thunder boomed and lightning crashed over their heads.

Shep ran to the window. "Jesus, I never saw a storm come up so fast."

Addy laid her hand on Brand's arm. "Relax. It's sweet that you're jealous, but this is something I have to do. Poo—*dammit!*—I mean Bruce is my friend. I promised him months ago I'd go with him. I can't back out on him now. He's counting on me. It would be rude."

"I am not jealous," Brand said. "The Dalvahni do not experience jealousy. It is a purely human emotion."

"Uh huh."

Shep jumped as another loud rumble of thunder shook the house. "Sounds like the damn storm's right over the house. 'Scuse me a sec. I'd better tell Nora to get off the porch."

He hurried out of the room, leaving Addy and Brand alone.

Addy sauntered over to Brand and poked him in the chest. "Your little atmospheric disturbance gives you away. Admit it. You're jealous."

"I am not jealous. I have to protect you. This Pootie human could be the djegrali."

"Oh." Addy pretended to think this over. "I'll admit it then. I'm jealous as hell of Elvira out there, *soul man*. What does that mean anyway? Is it thrall for boy toy or something?"

"No one toys with the Dalvahni. Sol' Van is a term of respect. It means 'most noble Lord.'"

"Aw, that's so cute in a submissive totally vomitous kind of way." Addy stroked Brand's hard-muscled chest through the shirt. "Well, Sol baby, since you're not the jealous type, I guess you won't mind if Bruce drives me home tomorrow night and kisses me at the door and—"

Brand grabbed her by the shoulders and kissed her. The storm broke with fury over their heads. Rain drummed on the tin roof. By the time he ended the kiss, she was weak in the knees and panting like she'd finished a 5-k run. Another minute and she'd have done him right there on the floor, and if Shep wandered into the room in the middle of it, too bad, too sad, oh Dad.

"Very well, I admit it," he growled against her lips. "I am jealous. I am consumed with it. The very thought of another man touching you drives me mad. I will allow this Pootie person to escort you to the ball, but *only* if I accompany you. And if he lays so much as a finger on you, I will rip his head off and use it for a chamber pot."

Maybe it wasn't a vow of eternal love or a promise of happily ever after, but it was darn sure *something*.

"Does that make you happy?"

"Damn skippy," Addy said.

Chapter Twenty-nine

The following night, Addy entered the Hannah Town Hall with Pootie and a second, unseen escort at her side—Brand. At her request, he made himself invisible.

"Bruce is this year's Grand Goober," she explained. "It's a big whoopee-do deal in Hannah, and I don't want to spoil it for him. He's a nice guy, Brand, and this means a lot to him. He won't understand if you tag along, and I have no intention of trying to explain it to him. Why don't you catch a ride to the ball with Muddy and Mr. C? They've got plenty of room in their car. I know you're trying to keep me safe, but Bruce is harmless, I promise."

"No," Brand said. "This I cannot allow. I will accompany you and this Pootie human, or you will not go."

"Wait a darn minute, bub, you can't tell me—"

He jerked her in his arms and kissed her. Instant lobotomy. Her brain dried up and fell out on the floor. She ought to be ashamed of herself. And she would, too, as soon as her hootie stopped running things.

"Your safety and the safety of those you love may be at stake," he said when he'd finished kissing her senseless. "I can and I *will* tell you what to do in this instance. The Pootie human will not see me. The Dalvahni have the ability to move among your kind undetected."

So she went to the Grand Goober Ball with Pootie Jones and the Invisible Man. Problem was *Pootie* might not be able to see

Brand, but she sure as shoot knew he was there. She could feel him glowering at her from the backseat. It was like his eyeballs contained little laser beams, and they were burning a hole in the back of her head. Pootie seemed to feel it, too. He kept looking over his shoulder.

"I keep thinking I see something in the rearview mirror," he said with an edgy laugh. "Little green flames. Crazy, huh? Guess that dog spooked me."

Poor Pootie. He'd taken her arm as they approached the car, but was drawn up short by a low rumbling growl.

He spun around. "What's that? Sounded like some kind of animal."

"He is not to touch you," Brand growled in her ear. The car door swung silently open, and she was lifted in strong, unseen arms and deposited in the seat. "This I cannot allow."

"Oh, for Pete's sake. He's just being a gentleman."

Pootie blinked in surprise when he saw her sitting inside the car. "You say something, Addy?"

"I said it was probably the neighbor's dog. We'd better get going if we want to make the lead-out at the dance."

"Yeah, sure thing."

Pootie got behind the wheel. But he kept checking the rearview mirror, as if he sensed Brand's presence.

"Rabbit keeps running over my grave," he confided. "Must be all the excitement."

They eased into a parking place with a sign that said RE-SERVED FOR THE GRAND GOOBER. Addy flung open her door and scrambled onto the sidewalk as Pootie rounded the car to help her out. He seemed a little taken aback by her lack of manners.

Addy gave him a bright smile. "Sorry, guess I'm a little excited, too."

Thank goodness Bitsy didn't see her. She'd have gotten lecture number fifty two on entering and exiting an automobile like a Southern lady. She'd flunked that one for sure. A lady waited for her escort to come around and open the car door for her. Once the gentleman opened the car door for her, a lady exited the vehicle with grace, taking care to keep her legs together and offering her date a grateful smile and a murmured thank-you. A lady didn't eject herself out of a car like her drawers were on fire. Most Southern ladies, however, didn't have an invisible ticked-off boyfriend with supernatural powers waiting to beat the snot out of their date if the poor guy laid so much as a finger on them. So, she chucked lesson number fifty-two in favor of saving poor Pootie's life.

The Town Hall was a three-story turn-of-the-century brick warehouse on the west bank of the Devil River, part of the Hannah Riverfront Project, an ambitious plan to revitalize the waterfront over the next two decades. Future plans for the project included provisions for a park, bike and running trails, and an open-air amphitheater. There was even talk of having a riverboat one day, but the first phase of the plan was the Town Hall. The ground floor of the building would one day house the mayor's office and the police department. Right now, though, it was one big open space, just right for a ball. Much better than the high school gym, where the ball had been held for the past four years. Floor-length arched windows overlooked the river, and French doors opened onto a brick veranda with wrought-iron railings. The raw Sheetrock walls had been draped in yards of filmy cloth that gave the room an *Arabian Nights* feel. Twinkle lights sparkled over the windows and in the greenery. Hired for the evening, an orchestra all the way from Mobile played soft music. Tickets sold for $50.00 each, or $90.00 a couple. Everybody who was anybody in Hannah attended the Grand Goober. It was *the* social event of the season.

Mayor Tunstall spotted them as they entered and made his way through the crowd. The mayor was short and round, and reminded Addy of an egg with hair and legs.

"There he is, the Grand Goober himself!" The mayor did a double-take when he saw Addy. "My, my, Addy, you look good enough to eat. I almost didn't recognize you with all that glamorous blond hair."

His gaze drifted downward and locked on her chest. Good

grief, the mayor was a boob man. He was salivating over her girls. Eww. Politicians were almost as creepy as dead people.

He gave her an oily smile. "You've been hiding your light under a bushel basket, young lady. You'll have to save me a dance."

"No," Brand said. The single word, deep and full of menace, echoed around the cavernous room, all the more startling because it seemed to come out of nowhere.

The mayor looked at Pootie in surprise. "Pootie, my boy, you mustn't keep this lovely thing all to yourself."

"It wasn't me, I swear," Pootie protested. He looked around in alarm. "Must have been somebody else. Maybe they're testing the sound system or something."

Addy shoved her elbow in the general direction of Brand's voice. She connected with solid flesh and heard a muffled grunt. "Behave," she hissed.

"I can read his foul thoughts." Brand spoke in her ear. "If you dance with him, he goes in the river."

"Oh, for Pete's sake."

The mayor raised his brows. "What's that, my dear?"

"Oh, nothing." Addy gave him a dazzling smile. "Thrilled to be here, that's all."

The mayor beamed back at her. "That's right, as Pootie's date, you get to dance the lead-out. It's a big honor." The orchestra launched into "Stars Fell on Alabama." "There's the signal." He grabbed Bruce by the arm. "Excuse us, Addy. Got to get the Grand Goober ready for his big entrance. We'll be back in a jiffy."

Mayor Tunstall pulled Pootie across the room and through a door.

"What is this lead-out?" Brand asked.

"It's the first dance of the ball. As the Grand Goober, Bruce gets to open the festivities. As his date, I dance the first dance with him."

She shivered as she felt Brand come up behind her. Heat radiated off his big body, and his masculine scent, a heady, spicy combination of sandalwood, cedar, and rock rose with a hint of cardamom and pepper, swirled around her until she felt drunk.

He kissed her on the neck. "Have I told you how beautiful you are tonight?"

"No, I don't believe you have."

She swallowed a squeak as he slid his hands around her and cupped her breasts. It took her straight back to that first night, when she thought she was being made love to by a ghost. Had it only been four nights ago? So much had changed. *She* had changed. For one thing, she was about to have a screaming orgasm in a room full of people.

"You are ravishing, a vision, the most beautiful creature I have ever seen," he murmured. "I've been rock hard and aching for you all night. I want to slide this indecent scrap of nothing you call a dress over your delectable ass and have hot monkey sex with you. I do not want to share you with anyone, not even this Pootie Jones."

Sigh. The man sure knew how to sweet-talk a girl. If they were any place else, she'd shuck her panties right then and there, and take him up on his offer.

She reined in her raging hormones and pushed his hands away. "No. You have got to behave, and so do I. It's one dance." An excited buzz from across the room drew her attention. "And in case you think I'm looking forward to it, look what's coming through the door."

Clapping and cheering, the crowd lined up on either side of the massive double doors as a tall, bizarre figure entered the ballroom. It was Pootie, the Grand Goober himself, wearing his official costume.

Brand grunted in surprise. "By the sword, what is it?"

Addy sighed. "That's my date. Now, if you'll excuse me, I have to dance with the big nut."

Brand prowled the edge of the ballroom, his eyes fastened on Adara as she moved around the dance floor in another man's arms. Or at least he thought the creature holding Adara was human. He could not be sure. From the shoulders down, the creature looked like a man dressed in the black garb called a tuxedo. But, the thing's head was monstrous, a wrinkled three-foot-high curved pod with large round eyes and a vacuous red-lipped smile. Hideous, as alarming as any demon he'd ever seen. And Adara was twirling around the room with it. He wanted to sweep her off the dance floor and carry her into the night. He longed to cleave the giant pod head in two and leave the smoking halves on the floor as a no-trespassing sign to all other males.

Adara spun closer. She seemed to sense his hot gaze upon her and glanced nervously about, her large brown eyes wide with apprehension. She should be afraid. He was near crazed with jealousy and desire and possessiveness. This was insanity. The Dalvahni did not feel such things.

Yet, he did. That and more.

His hungry gaze fastened upon her as she moved about the room. He had been in a near frenzy of lust since she came out of the bedroom earlier that evening dressed for the ball. The slinky blue gown she wore showed her white skin and pale hair to advantage and clung to her lovely body. The damn garment was so tight, it was a wonder she could breathe, hugging her deliciously rounded bottom and full breasts like a second skin. If not for the high slit on one side that exposed her long legs, she would not be able to move at all. Each step she took offered a tantalizing glimpse of those smooth, elegant limbs, legs she had wrapped around his waist the night before as he moved within her. All the men in the room watched her, panting with desire. He suppressed a snarl as he read their lustful thoughts. He wanted to kill them all.

In the darkness outside the long windows that overlooked the river, lightning flashed in jagged blue-white streaks, illuminating in ghostly gray relief the trees on the opposite shore. The orchestra ended the first song and launched into another. Thunder rumbled over the strains of music. A waltz, his internal guide told him, a voluptuous intertwining of the male and female bodies that was considered obscene and vulgar in the not-so-distant past. And rightly so. The creature with the elongated head dancing about the room with Adara held her much too close. He had one hand at her waist. Brand watched that hand with narrowed eyes. If it moved so much as a finger's breadth closer to Adara's breasts or inched lower by the space of a hair toward her luscious bottom, he would tear the man limb from limb. He would—

"You might as well show yourself, brother," Ansgar said. "All the growling and rumbling gives you away."

Brand shed his cloak of invisibility. Evie took a startled step back at his sudden appearance.

Ignoring Ansgar, Brand made Evie a deep bow. "Mistress Evangeline, you are a vision tonight."

Indeed, she was lovely. Hard to believe this creature with the glorious red hair and lush, hourglass curves was the shy, dowdy woman from the flower shop.

Evie's delicate skin flushed. "Thank you." She smoothed her hands down her green gown in a self-conscious gesture and slid Ansgar a quick, adoring glance. "This is my first Grand Goober Ball. Ansgar got me this gown and insisted on bringing me along."

"I told her I would not come without her." Ansgar surveyed Brand's formal attire with cool indifference. "I see the tailor met your needs as well."

"Yes, Master Gibbs has been most accommodating."

"You both look very handsome," Evangeline said. "All the women are drooling over you."

Ansgar raised her hand to his lips. "Are there other women here? I had not noticed."

Her blush deepened. "What a sweet thing to say, even though I know you're only being nice."

Ansgar gave her a smoldering look. "I assure you, Evangeline, I am neither sweet nor nice."

Ansgar's chilly hauteur was noticeably absent in his dealings with Evie, Brand noted. Perhaps he was not the only warrior affected by these damnable feelings. The knowledge cheered him.

He sought and found Adara once more on the dance floor. Her partner's grinning pod head bent closer to her shining head as though whispering something in her ear. Brand's hearing was unusually keen, but he could not hear the creature for the music.

"'T would be much simpler, brother, if you claimed the next dance," Ansgar said, sounding bored once more. "Or you could skulk in the shadows like a lovesick boy and allow one of these other drooling jackals to claim her instead." He shrugged. "I daresay it would be better if you did. It is not the nature of the Dalvahni to love."

Love?

Once during a battle centuries before in the Kingdom of Alba, a demon-possessed soldier attacked him from behind, striking him in the head with a mace. The blow had stunned him. He felt the same way now. He *loved* Adara? No wonder he had not been able to put a name to this baffling condition. What did he or any other Dalvahni warrior know of love? But, since he'd met Adara . . .

He thought of his life before her. The long years blurred behind him, empty and meaningless—a dreadful, unchanging drudgery of grim purpose and duty. He imagined the future without her. Endless, lonely years . . . unbearable. How pitiable a creature was he that one female could shake him loose from his moorings and send him drifting rudderless into an unknown sea? He was a warrior, focused, dedicated, determined in the eternal fight against the enemy. These feelings the woman stirred in him left him as weak and helpless as a newborn babe blinking in the light of a bewildering new world. He had no defenses against such an opponent, no previous experience to fall back upon, no one to counsel him. Ansgar and their brother warriors, the closest thing to family he knew, could not extricate him from this coil. The Dalvahni were unburdened by sentiment, had no concept of it. He sailed alone on uncharted waters, tossed about on a treacherous ocean by an ever-changing current of emotion, something his brothers would find incomprehensible, even contemptible.

Love? Unthinkable.

He *loved* her.

The knowledge blazed through him, certain, cleansing. *Right.*

He should be holding Adara in his arms and whispering in her ear, not the grotesque human with the unnaturally large head. Enough was enough.

He strode out onto the dance floor to claim his woman.

Chapter Thirty

There are some social situations that no amount of mothering or all the lectures in the world can prepare a girl for. Dancing with a demonically possessed giant peanut is surely one of them.

"*D-i-i-e,*" her partner said in a rattling hiss that shivered along her nerve endings.

Classic horror movie stuff, though the big peanut head kind of ruined it for him. Hard to take a supernatural malefic being seriously when he was dressed like a gi-normous goober pea, even if he was the Legume from Hell.

Addy blinked at him. "I'm sorry, could you say that again?"

"Tomorrow you die."

"What *is* that smell?" She wrinkled her nose. "Like rancid butter. Yuck. Is somebody burning popcorn *at a ball?*"

She winced as his hand tightened painfully over hers.

"Heed me, Addy. I have marked you. You are mine, and tomorrow I will come for you."

Addy was terrified. Not that she was about to let him know it. Clowns and mimes and that creepy Burger King guy gave her the willies. And now she could add vengeful, possessed peanuts to the list. She stiffened her spine and donned her favorite armor, smarminess, to disguise her fear.

"Yeah, I heard you. Tomorrow's the big day," she said. "But, why wait? Is the big, bad demon scared of a woman? And what have you done with Pootie? This is his big night. Did you *ask* him if he wanted to be possessed by a soul-sucking fiend from hell? Because if you didn't that's just rude. And speaking of rude, when are you going to get that statue off my aunt's lawn? It's killing the grass."

Violet light flashed behind the round, dark eyeholes of the Grand Goober mask. She'd pissed him off. Her alter ego, Miss Smarty Pants, had that effect on others. Nice to know her abilities extended to the vegetable world.

The curved head bent closer to her ear. "Even for one of your kind, you are singularly annoying, Addy Corwin. I look forward to your death with pleasure." He jerked upright in sudden alarm. "The Dalvahni approaches. Despair, for tomorrow you die."

He flung her away and strode off. She stumbled back into a pair of strong arms.

"Thanks," she murmured, regaining her balance.

She looked up at her rescuer, and her knees buckled. It was Brand, decked out in formal wear. The last time she saw him before they left the house he was still wearing jeans. Tweedy must have dropped the tux off while she was getting ready, God bless him. The evening clothes clung to Brand's muscular frame like a lover's caress, black tailcoat, matching trousers, white shirt and tie—the whole nine yards. Hot damn, he was gorgeous. He made her mouth water. He was a great big Dalvahni all-day sucker, and she was dying to see exactly how many licks it took to get to the center of his Tootsie Roll Pop.

The music ended, but she hardly noticed. She stood on the dance floor staring at him, her mouth open.

He frowned down at her, six feet plus of glorious male. "It is fortunate your friend left when he did, Adara, else I would have done him an injury. I do not enjoy seeing you in the arms of another man, even Pootie."

Brand was jealous of Pootie. Only Pootie wasn't Pootie anymore, but a soul-sucking, flesh-eating fiend that wanted to kill her.

It all came crashing down on her. Her blind panic when she realized her enemy lay hidden behind the frozen features of the grinning mask, the sick terror that filled her when the demon whispered in her ear. She heard again that chilling, raspy voice promising death and worse. The whole thing was downright spooky. Spooky, hell; she was scared out of her wits.

Heedless of her surroundings, she launched herself into Brand's arms. "I wasn't dancing with another man." She buried her face against his hard chest. His spicy, masculine scent filled her senses, calming her and making her horny as all get-out at the same time. "It was the demon. The demon has Pootie."

With a low curse, he swept her out of the ballroom, through the French doors, and onto the veranda. He reached behind him and drew his sword. The silver blade gleamed in the moonlight but did not burst into flame. Apparently satisfied they were in a demon-free zone, he sheathed Uriel.

"What did he say to you?" He gave her a little shake. "The djegrali. I saw him whisper something to you. What did he say?"

"He said I'm going to die tomorrow." Tears filled her eyes. Angrily, she blinked them away. Badass Addy may have taken a powder, but that didn't mean little Addy Corwin had to be a total wus. "Cheerful, huh?"

He jerked her into his arms, crushing her against his broad chest. "I should not have let you come here tonight. It is too dangerous. If anything happened to you . . ." His arms tightened around her, the expression on his handsome face fierce. "Adara, I—"

She heard a faint cry over the noise of the river and put her finger to his lips. "Shh. Did you hear that?"

"Adara, I am trying to tell you—"

"Help."

"There, you heard it that time, didn't you?" She slipped out of his embrace and went to the railing, peering out into the darkness. "I think somebody fell in the river."

The old Addy had terrible night vision, but the new and improved Addy could pick fly shit out of pepper. Below them, clinging to the branches of a fallen tree in the river, was Pootie Jones. The river was deep at this point, and the current pulled at his legs. The Grand Goober had lost his peanut head. He looked small, wet, and bedraggled.

"Oh, my goodness, it's Pootie!" She leaned over the railing. "Hang on, Pootie. We'll get help."

Brand yanked her back. "By the sword, are you trying to kill yourself?"

"Oh, pooh. The bank's not that steep. What are we going to do about Pootie?"

Brand frowned. "Why must we do anything about Pootie? Cannot the foolish human extricate himself from the river?"

"He can't swim," Addy said. "We took swimming lessons together at the club when we were kids. Pootie flunked."

"Is this not the same human that threatened to kill you but a moment ago?"

"That wasn't Pootie. That was the demon. Pootie wouldn't hurt a flea."

"Help," Pootie yelped again.

"He doesn't *sound* possessed. He sounds like plain old Pootie." She gazed anxiously up at Brand. "Maybe the demon has gone."

Brand shrugged out of his jacket. "Very well."

"What are you doing?"

"I am going to remove the Pootie human from the river. Is that not what you desire?"

"Y-yes. No. I changed my mind." She twisted her hands together. "What if the demon is playing a trick? Maybe we should get somebody else, like the fire department."

She whirled around to rush back inside.

Brand stopped her. "I do not think that is the case. I think the demon, having delivered its message and knowing that Pootie cannot swim, left Pootie in the river to drown. It is their way to dispose of their victims once they have no further use for them. I will collect him for you."

He motioned with one hand.

"No, wait, Brand. I'm worried—" She stopped. A glowing circle of light surrounded her. "What are you doing?"

"I have placed a spell around you to protect you from the djegrali in my absence. Do not leave the circle."

"But Brand—"

Pfft, he disappeared. Addy tiptoed to the edge of the circle and peeked over the railing. Brand materialized on the partially submerged tree trunk at a point downstream from Pootie. His white shirt gleamed phosphorescent in the dark. Brand, the glow-in-the-dark Dalvahni warrior. Better than a light stick.

"Who are you?" Pootie demanded shrilly.

"Is it Pootie?" Addy yelled over the sound of the water.

"Yes," Brand said.

"How can you be sure?"

"He does not stink, and his eyes are not purple."

Wha? Purple eyes? Later, he would explain that remark, but at the moment she was remembering the rancid odor that had emanated from Demon Pootie on the dance floor.

"Burnt popcorn," she shouted triumphantly. "The demons smell like burnt popcorn!"

"I am not familiar with this popcorn." Brand paused. She could almost hear him thinking. Probably checking his internal Dalvahni guidebook, something she imagined as a sort of GPS and encyclopedia all rolled into one. "Ah, yes," he said at last. "Corn is a cereal grain, also known as maize. This 'popcorn' you speak of is popular with humans. I do not understand the appeal of a food that reeks of demon."

"It only smells like that when it's burned," Addy said. "I noticed it when I was dancing with—"

Pootie interrupted them. "Hey, people. I'm freezing my butt off here."

Pootie sounded petulant. The Devil River was fed by a series of underwater springs, and the water was *cold*.

Brand said something to him in a low voice. Pootie shook his head and clung tighter to the tree branch. Brand clenched his jaw. She heard his deep voice rumble again and saw Pootie shake his head a second time. In the darkness, Brand's eyes glowed like green coals. The big guy was getting cranky. Not a good thing. She'd better think of something quick before Brand exhausted his limited store of patience.

She cupped her hands around her mouth. "Hey, Pootie."

Pootie looked up, his face the color of bleached bone in the moonlight.

"Tell Brand the joke about the string that walks into a bar."

"Addy, I don't thi—"

"Do it, Pootie."

Teeth chattering, Pootie mumbled something to Brand. Nothing.

"Okay, he didn't get that one. My bad," she said. "Try the one about the penguin, the hippo, and the one-legged nun."

"Addy, I'm trying to keep from drowning. I don't think—"

"Just tell him the damn joke, Pootie."

Addy heard Pootie mutter something else to Brand. Brand grinned. Even at a distance, Addy was sucker-punched by that smile. It had the same effect on Pootie. His face went slack, and he let go of the branch. Brand caught him as he swept past. *Pfft*, they vanished. A second later, Brand reappeared on the terrace with Pootie slung over one shoulder like a sack of potatoes. Brand looked as elegant as before. Pootie looked like a drowned rat.

"Oh, my goodness, he's soaked." Addy rushed forward and slammed onto an unseen barrier. She banged her fist against the invisible wall. "Okay, joke's over. Let me out of here."

Brand dumped Pootie on the veranda. "I should have locked you up the first night. It would have saved me no end of trouble."

She felt like a bug in a jar. "Ha ha, very funny. Let me out, Brand. I mean it. I'm claustrophobic."

"Relax, little one. The spell is temporary. You are Dalvahni now. I could not really keep you imprisoned for any length of time, much as I might like to for your own good."

As he spoke, the glowing circle faded.

Addy bent over Pootie. "You all right, Poo—uh—Bruce?"

Pootie sat up with a groan. "What happened? I feel awful."

"Brand pulled you out of the river."

"Thanks, mister," Pootie said. He removed his wet shoes and socks. "I owe you one."

"Think nothing of it."

"How'd you get in the river in the first place?" Addy asked.

Pootie gave Brand a nervous glance. "Don't know. I remember feeling small and sort of squished. And there was this voice in my head." He shuddered. "A horrible, evil scratchy voice that gave me a headache. When I woke up, I was in the river." He shoved a hank of wet hair out of his face. "My peanut head! What happened to my peanut head?"

Poor Pootie. Being Grand Goober was the highlight of his existence, and so far, he pretty much sucked at it. It was swim lessons at the club all over again.

"I guess it went in the river," Addy said.

Pootie groaned. "The mayor's gonna kill me. That costume came all the way from Chicago, Illinois. It was custom made, one of a kind. Cost the City fifteen hundred dollars. Some Grand Goober I turned out to be. How am I going to pay for this?"

Addy patted him on the back. "Don't worry, we'll think of something. Right, Brand?"

Brand gave a noncommittal grunt and helped Pootie to his feet.

The three of them stood on the dark terrace, looking through the long windows into the brightly lit ballroom. The orchestra music drifted through the doors. The dance floor was crowded with women in brightly hued gowns and their penguinesque partners. A tall man whirled past with a curvaceous redhead in his arms. The redhead had a look of abject misery on her face.

Small wonder it took Addy a moment to recognize her. The goddess in the green gown was Evie. She'd turned herself into a creature so glorious Addy hardly knew her. And that was wrong on so many levels.

Hadn't she told Evie a thousand times she was gorgeous? But did Evie listen? N-o-o-o.

And now the caterpillar had turned into a butterfly without warning. *Without telling her best friend.*

No doubt about it. She and girlfriend needed to talk.

Chapter Thirty-one

Addy didn't stay miffed with Evie for long. She was too happy for her. She couldn't wait to get her alone and talk about it, though. Addy suspected Blondy was behind Evie's transformation, which put her in the giant hemorrhoid's debt. Again.

The knowledge did not dull her happiness for her friend.

"That's Evie dancing with Trey Peterson. Doesn't she look fabulous?" Addy spied Meredith standing to one side and stifled a giggle. "Check out Meredith. She looks like she swallowed a bucket of worms."

Brand nodded. "If by 'check out' you mean assess another person based upon their physical appearance, you should 'check out' Ansgar as well. He also appears to have ingested a large quantity of invertebrates."

Poor Blondy looked miserable, like a dog that had lost a juicy bone. His gaze followed Evie as she glided around the ballroom in Trey's arms. If looks could kill, Trey would be buzzard food.

They left the terrace and went back inside. The mayor hurried over to them.

"Bruce, what in the world happened to you?" he asked. "Where's the Goober head? We've got the silent auction coming up, and you're supposed to preside."

Bruce hung his head. "I'm sorry, Mayor. The Goober head's gone. I fell in the river and lost it."

Mayor Tunstall's mouth dropped open. "Lost it? *Lost it.* This is a disaster. How could you—"

"I will pay to replace the mask," Brand said, cutting off the mayor's tirade. "In addition, my brother and I will match the amount you raise in the auction on the condition that the donation is made in Pootie's name."

Pootie's eyes widened. "That's awfully gen—"

"Hush up, Pootie, and let the man talk," the mayor said. He flashed Brand a wide smile. "And you are . . ."

"I am Dalvahni."

The mayor rolled his eyes at Addy. "Italian shoe magnate," she mouthed behind Brand's back. She rubbed the tips of her fingers together to indicate that he was loaded.

Mayor Tunstall's black eyes gleamed with avarice. "Will that be cash or check, Mr. Dalvahni?"

"If you refer to the physical form of what passes for currency here, then it will be cash."

"Generous of you, Mr. Dalvahni. Very generous. I'll let my secretary know. That's Florence over there in the pink gown carrying the rhinestone possum purse. Made that purse herself. Has a whole line of animal purses she calls 'Roadkill Chic.' You interested in handbags, Mr. Dalvahni? No? Thought you might on account of you being in the shoe business. Well, if you change your mind, she'll have a booth at the festival tomorrow. You can stop by my office before the parade and make your donation. This is most generous of you, I must say! But it's a good cause, a very good cause, I can promise you that." He gave Pootie a dismissive glance. "Bruce, you're dripping all over the floor. Go home."

The mayor waddled off, looking very pleased.

Brand watched him leave. "A singularly odd creature. Where do you suppose he got the notion that I am a cobbler by trade?"

"No idea," Addy lied.

Pootie wrung Brand's hand. "Thanks a million. You saved my butt again. I don't know what to say, Brand." He sneezed loudly.

"Pootie, you'd better get out of those wet clothes before you catch your death," Addy said.

Pootie tugged on the sleeves of his ruined jacket. "You're probably right. You still riding with me in the parade tomorrow, Addy?"

"Sure thing."

"And you, too, of course . . . uh . . . Brand."

"I would be pleased to accompany you. In fact, I insist upon it."

Pootie sneezed again.

Addy gave him a little shove toward the door. "Go home, Bruce. Brand will see me home."

Pootie waved good-bye and sloshed out the door.

Addy smiled at Brand. "That was a nice thing you did. Real nice."

Brand shrugged. "Money is of little consequence to the Dalvahni. What we need, we are given."

"Are you saying you're rich?"

"Yes, I suppose in human terms I am rich."

"Wow, health, wealth, and immortality. Sucks to be you, doesn't it?"

"This is sarcasm, is it not?"

"Yep."

"Looking at it objectively, I can see how a human would envy the Dalvahni lot, but since I've met you I've come to understand that—"

"Adara Jean, where's your brother?" Bitsy glided up to them on the chief's arm, looking very elegant in a silk charmeuse gown with an ivory bodice and a cappuccino skirt. "And what have you done with Pootie? Aren't you supposed to be his date?"

"I haven't seen Shep, Mama, and Pootie left. He was coming down with a cold."

"Humph," Bitsy said, which in mama-speak meant *Somehow I know this is all your fault, young lady, and I will get to the bottom of this later.* Mama would find a way to blame her for sun spots and global warming, too. Bitsy turned her attention to Brand. "You look very handsome tonight, Mr. Dalvahni."

Brand bowed. "And you are a vision, Mrs. Corwin."

"Yes, Mama, you look beautiful," Addy said.

Chief Davis squeezed Bitsy's hand. "Pretty as a picture, ain't she?"

Bitsy batted her eyes at the chief. "Oh, Car-lee." Fiddle dee dee, Mama was doing the Southern belle thing again. She inspected Addy, a small wrinkle forming between her brows. "That's a lovely dress, dear, but why are you *still* wearing that wig?"

"It's not a wig, Mama. I keep telling you."

"Humph," Bitsy said again.

In the space of a few minutes, she'd ticked off *two* supernatural malefic beings, first the demon and now Mama. Was she good, or what?

Muddy joined them with Mr. Collier. Mr. C. looked very dapper in his evening clothes, and Muddy was the picture of elegance in a black gown that exposed one shoulder and had a slightly ruched waistline accentuated with a rhinestone clip. Diamonds twinkled in her ears and on the bracelet on her left wrist.

"Wuz up," Muddy said.

Good grief. Mama was channeling Scarlett O'Hara, and her great-aunt was Muddy from the hood. Her family was so odd.

"This is a nice party, isn't it?" Mr. Collier said. "Been to the Goober Ball before, of course, but I've always been too pounded to remember much about it. I'm going to try not to throw up on anybody this year."

"Sounds like a plan," Muddy said.

Bitsy fanned herself. "It is warm in here with all these people. Muddy, why don't you and Amasa join me and Carl for a glass of punch? Seeing as how Pootie's not feeling well, Mr. Dalvahni can ask Addy to dance."

That was Mama, always on the lookout for a husband for Addy and about as subtle as a sledgehammer.

"An excellent idea," Brand said. "I have not danced with Adara this evening."

Muddy twiddled her fingers at Brand. "See you later, Mr. Dalvahni." She scooted up to Addy. "Enjoy your dance, darling," she whispered. "That fellow of yours is positively scrumptious. Uh uh uh, take a whole loaf of bread to sop that up, if you know what I mean."

She knew exactly what she meant, but Muddy was wrong. Brand was at least a two-loafer.

Muddy gave them another finger wave, and moved off with Mr. C. The orchestra began another waltz, and Brand took her in his arms. He was an excellent dancer, much better than she. That wasn't saying much since she was born with two left feet. When she was thirteen, she nearly gave Mr. Fancher, the club dance instructor, a nervous breakdown during cotillion classes. He'd finally pronounced her hopeless.

"So, tell me, where does a demon hunter learn to waltz?"

He smiled down at her. *Thwack!* Instant brain freeze. The guy smiled at her, and she turned into a woozy floozy, a total doof.

"The Dalvahni, of necessity, have many abilities that enable us to move from place to place and among differing races and species in pursuit of the djegrali. We are highly adaptable and learn quickly. I watched you dance with the Pootie human and picked up the steps."

He twirled her around to demonstrate.

"Just like that, you learned to waltz?"

He shrugged. "It is not hard. And I had excellent motivation." His arm tightened around her waist. "As I was saying, Adara, I have been doing some thinking and I—"

"There's Evie. Let's go talk to her."

Grabbing him by the hand, she dragged him off the dance floor.

She threw her arms around her friend. "Evie, you look absolutely beautiful."

Evie hugged her back, her cheeks pink. "Thanks, babe. You, too."

Ansgar gave Addy a haughty bow. "Evangeline is correct. You are lovely tonight, Adara."

She dimpled at him. "Thanks, Blondy. You don't clean up so bad yourself."

Addy studied him through her lashes. Like Brand, Blondy was very handsome in his evening duds. Brand was dark and brooding and dangerous, the perennial bad boy. In contrast, Ansgar was as cool and remote as a snow-capped mountain, unruffled and still, as full of hidden depths as an underground lake. He was always glacial, but tonight he seemed positively frosty. Probably sulking because Evie danced with Trey. She stole a glance at Evie. The voluptuous redhead in the revealing gown was an alien creature. Since puberty, Evie had been riddled with insecurity, hiding her body under baggy clothes, changing in the bathroom stall during P.E., and refusing to be seen, even by Addy, in shorts or a bathing suit. The teasing Evie endured from Meredith and her cronies made things worse, convincing her she was fat and unattractive. The joke was on the Death Starr, however, because girlfriend was stacked, a glamorous old-time pinup girl with large breasts, a tiny waist, and generous, curving hips. And inside all that voluptuousness was a loving, generous heart, not a dried-up prune like the undersized organ that beat inside Meredith's narrow chest.

And Blondy was behind this remarkable Cinderella transformation. The green gown fit Evie like a dream. No way she got that gown in Hannah. Ansgar and a generous dose of Dalvahni woo-woo were responsible, Addy suspected. But, the real magic he'd worked was in giving Evie the confidence to wear it.

Suddenly, what she had to say didn't seem so hard. "Thanks for taking care of my girl, Ansgar. I've always known she's beautiful. It's high time everybody else knows it, too."

"You are most welcome," Ansgar said with his customary pain-in-the-ass hauteur.

So much for that Hallmark moment. At least she tried.

Instead of being thrilled at having gone from ugly duckling

to swan, though, Evie seemed subdued and miserable; time for a little one-on-one with the BFF.

Addy grabbed Evie by the hand. "I don't know about you, but I'm dying of thirst. Let's get some punch."

Brand and Ansgar moved to follow, but Addy stopped them with a bright smile. "Down boys, we're going to get something to drink." She pointed to the table in the opposite corner of the room. "See? We'll be right over there."

"Hurry up"—she tugged Evie in the direction of the refreshment table.—"before they decide to come along."

She ladled punch into two cups and handed one to Evie. "Spill it. Why the long face? Is it Blondy? If he's done something to upset you, I'll thump him on the head, so help me, I will."

Evie shook her head. "No, Ansgar has been great, getting me this dress and bringing me to my first ball. We danced together, and oh, Addy, it was wonderful." Excitement glowed in her eyes and faded. "It's Trey." She glanced about the room. "He's always looking at me and touching me. He makes me so uncomfortable."

"The creep. Why didn't you tell me he was bothering you?"

"What could you have done, Addy? And besides, I need my job."

"How long's this been going on?"

"A while. I try not to be alone with him."

"Why'd you dance with him then?"

"I didn't want to," Evie protested. "He was waiting for me when I came out of the ladies' room. He dragged me out on the dance floor. I couldn't get out of it without making a scene."

Evie, the shy wallflower, would hate that. She'd wondered how Trey managed to snag a dance with Evie when Ansgar guarded her like she was the last drink before Prohibition.

Evie took a deep breath. "I always thought it was my imagination." She made a face. "I mean, who would be interested in Whaley Douglass, right?"

"Wrong. Take a good look in the mirror, girl. Half the guys in this place have a boner just looking at you."

"Addy," Evie said in a scandalized whisper.

Addy set her glass down. "I don't want to hear it, Evie. You've been out-ed. You're beautiful, and it's time you accepted it."

"Maybe." Evie worried her bottom lip. "How do I get Trey to leave me alone?"

"Kick him in the bean bags. Guys hate that."

Evie giggled. "Oh, Addy, you are so bad. You always know how to make me laugh."

"That's what friends do."

Addy looked around. Trey was on the other side of the ballroom. Meredith stood beside him, looking stylish in a pale blue strapless gown that probably cost more than the combined gross national incomes of several third world countries. Her pixie features were pinched in an expression of unhappiness. She spoke to her husband. He ignored her, his gaze fastened with unnatural intensity on Evie. Meredith put her hand on Trey's arm. He shrugged it off and strode toward them.

"Here comes Trey," Addy murmured.

"Oh, no." Evie looked frantically around the room. "What do I do?"

"Relax. The Death Starr's right behind him, and she looks mad as a hornet."

Trey Peterson moved across the dance floor toward them with the grace of a natural athlete. He was all that and a bag of chips in high school; quarterback, class president, prom king. The Petersons were old money, having made a fortune buying and selling timber at the turn of the twentieth century . . . some people claimed by less than legal means. The Petersons were a Big Deal in Hannah, and that made Trey Peterson a big deal, too.

Tall and fit, with dark blue eyes and light brown hair that was slightly thinning on top, Trey was still a handsome man. He wore his custom-made tuxedo with the unconscious arrogance of the terminally rich.

"Ladies," he said, sauntering up to them. The watchful, hungry way he looked at Evie reminded Addy of a snake sizing up its next meal. "Evie, would you honor me with another dance?"

"I-I," Evie stuttered.

Meredith charged up behind him, her size five silver designer evening shoes pumping up and down with the hammer-blow force of the driving wheels of a steam locomotive.

"Trey Peterson, how dare you humiliate me in front of the whole town like this!" Evie's soap must have worked. Meredith's pale, powdered complexion, though mottled with anger, had returned to its former smooth glory. "You haven't danced with me once all night, and here you are asking that fat sow to dance for the second time. I won't have it, I tell you. I won't!"

Her voice rose to a shriek, drawing attention.

Addy shook her head. "You should watch what you say, Meredith. All that negativity could bring on a relapse. Seems to me I warned you about being ugly to Evie."

"You don't scare me, Addy Corwin," Meredith said. "I won't stand idly by and let Whaley Douglass steal my husband."

Suddenly, Brand and Ansgar were there. Brand slipped his arm around Addy's waist, and Ansgar drew a trembling Evie to his side.

Ansgar eyed Meredith with icy distaste. "Adara is right. Sheath that tongue of yours, woman, lest it cut your own throat."

Meredith gasped. "Are you going to let him talk to me like that, Trey?"

"For God's sake, shut up, Meredith," Trey said. He turned and stomped off.

Meredith watched him leave, anger, hurt, and humiliation flickering across her face. For a moment, Addy felt sorry for her. It didn't last, though. Quick as a flash, Meredith pounced on Evie.

"You think you can take Trey away from me? But you're wrong. He won't divorce me. I know too many Peterson secrets, secrets they don't want to get out. Do you hear me?"

"I'm pretty sure people in the next county heard you, my dear." Blake Peterson, Trey's grandfather, appeared at Meredith's side. Distinguished and handsome, with gray hair at his temples and a physique kept trim by daily walks and golf, rain or shine, Mr. Peterson had always amazed Addy. He had to be in his midseventies, but looked and acted decades younger. "I think it's time I took you home."

"No!" Meredith shrank back. "I mean, I . . . I'd rather wait for Trey."

"Trey has gone." Taking Meredith by the elbow, he gave them an apologetic smile. A smile that did not quite reach his dark blue eyes, eyes so very like Trey's. "If you'll excuse us, Meredith is a little overwrought."

Meredith seemed to wilt. "I didn't mean—I won't tell, I promise," she babbled as Mr. Peterson led her away.

His voice drifted back to them, smooth and cultured with a hint of underlying steel. "Of course you won't, my dear. You're a Peterson now, and Petersons take care of their own."

Addy watched them leave. "Whew, that was uncomfortable. Wonder what she meant by secrets?"

"That man . . ." Brand's gaze followed Blake Peterson as he steered Meredith toward the lobby. "There was something about him . . ."

Mr. Collier rushed up to Brand. "Did you see him? Blake Peterson, I mean."

"Yes," Brand said.

"He's one of them, the demonoids."

Brand frowned. "What is this demonoid?"

Amasa made an impatient gesture. "Half human, half demon. Blake's daddy had him a demon. Cole Peterson was his name. I defended him against a murder charge when I first started practicing law. Got him off, too. Whole case was circumstantial, and half the men on the jury owed Cole money. I was right full of myself. Thought I was some kind of lawyer. Then I had that car wreck and started seeing demons. Ran into Cole a few weeks afterward and realized what he was. Got to worrying maybe he'd killed that woman after all. Couldn't get it out of my mind. Confronted him about it, and he admitted the whole thing. I think he enjoyed telling me about it. Wasn't a damn thing I could do, and he knew it. Double jeopardy had attached. He cut that poor woman into a million pieces, and I helped get him off. That's when I started drinking."

Addy stared at him. "You mean to say Trey's great-granddaddy was possessed by a demon?"

"Hell yeah," Amasa said. " 'Scuse my French. Town's full of demonoids."

"Wow." Addy tried to wrap her mind around this new revelation. Was *nothing* in Hannah what it seemed? "That would make Trey an eighth demon."

"Yep, more if he's got demonoid on his mama's side."

"I don't believe it."

People she'd known all her life, gone to school and church with, done business with, and greeted at the grocery store and pharmacy and on the street were part demon. She did a quick mental tally and counted half a dozen people of her acquaintance who had violet eyes, including Cassy Ferguson, the town "witch." Another dozen, including Trey and his father and grandfather had eyes so blue they looked deep purple.

Good God, Hannah was demon central.

There was a commotion on the far side of the room. Shep and Lenora had arrived. The thrall wore a slinky, blood-red gown. Shep looked dashing in his formal attire. The room buzzed with whispers and conjecture regarding the identity of the mysterious raven-haired seductress clinging to Shep's arm.

Apparently, the Dalvahni weren't the only ones who could bend space and time, because Bitsy appeared out of nowhere at Addy's side.

"Addy, who is that woman with your brother? Where is Marilee, and what's Shep done to his hair? He's a little old to be sporting Bama Bangs, don't you think? I swear, what is it with my children and their hair lately?"

"Mama, Shep does not have Bama Bangs. He doesn't have it lacquered to his head like he normally does, that's all. I think he looks handsome and younger."

"I guess I'm not used to it hanging on his forehead like that," Bitsy said, frowning. "It looks messy, like he just rolled out of bed."

Uh huh, or just rolled *off* somebody, say, for instance, a sex pot emotion-sucking vampire from another dimension.

"Here they come." Bitsy dug her nails into Addy's arm.

"Who *is* that woman, Adara Jean? You know something, I can tell."

Addy pulled away. "No freaking way, Mama. This is Shep's mess."

Bitsy bowed up. "That's another way of saying the 'F' word. You know I cannot abide vulgarity, young lady."

The "F" word? Good Lord, Hibiscus Corwin had acknowledged the existence of the "F" bomb.

"Adara is right, Mrs. Corwin. A man should handle his own affairs," Brand said. "It is Shep's place to tell you."

Addy gave him a grateful smile.

"Tell her what?" Shep asked, coming up to them with Lenora.

The wrinkle between Bitsy's eyes smoothed as if by magic. At once, she became the picture of Southern feminine gentility.

"I was asking Addy about your new friend, Shepton." Her voice was sweeter than cane syrup. She gave Lenora a sugary smile. "I don't believe I know this young lady."

"This is Lenora, Mama," Shep said. "She's my muse. I love her, and I want to marry her."

"Whoo." Bitsy gave a brittle little laugh and fanned herself with one hand. "I imagine Marilee might have something to say about that."

"Marilee can't say a damn thing to anybody. She's run off with that tennis coach from the club and filed for divorce."

"Oh, Shepton, that's so unlike her! What did you do to make her so unhappy?"

"I didn't do anything, except go to work and come home," Shep said indignantly. "What about me, Mama? Don't you want to know whether I'm happy?"

"Well, of course you're happy. Why wouldn't you be? You've got a home and a family and a business that you love."

"That's just it, Mama. I don't love Corwin's. I want to sell it."

"Sell Corwin's? Have you lost your mind, Shepton? And do what, pray tell?"

"I want to paint, Mama."

"Oh, fudge," Bitsy said.

Except that Mama didn't say *fudge*. Fudge was the word Addy's battered psyche supplied because it could not accept the truth. Her mother said *fuh*—

Addy's brain screeched to a halt. She took a mental breath and tried again. Bitsy Corwin said *fuh . . . fuh . . . fff . . .*

Nope, no way. It simply did not compute.

Chapter Thirty-two

The next morning as Addy waited in the parade line with Pootie and Brand, she still could not believe her mother had said the *T. rex* of swear words. And at the Grand Goober Ball, of all places, shattering at once two rules of Lady-tude; namely, that a lady doesn't swear and always behaves herself in public.

So what if she was no longer entirely human and her brother, the Rock of Gibraltar, was having a flaming affair with the hussy from hell and wanted to quit the family funeral business to paint nekked pictures of his new girlfriend? She could adjust.

So what if she had a talking dog and a flying cat, and a great-aunt with a psychic connection to her freezer and her front door bell? A little weird, but she could handle it.

Her best friend saw fairies, and her boring little hometown was populated by violet-eyed demonoids. No problem. Piece of cake. Chunk it in with the rest of the weirdness.

A crazed demon with a hard-on for her had threatened to kill her this very day. Death by demon? Puh-leeze.

But this . . .

Hibiscus Hamilton Corwin saying the mother of all cuss-words? It boggled Addy's mind.

She had still been wrestling with the shock of it that morning when she and Brand went by City Hall to settle with the mayor. The silent auction raised twenty-five thousand dollars and Brand made good on his promise to match it. At the mayor's office, he produced a leather pouch and counted out

250 one-hundred-dollar bills, plus fifteen more to pay for the peanut head Pootie lost in the river.

Funny thing about that pouch. It sure didn't seem big enough to hold all that money, but Brand kept pulling hundred-dollar bills out of it anyway. Addy had a notion he could have kept it up forever. That pouch was the money equivalent of the wishing mill that turned the sea to salt, grinding out an endless stream of Benjamins. Good thing Florence was too busy planting her double-D's on her desk and making goo-goo eyes at Brand to notice.

The mayor toddled in as they were winding things up.

"This is fine, mighty fine." He shook Brand's hand. "All the big contributors will get their names on a brass plaque in the lobby of the new building. You sure you don't want this donation in your name?"

Brand pulled his hand free. "My brother and I prefer our privacy. We want Pootie's name on the plaque."

"Sure, sure," the Mayor said. Humpty Dumpty sat on a wall, Addy thought, watching him rock back on his heels. "You two joining the parade today?" he asked.

Addy glanced at Brand. A muscle in his jaw twitched. The big guy was not happy she was riding in the parade.

Last night, he had made love to her with an almost desperate urgency, his fevered caresses and husky murmurings urging her to new heights and daring. Several times during the night as they lay entwined in the aftermath of lovemaking, their heated skin damp and flushed, she sensed him struggling with something. Something she wasn't ready for. Something she knew deep in her bones would make the hurt that much worse when he went away. The "L" word; her heart would crack wide open if he said it and left. And he *would* leave. He had no choice. So she shied away from it each time, distracting him with her body and her mouth.

As dawn approached, bringing with it the possibility of death by demon, panic set in. So little time . . . there was so little time. What if she died without telling him how she felt? She opened her mouth to tell him . . . and that's when he announced she would not be going to the parade. *This I cannot allow,* he had said. He wanted her to stay home where it was safe, and she was determined not to be controlled by a demonic bully with B.O. Besides, she told him, he would be there to protect her. She won the argument, but there had been no time to make things right.

"We're riding in the Goober Mobile with Pootie," she told the mayor.

"Splendid, splendid." He raised a plump hand in farewell as Brand dragged her toward the door. "See you there."

They had a few minutes to spare before they were supposed to meet Pootie, so she and Brand walked up and down the parade line. Addy loved the Peanut Parade. Anything on wheels was allowed as long as it had a leguminous or patriotic theme. People on go-carts, golf carts, and riding lawn mowers, as well as bicycles, tricycles, scooters, roller skates, and skate boards thronged the streets, their rides all decked out in goober regalia. Bubbas from as far away as Namath Springs were in the parade, their vehicles proudly adorned with peanut paraphernalia or red, white, and blue trappings. In addition to a bevy of newer model trucks, Addy counted fourteen antique pickups, three tractors, an Edsel, and two Model T Fords in the parade line. Hooting and hollering, the Hannah High cheerleaders hung from the open windows of a Camaro jacked up on monster truck tires, their toned cheerleader legs waving in the air like the feelers of a giant insect. Jeannine from the Kut 'N' Kurl had covered her Volkswagen Bug fender to fender in peanut shells, adding a red, grinning mouth across the front of the car and long eyelashes to the headlights. It was the Rose Parade on acid.

Addy directed Brand's attention to the Mobile Bay City Rollers and the Paulsberg Biker Babes, new to the event this year. She couldn't decide which was her favorite, Mamie Hall's power chair with the peanut-shaped toilet mounted as the seat or the lowrider pickup truck encased in an enormous yellow, blue, and green Styrofoam likeness of a can of Roddenberry Peanut Patch green-boiled peanuts. The Purple Hoo-Hahs, Muddy's coterie of eccentric friends, rode at the back of the parade in three convertibles festooned with banners and flags and balloons. The Hoo-Hahs had donned their signature purple hats for the occasion and a variety of purple shoes ranging in style from running shoes to slut pumps and designer flip-flops. Feather boas fluttered around their necks like plumage on a flock of exotic birds. Singing and cheering and blowing noise-makers, they draped themselves over the side of their vehicles, an older, better dressed, and more disturbing version of the Hannah cheerleaders.

Muddy was in the middle car, a purple plastic glass filled with some unidentified frosty liquid clutched in one ring-laden hand and a purple megaphone in the other. "Attention Kmart shoppers," she shouted into the megaphone. "Attention."

Oh, brother, the Hoo-Hahs were pickled. The Hoo-Hahs got snockered at the Peanut Festival every year, one reason they were placed at the back of the parade line. Thank goodness the chief had the good sense to assign three officers from Hannah's meager police force to drive the bunch of rowdy old ladies. Dan Curtis drove Muddy's car, a ten-year-old red Mercedes-Benz. Some Hoo-Hah had taken his police cap, replacing it with a downturn silk Fedora that sported a big, poofy bow. Purple ribbons fluttered from the back. Dan looked resigned. Addy thought he looked fetching.

A Hoo-Hah wearing a black and white polka dot silk hat trimmed with a purple taffeta sash leered at Brand. "Hey, baby, you know what I like," she said.

Muddy bonked the woman on the head with her megaphone, knocking her hat askew. "That's my niece's boyfriend, you old cougar," she said. "Stop drooling at him and reel that twat back in the car."

"Hey, Miss Hixie," Addy said to the woman Muddy had assaulted. "How you doing?"

Miss Hixie adjusted her hat. "Not near as well as you, shugah. Who's the cheesecake?"

"This is Brand Dalvahni, Miss Hixie."

"Hang on to that one, baby doll." The old lady winked. "Somebody might steal him."

"Yes, ma'am." Addy waved at her aunt, but Muddy couldn't see her for her hat, a flat brimmed platter-sized confection with a chiffon ruffle. "Muddy. *Muddy.*"

Muddy turned from conversation with the Hoo-Hah next to her. "Yes, dear?"

"Where's Mr. C?"

Muddy waved her glass. "Down at the river with the rest of the artists. He's got a booth this year. Already sold three Bear Bryants, two Elvises, and a Nativity scene." She gave Brand a beetle-eyed stare from beneath the brim of her big hat. "Amasa's an artist, you know. Wire sculpture." She paused, as though trying to remember something. "Oh, yes, he asked me to deliver a message to you. He said trouble's a-coming. His contrabulator's been humming all morning."

"Contrabulator?" Miss Hixie waggled her gray brows. "What's that, his willy?"

Muddy whopped Miss Hixie on the head again. "Never you mind Amasa's willy, Hixie Belle Lovelace."

Good grief, shades of Shirley and Bessie Mae.

Addy and Brand made a tactical retreat and joined Pootie in the Goober Mobile, a 1963 Lincoln Continental convertible with suicide doors, brown leather interior, and a gleaming faux peanut shell finish. Pootie sat behind the wheel. The front seat was covered with goody bags, so Addy and Brand climbed in the back. The Goober Mobile occupied a place of honor smack dab in the middle of the parade line. People stopped by to shake Pootie's hand and congratulate him. Pootie was one happy Grand Goober, resplendent in a brown western shirt and leather bolo tie with a big, silver "G" medallion, jeans, and snakeskin shit-kickers. His mama had whipped out her glue gun, transforming his plain straw cowboy hat into a glittering masterpiece. The letters "GG" were emblazoned across the front in rhinestones. A fey miniature dancing goober adorned the back. Privately, Addy thought the dancing goober looked more like one of Mr. C's cat turds than a peanut, but she kept it to herself. He'd topped off his outfit with a brown homemade cape trimmed in black braid that bore two big "G"s on the back.

Pootie gripped the wood-grained Lucite steering wheel. "You think folks will know I'm the Grand Goober without the peanut head?"

"Pootie, you're driving a car that's been painted to look like an eighteen-foot-long peanut on wheels," Addy said. "And then there's the hat and the cape, and the big banner on the side of the car that says 'Goober Mobile.' Everyone will know who you are."

"We should be starting soon. Don't you think we should be starting soon? Addy, see if you can tell what's going on up ahead," Pootie begged.

Addy scooted to the top of the backseat for a better view. She bounced a little with excitement. "The bands have cranked up, and I see movement up ahead. I think we're fixing to start."

The cars ahead of them moved a fraction.

Pootie gripped the wheel tighter. "Here we go."

Gunning his engine and tooting his horn, Pootie eased the big Lincoln forward. Addy suppressed a smile. He was a cowboy-esque Toad from *Wind in the Willows*, deep in the grip of motor car fever.

The parade crept across the railroad tracks and turned onto Oak Street in a merry cacophony of horn blowing, catcalls, and band music. People lined both sides of the parade route, some standing and others sitting in folding chairs and on top of coolers. Still others perched on the back of cars and pickup trucks. The crowd cheered and waved madly when they came into view.

"Quick, grab the goody bags," Pootie said.

Addy plucked two large-size paper bags off the front seat and handed one to Brand. "You throw to the left, and I'll throw to the right."

"I do not understand," Brand said. "Why do you wish me to hurl objects at these humans?" Reaching inside the bag on his lap, he removed a cellophane package. He sniffed the object in his hand, his nostrils flaring. "What do you call these little tarts?"

"It's a MoonPie." Addy threw another handful of goodies.

"Graham cracker cookies filled with marshmallow and dipped in chocolate."

He flapped a silver package in her direction. "And this?"

"That's a Goo Goo Cluster. Chocolate, peanuts, caramel, and marshmallow."

"I like chocolate." Brand sounded wistful. "But I will abstain. I must be at my best in case the djegrali attacks."

A finger of dread crept down her spine. The demon, she'd forgotten about the demon. Shoved it to the back of her mind, because she didn't want to think about it. Today could be the day that she . . .

She pushed the thought aside. Deal with it, Addy, she told herself. Compartmentalize, or you'll go bonkers.

"I appreciate the sacrifice," she said. "You can have all the MoonPies and Goo Goo Clusters you want when we get back home, I promise. But, unless you want people coming all up in this car with you, you'd best be throwing some candy. Folks around here take their parade goodies seriously."

They wound onto Main Street. The parade watchers lined the sidewalks four and five deep and dangled like overripe fruit from the branches of the live oak trees that shaded the store fronts. Addy recognized Ansgar's tall, broad-shouldered form among the people milling about on the sidewalks. He towered head and shoulders above the rest of the crowd, his long, pale hair gleaming in the sun. He arms were crossed on his broad chest, his gray eyes watchful as he scanned the press of humanity milling around him. Addy waved at Evie. Girlfriend wore shorts—*shorts!*—and a cotton top that emphasized her curves. Girlfriend was a babe.

Evie grinned and waved at Pootie. "Hey, Grand Goober. You look mah-velous!"

Pootie gave Evie a Homecoming Queen wave, fingers pressed together and slightly cupped. "Addy, throw that girl a MoonPie."

"Sure thing, Poot."

Addy reached into her bag, but Brand was quicker. He beaned Ansgar in the head with a MoonPie.

"Hey, no fair," she said. "*I* wanted to bop Blondy upside the head."

Brand stared at the grocery sack in his lap. "I do not know what came over me. I had the sudden overwhelming urge to smite my brother with a pastry."

She patted him on the arm. "Don't worry about it, babe. Happens to me every time I get around the guy."

She chunked another handful of candy over the side of the car and made eye contact with a man in the crowd. He gave her a death's head grin, his purple eyes glowing with a sickly radiance. Startled, she looked back, but he was gone. Probably a trick of the light, she decided. Mr. Nasty really had her spooked. She'd be seeing purple-eyed whoozits everywhere if she wasn't careful.

An obnoxious rumbling drew her attention to the left side of the Goober Mobile. Shep and Lenora pulled alongside them in the northbound lane.

Shep grinned and waved. "Hey, sis, what do you think of my ride?"

It was official. Shep had gone ape shit crazy. Never mind that her stick-in-the-mud big brother was breaking any number of parade rules by getting out of line and tooling down the middle of the street. Forget the fact that his girlfriend, Suzy Succubus, was drawing a buttload of attention with an outfit that consisted of a couple of yards of ribbon and nothing more. Or that a magical wind machine blew Vampire Chick's long black hair and the ribbons of her dress behind her in a languorous stream like Isadora Duncan's scarf.

And, yes, she was surprised to see Shep *in* the parade instead of standing on the sidelines as befitted a man in his somber line of work.

But, what really racked her back was his vehicle, a 1932 Ford Roadster with a steel casket welded to the chassis and sporting a set of racing slick tires. A coffin car; her brother was driving a coffin car.

"Shep, is that by any chance Granddaddy *Corwin*'s Roadster you're driving?" she said.

She had to shout to be heard over the steady *whump-whump-whump* of the coffin car's exhaust.

"Sure is. Ain't it cool? I've been working on it for months down at Rat's place. Surprised?"

Oh, she was surprised all right. But, that was nothing on what Bitsy was going to do when she saw that car. Bitsy was going to have a duck fit.

"See yah," Shep said.

He squealed his tires and roared off in a cloud of smoke.

Chapter Thirty-three

The parade route ended at the top of the hill on South Main. Honking his horn, Pootie eased the Goober Mobile into a parking place under an oak tree on the west side of the square and turned off the engine. There was a bare patch in the grass where Jeb Hannah had sat before the demon picked him up and plunked him on Muddy's front lawn. The roving statue caused quite a sensation. The story was picked up by the Associated Press. A photographer from Paulsberg was taking pictures of people in the shallow depression.

There were long lines at the inflatable moon walk and the water slide the city brought in for the festival. Parents and children swarmed around the Conecuh Sausage vendor and the snow cone machine. Folks gathered around the Goober Mobile, admiring Pootie and his ride and having their picture taken with the most successful Double G in Peanut Festival history. Pootie was on Cloud Nine.

Leaving Pootie to enjoy his big moment, Addy and Brand wandered over to the snow cone vendor. Addy was trying to work up the courage to try the new boiled peanut–flavored shaved ice when the chief's patrol car pulled up and Bitsy and the chief got out. Bitsy was a vision of goober couture in a pale yellow linen boat-neck shell and a pair of matching cropped pants with little brown peanuts embroidered on the hem.

"Hey," Bitsy said, waving. The temperature was in the nineties but she looked as cool and unwilted as the flowers

Addy kept refrigerated at the shop. "Y'all get something to drink and meet me and Car-lee under that tree."

Addy took Bitsy's timely arrival as a sign from God that she was not meant to ingest a frozen dessert that tasted like peanut-y brine and dragged Brand over to a lemonade stand. They purchased two big glasses of lemonade and joined Bitsy and the chief in the shade of a huge sweet gum tree.

"Get out of the sun, you two," Chief Davis said. "It's hotter 'n a goat's butt in a pepper patch."

Hard to believe her persnickety, socially nice mother was dating a good ole boy who talked about goat butts. Really, those two had about as much in common as . . . as a small-town hick florist and a sexy drop-dead-gorgeous immortal demon hunter. The universe was a strange and random place.

"Thanks." Addy took a seat on the circular bench that surrounded the tree.

Bitsy smiled up at Brand. "Don't you want to sit down, Mr. Dalvahni?"

"Thank you," Brand said. "I will stand."

He stalked to the edge of the circle of shade, his hard gaze on the people swarming around the little park. Now that the parade was over, he seemed edgy and tense. His mood was contagious. Addy thought about the guy on the street with the wide, creepy grin. Was the demon watching them? Did Brand sense it? She looked around. Parents stood in line with cranky children, waiting their turn on the moon walk and the water slide. People crowded around the snow cone and lemonade booths and the Conecuh Sausage guy was doing a land-office business, but she didn't see any purple-eyed whoozits. This was silly. Brand's stone-faced warrior routine was making her jumpy. She needed to think about something else. She needed a puzzle or a problem to gnaw on.

Like who made God or where does space end, and what comes after that? If light has a speed, does dark? What exactly is Spam made of, and why isn't there a product called Spicken or Speef or Splamb or Spish?

Nah, she needed something truly incomprehensible and perverse to ponder so she wouldn't think about Mr. Nasty.

Like her mother.

Sipping her drink, Addy contemplated Mama. The Bitsy she knew and loved was wound too tight. But today Mama seemed relaxed and freer. Probably had something to do with Mama saying the "F" word. Who knew how long that word had been fermenting inside Mama, swelling and growing and straining to get out? It was a miracle the woman hadn't erupted years ago from the pressure, swear words rat-a-tat-tatting out of her mouth at machine gun speed, her size four body slamming up and down like a jackhammer.

Mama looked younger today, too. Why, saying that one "F" word had knocked ten years off her age, living proof that a person ought to indulge in a little judicious cussing now and then. In private, of course, and under the right circumstances. Profanity lost its zing if overused. If Mama had done more closet cussing last night's unfortunate episode might not have happened, and Mama wouldn't have forfeited her crown of perfect Southern Lady-tude.

Tragic.

"You seen Shep this morning, Mama?" Addy asked.

"No, I haven't. I was about to ask you the same thing, Addy. I—"

Whump, wump, wump, Shep and Lenora drove up in the coffin car. People mobbed the modified Roadster, pointing and asking questions.

Bitsy leaped up. "What in heaven's name is that?"

"It's a coffin car, Mama," Addy said. "Shep and Rat Godwin built it in Rat's garage."

"He's got that floozy with him again." Bitsy pointed at the thrall. "What's that she's wearing, a bunch of string?"

"I think it's supposed to be a dress," Addy said.

"It's indecent, that's what it is. Shep is having some sort of crisis. I'm going to have a talk with him."

The chief rose and took her gently by the arm. "Shep's a grown man, Hibiscus. He don't need his mama running his life."

"But—"

"No buts, Little Bit. Leave him alone."

Bitsy was still huffing and puffing like a calliope when a blue Jeep Cherokee with the word SHERIFF emblazoned in big silver letters on the side pulled up to the curb and parked behind Chief Davis's patrol car.

"It's somebody from the sheriff's department." Addy set her lemonade down on the bench and got to her feet. "Reckon what they want?"

A tall, broad-shouldered man wearing mirrored Ray-Bans got out of the SUV and looked around. He spotted the chief under the tree and started toward them, moving with a rangy grace that had female heads bobbing up and down like a colony of meerkats.

Brand strode over to stand next to the chief. "You know this man?" he asked.

"Sure, that's Dev Whitsun, the new sheriff." The chief grunted. "Wonder what he wants."

Bitsy gave the man approaching them a squinty-eyed stare. "That's the new sheriff?"

Uh oh. Addy knew that look. Mama was matchmaking again, looking for a back-up in case things didn't work out with Brand. Mama was all about the Plan B.

Bitsy sidled up to her. "He's a real nice-looking man, isn't he? According to Jeannine down at the Kut 'N' Kurl, he's single. He's got a steady job . . . for the next four years, anyway. And the county gives good benefits. Sick leave and health insurance and a nice retirement package."

"Forget it, Mama."

"But don't you think he's handsome?"

"Yeah, but I'm not interested."

"I declare, Adara Jean, you are too picky. That sheriff is a real catch. If you two got married you could stay here, not run off to Europe with Mr. Dalvahni."

Europe? Oh, good grief. Mama thought Brand was European. Okay, so maybe that was the teensy weeniest bit her fault, but what choice did she have? She could hardly tell Mama her

new boyfriend was not from Earth. But, Mama thought Brand
would take Addy away, and that was not a good thing. Mama
Hen liked her chickens close to the nest.

Right now she seemed to have her heart set on fixing Addy
up with the sheriff. Mama was as tenacious as a badger. If she
latched her jaws around a bachelor morsel by the name of Dev
Whitsun, neither man nor God could tear her loose.

"I don't care how hot the guy is, Mama," Addy said. "I love
Brand."

Oh, crap, she said the "L" word. For days, she'd held it in.
But the damn thing slipped out anyway. Maybe it was like that
"F" word Mama had been sitting on all these years. Lurking on
the back of her tongue, waiting for the right moment, and
then—*bam!*—springing forth like a dog freed from a kennel.

Love.

Man, she was so going to get her heart busted all to pieces.

Bitsy sighed. "I was afraid of that. Have you told him?"

"No."

"Adara Jean! What are you waiting for, a sign from the Lord
God Almighty? If you love the man, you ought to tell him."

"I know, I know. I'm going to. Things have been crazy."

Sheriff Whitsun walked up and shook the chief's hand. He
looked Brand up and down, his eyes unreadable behind the
mirrored sunglasses. Chief Davis introduced Brand to the sheriff. The sheriff said something in a low voice to the chief. Addy
edged nearer. Mama scooted closer, too.

"—warn you," Sheriff Whitsun was saying. "Sorry to be the
bearer of bad tidings, but I thought you'd want to know."

He glanced at Addy and Bitsy and muttered something in the
chief's ear. Brand's lips thinned. Whatever the sheriff said,
Brand didn't like it.

"Thanks, Dev," Chief Davis said. "I appreciate the heads-up.
You need any help, you let me know."

"I'll do that," Sheriff Whitsun said. "The news has gone out
over the wire. The State Troopers are on the lookout, and the
sheriff's departments in Monroe and Escambia counties have

sent men. We'll catch the sum bitches." His head turned in their direction, his eyes hidden behind the Ray-Bans. "Excuse my French, ladies."

Bitsy gave him a sugary smile. "That's quite all right, Sheriff."

With a curt nod, he walked back to his Jeep, climbed in, and drove off.

Bitsy gave Addy a sideways glance. "Easy on the eyes and smells like heaven, too. Sure you don't want to change your mind, Addy?"

"Positive."

Bitsy shrugged. "Oh, well. What did the sheriff want, Carlee?"

The chief pushed his hat back. "Been a prison break. Six convicts busted out of Newsome Correctional Facility last night. Killed three guards in the process. Soon as they got out, they robbed a convenience store over by Jordan's Crossing. Killed the owner and two customers. Dev said the place looked like somebody butchered a hog. Forensics guys are having a hard time identifying the bodies."

Bitsy gasped. "Oh, my goodness, how horrible! What if those terrible men come to Hannah?"

The chief put his arm around Bitsy. "Relax, Hibiscus. That scum is a hundred miles away from here by now."

Dan Curtis barreled around the square in Muddy's convertible and screeched to a stop.

Muddy sat up and straightened her hat. "Yi-ha, ride 'em cowboy," she yelled into the megaphone.

Dan Curtis leaped out of the convertible and loped across the grass.

Chief Davis watched him approach, his expression sour. "What's that damn fool up to now?"

Officer Dan's eyes were alight with excitement. "Alarm's going off at the First National Bank, Chief. Probably a squirrel in the wiring again, but I thought I'd better tell you."

"God almighty." The chief threw his hat on the ground. "If this ain't the damndest town. Wandering statues and burgling squirrels." He picked up his hat and jammed it back on his head. "Well, don't stand there, Officer Curtis. Let's go arrest some rodents."

Muddy climbed out of the convertible. She was wearing purple high-top Converse tennis shoes that matched her purple skirt and silk blouse. "I'm coming with you. I always wanted to ride in a police car."

Officer Dan adjusted his gun holster. "You can't come, Miss Muddy. This here is official police business."

His officer-of-the-law persona would have been a lot more impressive without the big purple hat.

"Oh, let her come along." The chief shook a warning finger at Muddy. "But you're staying in the car while we check this bank thing out, understood?"

"Ten-four," Muddy shouted into the megaphone.

"God almighty," the chief said again.

They jumped in the chief's patrol car, Muddy in the back, and sped off.

Bitsy sighed. "Oh, dear, I do hope they'll be all right. You know how Muddy is."

"They'll be fine, Mama," Addy said. "Like the chief said, it's a bunch of squirrels. You know nothing exciting happens around here."

What was she saying? That might have been true five days ago, but it sure as shoot wasn't true anymore. Sleepy, boring little Hannah had turned out to be a sinkhole of weirdness.

As if the cosmos were attuned to her thoughts, she heard a low rumble from the direction of the river. The sound was too steady to be thunder. It grew louder, coalescing into the excited murmuring of many voices.

The white stag trotted up the broad, azalea-lined steps that went from the park down to the river, Hannah's version of the Spanish Steps in Rome. The stag's antlers shone in the sun. A mob of exultant, shouting people came up the stairs behind him. The men in the horde, and a few of the women, too, looked wild eyed and feverish. Addy knew that look: hunting fever. Screw the fact this deer was one-of-a-kind in its magnificence; didn't matter. It had silver antlers and glowed like a nuclear reactor; didn't matter. Deer season was long past. That didn't matter, either. The granddaddy of all deer was in Hannah, and every bubba and bubbette with a gun or a hunting bow wanted to shoot that sucker and hang it on a wall.

The stag loped across the park. Vendors abandoned their booths, and the festivalgoers in the square flowed into the horde as it passed, thickening the crowd that followed the snowy deer.

"Holy freaking shit, it's an albino elk," Shep yelled. He leaped out of the coffin car. "That thing's the size of a baby elephant. Where the hell's my gun? Look at the rack on that bad boy!" He waved his arm at a man in a ball cap. "Jimmy Lee, you got your gun in your truck?"

"Hell yeah, I got it."

"Let me borrow it."

"Get your own friggin' gun, Shep. This baby's all mine. Have you ever seen such a beaut in all your born days?"

"Shit," Shep said. "Shit. Shit. Shit."

Bitsy flew up to him, an avenging fury. "William Shepton Corwin, you watch your language."

Do as I say, not as I do. It was Jim-Dandy-fine for Mama to say a wordy-dird in public, but that didn't mean her kids were allowed. Mama needn't have worried. No one was paying Shep any mind. People scattered up and down Main Street in a mad dash for their vehicles and their firepower. Those folks that didn't hunt trailed behind the glowing stag in a ragged line, a look of stupefied amazement on their faces. It was better than an Elvis sighting. The stag seemed unfazed by all the commotion. He pranced across the grass, leading the clamor of people in a weaving circle through the little park.

The air shimmered, and Ansgar materialized in the square with Evie in his arms. Bitsy was too busy chewing on Shep and shaking her finger in Lenora's direction to notice. How 'bout that? Shep was on Mama's list for a change. Addy had been on that list for the better part of twenty-seven years. She should be relieved. Instead, she felt sort of funny and confused and a little left out.

Ansgar set Evie on her feet.

Evie grinned and fluttered her hand in Addy's direction. "Hey, Adds."

"Hey yourself," Addy said.

Ansgar took Evie by the hand and dragged her over to Brand. Huh. Mr. Personality was acting like more of a butthead than usual. Something was up.

Giving Mama and Shep a last worried glance, Addy hurried after them.

"—meaning of one of the Lesser in this realm," she heard Ansgar say as she walked up. "There is more here than meets the eye. Conall should be apprised."

Conall again. He must be like the big cheese among the Dalvahni.

"Who's Lester?" she asked.

Ansgar looked down his nose at her. "I said 'Lesser,' not 'Lester.'"

Ooh, she hated that disdainful "you are such a big stupid head" tone of his. It made her want to bop him upside the head with something a whole lot harder than a MoonPie. A two-by-four, for instance, or maybe a ball-peen hammer.

She scowled at him. "Pull the stick outcha butt, Blondy. Who's this Lesser guy, another Dalvahni?"

"Gently, little one," Brand said, taking her hand in his. "Ansgar refers to the celestial being in our midst, one of the Lesser gods of Gorth."

Addy blinked at him. "Say what?"

"The stag leading yon town folk such a merry dance is a forest deity."

"You're kidding me, right?"

His expression grew distant. "Ah, you are asking if I jest. I assure you, I am not. From your expression of disbelief, I take it you do not practice polytheism?"

"This is Alabama. We got two religions. God and football."

"Levity again."

"Dude, around here we don't joke about football. So Malibu Bambi over there is a god?"

"Yes, but his name is Sildhjort, not Bambi."

"That's a terrible name. Was his mama mad at him or something? I'll call him Sid instead." She rolled the name around on her tongue. "Yeah, Sid. Way better than Sildhjort."

His lips twitched. "Perhaps you should tell him that, although I do not think this is the proper time."

The stag skimmed across the grass on weightless silver hooves, a bevy of ecstatic people in his slipstream.

"So, what's Sid doing in Hannah?"

"I am not certain," Brand said. "His presence is most unexpected."

"You can say that again. Some people would be having a religious crisis right now trying to square old Sid with their concept of God and the universe. But here's the way I see it. God is the creator, right? That's what He does. I always figured He didn't stop with us. How boring would that be? And God is anything but boring. So He made us and this world and many more besides and filled them with all kind of fantastic, wonderful creatures. Things I can't even imagine. And He made Sid over there, and gave him some cool powers and made him immortal, but he's still a child of God like you and me."

"Very wise, little one. You constantly surprise me," Brand said.

"Yeah, I'm a stone hoot."

They watched the stag make a final turn around the park and canter over the hill. People swarmed after him, and the little square emptied. Shep, Lenora, Pootie, and Bitsy were swept up by the multitude and washed down Main Street with the rest of the crowd. Addy ran across the park and looked down the hill. Jimmy Lee Butler was parked in front of the drug store. He dove inside his truck, emerging a moment later with his deer rifle in hand.

"Whoo hoo, I got mine," he shouted, brandishing his weapon in the air.

"Me, too," Taz Phillips hollered, waving his shotgun from the truck next to Jimmy Lee's.

Thunk, thunk, thunk. Up and down Main Street, truck doors slammed as men and women retrieved their weapons from their vehicles and ran after the prancing stag. Addy could almost hear the collective *cha chung* as weapons were checked and loaded. People from the arts and crafts booths down by the river heard the shouting and came up to see what all the commotion was about, further swelling the crowd. Addy thought she spotted Mr. Collier waving his contrabulator around in all the chaos. In a matter of moments, Main Street was clogged with a mass of people in pursuit of the white stag.

Addy ran back over to Brand. "You better do something quick. The bubbas are armed to the teeth down there. I think they mean to kill Sid."

"Do not be distressed, Adara. They cannot harm him. He is a god. He plays with the humans, though to what end I cannot say." He turned to Ansgar. "Do you not agree, brother?"

"I believe I can guess his intent," Ansgar said. He pointed to the press of humanity pouring down Main Street toward the northeast. "He is leading them to safety across the river bridge."

"Leading them to safety from *what*?" Addy asked.

A low, throbbing boom came from the hills that surrounded the town. Addy's heart lurched out of rhythm with a sickening thud. The sound vibrated against her skin and thrummed in her ears, menacing and terrifying, the single, steady heartbeat of an unseen monster beating out a death knell on an enormous drum.

She clutched Brand's arm. "What in God's name is that?"

Ansgar gave her the big stupid-head look again.

"You mean, you do not know?" He arched a blond brow at her. "The demons are coming."

Chapter Thirty-four

*B*oom, *boom, boom.* The drums sounded again, harsh and hollow, a ravenous giant promising bloody retribution. *Fe-fi-fo-fum.* The drumbeat pulsed inside Addy's head. *I'll grind your bones to make me bread.*

The relentless pounding drew closer, the jaws of the trap tightening around them. The demons were almost upon them, closing in on all sides. Taking their time and playing with their food.

Boom, boom, boom.

Drums in the deep. We cannot get out. Balin's anguished words from the belly of Moria echoed in her mind.

Like Balin and his kinfolk, they were doomed. The goblins were coming. There would be no escape.

Addy's heart thudded with terror. She wanted to scream, to run blindly down the steps, and jump into the river. It was hopeless though. She could not run, could not reach the river in time. They were hemmed in on all sides by the ceaseless thunder of the drums, trapped like rats in a rain barrel.

Besides, she wouldn't leave Brand and Evie. Heck, she wouldn't even leave Blondy to face the demons alone.

Not that she could do much more than give moral support. What did she know about fighting demons?

The world tilted sideways as Brand lifted her in his arms. "Do not be afraid, little one," he said, striding across the grass. "The demons will not harm you. I will not allow it."

"What's the big idea? Put me down."

He dumped her under the big sweet gum tree and stepped back. Ansgar stomped up with Evie in tow. He gave her a little shove and stalked over to stand next to Brand. Brand pointed, and a glowing circle appeared around the tree; a protective spell to keep her and Evie safe. How sweet. Her heart began to race. Being confined made her feel hot and woozy and panicky. Hadn't she told the big lug she was claustrophobic?

Metal flashed in the sunlight as Brand drew a wicked-looking knife from his boot.

She eyed the weapon uncertainly. "What are you doing?"

"Keeping you safe."

He swiped the knife across his palm.

She gasped. "Brand, your hand! Are you crazy?"

"I do not believe so. But no doubt your question was rhetorical and you do not, in reality, question my sanity. Do not worry about my hand. It is nothing."

He turned his palm over and dripped blood onto the ground. It was like adding grease to a fire. The spell line flared brighter. When he lifted his hand, the deep cut was gone. He handed the knife to Ansgar. Without a word, Ansgar slashed his hand and added his blood to the pulsing ring of light. The gash on his hand quickly closed and faded. He wiped the blade clean and handed the knife back to Brand. Brand slid the weapon back in his boot.

"It's gone." Addy stared in bemusement at Brand's hand. "The cut on your hand is gone."

Ansgar gave her that "my poop don't stink but yours sure does" look she was *so* crazy about. "Foolish woman. The Dalvahni heal quickly. Do you not know that?"

That did it. She was going to read his beads for whale shit. She opened her mouth to tell him where to stick his condescending attitude, but Brand spoke first.

"She knows, brother. She is having trouble accepting it. That is all."

Evie put her arm around Addy's shoulder. "There's no need

to be so stuffy, Ansgar. Addy has had a lot to deal with lately. *I think she's handled things remarkably well, considering all that has happened. You've had ten thousand years to get used to who and what you are. Maybe you should spend the next ten thousand years developing a little patience."*

Whoa, did shy little Evie just give Ansgar a verbal smack-down?

To Addy's surprise, Ansgar bowed. "You are right, Evangeline. Adara, I regret my impatience with you. Please accept my apology."

"Sure thing, Blondy." Evie poked her in the side with her elbow. For a curvaceous gal, girlfriend's elbows were *sharp*. "Ouch, I mean Ansgar."

"Enough," Brand said. "They are coming. It is time."

Addy glanced at him, startled by his sharp tone, and received a shock. Brand's eyes were hard and flat. He radiated a combination of lethal eagerness and raw, primal power. Ansgar exuded the same restless, coiled energy. They were in warrior mode, she realized with a stab of dismay, two predators on the hunt, *eager* for the hunt. But, there was no *need* for them to do the macho warrior thing. Not when there was an alternative.

They turned to leave.

"Wait, where are you going?" Addy cried. "Stay here, where it's safe."

Brand turned around, his expression of chilly hauteur reminding her uncomfortably of Ansgar's. "Dalvahni warriors do not cower behind a shield spell like frightened children. Fighting the djegrali is what we do."

Oh, great. She'd insulted his masculinity. Heaven forbid they do the sensible thing and get inside the shield. Oh, no. The big bad Dalvahni warriors had to take on a bunch of crazed, blood-thirsty, soul-sucking demons.

Fighting the djegrali is what we do. Ooh, he was infuriating, the big, macho jerk. Who knew how many demons were out there or what twisted form they would take? Sure, he and Ansgar were seasoned warriors, but what if they were outnumbered?

What if Mr. Nasty brought reinforcements? No one was infallible. What if Brand got hurt . . . or . . . or . . .

Terror streaked through her, mind numbing, petrifying. Terror for *him*. And did he care? Oh, no. He was an adrenaline junky, hooked on a djegrali fix, chomping at the bit to kick a little demon boo-tay. He was going to go out there and fight the demons *right in front of her,* and he expected her to sit in a safe little bubble and watch like a good little woman. No. She did not think so.

Suddenly, she was furious.

She slammed the flat of her hand against the invisible wall. "Well, excuse the hell out of me for being worried you might get hurt. Go ahead then. Get yourself killed. See if I care."

Hurt flashed in his eyes and was gone. He shrugged and strode after Ansgar.

Addy flung herself against the shield. "Wait, Brand, I didn't mean it! I do care. I—I . . ."

She stopped. Her throat closed up, and the words shriveled on her tongue. What was the matter with her? It was like her brain and her mouth were disconnected. She could not say it. Neither could she let him go like this, facing death with her hateful words ringing in his ears.

Tears of frustration streamed down her face. She pounded her fists against the shield. "Brand, come back. I'm sorry. I didn't mean it. *Brand.*"

He heard her. He must have heard her, because he came back. She watched him stride across the grass, her heart hammering in her chest. The way he moved was a thing of beauty, lithe, fluid, powerful—the heavy muscular grace of a predator in his prime. She loved the way he moved. She loved everything about him. She loved *him*.

He stopped a few paces from the tree, his beautiful archangel features strained and taut, as though he were in the grip of some ferocious inner battle. He took a deep breath. She shrank back instinctively, knowing what was coming. She forgot about the demons, watching with helpless longing and dread as his wicked, beautiful, sensuous mouth curved into a rueful smile. He was going to say it. He tried to tell her last night more than once, but each time she stopped him. It was right there in his eyes, in the hot, aching melting way he looked at her. He loved her. He was going to say it and walk into danger, and leave her with an agony of bitter regret because she was too big a coward to say it back.

Like hell she was.

"I love you, Brand," she blurted.

A terrible weight lifted from her heart with the words. What a relief it was to say it, how easy and *right* it felt. I love you. She wanted—no, *needed*—to say it. What an idiot she had been. She loved him. And he loved her . . . although he hadn't said it yet.

He stared at her like she was some strange, exotic animal, this man from another dimension who'd seen dwithmorgers and fought demons in the far reaches of Gorth.

"What did you say?"

She gave him a giddy grin. "I said 'I love you.' What do you think about that?"

Thwack! He grinned back and she was a goner, high as a kite from that smile.

"I think you are the most infuriating, impossible, maddening female I ever met." His eyes were alight with amusement and enough love to burn her to cinders. "I have been trying to tell you of my damnable *feelings* since last night, would you but let me. But you defeated me at every turn. You are the most exasperating creature."

"Those things you said, maddening, impossible, infuriating and . . . uh . . . uh . . ."

"Exasperating?"

"Yeah, that's the one, exasperating. Those are good things, right?"

He chuckled and turned again to leave.

"Hey!" She pounded her fists against the shield. "You can't walk away without saying it back. That would be rude."

"Heaven forbid," he said without slowing.

"I mean it, Brand. *Brand.*"

He looked back at her then, his gaze hot enough to melt stone. "Very well, if you insist. I love you, Adara Jean Corwin. You have taken my heart by storm. Satisfied?"

"No, but it'll do for now."

Swallowing the lump of tears in her throat, she watched him stride off to join Ansgar near the center of the park. The drums throbbed closer, louder. It sounded as though the demons had reached the foot of the hill. Any moment they would come over the rise and the battle would begin. Brand could be . . . Brand could be . . .

Brand and Ansgar drew their weapons. Liquid tongues of flame danced down the blade in Brand's hand, and the silver and white bow Ansgar held shone with an unearthly light.

Beside her, Evie made a small sound of dismay. Addy felt a twinge of remorse. She'd been so wrapped up in Brand that she forgot all about Evie. She hurried over to her friend. Evie clung to her, staring in wide-eyed horror across the field.

"Look," Evie cried, pointing.

Two men came up the rise on Main Street dressed in prison whites. Addy recognized the uniforms. Work gangs were a common enough sight on the highway that ran between Hannah and Jordan Springs, where the state penitentiary was located. These men were some of the escaped convicts the sheriff warned them about. If she hadn't known them by their garb, the words PROPERTY OF THE ALABAMA DEPARTMENT OF CORRECTIONS stamped in big black letters on their loose cotton pants and shirts were a big, fat clue. They looked like ordinary men, not demons. No twisted horns or gnarled limbs or bristling, tusk-filled mouths. Except for the gooey purple eyes that wobbled above their snarling mouths like bits of jelly left out in the sun and the blood that stained their clothes and the severed human heads they carried, they looked like ordinary men.

They saw Ansgar and Brand and swung their gruesome trophies. The heads slammed together with a dull boom. *Fe fi fo fum.* The hollow sound made Addy want to cover her ears and scream in mindless terror. It vibrated against her skin and rattled her bones, dark music from the bowels of hell. This was demon magic, she realized dimly, through her fright. It stripped the mind of reason and replaced it with stark, primitive fear, fear of the boogie man and the thing under the bed and the horror of the unknown.

Boom, boom, boom. She whirled around. Two more convicts entered the park from the south. Each held a severed human head. Three prison guards had been killed in the breakout, the sheriff said. And a store owner and two customers at Jordan's Crossing. *Boom* and *boom* again. The last two escaped prisoners came, one from the east and one from the west, ghoulish plunder in hand. Addy counted. Six heads, six victims. *Boom, boom, boom.* The convicts thumped the heads with their fists, sounding their dreadful song. The ground boiled, and a cloud of insects rose in the air, bringing with them the smell of wet earth and moldering leaves, rotting bugs, and worms and other small creatures. The damp, musty stench penetrated the shield, filling Addy's nostrils and mouth with the smell and taste of detritus and decay.

She coughed and spit to get the taste of death out of her mouth. "Brand's spell might work on demons, but it sure doesn't work on stink."

Evie was red faced from holding her breath.

Addy pounded her on the back. "Breathe, Eves. Spit it out before you choke on it."

Evie sucked in a lung full of air and coughed. "La . . . dies don't spit," she said with a gasp. "Bitsy says."

"They do if they got bug funk in their throats."

The black column of insects swirled in a dizzying pattern over the convicts' heads and settled back down, covering everything in a blanket of tiny, moving bodies. Evie screamed as the shield was enveloped by thousands of roaches, stinkbugs, beetles, and other winged insects.

"Bugs." Evie did a shivery little dance. "Oh, my God, we're buried alive in bugs! *I hate* bugs, especially roaches. And stinkbugs. They crackle when they walk. Yuck!"

Crackle when they walk? No time to think about that one. Addy was too worried about Brand.

She rushed to the edge of the shield, frantic to see what was happening. "I can't see. I can't see Brand."

Frustrated, she smacked her hand against the shield, her fear and anger fueling the blow. She felt a pulling sensation. Her palm burned. The shield crackled and flared, bright blue and then white. The curtain of bugs slid to the ground in a smoking heap. The once green park was covered in a thick carpet of dead bugs.

"You got 'em, Addy." Evie jumped up and down with excitement. "You got 'em!"

Addy barely heard her. Her attention was focused on the two warriors. They stood back to back. The inmates surrounded them in a loose circle. Grinning, three of the men dropped the heads they carried. Bones cracked and skin and clothing split as the demons inside them took full control. A convict's head and jaw elongated grotesquely. His enormous, gaping mouth bristled with a double row of sharp teeth. Flesh tore with a wet, meaty sound as a row of steely red spikes sprang from the man's hunched back. His arms and legs grew into long, leathery limbs that ended in cruel claws. A second man took the form of a gigantic wolf with six legs and three heads with vice-like, slavering jaws. The third man stretched and grew into a ten-foot ogre with one eye in the middle of his bulging forehead, and a wide, drooling mouth. A *naked* ten-foot ogre with skin like tanned hide and feet like concrete blocks. And a gi-normous ogre-size hairy arse. Eww.

With a guttural roar, the ogre pulled up a flowering pear tree by the roots and swung it at Brand and Ansgar. They ducked, avoiding the blow with ease.

Brand straightened. "Hear me, djegrali."

His deep voice rang around the square. He sounded calm and unafraid, like a man who had things under control.

As if.

Not if Cerberus the three-headed wolf or Mr. Hairy Butt Cheeks or the guy that looked like somebody had mated the monster from *Aliens* with a horny toad had anything to say about it.

"Return with me and my brother peaceably," he said, "and you will be banished to the Pit. Fight and we will destroy you." He held out his left hand, palm side up. A small, curved bottle with a stoppered top appeared in his hand.

Was he serious? He was threatening a Cyclops with a *perfume bottle?* The three convicts still in human form jeered and beat on their drums.

Brand shrugged and closed his hand. The bottle disappeared.

The ogre opened his slack, lipless mouth and bellowed. The sound was deafening, a hundred rampaging elephants trumpeting their rage at once. He lurched forward, swinging his makeshift club like an enormous mace. One blow from that club and Brand and Ansgar would be smashed to bits.

"Mine," Ansgar said as cool as you please.

Stepping forward, he fitted an arrow into his bow and fired in one smooth motion. The arrow whistled through the air and skewered the ogre in his one eye. The ogre bawled like an injured calf and crashed to the ground. The mountainous, fleshy body trembled in gelatinous waves, and the ogre disappeared. In the monster's place a dead convict lay on the ground, a shining silver arrow between his eyes. Something dark oozed out of the corpse and pooled on the ground. A despairing wail rose from the puddle. The hair on Addy's arms and neck stood on end at the eerie sound. The liquid patch of darkness solidified and cracked, then shattered into dust that was caught and blown asunder by a sudden rush of wind.

After that, things seemed to happen at once. Howling with rage, the gigantic wolf and the lizard monster attacked. Addy saw Brand's sword flash in a flaming arc and heard the sharp twang of arrows as Ansgar fired his bow. A wolfen head hit the ground, jaws snapping. Arrows bounced off the lizard monster's leathery skin.

"Aim for the throat, Ansgar," Brand shouted, stabbing one of two remaining wolf heads in the neck. The huge animal shuddered and snarled, snapping at Brand as the wounded head sagged. Brand dove under the wolf, stabbing it deep in the belly. It gave a gurgling cry and collapsed. Brand rolled free and sprang to his feet, chopping off the third and last head with a swinging blow. The wolf vanished, leaving in its place a dead convict with a severed head and a deep slash across his abdomen.

Ansgar smiled as he battled his monster. And he was *singing*. He danced between the monster's clawed limbs on nimble feet, a strapping, flaxen-haired, six-and-a-half-foot Viking god, Fred Astaire doing the quick step with a nightmarish Ginger Rogers. He sang as he dodged the thing's biting jaws, belting out a song in a language Addy did not recognize. Evie giggled. Oh, boy. Ansgar's singing made girlfriend giddy even at a distance. On the bright side, his yodeling seemed to annoy the monster, even cause it pain. The creature opened its toothy maw with a roar of protest. Ansgar stopped singing and fired a swift volley of arrows down the monster's throat. The thing stiffened and crashed to the ground. A moment later it disappeared. A man lay on the ground, half a dozen arrows sticking out of his neck.

Dark sludge leaked out of the dead men's bodies and stained the ground, hardened and cracked. The wraiths shrieked, turned to dust, and blew away.

"Look, Addy." Evie pointed to the three corpses on the ground. She sounded a little woozy from the aftereffects of Ansgar's singing, but otherwise okay.

The bodies of the men collapsed and folded in on themselves, like deflated balloons, leaving a big clump of loose skin on the ground. The skin dissolved and melted away.

"Gross," Addy said. "What happened?"

Evie came over to take a closer look. "I don't know. It's like the demons used them all up."

"Maybe so. Something sure happened to them."

The three demons still in human form shouted something in a foul, guttural language.

Evie clutched Addy's arm. "What are they saying?"

"I don't know, but I got a feeling it's not good."

The earth shook in response to the demons' call and vomited out a horde of mud critters. Roughly the size of a hub cap and clam shaped, the demons' soldiers were all mouth, with row upon row of serrated teeth. They clattered across the park on slender, birdlike legs, consuming all within their path like an army of hungry Pac-Men gobbling up pac-dots.

The gobblers swarmed over Brand and Ansgar, and the warriors disappeared.

Chapter Thirty-five

Brand and Ansgar shook off the nasty little gobblers like a couple of big dogs shaking water from their fur. Their clothes were in shreds, and dozens of vicious bite marks marred their powerful bodies. Brand held out his hand, and there was a blinding flash of light. When Addy's vision cleared, she saw the warriors standing on top of a big mound of dead gobblers. Their wounds had healed—score another one for the miraculous Dalvahni constitution. Their tattered jeans and shirts were gone and they were once more clad in their leather clothing. What, did they have a secret cosmic Rubbermaid compartment where they kept their warrior duds?

To her relief, they seemed to be holding their own in the fight. Brand swept his sword back and forth, cleaving mud critters left and right. Ansgar fired his arrows with the rapidity of a well-oiled machine gun, his movements a blur. Addy felt a glimmer of hope. Maybe things were going to be okay. Brand and Ansgar were professionals. She was worried for nothing. Fighting demons and creatures of darkness was their job, something they were *created* to do. They had to be good at it to have survived this long, right?

Her relief was short-lived. The demon-men shouted something harsh, and the earth belched out a second wave of gobblers. The insatiable creatures darted toward Brand and Ansgar like a crazed army of sandpipers wearing clamshell hats with teeth.

"There are too many of them," Addy cried. "They can't stop

them all. Oh, my God, they're going to be eaten alive." She flung her body against the shield, pounding it with her fists. "Brand. *Brand*."

Terror streaked through her, and a surge of energy that started at the soles of her feet, moved up her legs and torso, and burst from her fingertips in a brilliant flash of light. The shield exploded in a shower of sparks, and she pitched forward onto her knees. Shaken, she scrambled to her feet. Crap, she'd broken the shield. How the heck did she do that? Brand was not going to be a happy camper.

"Addy?" Evie stared at her open mouthed. "You busted the shield."

"I didn't mean to. It just happened."

They both turned at the sound of hoofbeats from the north. Whooping at the top of his lungs, Shep galloped over the hill on Sildhjort's back, a makeshift club in one hand. He swung it back and forth like a polo mallet, scattering gobblers left and right, an avenging angel wearing faded jeans and a Polo shirt. Sildhjort's antlers shone with sapphire light, like a ship's mast ablaze with Saint Elmo's fire. He lowered his shining white head. Blue light spread out from his antlers in waves, pulverizing the mud gobblers. Dust and grit rose up in a choking cloud.

Enraged at the destruction of their rapacious army, the demons attacked Brand and Ansgar. Earth and sky groaned beneath their assault. The demons clouted the warriors with lightning. Brand and Ansgar caught the bolts and flung them back. It was like watching an epic battle, the Titans against the young gods of Olympus or the Frost Giants at war with the Aesir. But the demons were outgunned and outclassed, Addy soon realized with a dawning sense of awe. The demons called forth fire and the Dalvahni doused it with rain. Wind howled, and Brand and Ansgar swept it aside. The demons rained down a hailstorm of black ice daggers, and Brand and Ansgar ground them to powder.

Frustrated and furious, the demons loosed their wrath on Sid and Shep, hurling molten balls of flame at them. Sid snorted, his breath steaming from his nostrils in enormous white puffs. The vapor struck the demons' burning orbs, and they spun across the park. One of the fireballs took out the Conecuh Sausage stand, and another one rolled into Shep's coffin car. The car burst into flames and exploded in a shower of parts.

"My car! That was my *car,* you son-of-a-bitch." Swinging his mallet, Shep jumped off Sildhjort's back and charged the nearest demon-man.

"Shep, no!" Addy shrieked.

The demon lifted his hand in a negligent manner, blasting Shep with a burst of energy. He flew through the air like a rag doll and landed hard on the ground, rolling to his side with a groan. Grinning in triumph, the demon stalked toward him.

Oh, God, Shep was in big trouble. Frantic, Addy looked around for something, *anything,* to use as a weapon. The park had been cleaned for the festival. Not so much as a stick lying around. The demon was almost on top of Shep. Time, she was out of time. She spied an aluminum pole on the ground amid the shambles of the sausage stand. She beckoned. The pole flew through the air and into her hand.

"Addy?"

She hefted the pole like a lance. "Stay put, Evie."

"Addy, I know that look. You're fixin' to do something stupid."

Addy took off at a run. Grinning, the demon raised his hand to finish Shep.

"Adara, *no,*" she heard Brand shout.

She rammed the demon with the aluminum pole. He reeled back.

She stood between Shep and the demon. With shaking arms, she raised the pole. "Leave my brother alone."

The demon straightened with an evil leer. "Hello, Addy."

A cold shiver of recognition slithered down her spine. Brain-numbing fear slammed through her, and the aluminum pole slipped from her grasp. That voice . . . that horrible, raspy voice. It was Mr. Nasty, alive and in the flesh. He said he was coming for her, and he was here.

She couldn't move, couldn't think; watched helplessly as he raised his hand to strike her.

Lightning danced from his fingertips. "Time to die, pretty girl."

She heard Brand's shout of alarm as the demon drew back his arm and flung a ball of flame at her. Too fast, she thought, watching the comet streak toward her like a miniature sun. It was coming too fast. She was going to die and never see Brand again. Grief flashed through her, agonizing and sharp, and then she was flung aside. The flaming comet slammed into the ground a few feet away from her, pelting her with rocks and dirt. Bruised and shaken, she rolled to her feet. Sildhjort stood over Shep. The stag lowered his head and charged, catching the screaming demon-man on his antlers. With an angry snort, Sildhjort flung the demon to the ground and stamped it beneath his sharp hooves, crushing the human vessel into a bleeding, unrecognizable thing. A thin stream of black smoke puffed out of the body and wafted away.

Sildhjort tossed his head and cantered out of the park. Addy staggered toward Shep. Before she could reach him, strong arms caught her in a crushing embrace.

"Damn you, Adara." Brand hugged her close. "Of all the foolish, hardheaded females . . ." Tremors racked his big body. Holding her away from him, he gave her a little shake. "I thought you were dead. I saw the demon raise his hand to strike you. I died a thousand deaths in that moment, knowing I could not reach you in time."

He jerked her back into his arms as though he could not bear to let her go. And that was fine with Addy. She didn't want to let him go, either. She buried her face against his hard chest, soaking up his glorious strength and the warmth of his arms around her. The salty odor of sweat and the spicy, masculine scent that was all Brand tickled her senses. He was alive. Oh, God, he was alive, and so was she.

And Mr. Nasty was dead.

"I was scared for you, too." She ran her hands down his hard muscled back to assure herself he was all right. "It was awful."

"Scared? Scared is too paltry a word to describe what I felt when I saw the djegrali raise his hand against you." His arms tightened around her. "Why did you not do as you were told and stay where it was safe?"

"The shield broke."

"Broke?" His brow creased in a black scowl. "Ansgar and I bound that shield with our blood. Such a thing is not possible. The djegrali could not break that spell."

Oops, someone had their masculinity bound up in a certain little shield spell. Time to change the subject. "What happened to the other demons?"

"Ansgar slew one with his arrows. The last one surrendered and is in our custody."

Curious, she lifted her head to take a look. A dead convict lay on the ground, his body pierced by a dozen or more silver arrows from Ansgar's bow. Something black drained out of the corpse, hardened, and turned to powder. The empty body collapsed and melted away.

The last convict sat on the ground, head and shoulders bowed, his hands and feet bound with sturdy rope. He rocked back and forth, mumbling to himself. Addy didn't bother to ask where the rope came from. She probably wouldn't like the answer, anyway. Ansgar stood over the prisoner, his icy, detached demeanor back in place, a poster child for the giant frozen hemorrhoid.

She eyed the hostage with unease. "Suppose he gets loose? That rope won't hold him for long."

"The demon has relinquished its human receptacle. We have the djegrali in custody."

She took a quick glance around the park. "Oh, yeah? Where you keeping him, your shirt pocket?"

"I do not have a shirt pocket. At any rate, such a mode of transport would be highly inefficient. The djegrali is over there."

Brand pointed. On the ground beside the mumbling man was the delicate glass container Brand had earlier when he gave the demons his "stop in the name of the law" speech.

"You're kidding. You got a demon in a wussy little perfume bottle?"

"It is not a perfume bottle, Adara. It is a djevel flaskke, a special container that holds the djegrali."

"Oh, yeah, a devil flask. I knew that."

Shep grunted in pain and sat up, his expression dazed. "What happened?"

Addy slipped out of Brand's arms and hurried to his side. Poor Shep. He had two black eyes, a split lip, and a busted nose. And those were the injuries she could see.

She knelt beside him and put her hand on his forehead. "Take it easy, Shep. That was a nasty wallop you took. I wouldn't be surprised if you have a concussion."

He gave her a groggy look. "Real slobberknocker, huh? Are we winning?"

"Yep."

"Good. That's real good. My head hurts, Coach. But I can still play. Put me back in. I wanna whup some Wildcat ass."

Good grief. Shep thought she was Coach Latham and he was back in high school playing for the Blue Devils again.

A shadow fell over them, and a pair of booted feet appeared at her elbow.

"Adara, where is Evangeline?" Ansgar asked.

She flapped a hand in the direction of the sweet gum tree. "Over there."

He moved off, and she returned her attention to Shep, who was pale and sweating.

Ansgar reappeared a moment later. "I do not see her."

Ansgar's grim tone sent a frisson of uneasiness through her. She jumped to her feet. "You're benched, Corwin," she told Shep sternly.

"Aw, Coach, I wanna play."

She hurried after Brand and Ansgar. They looked all around the tree. Evie was gone. A low, tortured groan sent chills up and down her spine.

"There!" Addy pointed to the steps that led from the park down to the river.

Evie wavered at the top of the stairs and staggered back down again, an expression of stark terror in her eyes. Her movements were jerky and strained, as though she was no longer in control of her own body.

"Evangeline," Ansgar shouted, breaking into a run.

Evie struggled up the steps once more, panting like she'd run a marathon. Tears streamed down her cheeks.

"Evie!" Addy cried, lunging for her friend.

Brand pulled her back.

"Let me go!" Addy struggled to break free of his grasp. "Something's wrong with Evie."

"You cannot help her, Adara," Brand said. "The djegrali has taken her."

"No, that's not possible! You told me they were all dead."

"I was wrong. The human that Sildhjort slew, did you see anything rise from the body?"

"Oh, my God," Addy whispered. Sick with horror, she saw it all again. Sid's hooves crushing the convict's body to a bloody pulp, the curling wisp of smoke rising from the smashed and bleeding husk and wafting away.

Evie was possessed, and it was all Addy's fault. She broke the shield and left Evie alone. It was all her fault.

"Ansgar, please," Evie pleaded, reaching out to the blond warrior. Claw marks marred the porcelain skin on her cheeks and neck. "I can't stand it. It burns. Help me. I can't fight it much longer. Don't let it take me."

Ansgar stood silently in front of her, his face an icy mask.

Fury gripped Addy. How could he be so cold when Evie was in agony?

"What's the matter with you?" she screamed. "Help her."

"She should not have left the shield," Ansgar said, his words toneless and without emotion. "She was safe there."

"That was *my* fault." Addy flung herself at Ansgar, but Brand held her back. "I broke the shield. I thought you *cared* about Evie. But you don't care about anybody, you heartless bastard."

"Adara," Brand said. "You do not understand."

"I understand plenty. He can help her, but he won't."

Evie's face twisted. "Ansgar, *please.*"

A muscle twitched in Ansgar's jaw, the only sign that he heard her.

"Very well," he said.

In one smooth motion he drew a silver arrow from his quiver, fitted it in his bow, and shot Evie through the heart. Blood bloomed on the front of her blouse and spread. She clutched the arrow in her chest, her wide-eyed, startled gaze fixed upon Ansgar. The light in her hazel eyes flickered and dimmed. She sighed and crumpled to the ground.

"*Evie,*" Addy screamed.

She felt herself falling away, tumbling down a long, dark tunnel. Someone was screaming. The sound went on and on. Through her tears, she saw a trail of black smoke drift out of Evie's body, saw Ansgar fire a silver arrow into the dark mist. Watched as the arrow pierced the black shadow and splintered into a million silvery shards. Heard the long, keening wail of despair as the djegrali vanished into the nothingness.

The djegrali was dead. But Evie was dead, too.

Brand still held her, Addy realized, floating out of the blackness. Ansgar clasped Evie's limp form in his arms, his expression impassive.

Rage washed away her grief. He had no business touching her. He had no *right* to touch her.

"Let me go," she said, twisting in Brand's arms.

"No."

Unable to break free of Brand's iron grip, Addy watched, seething with fury, as Ansgar tenderly smoothed Evie's hair from her brow. Grasping the arrow, he pulled it from her chest and tossed it aside. He bent over her, one hand resting upon her wounded breast, the other hand grasping the back of her head, and kissed her. Light pulsed around them, soft and luminous, pale as the milky gleam of a new moon on a lake, and was gone.

Evie opened her eyes and gazed up at Ansgar. "What happened?"

"You were hurt." Ansgar touched her cheek with the tip of

one finger as though she were something fragile and infinitely precious. "You do not remember?"

Evie straightened and stepped back. "No. Who are you?"

His arms dropped to his sides. "I am Ansgar."

She looked down at her shorts and blushed. "Why am I dressed like this? What happened to my clothes?"

Brand released Addy. She ran over and flung her arms around Evie. "Evie," she cried, bursting into tears.

Evie patted her on the back. "Addy, you're crying. You never cry."

Addy wiped her eyes and hugged her again. "I'm so glad you're all right."

"Well, of course I'm all right. Why wouldn't I be?"

"Brother?" Brand's expression was solemn as he addressed the other warrior. "Her memory can be restored."

"It is better this way."

"Ah," Brand said. "I see."

Addy was glad somebody did, because she sure as hell didn't understand any of it. Not Ansgar's strange, cold behavior or what had happened to Evie. Blondy shot her with an *arrow*, for God's sake. Addy felt dizzy and sick from the emotions roiling within her—terror, anger, grief, sadness—and an overwhelming, knee-weakening relief that Evie was alive.

A horn sounded in the distance, tinny and faint.

Ansgar lifted his head like a hound to the scent. "Brand."

"I heard, brother."

The horn sounded again, this time closer. Three leather-clad warriors materialized in the square, big, muscular and armed to the teeth. And drop-dead gorgeous, bless their hearts. They had to be Dalvahni. No human looked like that.

They surveyed the square, a trio of hunky guys wearing identical wooden expressions. Brand had worn that same expression only a few days ago. A lifetime ago.

A warrior with long red hair and the unblinking, flinty gaze of a hawk spied Brand and Ansgar and strode over to them. "Brothers," he said curtly. "We have come to escort you back to the Hall. Conall is desirous of speech with you."

Ansgar inclined his head. "As you wish."

Addy's heart squeezed painfully in her chest. "Brand?" she whispered.

He looked at her. His bleak expression told her all she needed to know.

"Adara," he said.

That was it, her name and nothing more. But the aching, hollow way he said it spoke volumes. A yawning chasm opened at her feet.

Two guards flanked Brand and Ansgar, one on either side. The grim-faced warrior with the red hair fell in behind them. Moving as one, the five Dalvahni strode across the green. They flickered briefly in the summer sunshine, like a mirage in the desert heat, and disappeared.

Chapter Thirty-six

He was gone.

Grief settled like a leaden weight around Addy's heart. Gone. Gone. Gone.

The unbroken litany pounded in her brain as she cared for Evie and Shep. It played beneath the clamor of the crowd as folks drifted over the bridge and back up the hill exclaiming about the first-rate fireworks they'd seen by the river. In broad daylight, no less. Mass hallucination. The entire town of Hannah had drunk the Sid Kool-Aid.

Mama and Pootie came back, jabbering excitedly about the light show. Lenora was with them. *She* didn't say anything about the fireworks. She looked a little green around the gills, though, like someone who'd eaten three Thanksgiving dinners. Someone had glutted herself on the Post-Sid euphoria. Like a kid in a candy shop. The whole damn town was high, and all that bliss had given Lenora the mother of all bellyaches.

When Lenora saw Shep lying on the ground, she seemed to forget her own discomfort. Exclaiming in dismay over his injuries, she dropped to her knees beside him, the strands of her dress fluttering around her. Jeez, she looked like one of those alien barbarian warrior chicks straight off a Boris Vallejo cover. Shep opened one swollen eye and gave the thrall a crooked grin.

Oh, man, he was eating this stuff up. And he really liked the string dress. Addy could tell.

Mama hurried over to see about Shep, too. Mama, of course,

wanted to know what happened. Addy considered telling Mama the truth . . . for about a millisecond, and pointed to the coffin car. Or what was left of it. That seemed to sober Mama right the hell up. Pootie pulled the Goober Mobile over the curb and onto the grass, and Addy helped Mama and Lenora load Shep into the car so they could take him to the hospital. She waved good-bye with a promise to check on Shep later.

No one could see her bruised heart, of course.

Gone.

The knowledge throbbed inside her, a wound that would not heal.

Numbly, she watched the chief and Officer Dan arrive, and Sheriff Dev Whitsun right after them. They found the inmate sitting on the grass where Brand and Ansgar left him. The ropes around his feet and ankles had vanished, but he made no move to escape. He sat there, carrying on a conversation with the six human heads lined up in a row in front of him. A one-sided conversation, thank God. Addy looked around, noting with dull surprise that all traces of the battle were gone, except for the demolished coffin car. The grass was once more a pristine green carpet, and the Conecuh Sausage stand looked good as new. The Dalvahni must have cleaned up before they left. She was too busy having her heart ripped out of her chest to notice.

Why leave the coffin car? she wondered. Maybe the Dalvahni didn't know what to do with a coffin car. Whatever the reason, she was glad they left it. She'd have been hard pressed to explain Shep's injuries without it.

It provided an excuse for her and Evie as well. The chief and Sheriff Whitsun had a ton of questions, which neither of them answered. Amnesia from the explosion, Addy explained. Evie's was genuine, hers feigned. A little amnesia would have been a blessing at this point. She remembered everything. That was the problem.

He was gone.

The park was enclosed in crime scene tape, the grisly evidence of the murders photographed and collected, and the raving inmate loaded into the sheriff's car.

"Crazy as a loon." Chief Davis shook his head. "Babbling on about demons and avenging angels. There's one murderer who won't see the inside of a prison again. Headed for the nut house and a straitjacket, if you ask me. Thorazine City. Too bad. No closure for the victims' families."

Sheriff Whitson grunted. "Yeah, I'll be surprised if that one stands trial. But his buddies are out there somewhere. I'll find 'em. Those sons-of-bitches are going down. We got the whole thing on video at the store. I think they knew they were being filmed and didn't care. It was like they were posturing for the camera." He looked at Addy, his expression unreadable behind the sunglasses. "You sure you don't remember anything?"

"I remember drinking lemonade and the chief and Dan going off to check on the bank alarm. That's it."

The sheriff turned his attention to Evie. "What about you, ma'am?"

Evie huddled in a knot on the bench under the sweet gum tree, her arms crossed over her chest and her legs drawn under her. The big bloodstain on the front of her shirt was gone. So was the arrow hole. She looked confused and embarrassed, and utterly miserable.

"The last thing I remember is coming into the flower shop." Her brows drew together. "What was that, Addy, Friday morning?"

"Saturday," Addy murmured.

Saturday morning Evie met Ansgar, and Tuesday night Evie burst out of her cocoon and danced at the Grand Goober Ball, a beautiful, soaring butterfly. And now she was a caterpillar again.

"Saturday morning, and what's this, Wednesday?" Evie asked.

"Right," the sheriff said.

Evie tightened her arms across her chest, as if she could make herself smaller. "I don't know how I got here or why I'm dressed this way. These aren't my clothes. I don't wear shorts." Her chin quivered. "I don't feel well. My chest hurts. I want to go home."

"Of course you do." The chief patted Evie on the shoulder.

"Addy, you take Evie on home and call Doc Dunn. He still makes house calls. I think he ought to take a look at the both of you. A lick on the head is nothing to sneeze at. Y'all could have a concussion same as Shep."

"Thanks, I'll do that," Addy said.

"Your aunt Muddy went home with Mr. Collier," Chief Davis said. "Wedding plans, you know."

Addy felt a surge of relief. Thank God she didn't have to face Muddy. Not now, not when the pain was still so raw. She needed time alone. Time to grieve. Time to figure out how to go on without Brand. The future stretched ahead of her, a gray, meaningless void.

Somehow, she got Evie home and called Doc Dunn. Waited until the irascible old man completed his examination of Evie and prescribed bed rest. Thanked Old Doc and helped Evie into her pajamas and tucked her into bed. Addy refused treatment for herself. All the medicine in the world couldn't fix what ailed her.

She stopped by the hospital to check on Shep. He had a concussion, all right. Big bro was puking up his toenails. Lenora and Mama were with him. She and Mama seemed to have established an uneasy truce. Lenora had ditched the string dress and was wearing a pair of pink sweatpants and a matching T-shirt that said HANNAH MEMORIAL HOSPITAL across the front. Addy detected Mama's subtle influence at work here. As in Mama marched down to the gift shop and bought her son's new girlfriend-the-pole-dancer some decent clothes to wear. Too bad Mama didn't buy Lenora a bra while she was at it. The thrall's puppies were straining at the leash. A woman who dressed in yarn probably didn't rank undergarments high on her list of must-haves.

Addy drove home in the Van of the Sacred Hump in a fog of misery. Gone. Gone. Gone.

Dooley met her in the foyer. *"Addy home. Dooley miss Addy."* The Lab ignored the flying kitten sailing around her head and stuck her nose in Addy's crotch. *"Addy home."*

Addy shoved Dooley's head away. "Dooley Anne, that is so rude. Lord."

Dooley wagged her tail. *"Addy. Dooley love Addy."* She pushed past Addy, feet scrambling on the wood floor and ran to the front door. *"Where Brand man?"*

That was it. The tears started to flow and would not stop.

She cried, great wracking sobs that came from some bottomless well of grief. Dooley and Mr. Fluffy hovered around her, anxious and eager to please. Only this couldn't be fixed. Wailing like a banshee, she stumbled out of the foyer and into the living room. She caught a glimpse of her reflection in the foyer mirror as she went past. She was not a pretty crier. Her eyes swelled shut and her face turned red and scrunched up like a constipated Cabbage Patch doll. Who cared? Bump it. Nothing mattered. Brand was gone.

She staggered over to the couch. She would bury her face in the cushions. With any luck, she'd smother to death. Her heart hurt. Her chest hurt. Her damn brain was whirling with images and memories of Brand—his scent, his touch, his kisses. She could smell him. She could still taste him. She felt his body moving on her, *in* her. He'd left her drowning in an ocean of misery. She wanted to die. She wanted to—

A man stared at her through the double French doors that looked out on the backyard, a man with a familiar hollow-cheeked grin. The man from the parade. The doors burst open and he stalked inside, his horrible, wobbly purple Jell-O gaze fixed on her.

"Addy."

That grating sibilant whisper made her shudder with dread.

"You're dead," she said through lips stiff with disbelief.

"Hardly. I told you I would come for you. I always keep my promises."

"But, I saw you! I-I *heard* you! It was you!"

Mr. Nasty chuckled. "Foolish girl, that was one of my minions, a lesser demon, not one of the *morkyn* such as I."

"Morkyn?"

"A powerful, ancient race of demons far superior in strength and magic to the dross you saw today. You should be honored to be chosen by one of the *morkyn*."

"Yeah? Well, before I do the superior dance, what exactly is this honor you're thinking of bestowing on me?"

"I have been watching you. You are no ordinary mortal. You proved that when you resisted me. You reek of Dalvahni. At first, I thought it was because you took one of the spawn as your lover. But soon I realized it was something else. The Dalvahni saved your life the other night after I stabbed you, did he not? He gave you part of his essence, making you something greater, something *more*. You are part Dalvahni, part human. The first of your kind. I have been drawn to you since I marked you. But, now that you are Dalvahni, you are irresistible."

"Whoopee."

"You jest, because you do not understand. I could kill you and feed upon your soul, but I have chosen you to be my vessel."

"Wow, I'm flattered. Really, I am. But, it looks to me like you already got a vessel, so I'm going to say no."

"This shell? It is nothing. Less than nothing. I will prove it to you."

The man's body contorted and twisted, like a fleshy towel being wrung by unseen hands. Repulsed, Addy staggered back. She tripped over something and sprawled onto the floor. Dooley and Mr. Fluffy were lying in a furry heap under her legs.

She looked back at the demon. The once human body was a thing out of a nightmare. Muscle, tendon, and flesh shrank and dried up, exposing the skeletal frame underneath. As she watched, the bones crumbled to dust. A black mist rose from the pile of ashes and floated over the couch. Wind howled through the open French doors, scattering the powdery remains of the demon's victim into the night.

"The human body is too frail to contain the djegrali for long." Mr. Nasty's voice slithered inside her head, a raspy, husky sound that made her shiver. "Aside from the obvious drawback of a short life span, mortals cannot sustain us for any great length of time," he said. "A few years, a few decades if we are frugal, no more. Perhaps it is their fault. Perhaps it is ours. Our desire for physical sensation and pleasure is our great weakness. It leads us to excess and, too often, we consume our human vessels from within. Certainly, if we use any great magic or shape-shifting, the process of degeneration is hastened. I believe you saw evidence of that today. But you are part Dalvahni and thus imbued with their strength and immortality. You will be a fitting container for me. We will do great things together."

"What have you done to Dooley and Mr. Fluffy?"

".The creatures are alive, lying in slumberous state. Cooperate, and I may let them live."

"I get it. I let you possess me and eat my soul and turn me into a purple-eyed whoozit, and you *might* let Dooley and Mr. Fluffy live. But no promises."

"Exactly," Mr. Nasty said.

Addy got slowly to her feet. The demon was right about one thing. She was part Dalvahni now, part *warrior*. She needed a kick-ass weapon, something befitting a foe of darkness. She needed a weapon, something really cool. Something like . . . like . . .

She looked down. She held Muddy's portable mixer in her hand. It was top of the line as far as hand mixers went, but it was a mixer all the same. Brand got a flaming sword and Blondy got a bow and arrows . . . and she got a hand mixer. Jeez, the damn thing wasn't even connected to a socket. The cord and the three-pronged plug dangled at her feet.

She heard a dark chuckle inside her head. Mr. Nasty swooped down. She slid the power button to high. The stainless steel turbo beaters whirred to life. It wasn't a light saber, but at least it worked. Her own bit of magic, it would seem. She thrust her arm and the mixer into the dark mist. She screamed in pain. The demon was cold, the heart of an Arctic glacier, liquid fire. Her arm burned and went numb. The spinning blades caught the shrieking demon, whipped him to pieces, and flung him back out again. He floated in the air like bits of foamy licorice meringue.

Mr. Nasty's spell was shattered, too. Dooley and Mr. Fluffy sprang up. Mr. Fluffy hissed at the bits of dark fluff wafting around the living room and flew up to sit on the ceiling fan, tail twitching in agitation.

Lenora materialized by the couch. Dooley barked and then looked embarrassed, like she just remembered she could talk.

"Addy, Addy! Stranger! Stranger!"

"It's okay, Dooley. I know her."

Dooley trotted over and inspected the thrall. Dooley was an equal-opportunity crotch sniffer.

Lenora looked around the room. "I thought I heard something as I arrived, a scream and then a terrible wail. Is something wrong?"

"Demon," Addy said through her teeth. Searing pain shot through her right arm, which hung useless by her side. The mixer clattered to the floor.

Lenora glided toward her. "You are in pain. I can help you."

"Not on your life, lady. You keep your sharp little succubus fangs away from me. I'll take an aspirin instead. What are you doing here anyway?"

Lenora shrugged. "I came to tell you your brother is doing better, although he will have to remain in the Hall of Healing for a few more days."

"Thanks." Addy limped over to the cabinet and found a bottle of pain reliever. Her arm hurt like hell. She shook three pills out of the bottle and swallowed them. "Mama didn't see you do the time warp, did she?"

"Of course not. I am not a fool." Lenora gazed at the shreds of black confetti that wafted about the room. There was a strange, almost hungry look in her eyes. "Is that the djegrali?"

"Yeah, what's left of it."

"You do realize it is weakened, but not dead?"

"What?" Addy looked around for another weapon. What was she supposed to do for an encore, microwave the damn thing?

Lenora plucked a wafting piece of black confetti out of the air and popped it in her mouth.

Addy's stomach heaved. "Gross, you did not just do that."

Lenora licked another floating shred of demon out of the air.

It melted on her pink tongue like cotton candy. "It has a spicy tang. Probably all that concentrated evil. It is quite delicious. May I consume the rest?"

"Uh, sure," Addy said. "If you'll excuse me, I think I'll take a shower."

"But of course. Do you mind if I watch television while I eat?" Lenora snatched a black wisp as it sailed past and ate it in two bites. "I have become quite fond of the show *Loins of Lust.* So much melodrama and strong emotion. Quite addictive."

"Knock yourself out."

Turning, Addy fled into the bedroom and shut the door.

Chapter Thirty-seven

Addy leaned against the bedroom door and closed her eyes. She needed a shower. She could not remember feeling dirtier in her life, not after mud bogging with Shep or cleaning fish down by the river. She was covered in bug funk and gobbler funk and demon funk, and sweat and plain old dirt. She was bone tired, and there was a ball of sadness the size of a Buick lodged in her chest. Her arm hurt. She could add grossed out to the list, because her brother's freaky girlfriend was in the living room eating what was left of the creature of darkness she'd almost killed with a kitchen appliance. Her life was so weird.

Stripping off her clothes, she went into the bathroom. She stood in front of the mirror. From fingertips to elbow, her right hand and arm were bone white and stiff as marble. How was she going to explain this one to Bitsy? *Well, you see, Mama, I shoved my arm up this demon's butt and then . . .* Oh, yeah, that would go over like a lead balloon. A tear ran down her cheek and dripped off her chin. She wiped it away angrily. She would not do this. She would *not*.

Getting in the shower, she washed her hair and body as best she could one-handed. She dried off and put on an old pair of sleep pants and a T-shirt. By the time she was dressed, her arm and hand felt better. They were still hard to the touch and white as alabaster, but at least a little of the feeling was coming back. By tomorrow morning, her hand and arm would probably be good as new. That Dalvahni DNA was strong stuff. If only her broken heart would mend as easily.

Unbidden, the hurt welled up inside her, choking her. OhGodOhGodOhGod. He was gone. How would she bear it? How would she go on without him?

A gray shroud of grief enveloped her, heavy, unbearable. She sat down on the floor and burst into tears.

"Why are you crying, little one?"

Addy squeezed her eyes shut. That deep, husky growl *sounded* like Brand. Holding her aching arm next to her chest, she rocked back and forth. "I'm losing my mind."

"Why do you say this?"

"Because you're gone, and this isn't real," she wailed. "But it *feels* real, and I want it to be real. I want it like crazy. I can *smell* you, for Pete's sake. But I know I'm imagining it because I miss you so much. And now I'm *talking* to you, and that means I'm losing it. Big time."

A pair of strong hands lifted her to her feet. "Adara, you are not crazy. Look at me. I am here."

She opened her eyes. Brand stood in front of her. She drank in the sight of him, his beloved face, the sexy mouth and chiseled features, his big, hard-muscled body. How could she have forgotten how gorgeous he was? It had only been a few hours.

"Brand?" Her mouth widened in a grin of delight. With a squeal of happiness, she flung herself against him. "I thought you were gone. I thought I'd never see you again." She rained kisses along his neck, shoulder, and chest. "Oh, God, I've been so unhappy. I wanted to *die* I was so miserable."

He put his hands on her shoulders and stepped back. He scowled down at her, his expression stern and disapproving. Why wasn't he glad to see her? Her stomach did a sickening little flip-flop. He couldn't stay. He'd come back to tell her he couldn't stay. OhGodOhGodOhGod.

"You are hurt." His tone was accusing. "How did this happen? You were uninjured when I left. I am sure of it."

Suddenly, she was furious. Balling up her good fist, she slugged him in the chest. It was like slamming her hand into a brick wall. "How the hell would you know? You walked off into the sunset without saying good-bye."

"I did not walk into the sunset. The sun was at its zenith when I left. But that is beside the point. How did you injure your arm?"

Addy squelched a sigh of exasperation. He was *so* literal. "Mr. Nasty did it. Or to be more accurate, *I* did it when I killed him." She made a face. "Well, I sort of half-ass killed him. Lenora's doing the rest."

"Adara, you are not making sense. Ansgar and I slew the dje-grali."

"Yeah, but Mr. Nasty wasn't at the park. He was waiting for me when I got home."

Brand looked momentarily confused, and then outraged. Yikes, somebody had their leather panties in a wad.

"I leave you alone for a moment and you fight a djegrali?" he roared. *"You could have been killed."*

Addy winced. "Brand, my ears."

Ignoring her protests, he picked her up and strode over to the bed. He sat down with her in his lap and examined her arm. Bending his dark head, he kissed her frozen fingers, nibbled her palm and the top of her hand, and trailed his lips past her wrist and up her arm. She gasped in pain. Heat flowed from his hands and lips, thawing her frozen flesh. Her injured arm and hand tingled and grew warm. Healthy color returned to the tissue. She flexed her fingers. Good as new.

"Thanks," she said, snuggling against him with a happy sigh. She kissed his chin, his neck, his chest, breathing in the scent of him and savoring the feel of his arms around her. He was big and warm and smelled oh-so-delicious, and he was *here.* "My arm feels all better now."

"I am glad."

His deep voice rumbled beneath her ear, and she thought she might die from the joy of it.

He wrapped his arms around her. "Tell me about the dje-grali. How did you manage to defeat it if you were unarmed?"

He was patronizing her. She heard it in his tone. He didn't really believe her. "I wasn't unarmed. I had a hand mixer."

"There is a device that mixes hands? To what purpose?"

"Not a *hand* mixer, Brand. That would be painful. I'm talk-ing about something that mixes things *by* hand. You know, cakes and cookies and stuff."

"You used a *cooking device* to defend yourself against the dje-grali?"

"Yeah, and it worked, too. Maybe it isn't flashy like a flam-ing sword, but it's what the cosmos gave me."

"Madness. Where is the djegrali now?"

"In the living room with Lenora, what's left of it anyway."

"*What?*"

He set her down and drew his sword. "Stay behind me," he ordered, stalking out of the bedroom.

He looked around the living room, his green eyes ablaze and his beautiful face hard as stone. "Where is the djegrali?"

Addy trailed after him. "Relax, big guy. The demon is gone. Well, mostly."

Mr. Fluffy saw Brand and sailed off the ceiling fan. Dooley leaped to her feet with a happy *woof* and galumphed across the room, tail wagging.

"Brand man? Dooley love Brand man."

"Yes, yes, I am happy to see you, too." Brand sheathed his sword and patted Dooley.

The cat flew in ecstatic circles around Brand's head.

"Cat, Brand man, cat."

"Yes, I see him, Dooley." Brand looked up at the kitten hov-ering over his head. "Well met, my winged friend."

Mr. Fluffy executed a double loop in the air. "Meow."

"I think it's time you two went outside." Addy waved the dog and the cat out the French doors. "Be good, and you'll both get treats in a little while."

Crickets chirped and dusk painted the backyard in mysteri-

ous shades of silver, black, and muted green. Dooley and
Mr. Fluffy romped on the lawn, enjoying a vigorous game of
catch the flying cat.

Dooley was singing her favorite song, *"Cat. Cat. Stupid Cat,"*
as she bounced stiff-legged around the yard in pursuit of Mr.
Fluffy.

Addy closed the door. Brand stood in front of the couch
glaring down at Lenora. Lenora was absorbed in her soap opera
and did not seem to notice. She held a large white bowl that
said POPCORN in red letters on it in her lap. Inside the bowl was
a wiggling black mass that looked like scraps of crepe paper.

"Greetings, Sol' Van." Lenora did not look up from the television. "I thought I heard you."

Addy rolled her eyes. A few minutes ago, Brand had been
bellowing like an injured bull. People in Paulsberg probably
heard him.

"Lenora," Brand said in a dangerous voice. "What are you
doing here?"

"I am having a snack and watching the device humans call
'television.' It is vastly entertaining."

She dug her hand in the bowl and shoved a large handful of
black scraps in her mouth.

"What are you eating?"

"Demon froth. Adara whipped it up." Lenora held out the
bowl to Brand. "Would you care for some?"

"No."

Lenora shrugged and went back to her show.

Brand watched the thrall, an expression of sickly unease on
his face.

"You had no idea she could do that, did you?" Addy asked,
coming to stand beside him.

"No. It is . . . most unsettling."

"I'll bet it is. Maybe y'all had this thing bass-ackwards all
along. Maybe you Dalvahni pretty boys should have stayed in
the bedroom and let the thralls do the demon hunting. I mean
look at her. She's eaten the whole thing."

Lenora set down the empty popcorn bowl with a loud burp.

"Why are you still here, Lenora?" Brand asked.

The thrall turned her fathomless gaze on Brand. "I like this place. I have decided to stay a while."

"That is not possible."

Lenora shrugged. "I have served the Dalvahni more than three thousand years. I need a respite. A . . . a . . . what is the word?"

"A vacation?" Addy said.

"Yes, that is it! I need a vacation." She tilted her head, surveying Brand with a speculative gleam in her slanted blue eyes. "What about you, Sol' Van? I felt you depart with the other Dalvahni. Why have you returned?"

Brand raised his brows. "Unlike you, Lenora, I have permission to remain here."

Hope grew in Addy's heart, fragile and tender. "Whoa, back up." She felt breathless and shaky. "What did you say?"

"Ansgar and I told Conall about the unusual demonic disturbances in this place. He has ordered further investigation. I have been placed on permanent assignment here."

Addy's heart soared. "Here, as in Hannah? For good?"

"For the foreseeable future. Conall wants regular reports on the demon activity in Hannah. He is most curious about this place and about the demonoids."

He was going to *stay*? It was too good to be true. "But how in the world did you convince him?"

He jerked her into his arms and kissed her until her head spun. "I told him that I love you." He dragged his lips down her throat in a hot, lingering kiss that sent a thrill of longing down her spine. Magic man, she thought, dazed by a heady mixture of joy and desire. "That I cannot live without you, and have no intention of trying. I informed Conall that he could lock me in the bottommost dungeon of the Pit and place a thousand armed guards to keep me there, and still I would fight my way back to you."

"Fascinating." The thrall watched them with the same intensity she reserved for her soap opera. "What did Conall say?"

"I fear he does not understand." Brand shook his head. "In truth, I do not understand it myself, only that it *is*."

"If you love the human, you should ask her to marry you," Lenora said matter-of-factly. "That is what they do on television."

Brand tightened his arms around Addy and smiled at her, love and laughter in his eyes.

"I think she is right," he said. "Will you marry me, Adara? I love you. I want to bind you to me with the human ritual called marriage, and then I want to take you to the Hall of Warriors and write your name in the Great Book, proclaiming you as my life mate and my woman."

"Oh, this is better than *Loins of Lust*," Lenora said. She frowned down at the empty popcorn bowl. All that was left of the djegrali was a greasy black smear. "Strange, the demon should have sated my appetite, but I feel hungry and dissatisfied. If you will excuse me, I think I will go see Shep."

She vanished.

"Adara," Brand said between kisses that left Addy panting and dizzy with lust. "I would have my answer. Will you marry me?"

As if on cue, the front door bell rang and Bitsy buzzed into the house. "Who's getting married?"

Brand straightened with his arm around Addy's waist.

Addy took a deep breath. This was going to be seismic. "Mama."

"Yes, dear?"

"Brand has asked me to marry him."

Bitsy clasped her hands together. "Oh, this is so exciting! I have two weddings to plan. We'll have the ceremony at Trinity, of course, followed by a reception at the club. It will be the biggest party this town has seen in an age. I'll have to call that caterer in Paulsberg, and we'll go to Mobile to look for a wedding dress. You and Muddy can go together. It'll be fun. And then we'll have to decide on the cake—you know, three tiers or four and whether you want buttercream icing or the fondant, and—"

"Mama."

Mama blinked. "Yes, dear?"

"I haven't given Brand an answer yet. You want me to give him an answer, don't you?"

"Of course, dear! Color me gone." Mama trotted into the foyer, fluttering with excitement. "Don't you worry about a *thing*. I've been dreaming about this day since you were born. Oh, Addy, it's going to be wonderful! But there's so much to do! Flowers and invitations and how many attendants you'll have. Oh and a date, of course, and a color scheme and music and—"

Addy pushed Mama out the door. "Goodnight, Mama. Talk to you tomorrow."

Mama paused on the front porch, her eyes bright with tears. "Love you, Pookie."

"Love you, too, Mama."

"He's the one, isn't he baby? You love him?"

"So much, Mama. More than I can say."

"To the universe and beyond?"

"Squared and cubed, Mama."

Mama gave a sigh of happiness. "I'm so glad, Pookie. That's what I always wanted for you."

Addy shut the door. There was an ear-shattering yell from the front porch.

"I think she's happy," Addy said, walking into Brand's arms.

He picked her up and carried her into the bedroom. He stripped her clothes off her in seconds and dropped her lightly on the bed. His own clothes disappeared. Bloop, one second he was fully dressed, the next he was gloriously naked.

"You know, one of these days you're going to have to show me how you do that. Do you keep a whole wardrobe in that invisible closet of yours, or one or two outfits?"

He stretched out on the bed beside her. "If I tell you all my secrets you might become bored with me."

"Ha, fat chance. You're the one who's likely to get bored with *me*. You've probably seen more coochie than a herd of gynecologists."

"Am I to surmise from that confusing remark that you are insecure?" He ran his fingertips lightly over her breasts and blew on the sensitive tips. His hair brushed her belly and his spicy masculine scent filled her senses. Raising his head, he smiled down at her. She blinked up at him, dazed by desire and the sheer masculine beauty of him. "I am the one who should be feeling uncertain," he said. "I bare my heart and beg you to marry me, something no Dalvahni warrior has ever done, and you leave me wandering in a wilderness of despair awaiting your answer."

She gasped as he settled between her legs and pushed inside her. Little pulsing shimmers of delight shot up from the place where they were joined, making her dizzy with need. She clenched around him.

He withdrew slowly and entered her again, slow, exquisite torture. "A warrior only has so much patience, Adara. I would have your answer. I love you. You are life and breath and heart's blood to me. Will you marry me or not?"

She wrapped her legs around him and arched her back, taking him deeper. "Well, when you put it like that, how can I resist? Yes, Brand, I will marry you. I love you, too, you know."

"Say it again."

The husky command sent a thrill through her.

She tangled her hands in his silky hair and kissed his wicked, sexy mouth. "I love you, Brand. I love you . . . love you . . . love you."

"*Adara.*"

He told her then without words how he felt, although the words had been fine, too, heart's blood and all of that. He poured himself into her, and she shuddered around him, and all was right with the world.

Some time later, she floated back down in his arms. She was so happy. She couldn't wait to tell Evie. She frowned, realizing something.

"Brand, where is Ansgar?"

"He stayed in the Hall of Warriors."

"But he's coming back, isn't he?"

"I do not think so."

"What about Evie?"

"She does not remember him. In his estimation, it is better this way."

"Better for whom, him or her? 'Cause it sure isn't better for *her*. She loves him! She was finally coming out of her shell."

"I think Ansgar cares for Evie, but I do not think he is ready for this."

"*This*? What's that supposed to mean?"

Brand sighed. "Love is a most unsettling thing for a Dalvahni warrior. Give him time. If he loves her, he will not be able to stay away, any more than I could stay away from you."

"Okay, I'll give him time. But he better not wait too long, or I'm gonna kick his butt, even if I have to climb a stepladder to do it."

"A terrifying prospect, to be sure." He stroked her stomach and the underside of her breasts. "Tell me, what is the meaning of this 'Pookie'?"

She made a face. "Oh, that. That's Mama's pet name for me. You know how it is."

"No, I do not."

Pushing herself up on one elbow, she stared at him in disbelief. "You mean, you've never had a nickname in ten thousand years?"

"No."

"Well, we've got to do something about that. Let's see." She tapped her chin as though in thought. "You could be Brandy-kins or my Widdle Stud Muffin or Sweet Cheeks. No, that's what Pauline calls you." She snapped her fingers. "I've got it. Sugar Scrotum."

"Sugar Scrotum?" He pounced on her, his dark hair streaming down his broad shoulders and muscled chest. He looked wild and dangerous, forbidding, an untamed warrior out of some fantasy. *Her* fantasy. "I love you madly, Adara Jean Corwin, more than I can say, but this I cannot allow."

Ansgar stood in the darkness outside the house listening to the happy sound of their laughter. What ailed him? Why the heavy sense of gloom and oppression that weighed him down, as if he carried all the vast, unending blackness of the Pit within his aching chest?

Lonely. The word drifted from the deep recesses of his mind. He pushed the notion aside. Ridiculous. His brief, but admittedly pleasant, interlude with the woman had made him soft. He was right to walk away. Stay and he would soon be as pathetic and hag-ridden as Brand.

Unthinkable.

He would lose himself in the hunt. He would not remember the woman or her sweetness.

She did not remember him. It was better this way.

As for her . . . She was already forgotten.

There's nothing sexier than a
BIG BAD BEAST.
Keep an eye out for Shelly Laurenston's latest,
out now!

Ulrich Van Holtz turned over and snuggled closer to the denim-clad thigh resting by his head. Then he remembered that he'd gone to bed alone last night.

Forcing one eye open, he gazed at the face grinning down at him.

"Mornin', supermodel."

He hated when she called him that. The dismissive tone of it grated on his nerves. Especially his sensitive *morning* nerves. She might as well say, "Mornin', you who serve no purpose."

"Dee-Ann." He glanced around, trying to figure out what was going on. "What time is it?"

"Dawn-ish."

"Dawn-*ish*?"

"Not quite dawn, no longer night."

"And is there a reason you're in my bed at dawn-ish . . . fully clothed? Because I'm pretty sure you'd be much more comfortable naked."

Her lips curved slightly. "Look at you, Van Holtz. Trying to sweet talk me."

"If it'll get you naked . . ."

"You're my boss."

"I'm your supervisor."

"If you can fire me, you're my boss. Didn't they teach you that in your fancy college?"

"My fancy college was a culinary school and I spent most of my classes trying to understand my French instructors. So if they mentioned that boss-supervisor distinction, I probably missed it."

"You're still holding my thigh, hoss."

"You're still in my bed. And you're still not naked."

"Me naked is like me dressed. Still covered in scars and willing to kill."

"Now you're just trying to turn me on." Ric yawned, reluctantly unwrapping his arms from Dee's scrumptious thigh and using the move to get a good look at her.

She'd let her dark brown hair grow out a bit in recent months so that the heavy, wavy strands rested below her ears, framing a square jaw that sported a five-inch scar from her military days and a more recent bruise he was guessing had happened last night. She had a typical Smith nose—a bit long and rather wide at the tip—and the proud, high forehead. But it was those eyes that disturbed most of the populace because they were the one part of her that never shifted. They stayed the same color and shape no matter what form she was in. Many people called the color "dog yellow" but Ric thought of it as a canine gold. And Ric didn't find those eyes off-putting. No, he found them entrancing. Just like the woman.

Ric had only known the She-wolf about seven months but since the first time he'd laid eyes on her, he'd been madly, deeply in lust. Then, over time, he'd gotten to know her, and he'd come to fall madly, deeply in love. There was just one problem with them becoming mates and living happily ever after—and that problem's name was Dee-Ann Smith.

"So is there a reason you're here, in my bed, not naked, around dawn-*ish* that doesn't involve us forgetting the idiotic limits of business protocol so that you can ravish my more-than-willing body?"

"Yep."

When she said nothing else, Ric sat up and offered, "Let me guess. The tellin' will be easier if it's around some waffles and bacon."

"Those words are true, but faking that accent ain't endearing you to my Confederate heart."

"I bet adding blueberries to those waffles will."

"Canned or fresh?"

Mouth open, Ric glared at her over his shoulder.

"It's a fair question."

"Out." He pointed at his bedroom door. "If you're going to question whether I'd use *canned* anything in my food while sitting on my bed *not* naked, then you can just get the hell out of my bedroom . . . and sit in my kitchen, quietly, until I arrive."

"Will you be in a better mood?"

"Will you be naked?"

"Like a wolf with a bone," she muttered, and told him, "Not likely."

"Then I guess you have your answer."

"Oh, come on. Can I at least sit here and watch you strut into the bathroom bare-ass naked?"

"No, you may not." He threw his legs over the side of the bed. "However, you may look over your shoulder longingly while I, in a very manly way, walk purposely into the bathroom bare-ass naked. Because I'm not here for your entertainment, Ms. Smith."

"It's Miss. Nice Southern girls use Miss."

"Then I guess that still makes you a Ms."

Dee-Ann Smith sat at Van Holtz's kitchen table, her fingers tracing the lines in the marble. His kitchen table was real marble, too, the legs made of the finest wood. Not like her parents' Formica table that still had the crack in it from when Rory Reed's big head drunkenly slammed into it after they'd had too many beers the night of their junior year homecoming game.

Then again, everything about Van Holtz's apartment spoke of money and the finest of everything. Yet his place somehow managed to be comfortable, not like some spots in this city where everything was so fancy Dee didn't know who'd want to visit or sit on a damn thing. Of course, Van Holtz didn't come off like some spoiled rich kid that she'd want to slap around when he got mouthy. She'd thought he'd be that way, but since meeting him a few months back, he'd proven that he wasn't like that at all.

Shame she couldn't say that for several of his family members. She'd met his daddy only a few times and each time was a little worse than the last. And his older brother wasn't much better. To be honest, she didn't know why Van Holtz didn't challenge them both and take the Alpha position from the mean old bastard. That's how they did it among the Smiths, and it was a way of life that had worked for them for at least three centuries.

Hair dripping wet from the shower, Van Holtz walked into his kitchen. He wore black sweatpants and was pulling a black T-shirt over his head, giving Dee an oh-too-brief glimpse at an absolutely superb set of abs and narrow hips. No, he wasn't as big a wolf as Dee was used to—in fact, they were the same six-two height and nearly the same width—but good Lord, the man had an amazing body. It must be all the things he did during a day. Executive Chef at the Fifth Avenue Van Holtz restaurant; a goalie for the shifter-only pro team he owned, The Carnivores; and one of the supervisors for the Group. A position that, although he didn't spend as much time in the field as Dee-Ann and her team, did force him to keep in excellent shape.

Giving another yawn, Van Holtz pushed his wet, dark blond hair off his face, brown eyes trying to focus while he scanned his kitchen.

"Coffee's in the pot," she said.

Some men, they simply couldn't function without their morning coffee, and that was Van Holtz.

"Thank you," he sighed, grabbing the mug she'd taken out for him and filling it up. If he minded that she'd become quite familiar with his kitchen and his apartment in general, after months of coming and going as she pleased, he never showed it.

Dee waited until he'd had a few sips and finally turned to her with a smile.

"Good morning."

She returned that smile, something she normally didn't bother with most, and replied, "Morning."

"I promised you waffles with *fresh* blueberries." He sniffed in disgust. "Canned. As if I'd ever."

"I know. I know. Sacrilege."

"Exactly!"

Dee-Ann sat patiently at the kitchen table while Van Holtz whipped up a full breakfast for her the way most people whipped up a couple of pieces of toast.

"So, Dee . . ." Van Holtz placed perfectly made waffles and bacon in front of her with warmed syrup in a bowl and a small dish of butter right behind it. " . . . what brings you here?"

He sat down on the chair across from her with his own plate of food.

"Cats irritate me."

Van Holtz nodded, chewing on a bite of food. "And yet you work so well with them on a day-to-day basis."

"Not when they get in my way."

"Is there a possibility you can be more specific on what your complaint is?"

"But it's fun to watch you look so confused."

"Only one cup of coffee, Dee-Ann. Only one cup."

She laughed a little, always amused when Van Holtz got a bit cranky.

"We went to raid a hybrid fight last night—not only was there no fight, but there were felines already there."

"Which felines?"

"KZS."

"Oh." He took another bite of bacon. "*Those* felines. Well, maybe they're trying to—"

"Those felines ain't gonna help mutts, Van Holtz, you know that."

"Can't you just call me Ric? You know, like everyone else." And since the man had more cousins than should legally be allowed, all with the last name Van Holtz, perhaps that would be a bit easier for all concerned.

"Fine. They're not going to help, *Ric.*"

"And yet it seems as if they are—or at least trying."

"They're doing something—and I don't like it. I don't like when anyone gets in my way." Especially particular felines who had wicked right crosses that Dee's jaw was still feeling several hours later.

"All right," he said. "I'll deal with it."

"Just like that?"

"Yep. Just like that. Orange juice?" She nodded and he poured freshly squeezed orange juice into her glass.

"You don't want to talk to the team first?"

"I talked to you. What's the team going to tell me that you haven't? Except they'll probably use more syllables and keep the anti-feline sentiment out of it."

She nodded and watched him eat. Pretty. The man was just . . . pretty. Not girly—although she was sure her daddy and uncles would think so—but pretty. Handsome and gorgeous might be the more acceptable terms when talking about men, but those words did not fit him.

"Is something wrong with your food?" he asked, noticing that she hadn't started eating.

She glanced down at the expertly prepared waffle, big fresh blueberries throughout, powdered sugar sprinkled over it. In bowls he'd also put out more fresh blueberries, along with strawberries and peaches. He'd given her a linen napkin to use and heavy, expensive-looking flatware to eat with. And he'd set all this up in about thirty minutes.

The whole meal was, in a word, perfection, which was why Dee replied, "It's all right . . . I guess."

A dark eyebrow peaked. "You guess?"

"Haven't tried it yet, now have I? Can't tell you if I like it if I haven't tried it."

"Only one cup of coffee, Dee. Only one."

"Maybe it's time you had another."

"Eat and tell me my food is amazing or I'm going to get cranky again."

"If you're going to be pushy . . ." She took a bite, letting the flavors burst against her taste buds. Damn, but the man could cook. Didn't seem right, did it? Pretty and a good cook.

"Well?"

"Do I really need to tell you how good it is?"

"Yes. Although I'm enjoying your orgasm face."

She smirked. "Darlin', you don't know my orgasm face."

"Yet. I'm ever hopeful."

"Keepin' that dream alive."

"Someone has to." He winked at her and went back to his food. "I'll see what I can find out about what's going on with KZS and get back to you." He looked up at her and smiled. "Don't worry, Dee-Ann. I've got your back."

She knew that. She knew he would come through as promised. As hard as it was to believe, she was learning to trust the one breed of wolf her daddy told her never to trust.

Then again . . . her daddy had never tasted the man's blueberry waffles.

"But do me a favor, Dee," he said. "Until I get this straightened out, don't get into it with the cats."

Dee stared at him and asked with all honesty, "What makes you think I would?"

Don't miss Mia Marlowe's newest,
TOUCH OF A THIEF,
available now . . .

Only once more, Viola vowed silently. Though, like the Shakespearean heroine for whom she was named, she'd miss wearing men's trousers from time to time. They were ever so much more comfortable than a corset and hoops.

From somewhere deep in the elegant row house came a low creak. Viola held her breath. The longcase clock in the main hall ticked. When she heard nothing else, she realized it was only the sigh of an older home squatting down on its foundations for the night.

The room she'd broken into still held the stale scents of cigar smoke and brandy from the dinner party of the previous evening. But there were no fresh smells, which meant Lieutenant Quinn had taken Lord Montjoy up on his offer to introduce him at his club this evening.

Probably visiting a brothel instead. No matter. The house was empty and why made no difference at all.

She cat-footed up the main stairs, on the watch for the help. The lieutenant hadn't fully staffed his home yet, but he'd brought a native servant back with him from India. During the dinner party, Viola had noticed the turbaned fellow in the shadows, directing the borrowed footmen and giving quiet commands to the temporary serving girls.

The Indian servant would most likely be in residence.

So long as I steer clear of the kitchen or the garret, I'll be fine, Viola told herself.

Besides, the stones would be in Lieutenant Quinn's chamber.

Her fence had a friend in the brick mason's guild who, for a pretty price, happily revealed the location of the *ton's* secret stashes. Townhouses on this fashionable London street were all equipped with identical wall safes in the master's chamber. The newfangled tumbler lock would open without protest under Viola's deft touch.

She had a gift. Two, actually, but she didn't enjoy the other one half so much.

Slowly, she opened the bedchamber door. *Good.* It had been oiled recently. She heard only the faint scrape of hinges.

The heavy damask curtains were drawn, so Viola stood still, waiting for her eyes to adjust to the deeper darkness. There! A landscape in a gilt frame on the south wall marked the location of the safe.

Viola padded across the room and inched the painting's hanging wires along the picture rail, careful not to let the hooks near the ceiling slide off. She'd have the devil's own time reattaching them if they did. With any luck at all, she'd slide the painting right back and it might be days before Lieutenant Quinn discovered the stones were missing. After moving the frame over about a foot, she found the safe right where Willie's friend said it would be.

Viola put her ear to the lock and closed her eyes, the better to concentrate. When she heard a click or felt a slight hitch beneath her touch she knew she'd discovered part of the combination. After only a few tries and errors, the final tumbler fell into place and Viola opened the safe.

The dark void was empty. She reached in to trace the edges of the iron box with her fingertips.

"Looking for something?" A masculine voice rumbled from a shadowy corner.

Blast! Viola bolted for the door, but it slammed shut. The Indian servant stepped from his place of concealment behind it.

"Please do not make to flee or I am sorry to say I shall have to shoot you." The Hindu's melodious accent belied his serious threat.

Viola ran toward the window, hoping it was open behind the

curtain. And that there was a friendly bush below to break her fall.

Lieutenant Quinn grabbed her before she reached it. He crushed her spine to his chest, his large hand splayed over one of her unbound breasts.

"Bloody hell! It's a woman. Turn up the gas lamp, Sanjay."

The yellow light of the wall sconce flooded the room. Viola blinked against the sudden brightness. Then she stomped down on her captor's instep as hard as she could.

Quinn grunted, but didn't release his hold. Instead, he whipped her around to face him. His brows shot up in surprise when he recognized her. "Lady Viola, you can't be the Mayfair Jewel Thief."

"Of course I can." She might be a thief, but she was no liar. "I'd appreciate it, sir, if you'd remove your hands from my person."

"I bet you would." The lieutenant's mouth turned down in a grim frown and he kept his grip on her upper arms. His Indian servant didn't lower the revolver's muzzle one jot.

"Did I not tell you, *sahib*? When she looked at the countess's emeralds, her eyes glowed green." The servant no longer wore his turban, his coal-black hair falling in ropey strands past his shoulders. "She is a devil, this one."

"Perhaps." One of Quinn's dark brows lifted. "But if that's the case, my old vicar was right. The devil does know how to assume pleasing shapes."

That was a back-handed compliment if Viola ever heard one. She hadn't really considered Lieutenant Quinn closely during the dinner party. She made little time for men and the trouble they bring a woman. Once burned and all that. Besides, she'd been too intent on Lady Henson's emeralds at the time. Now she studied him with the same assessing gaze he shot at her.

Quinn's even features were classically handsome. His unlined mouth and white teeth made Viola realize suddenly that he was younger than she'd first estimated. She doubted he'd seen thirty-five winters. His fair English skin had been bronzed by fierce Indian summers and lashed by its weeping monsoons. His stint in India had rewarded him with riches, but the subcontinent had demanded its price.

His storm-gray eyes were all the more striking because of his deeply tanned skin. They seemed to look right through Viola and see her for the fraud she was—a thief with pretensions of still being a lady.

And keep an eye out for Cynthia Eden's
NEVER CRY WOLF
coming in July

L ucas Simone paced the confines of the eight-by-twelve foot jail cell, a snarl on his lips. The wolf within howled with rage, and the man that the world generally saw, well, he felt more than a little pissed, too.

Collared for a murder he hadn't committed. Talk about shit-luck. Yeah, Lucas had played on the wild side, he'd even killed before, and the bastards had more than deserved the death he'd given them.

But this time, for this crime, he was innocent. Right. Like the cops would buy that story.

His hands tightened around the bars. If he wanted, he could rip those bars apart, and if they didn't let him out soon, he would. "I want my lawyer! Now!" His pack had to know where he was. A leader didn't just vanish, and if he didn't make contact with them soon, Lucas wasn't exactly sure what would happen.

Probably hell on earth . . . or wolves running wild in LA, which, yeah, that equaled hell on earth. Especially if he wasn't there to keep the wilder wolves on their leashes.

Everyone already knew that wolf shifters had a tendency to dance on the edge of sanity. Once those leashes were gone . . . *hello, hell.*

The bars beneath his fingers began to bend as the rage swelled inside him.

A human was dead. Tossed on his doorstep like garbage. *Not my kill.*

Because Lucas had a rule. Just one. *Don't attack the weak.*

As far as he was concerned, there wasn't any being weaker than a human.

"Guard!" His teeth burned as they lengthened in his mouth. No more fucking nice wolf. He was getting out, one way or another. The metal bars groaned within his grasp. "Simone!" Not the guard's voice. The dumbass detective who'd brought him in for "questioning." Only he hadn't been questioned. The cop had just thrown his ass into a cage.

Lucas's kind didn't do so well with cages.

He'd make sure the detective didn't make the same mistake again.

His eyes lifted, tracked to the left to meet that beady gray stare—

And instead got caught by a pair of green eyes.

His nostrils flared. The woman stood behind the detective, a slight frown between her brows. She was tall, curved just the way he wanted a woman to be, with sensual, full breasts and hips that would let a guy hold on tight for a wild ride.

Pretty face. Straight nose, tilted just a bit on the end—kinda cute. A light spray of freckles across her high cheekbones. Sexy red lips. Jaw that was a bit stubborn.

And gorgeous hair. A thick mane of dark, dark brown hair that curled around her face.

Her stare widened as he gazed at her. She licked her lips, a quick swipe of her tongue.

His cock began to swell, an immediate and instinctive response, even as suspicion rose within him. What was the sexy little human doing at his cell? Was she another cop? A lawyer?

Her eyes—the greenest he'd ever seen—stayed locked on his. That emerald stare didn't waver at all. Not even to glance toward the right, to catch sight of the jagged remains of his ear.

Most women looked. Like they couldn't help it. Looked, flinched. So did the men.

Lucas had never really given a damn. The top of his ear had been ripped off years ago in the worst fight of his life. He'd been ten at the time.

But she didn't look.

A guard came scurrying into the holding area, keys loose and jingling in his right hand.

"Get him out." The order came from Detective Dickhead.

Lucas let go of the bars, even as he tried to chain the beast that demanded he lunge for the ass's throat.

Playing it civilized sucked.

The door opened seconds later with a harsh moan.

The woman smiled—with her lips, not her eyes. "Lover . . ." A sexy purr of sound.

He felt that purr run the length of his body, even as the lie burned in his mind. He knew he'd never been *this* lady's lover.

Not yet, anyway.

"You're free to go, Romeo," Detective Dickhead drawled. "Your lady gave you an alibi for last night, one that we were able to back up with accounts from three other witnesses."

Bullshit.

Last night, he'd gone running solo. He'd let the wolf out so that he could howl and hunt as much as he wanted.

He'd come home with the taste of blood on his tongue, and then he'd found blood staining his front steps.

Lucas rolled his shoulders, trying to force the tension back, and stalked out of the cage. Then she was in his arms. Throwing herself against him. Wrapping slender arms around his neck and pressing her mouth to his.

Lucas wasn't a stupid man. If a sexy woman wanted to plaster her curves against him, he wasn't gonna argue.

But he was most certainly gonna take.

His hands lifted, caught her, locked right around the firm flare of her ass, and he pressed her closer. His mouth took hers, his tongue plunged deep.

Oh, but she tasted sweet.

Not the wild tang of his kind. Women like him, women who could shift into the powerful form of a beast, usually tasted like aged wine.

She tasted like candy.

He'd always had a sweet tooth.

Her tongue moved against his, soft strokes, like a kitten, licking. A moan trembled in her throat.

His cock strained against the front of his jeans. Okay, so he didn't know who she was. Not gonna stop him. Because he'd sure like to screw h—

"Ahem." The Dickhead again.

The woman in his arms stiffened, just a bit.

For show. He knew she hadn't forgotten the detective's presence. And neither had he. Lucas just hadn't given a damn that they were being observed.

"Sorry I wasn't here sooner." Her voice was husky, sexual. Like a silken stroke right over his groin.

"No problem, babe." He curved his fingers under her chin. Two could play. He saw the small tremor that shook her, and he smiled. Deliberately, he let her see the sharp edge of his teeth. Way sharper than a human's.

But no fear flashed in her eyes.

Interesting.

The lady knew the score, he'd stake his pack's reputation on that fact. She knew he wasn't human. Probably knew exactly *what* he was.

And she was still coming to his aid.

Now, as a rule, Lucas didn't believe that people were good. No, he knew they were more apt to be influenced by the devil than any pure motivation . . . so he figured the lady had an angle.

"The Los Angeles police department apologizes for any inconvenience." The nasally voice of Dickhead told him.

Lucas released the woman. Gently, he pushed her to the side. His eyes narrowed as he cocked his head and waited for Dickhead to finish.

"Of course, you have a known history of affiliation with certain—"

He moved in one quick lunge. Lucas grabbed the detective, lifted the jerk by his too-thick throat, and slammed him against the bars.

The guard stepped forward.

Lucas's head snapped to the right. "Don't even think about it." Guttural. Because really, a guy's patience could only last so long.

The guard's Adam's apple bobbed.

"Good." He glanced back at the detective. "Bruce, I think you and I need to clear the air." So others were there watching—big deal. He wouldn't play subtle. "You've got a hard-on for me. You been dodging my feet for the last two months." He let the beast show in his eyes. Lucas knew the glow of the wolf would burn from his blue eyes. "You stay out of my way from now on . . . or you'll find out just what I do to bastards who piss me off."

The detective's skin bleached. "You—you can't threaten a cop—"

He let his claws dig into Bruce's flapping flesh. "I just did."

"*What are you?*" A whisper.

His smile faded. "Someone"—*something*—"you don't want to have as an enemy." His fingers loosened. The detective slid from his grip. Dropped to the floor. Probably pissed himself.

Lucas glared down at the man. He let Bruce see the intent in his eyes. Then he caught the woman's hand. "Let's get the hell out of here."

GREAT BOOKS,
GREAT SAVINGS!

When You Visit Our Website:
www.kensingtonbooks.com
You Can Save Money Off The Retail Price
Of Any Book You Purchase!

- **All Your Favorite Kensington Authors**
- **New Releases & Timeless Classics**
- **Overnight Shipping Available**
- **eBooks Available For Many Titles**
- **All Major Credit Cards Accepted**

Visit Us Today To Start Saving!
www.kensingtonbooks.com

All Orders Are Subject To Availability.
Shipping and Handling Charges Apply.
Offers and Prices Subject To Change Without Notice.